Rachel Lee was hooked on writing by the age of twelve and practised her craft as she moved from place to place all over the United States. This *New York Times* bestselling author now resides in Florida and has the joy of writing full-time.

Elle James, a *New York Times* bestselling author, started writing when her sister challenged her to write a romance novel. She has managed a full-time job and raised three wonderful children, and she and her husband even tried ranching exotic birds (ostriches, emus and rheas). Ask her, and she'll tell you what it's like to go toe-to-toe with an angry 350-pound bird! Elle loves to hear from fans at ellejames@earthlink.net or ellejames.com

D1077667

CONARD COUNTY: MISTAKEN IDENTITY

RACHEL LEE

HELD HOSTAGE AT WHISKEY GULCH

ELLE JAMES

MILLS & BOON

First Published in Great Britain 2022
by Mills & Boon, an imprint of HarperCollins*Publishers* Ltd
1 London Bridge Street, London, SE1 9GF

www.harpercollins.co.uk

HarperCollins*Publishers*
1st Floor, Watermarque Building,
Ringsend Road, Dublin 4, Ireland

Conard County: Mistaken Identity © 2022 Susan Civil-Brown
Held Hostage at Whiskey Gulch © 2022 Mary Jernigan

ISBN: 978-0-263-30329-2

0222

MIX
Paper from
responsible sources
FSC® C007454

This book is produced from independently certified FSC™ paper to ensure responsible forest management.

For more information visit: www.harpercollins.co.uk/green

Printed and Bound in Spain using 100% Renewable electricity at CPI Black Print, Barcelona

CONARD COUNTY: MISTAKEN IDENTITY

RACHEL LEE

Chapter One

Jasmine Nelson picked up the phone to hear her twin sister's welcome voice.

"Hey, Jazz," Lily said. "How are you making out with Iris?"

Jazz smiled into the phone. For a fifteen-year-old, her niece was an easy kid to deal with. "We're doing fine. How's Stockholm?"

"As usual. Someday you'll have to come with me. I can attend conferences and meetings and you can take in the sights. There are a lot of good ones."

"I bet."

Just then Iris burst through the front door, an energetic girl with tightly curly red hair that was amenable to no brush and required a short cut to easily fit under her swim cap. Her hair also got curlier in the rain and sometimes frizzed. None of this bothered Iris in the least.

"Hey, Iris. Want to talk to your mom?"

Iris screwed up her face.

"Let me guess," Lily said. "I'm the last person on earth she wants to talk to."

"Only because you're her mom." Jazz laughed. "She treats me *ever* so much better."

Iris screwed up her face again, stuck out her tongue and headed for the kitchen with her backpack.

"So no problem," Lily said. "I hope that continues. I'll call again in a couple of days. And obviously you know how to reach me if Iris gets arrested."

"In *this* town? If she does anything that bad, I think the cops will bring her home and present her for house punishment."

It was Lily's turn to laugh. "You're probably right. So after only three days you've figured out Conard County?"

"Well, that's debatable, but I'm learning."

Lily made a kissie sound over the phone. "Later, sis."

Iris bounced back into the small foyer, a peanut butter sandwich in hand, bag in the other. "I got the mail," she said, tossing her backpack onto a nearby straight-backed chair. "I just threw out all the flyers. I don't know why Mom gets any mail anyway. She pays all the bills automatically."

Before Jazz could answer, Iris bent and pulled a slim stack of envelopes from her pack and tossed them into a basket on top of the envelopes that had begun to build up over the past few days. Jazz never looked at them, preserving Lily's privacy. Neither of them guessed there was a bombshell in that stack.

"I am so glad you're not twins," Jazz announced.

Iris giggled. "I've heard some of what you and Mom got up to. I could be double trouble."

She wasn't much of a problem to begin with, but Jazz didn't say so. No reason to encourage it. "I wish you'd talk with Lily next time she calls."

Iris shrugged. "She's the one who went to Stockholm."

"And you're the one who chose to stay here. What do

I recall? Something about friends and school and swim team and oboe lessons."

Iris grinned. "Yeah, well."

"Well." Her niece always made Jazz smile. "What's the agenda?"

"I do my homework and you cook dinner."

"I knew you had it figured out. Why don't you help me cook?"

"Too much homework." With that, Iris vanished into the dining room with her backpack.

Jazz found it impossible to get annoyed with the girl. She was like a ray of sunshine coming through the door and she usually stayed that way all through homework, washing dishes and spending countless hours on her cell phone with her friends.

Nope. No problem. At least not yet.

Although Jazz wondered why Iris spent so many hours on the phone in the evenings. A teen thing? Or that there was no good place for them to meet up? She had no idea. Maybe she should ask.

Iris poked her head out the dining room door. "Hey, Aunt Jazz?"

"Yes?"

"It's a good thing Grandma didn't have another set of twins. Can you imagine the names? Begonia and Hibiscus."

Jazz cracked up as Iris disappeared once again. Iris's grandmother had been a fan of flowers, obviously, but she hadn't gone *that* far. She *had*, however, suggested Iris's name. A lovely one.

Jazz returned to her office. Well, Lily's office, but Jazz had made her own workspace in there with a laptop. Not difficult, considering Lily had a big wraparound desk. Jazz easily fit her own items along one side. As a writer of fantasy novels, she had a portable job, which was why Lily had asked her to stay with Iris.

Her niece was a joy and the climate here in Wyoming, even in springtime, had Miami beat hands down. At least at this time of year.

She surveyed her work area, surrounded by Lily's things. Lily was neat, so that wasn't a problem, but Jazz was much less so. Her only neatness came from the laptop, and a pencil cup that was decorated with a pen that had a colorful flower on the top. A gift from Iris when she'd been eight.

Then, of course, there was her notepad, essential for jotting down everything from ideas to shopping lists. A coaster for her bottle of water or cup of coffee. And the inevitable mess of papers that she'd printed out for one reason or another, and forwarded mail. She didn't even bother to try to straighten up the papers because they had a mind of their own.

She leaned back in the comfy office chair, not really inclined to write, and thought about her niece and her sister.

She'd never visited them here before because Lily and Iris preferred to come to Miami to visit, for beaches, sand and sun, especially during winter months. That was okay by Jazz. She'd never felt any urge to come to the back of beyond.

Now here she was, and she was enjoying it.

Well, she'd finished her day's allotment of writing anyway, so perhaps she should just go to the kitchen to start dinner. Because she rarely cooked just for herself, she was having an adventure with that. She was trying to prepare *real* meals, not just something frozen she could toss in the oven or microwave.

Jazz suspected that Iris would have been happy to survive on hamburgers, but she tried to stick to a training diet for her swimming.

Jazz was all for it, but that meant that a tray of frozen lasagna wasn't a great idea. Anyway, all that swimming created an astonishingly large appetite.

Which left Jazz standing in the kitchen trying to figure it out. Veggies, of course, but Iris also had a need for carbs. Jazz repeatedly felt surprised by the way Iris tucked into them.

Whole wheat and multigrain bread. Usually, but that didn't keep her from eating ordinary rye bread by the ton. Peanut butter was another favorite, but that list wasn't going to turn into a dinner.

Heck, she'd gone grocery shopping after her arrival three days ago and she already realized she hadn't bought enough.

Startling her, there came a knock on the front door. She'd hardly moved three steps when she heard Iris's happy voice.

"Adam! Oh, and you brought Sheba, too."

Sheba? Jazz could hardly imagine. As she rounded the corner into the foyer, she saw a tall, well-muscled man with military-cut light brown hair. He wore jeans, work boots and a khaki work shirt. Accompanying him was a dark red Irish setter whose feathery tail swished the floor happily as she sat.

Iris was already on her knees with her arms wrapped around the dog's neck. "Ooh, you good doggie."

Good doggie returned the hug with a wide grin and repeated laps of her tongue on Iris's face.

"She'll lick you to death," the man said.

Jazz raised her gaze and saw him smiling at her. He was good-looking, too, his face lightly lined from weather.

"Hi," he said. "I'm Adam Ryder. You must be Jazz. And this furry critter is Sheba. Don't ask me why, I still don't know where the name came from. Just popped out of my mouth when I adopted her."

Iris turned her head, still hugging the dog, and said, "Aunt Jazz, I want a puppy."

Jazz shook her head. "And I don't want your mother to kill me." She smiled at Adam. "Come in, if you have time. I'll make some coffee and pour orange juice into Iris."

Man, girl and dog followed her into the kitchen where she started the drip coffee pot. Iris grabbed her own bottle of juice from the fridge. At a quart a day, it wouldn't last long. Iris's appetite amused her.

"I'm sorry I didn't get over sooner to introduce myself," Adam said. "But I was in Cheyenne for a few days. Anyway, I'm your across-the-street neighbor."

Iris planted herself at the small kitchen table, drinking juice from the bottle with one hand while petting Sheba with the other. The dog's tail still swished happily.

When Jazz realized Adam was still politely standing, she said, "Grab a seat. Can I offer you a snack?"

"Unlike this young lady here, I can't afford to snack much. Gone are the youthful days when I could eat any amount."

"I heard," Iris said. "Twenty tacos once, wasn't it?"

Adam chuckled. "I was a string bean with a fast metabolism. After I left the Army, that didn't work anymore."

His smile was engaging, Jazz thought. It lit up his face.

"I still want a puppy, Aunt Jazz."

Jazz looked at her niece. "I'm not doing an end run around your mother. No way. You convince *her*. Besides, who'd take care of it when you're gone all day at school or lost in a swimming pool? Me?"

Iris shrugged. "Walking a dog would be healthy."

Jazz couldn't contain her laughter. "I can walk without a dog."

Iris gave her a sidelong look. "Not as often, though."

Adam spoke to Jazz. "You can't win with this one."

"Apparently not, but I can stand firm."

Iris sighed. "Okay, okay. But I need to get back to my homework. Can I take Sheba?"

Adam answered. "I think she'll follow. She's got kind of a thing for you, Iris."

"Sheba needs a cousin." Iris left the room with the orange juice and the dog at her heels.

Jazz poured the coffee. "Milk? Sugar?"

"Black, please."

Jazz joined him at the table. "Lily mentioned you a couple of times. It's nice to meet you at last."

"Lily mentioned you more than once. Twins are close."

"Sometimes it's like we still share the same umbilical cord. So how about you? Something about you being a carpenter?"

"Handyman. Odd jobs. I like fixing things." His eyes crinkled at the corners as he smiled. "And you're an author?"

"So my fingers and computer claim."

"More than that. Lily showed me a row of your books on her shelf. Must be special."

"First it starts as a hobby. Then it becomes a job. Different feeling altogether."

"I guess I can see that." He sipped his coffee, and silence fell between them.

Small talk between strangers could be awkward, Jazz thought. She sought something to say, then, "How'd you get Sheba?"

"Well..." He drew the word out, teasing the story along. "You see, I was visiting my buddy up north. The guy has a big spread and I like to ride horses. He's always happy to lend me one and send me out into the wide-open spaces."

"Sounds nice."

"It is. Peaceful. Anyway, he has this thing."

"A thing?"

"Yeah. He says he read a veterinary study that said it was better not to fix dogs until they were well over a year old. Something about them being less likely to get overweight. So..."

Jazz chuckled. She guessed what was coming. "Unintended consequences?"

"You could call them that, although Sam didn't seem too upset about it. He's got quite a collection of Irish setters. They're great hunting dogs and pointers. Anyway, a couple of them got together and when I arrived on one visit he had six weaned puppies. The rest, as they say, is history. I've never regretted bringing Sheba home with me."

Then he cocked a brow. "I think I should have come up with an Irish name for her. I keep getting asked about Sheba."

"It's unique."

"Maybe. It seems there is a list of popular dog names

with Molly at the top. Bet you Sheba isn't as low as we'd think."

"Do you take her hunting?"

Adam shook his head. "I didn't get her for that. She's a great companion. And I've learned a lot of breed traits from her."

"How so?"

"Well, I never taught her to point, but she does."

"Wow. Really?"

"Yep. And another thing that still floors me. A friend of mine has a parakeet. He was out of his cage one day, flying around and perching on high things, like curtain rods. I'll never understand why Nibbles decided to fly low."

"Nibbles?" Jazz felt her eyes widen.

Adam grinned. "Yeah, because the bird used to bite my friend when it was a baby. So Nibbles."

"Makes sense."

"Anyway, Nibbles got too close to Sheba. Next thing all we can see is feathers sticking out from her jaw. I yelled *drop it* and the dog did."

"Oh my God. I can't imagine!"

"What I couldn't have imagined was that Nibbles was just fine. He shook out his feathers then started squawking at Sheba right in her face. A total scolding."

"How did Sheba take that?"

"She hung her head and took it until the bird flew away."

Jazz thought about it, amused. The image was just too much, but she had to ask, "You're not kidding?"

"I swear I'm not. Bird dog in her, I guess. She never bit down."

"Holy moly."

"That's what I said, only a little more colorfully. That dog is a trip, I can tell you."

"Sounds like it."

Then they fell silent again. Eventually Adam asked, "You haven't been here long yet, but what do you think of our town?"

"So far it's charming."

"It's also small enough to have one hell of a grapevine. As the saying goes, if you don't know what you're doing, ask a neighbor."

"Uh-oh."

Adam shrugged. "It rarely gets nasty, but when people gossip it's bound to happen. I just haven't heard anything like that."

"Thanks for the heads-up. I'll be sure to behave myself."

He laughed. "Always wise, don't you think?"

He rose then, and took his cup to the sink and rinsed it. "I've kept you long enough and I need to get ready for a meeting. If you want anything, I'm right across the street. Or Iris can show you."

Jazz rose, too. "You're fond of Iris."

"Hard not to be. I could say the same for Lily. You got a nice sister. But you got the better name."

He called Sheba when he reached the front door and clipped a leash on her. "Time for a short walk before my meeting. Nice to meet you."

It had been nice to meet him, too. But then Jazz faced the conundrum of dinner again. Maybe she ought to get some cookbooks. No help now, though, when the larder and fridge looked as if a horde of locusts had passed through.

"Hey, Iris," she said, sticking her head into the dining room.

Iris looked up from her laptop. "Writing a term paper," she said. "For physics, if you can imagine." She looked disgusted. "I can see it for English or history, but this?"

"I'd have no idea where to begin."

Iris asked, "What did you need?"

"A grocery list. Or better yet, for you to come shopping with me. I have almost no idea of what your training diet involves, or how much. Man, a quart of orange juice would have lasted me over a week."

Iris looked impish. "You need to walk more. Okay, let's go now."

"But your paper…"

"Can wait. It's not going to get any harder if I come back to it in an hour. Besides, I noticed we're pretty much down to peanut butter sandwiches."

"And I can't even figure out something for dinner."

"The horror! Okay, let's get going."

JAZZ PULLED ON a sweater because she was acclimated to a much warmer client. Iris teased her about it. "This is wonderful weather."

"For those who haven't lived in Florida most of their lives. You're just going to have to deal with me being chilly."

Iris suggested they drive to the store, which gave Jazz an idea of the size of the coming shopping trip. The grocery was fairly busy with people looking for last-minute meal needs, but Iris kept them moving, filling the cart with enough groceries for a football team. As they worked their way along the aisles, greetings were exchanged but there was no time for introductions. Everyone was busy, and Iris didn't slow down enough to talk.

Jazz was astonished by the heap in the cart, but a little more concerned about knowing how to cook everything. Frozen vegetables fine, but some of the fresh ones were unfamiliar to her. A mound of protein bars. Then there was fish, all of it frozen, but it was still a lot.

"I guess I'm going to have to learn to cook fish," Jazz remarked.

"Look it up online. Don't you cook at home?"

"For one? Not often."

Iris just shook her head. "Not healthy, Aunt Jazz."

"So I should crawl under a rock?"

"No," Iris answered pertly. "Just learn. Are you sure I can't get a dog?"

Jazz gave her a humorous frown. "Talk to your mother."

Multiple loaves of whole grain breads, two dozen eggs. Three gallons of milk. Instant grits. How was Iris going to eat all of that?

Well, she must be able to, and she had a perfect figure.

Jazz could have sighed. Her sedentary job made it so much more difficult.

At home, putting everything away proved to be a bit of a challenge. Iris, at least, had a good idea of where things could go. A bit of rearranging in the fridge was necessary, but after a half hour or so everything was put away.

"Now that looks better," Iris announced approvingly with her hands on her hips.

"At least you won't starve to death."

Iris giggled. "The benefit of athletics."

"So...dinner tonight."

"I'll take pity on you."

Jazz cocked an eyebrow. "How?"

"Red beans and rice." She waved a box. "The only hard part is lightly browning the andouille sausage."

"What about your paper?"

Iris shrugged. "It's not due tomorrow, and anyway this doesn't take long."

Nor did it, especially with the rice cooker.

"Now you know how to cook this," Iris said.

"Yeah, and I can buy a dozen boxes now."

Iris laughed. "Check online. Loads of recipes."

"But *I* get to cook."

Iris laughed again. "Thirty minutes. I'll be back for dinner."

Jazz didn't doubt it as she watched Iris head back to her studying.

AFTER THE MEETING with other vets that Adam helped counsel, he took Sheba for her late-night walk. The streets were peaceful, quiet. His favorite time of the day.

He also thought a lot about Jazz. She was definitely Lily's twin, so alike in appearance that it was hard to tell them apart. But Lily had never appealed to him the way Jazz had managed to in just a few minutes. An interesting reaction.

Both sisters were striking, with long inky hair and bright blue eyes. *Black Irish*, Lily had once told him. Iris had the same brilliant blue eyes, but with that tightly curly red hair. Red Irish, he supposed, although the family tree probably wasn't purely Irish. Maybe he'd ask Jazz a bit about that.

Any reason to have another conversation.

He also had plenty to consider after the night's support group. Together, vets talked a lot more than they could with people who'd never walked in their boots. Stories they never could have shared because they were raw, open wounds that others wouldn't understand. Tonight had been especially hard for Winston, a man who'd led his platoon into dangerous places, places where death had stared them in the eyes. They'd done what was demanded of them, but had to live forever after with appalling images, horrifying memories and grief that plagued them almost constantly. Some even hated themselves.

War was an atrocity-making situation, a situation soldiers had to harden themselves against in any way they could. Then they came home. In a couple of days they transferred from war to peace. To a life with different rules and different expectations, and the transition rarely felt like slipping into an old, comfortable shoe. They'd been indelibly changed. Hardly to be wondered that they often had difficulty coping.

Winston had come home to a wife and two young children. Video calls couldn't make up for the loss of shared experiences. He might have taken the family with him to Germany before his deployments but he and Sherri had decided not to uproot the kids that way. In the end it wouldn't have made much difference.

He had come home to a family, especially children, who were virtually strangers to him. The man he had become was a stranger to them.

To top it off, Winston had a truly severe case of PTSD. He'd put up a steel shed in his backyard, then had used it as a bolt hole. For days at a time he wouldn't emerge while he hunkered inside, possessed by his demons. Sherri had left food and drink outside the locked door of the shed, but sometimes he didn't come out long enough to even grab bottled water.

Then Sherri had left him. Now *she* couldn't handle any more and she believed it wasn't good for the kids. In that Winston had agreed with her.

He'd come to this town alone, wandering the back roads, finding secluded places in which to hide when he needed to.

Then he'd parked here, but no one knew for how long. Adam wished for some way to ease the guy's suffering but so far even the meds the VA had prescribed for him made no noticeable difference. Winston was a broken man.

Tonight for the first time, Winston had cut through his reserve and dumped some of his ugly backstory to a group that understood. Winston had wept and raged while he talked, and some of the others had, too, recognizing themselves in Winston's story.

God! Each one of these gatherings evoked a lot in Adam as well. Memories and emotions he kept under steely control but were nevertheless part of him.

Which made him a lousy candidate for feeling an attraction to Jazz. To any woman. Nope, no innocent deserved to be exposed to his backpack of sorrows, hatred, ugliness. Winston was proof of that.

Firm in his decision, he led a happy Sheba back to the house. That dog was a comfort to him. The only real comfort he allowed himself.

Chapter Two

Morning brought bright sunlight and cool temperatures. Before starting her work, after Iris had left for her Saturday training, Jazz set out for that small bakery she'd seen near the sheriff's office. The time shift from Florida had changed her best writing hours, which left her some more time in the morning. She couldn't understand it, but since coming here she didn't at all feel like writing until midafternoon. It should have been the opposite because the time here was two hours earlier.

She figured Iris would be delighted with a bag full of delicious sins and would probably dive into them. As for dinner tonight…well, she was going to have to take stock of the larder and figure out something. Iris had been right about searching recipes online, but it now occurred to her that a list of menus for a week would help her organize the shopping better, with necessary ingredients. At this point she didn't know which items would fit into what recipes and thus she didn't know what to look for. Maybe she ought to try to lay out menus for this week and find out what she still needed.

God, she had a lot to learn. She wondered if Lily had done much cooking, or if Iris's rapacious run through the grocery had simply met *her* desires.

Sheesh.

Well, there was the fish. Lots of it. She should start with that.

What mundane thoughts, a far cry from the adventures she wrote. Did any of her characters cook? Hah. Not beyond the requisite pot of something hot, or something easy like beans—her own version of course.

She smiled and nodded at people she passed, all of whom called her Lily. She didn't mind in the least. No point in stopping every time to try to straighten it out or, worse, humiliate people for an understandable mistake.

She just wished she could slip into Lily's shoes in other, more important, ways. Well, she'd only be here for a month or so and developing an inferiority complex wouldn't help much.

At the bakery she met Melinda, a lovely middle-aged woman wearing a white apron and only too ready to show her the contents of her case.

"For Iris?" she asked. "I know what she likes."

"For Iris," Jazz answered with a smile. Last thing she wanted to do was mess this up. She'd have plenty of opportunities to mess up other things.

Ten minutes later she left the bakery with a box full of treats. A breeze had kicked up and she buttoned her sweater. She just hoped she didn't get used to these cooler temps before she headed back to swelter in Miami.

She left the box of pastries on the kitchen island for Iris, then headed to her computer. The nice thing about this change in time zones was that when her best writing hours rolled around, she'd already had time to do quite a bit of other stuff, like going to the bakery. Except the writing defied her.

Man, this was a whole new way of thinking, not just a

new lifestyle. The mundane thoughts that were running around in her brain were unusual for her.

And they'd become boring even to her if she let herself ramble in those weeds for too long.

She put in her earbuds and turned on some moody music that would fit her writing. Music always made it easier for her to write.

JAZZ WAS DEEPLY absorbed in her work when Iris interrupted. "I'm home, Aunt Jazz. Need more time to work?"

Jazz scanned her page and word counts. "I'm almost done for the day. How about I just stop?"

Iris grinned. "What about that pastry box?"

"Oh, that? Some woman wrestled me to the sidewalk this morning and told me to take them for you."

Iris giggled. "Right. Say, can we invite Adam over?"

Jazz blinked. "Sure. I guess. Why?"

"Because he's sitting on his front steps with Sheba and he's not looking very happy. Maybe gloomy."

"You just want Sheba to come over," Jazz teased her. "Okay, round him up. I have enough pastries for an army."

"Better make coffee," Iris said over her shoulder as she hurried away. "From what I've seen, it's essential to life for him."

Jazz closed her document, turned off her music and went to the kitchen to make coffee as ordered.

It must have taken a little effort on Iris's part to persuade Adam to come over because the coffee had finished brewing before she heard Iris return, the click of Sheba's claws on the wood floor and Adam's heavier tread.

One after the other they entered the kitchen, Iris in

the lead. "I dangled pastries under Adam's nose," she said. "I think it was Sheba who made up his mind for him, though."

Adam spoke. "I told you that dog would follow you anywhere."

"Only because she has good taste," Iris retorted.

"Hi, Adam," Jazz said when she could get a word in. "Have a seat, and I'm just putting the box of pastry on the table with napkins. Finger food time and no plates for Iris to wash."

"Fine with me," he answered.

Jazz noticed the heaviness in his voice, nothing like yesterday. Iris was right, he was looking gloomy.

Iris brightened the moment. "You hear Aunt Jazz, Adam? She *assumes* I'll do dishes."

Adam half smiled. "I'm surprised she doesn't assume more."

Iris feigned a sigh as she helped ferry coffee and napkins to the table. She even poured coffee for herself. "Better with pastry," she remarked. "Orange juice with this? Blech."

Jazz chuckled. The girl was irrepressible.

"You know," Iris said as she chewed a mouthful of jelly-filled doughnut, "Aunt Jazz isn't correcting anybody when they call her Lily."

Adam looked at Jazz. "Why not?"

"Because it doesn't matter. I'll only be here a few weeks. Anyway, Iris's mom can come home and apologize for *my* mistakes."

That drew giggles from Iris. "I like that." Then she turned her attention to Adam. "Aunt Jazz has the best name of all the girls Grandma named. I mean, think about it. At least Jasmine can be shortened to Jazz. Very cool."

One side of Adam's mouth remained lifted, but the smile didn't reach his eyes. "I agree. Very cool."

What was going on, Jazz wondered. Adam seemed like a very different man than the one she'd originally met. Withdrawn. Iris had been right about him looking moody. His heart wasn't in this little coffee klatch. Sheba sat right beside him, and she looked a bit down, too. God, dogs seemed to have expressions. Maybe more importantly, her tail wasn't happily swishing the floor.

Iris was doing all the bright and cheerful for them, and Jazz felt uncomfortable because she couldn't think of much to say that might lift Adam a bit. But Iris had picked up his mood and dragged him over here. Maybe this would help.

He finished his coffee, without touching the pastries, and looked about ready to leave. Iris forestalled him, jumping up to refill his mug.

She spoke pertly. "You can't leave until you drink that. Anyway, you need to eat a donut or something. Sugar will perk you up and if I eat all of that, I'll get fat."

"Small chance of that," Adam remarked. "How many miles a week do you swim?"

"I don't count the miles, only pool lengths." Iris resumed her seat and reached for a cruller. "These are the best."

Jazz spoke. "Well, that explains why Melinda gave me six of them. She said she knew what you liked."

"She knows me all right."

"And just how, pray tell, do these pastries fit into your healthful diet plan?"

Iris grinned. "Pure ugly calories. Sometimes I need a bunch of them. Just not too often."

A smile finally creased Adam's face. "You mean you need to indulge once in a while."

"Well, that too." She pushed the pastry box toward him. "So do you."

At last he took a cruller. "Saving you from yourself."

Jazz, who'd been picking on her own bit of muffin, was glad to see the interaction between the two of them. She suspected that Iris got further with him than most people.

Jazz decided to stick her toe in the water. "Adam, you said you're a handyman. Does that mean you do everything, or do you limit your skills?"

"I do pretty much everything household. I stay away from cars, though. Not because I can't do them but because I don't want to take any business from Roger's garage. I have enough work anyway. A lot of people are pretty handy themselves, but there are jobs they don't want to do. Like squeeze under a sink to fix the pipe fitting on a dishwasher. Or to actually repair one." He tilted his head. "Dishwasher pumps always get them to call. Washers, dryers, stoves, refrigerators. A little of everything, which I guess was a long answer to your question."

At least he was talking, Jazz thought. "That's a pretty useful skill set. So plumbing? Carpentry?"

"Depends on the job. I install water heaters, faucets. As for carpentry, small jobs."

"He's done some work for Mom," Iris announced.

"But I couldn't fix the washer," Adam reminded her. "When those tubs go out of balance permanently, that's pretty much all she wrote."

"Noisy, too." Iris wrinkled her nose. "I was surprised it didn't fall apart."

"Might as well have."

"So now we have this fancy-schmancy one. I think Mom cringes every time I use it. But she still makes me do my own laundry."

Jazz was startled. "Of course she does! She's not a maid."

"That's what she says." Iris looked mischievous. "Darn, expecting me to keep up with all those towels."

"Trust me," Jazz answered, "I'm not the laundress, either."

Another giggle escaped Iris. "I'm not as bad as I pretend. Mom works. You work. But that doesn't mean I can't try to wriggle out of things."

"Wriggle harder," Adam suggested. "Maybe you can fool your aunt into letting you out of more."

Iris sighed. "I wouldn't like it if Mom heard about it. She's not as nice as you are, Aunt Jazz."

"You only think I'm nice."

After a bit, Iris excused herself, announcing that she still had that paper to finish.

Jazz looked at Adam, and thought he appeared uncomfortable. "Would you rather be somewhere else?" she asked him point-blank.

"I don't mean to be rude." His brown eyes met hers, then slid away. "Sorry, there are times when I'm just not good company."

"We all have those times." But she sensed he meant something more than an ordinary mood. No way to ask him, however, but she couldn't help feeling bad for him.

"I'd better go," he said, rising and reaching for his cup.

"Leave it. I'll get it."

Then she watched him walk away, a subdued Sheba at his side. What the hell was going on?

Chapter Three

Four more weeks before Lily returned. Jazz was settling into a routine, and she'd learned how to cook fish with several different recipes. Fish was great but she needed something more for herself.

She opted for walking to the grocery. It wasn't that far, the walk would be good for her and besides, the eco awareness in her made driving seem like a sin when it wasn't necessary.

However, she soon noticed something different. Yes, the trees had begun to don cloaks of spring leaves, a beautiful feathery view.

People still greeted her when they passed, still calling her Lily.

But something had changed.

She felt watched. Not casually, as locals might have done, but something more intense. Awareness made her neck tingle.

Man, was she losing her mind? Why would anyone watch her in this pleasant town? She hadn't had a chance to annoy anyone.

But the feeling persisted, and she put it down to the different environment. Maybe she'd just been too busy adjusting to all the newness to notice the sensation before. Or maybe her mind was creating it. Yeah. Why not? Minds did strange things sometimes.

Shrugging it off, she reached the grocery and purchased a few items that Iris, in her drive through there nearly a week ago, had missed. For cooking. Damn, she was cooking, and every night, too. Lily must have done *something* when she was home. Iris sure didn't expect to take part often.

She guessed she was learning some new things about her sister. The high-flying businesswoman cooked.

Hah! She could hardly wait to tease Lily about it.

Every single day, Iris had something going on, whether it was swimming or oboe lessons. Even some after-school tutorials.

The girl was sure driven, and she didn't expect to be carted around. In fact, she kept needling Jazz to do some more walking. Regardless, Iris was too busy to get into trouble, even the ordinary teenage kind.

As she approached the house, she saw Adam sitting on his front steps again, Sheba at his side. She waved, intending not to bother him, but he rose instantly and came toward her.

"Need some help with those groceries?"

She didn't really. Just three paper bags with handles, but she suspected that rejecting his help might be taken the wrong way. "Thanks." She smiled, and let him take two of the bags. Sheba, she noticed, was off leash but glued right to Adam's side.

"She's a well-behaved dog," Jazz remarked to Adam. "I couldn't imagine a dog being so good without a lead."

"She's special, all right. The only time she leaves me is when Iris is bouncing around. I wasn't kidding when I said the two of them have a special relationship."

Once inside the house, she offered him the inevitable coffee, and brewed it while she unloaded the bags. She hoped she was making him feel welcome. She sensed he needed that, though why she couldn't imagine. This town, so friendly, ought to be sitting on his front porch. It never seemed to be. Was he standoffish as a rule?

"Looks like you went with special items in mind," he remarked. He stroked Sheba when she laid her head on his thigh.

"Well, I'm learning to cook," she replied as she put the last item, green onions, in the refrigerator drawer. "That means as I come up with recipes to use the meat and fish, I have to pick up some items. Right now it's all complicated. For me, anyway. Iris barrels through that store and heaps the cart full according to her own tastes, I guess. Then I have to figure out what to do with it."

He snorted. "Easy for her, hard on you."

"That's the way it is, and I'm not going to be here long enough to try to change her habits."

"That might take forever anyway." This time he poured coffee for them both and they sat together at the kitchen table. "Did you know what you were getting into when you agreed to do this?"

"Mostly, I think. Lily and Iris like to visit me in Miami, although I could feel offended and think they come for the beaches." She laughed. "At least twice every winter. That's okay."

"But you've never come up here to visit."

She shook her head, still smiling. "No beaches and no ocean."

That at last drew a genuine smile from him. "Feel like the Hotel Paradise?"

"I know some people who do, but not me. Iris and

Lily are easy guests. Besides, they get my nose out of the computer and introduce me to good restaurants."

"So no cooking?"

Jazz laughed again. "No cooking. No extra laundry or cleaning, either."

"Good houseguests." His face grew thoughtful. "Remember how Iris complained her name didn't allow for a cool nickname like yours?"

Jazz nodded. "Interesting thing to notice."

"That young lady has some interesting thoughts in her head. Anyway, I was thinking about a nickname for her, and wondered what you'd think of *Irish*."

Jazz rolled it around in her head for a few moments, then said, "I like it. Her opinion is the one that matters, though."

"Of course, but if you didn't want me to come up with anything like that, I'd rather know it before I try it. Lily would be okay, too?"

"I'm sure. We're the same head in two bodies, basically. And anyway, the family *is* Irish."

He nodded. "That's what Lily said. All the way back until forever?"

Jazz shook her head. "That's the family story. Mom could prove it at least back to my great-grandmother. Lily hired a genealogist out of curiosity and, sure enough, our first Irish ancestor came over with the British Army during the Revolution. He wound up living in Canada. However…" She drew the word out.

Adam arched his brow. "However?"

"However, as is to be expected of almost any lineage, it's not pure. My sister decided not to show it to Mom when some Welsh and British showed up there. We didn't want to break her heart. But yeah, Irish enough as Lily said."

"I'm a mongrel by comparison."

"I bet you didn't have to grow up with family history being drilled into you."

"No, I didn't. You're right. But Irish is okay?"

"I think so." Jazz shrugged with a faint smile. "See what she thinks, but I'd be surprised if she doesn't like it. Whether she starts using it is something else."

"Might be kinda hard to change her name now."

The gloom started to settle visibly over Adam again. Jazz wondered what she might say to get him to talk about what was bothering him. The best way, she decided, was to confide in him herself. Maybe start the first bridge of trust. Although with only a few weeks, it might be a waste of time.

She smothered a sigh and dove in. "You ever feel like you're being watched?"

He nodded slowly. "Sure, but not for a while."

"You'll think I'm nuts, but I felt that way this morning."

His gaze immediately snapped to her, his face settling into grim lines. "I don't think you're nuts. How bad was it?"

"It made the skin on my neck crawl. I started to get pretty creeped out."

"You would." He nodded thoughtfully. "Did the feeling last for a while?"

"The whole time I was walking to the store. I told myself it was my imagination, but I couldn't totally ignore it. Weird. Anyway, in this town there isn't much to worry about."

"Really? When I was a kid, I remember the old sheriff saying this county was going to hell in a handbasket. Since then we've had some growth, but nothing phenomenal. Anyway, nobody's a hundred percent safe anywhere."

"Oh, thanks!" she said sarcastically. "You just made me feel a whole lot better."

He smiled, a real smile. "I wouldn't give it much thought. We're still a place where almost nobody locks their doors. That sense of being watched might have been nothing. But if it continues, let me know."

"Why? You going to run around looking for someone who's staring at me?"

He flashed a grin. "That's me, fool without a cape. No, I just want to know. I don't like the idea of you feeling creeped out. That's all."

"It won't happen again," she said decisively. "No reason it should. Maybe just a curious person. *Some* people can tell the difference between me and my sister."

"Then they're very observant."

She regarded him curiously. "Can you tell?"

"Just. You have mirrored smiles. When you half smile, the right side of your mouth curves upward. With Lily it's the left side."

She shook her head. "Now that's something I never noticed."

"Why would you? When you look at each other, you're looking into a mirror."

She visualized what he was saying. "You're right!"

"There are probably other things I haven't noticed yet, but I will."

Now his smile was natural and it was good to see. She only wished she dared ask him what haunted him. Then she realized she might not want to know. He didn't appear to be in any hurry to share anyway.

Iris returned very early from school, breezing through the doorway and heading directly for the refrigerator, where she rescued the remaining orange juice. "Hi," she said as she walked through, pausing just long enough to pat Sheba.

"Iris? You're home early."

The girl shrugged one shoulder, the other bearing her backpack. "Teacher education day or something." She flashed a grin. "I think it's actually teacher sanity day."

"It wouldn't surprise me," Jazz admitted. Dang, she loved Iris's view of life.

"Homework," Iris announced.

Jazz stopped her. "Hold on a second. Adam thinks your name has the potential for a cool nickname like mine."

Iris wrinkled her nose. "Nothing as cool as Jazz." Then she asked, "What nickname?"

Adam answered. "Irish."

Iris hooted. "Doesn't that fit, me being red Irish and all. I like it, but nobody will use it."

"Maybe when you get old enough to get tipsy," Adam suggested, which set Iris off into fresh laughter.

"Homework," she announced again, still holding the orange juice. "Then later I've got a training workout at the college. See ya." She headed for the dining room with Sheba on her heels.

"We ought to move to the living room," Jazz suggested.

"Closer to the coffee pot here. Anyway, I've got to get ready for a three o'clock appointment. There's a whistling water heater."

"Whistling? What in the world?"

"Most people never experience it, but there's a pressure relief valve on the top of the heater tank. If the water gets too hot, it starts releasing the pressure. It's a safety mechanism to prevent the thing from blowing up."

"Wow, the things I never knew."

"Most people don't know. Anyway, I need to stock my truck to get ready, and you probably need to get to your own work."

It was true. Since arriving here, she'd begun to have trouble concentrating on her book. That couldn't continue.

"Thanks for the coffee," Adam said, then called to Sheba. He and the dog left quickly.

Jazz stared at the empty space where Adam had been and wondered why she felt so discombobulated. It wasn't just the change of residence. It wasn't taking care of Iris.

It was something more. Some weird kind of unease, and not just because she had felt watched earlier.

She and Lily had often joked that they were psychic, but that usually meant between themselves. This was different.

And it carried a vague sense of doom.

As ADAM WAS loading his truck with water heater parts, hoping something hadn't gone wrong with the heating coil because that was god-awful to fix, he suddenly had the sense of being watched, a feeling he hadn't experienced since his days in the Army.

He looked around, but all he saw was a man parked a few doors down. The guy appeared to be reading a map.

Adam could have chuckled. If the man had wound up on this street and needed a map, he was certainly lost.

He was about to go over and ask if he could help when the driver put the map aside and drove off.

Adam went back to loading his truck, but he remembered what Jazz had said earlier about feeling watched. Now he'd felt it, too, but only briefly.

Something must have gotten into the air, he decided. There could be no other explanation for it, not around here.

But he didn't quite believe it.

It was nicer to think about Jazz anyway. She'd managed to drag him out of his morose thoughts, at least temporarily. Much as he tried to avoid these bouts, there wasn't much he could do.

Memories and emotions washed over him like a massive flood, and the gates of the dam only held so long. It was better than it had been a few years ago, but it still overwhelmed him at times.

Not like Winston, though. He didn't think anyone in that support group was as bad off as Winston. But then none of them had rotated through as many tours as he had. Winston had made his twenty years, giving him retirement, but he'd also fought in two wars, Iraq and Afghanistan. Rotation after rotation.

Then he'd come home and his retirement had turned into its own kind of hell. No rest, no peace, no family.

It was a wonder he was still around.

Sometimes Adam wished he wasn't around either. He'd finally found a balance between work that kept him busy enough and the weight room he'd pieced together in his extra bedroom. Working out with those weights caused a rush of endorphins that made him feel much better. Working with his hands helped him to think about other things. The support group, while it freshened some of his mental and emotional scars, gave him a place to vent when he needed one.

And helping his fellow vets in any way gave him a sense of purpose.

Not bad for a guy who'd considered building himself a hermitage in some isolated place, then realized he'd only be reinforcing his sense of isolation.

Because he was different now. Different from most people, and that bridge could never be completely crossed. He was now on a lifelong journey where he'd always feel mostly alone.

Ah, hell. He forced his thoughts away from dark places and turned them instead to Jazz.

Much as the twins might believe they were carbon copies, he was beginning to notice differences, and not minor physical characteristics. Slight differences in outlook, in reactions.

Very slight, probably arising from their different paths in life. At least discovering those differences was a journey he'd enjoy.

Feeling better he set out to take care of an overheating water heater, one that he hoped only needed a new thermostat.

Now that would add another bright spot to his day.

JAZZ MANAGED TO grind out another five pages in her book. Five pages. She sighed, but it *had* been a grind. Well, it happened sometimes. Waiting for a muse achieved nothing. Muses were unreliable, she thought with a spark of humor. When one arrived to sit on her shoulder, writing carried her away to a place where words and ideas flowed effortlessly.

But more often an editor sat on her shoulder, making her aware of every flaw, every poor word choice, every instance of passive voice. Years of critiques and suggestions had affected her writing. Maybe not all of it good, but she knew her editor would catch it when she screwed up.

How many times had she submitted a manuscript with the feeling she'd screwed up, and with the belief her editor would catch it? A lot of times.

Hah! Most of the time these days she received little criticism, but her confidence still needed some work.

She had just closed her laptop when Lily's landline rang. Lily kept it for business purposes because it was more reliable than a cell for professional calls.

"I hate it when the cell crackles and I miss words," Lily had explained. "Or the famous *I'm losing you* line. I love my cell phone for ordinary calls and texting, but business conversations just don't always make it."

Jazz had noticed that since arriving here. Atmospherics or too few cell towers?

She reached for the phone and heard Lily's welcome voice.

"How's it going, twin?"

"Just fine," Jazz answered. "But I'll never forgive you for putting me in a situation where I have to learn to cook."

Lily's laugh reached across the continents. "It'll do you good. And my peripatetic daughter?"

"Still constantly on the move. I wish I had her energy."

"We used to," Lily reminded her. "When we were her age. Anyway, I figure she's too damn busy to get into any serious trouble."

"That would be my guess. Although how she'd get into much trouble around here beats me."

"Well, there are a few unsavory elements, but not like Miami."

"Yeah," Jazz answered. "I'm still a little uneasy about letting her walk just anywhere, like out to the college."

"You've changed venue. Accept that you need to change perspective, too."

Maybe she was right, Jazz thought. Iris certainly believed she was safe walking everywhere, and Jazz's concern evidently had little to do with here and much to do with where she lived. "How are your conferences and meetings going?" she asked Lily.

"As usual. Much agreement punctuated by even more disagreement about whether, about how, about money. I'm sometimes not sure there's any real agreement at all."

Jazz sighed. "How frustrating."

"I'm used to it. I always bring my mental flak jacket to these meetings. Sometimes I think there are as many opinions in the world as there are people. Or at least cultures. Anyway, we muddle through until we settle on a few things we can do. A step at a time. Or maybe baby steps."

"I don't think I'd have the temperament."

"No," Lily answered frankly. "You've always been the relative introvert between us. You'd rather sit and listen, make your own judgments and keep them to yourself. Me, I'm always getting into it."

"Always to good effect."

Lily laughed again. "Right. Remember Dolly Moore in high school? She wanted to shut my mouth with a good punch."

Jazz smiled, remembering. "She might have, too, except we confused her so much she didn't know *who* she wanted to punch."

"Ah, the good old days. Are you getting mistaken for me?"

"All the time. I let it go. You can make apologies for me when you get back."

Lily hooted. "I'll just blame it on my bad twin. So nobody has figured it out yet?"

"If they have, it's only because they've heard Iris call me Aunt Jazz. And maybe half of *them* are still wondering. Didn't you tell anyone you have a twin?"

"Never seemed to matter. So no one yet for sure?"

"Well, Adam Ryder. He's seen a difference in our smiles. He said the difference wouldn't be apparent to either of us because when we look at each other it's like looking in a mirror."

"Interesting. I never thought about that."

"About Adam," Jazz said hesitantly.

"Yes?"

"I like him, he's nice, but... I don't know. I haven't been here long enough to really judge, but he seems moody."

"That's more of a problem for him than anyone. Army. Afghanistan."

Jazz drew a long breath. "I guess that would explain it."

"Anyway, don't worry about him. Nothing you can do, he has that wonderful dog of his, and he's always great with Iris. He's always struck me as isolated, though, so if he reaches out, just welcome him."

"Absolutely."

Just then Jazz heard the front door open and the unmistakable sounds of Iris's return. She held the phone away from her mouth and called out, "Iris, your mom is on the phone and I really think she'd like to hear your voice. If you can spare a whole minute."

She heard Iris laugh and then the girl appeared. "Oh, all right. I think I can manage." She took the receiver from Jazz's hand.

Jazz left them relative privacy to talk and made her way to the dreaded kitchen. Flounder tonight. She'd never met a flounder that hadn't been on a restaurant plate. Now she was going to get up close and personal.

AN HOUR LATER, after Jazz had unwrapped the now-thawed fish, Iris took the trash out. Another thing the girl never had to be asked to do.

"How'd the swimming go?" she asked over her shoulder as she patted the fish with a paper towel. When Iris didn't answer, she turned around.

Iris stood there, looking confused. She held up a plastic-wrapped bundle of flowers.

"These weren't on the doorstep when I got home, Aunt Jazz. I found them just now. Why would anyone leave dead flowers?"

Chapter Four

The package of dead flowers lay on the kitchen table. Jazz had told Iris to go take her shower and do her homework, pretending to dismiss the whole thing. Of course, it being Saturday, Iris had no essential homework, and she'd already taken a shower at the pool.

Seeming to understand, however, Iris announced she was going to start her laundry.

But the instant Jazz had seen the dead flowers, for some reason it had clicked with the sense of being watched she'd had earlier.

Her heart still clogged her throat from her initial reaction, and she tried to ignore the way her hands had begun to shake. It had to be a prank. Surely.

But she couldn't escape the sense that it was an ugly message.

She heard the washer start filling, then Iris walked by. "Adam's home. I'm going to visit Sheba."

"Mmm," Jazz answered, the only sound she could make just then. She couldn't take her gaze off those sinister flowers.

Enough, she told herself. Enough. Why get all in a tizzy about something like this? She still needed to make dinner. Flounder. Hell, it would spoil if she didn't cook it somehow.

It also felt like the least important thing just then.

Oh, for heaven's sake!

She was just rising from the chair, planning to toss those flowers in the trash bin, when the front door opened. At once she heard Iris accompanied by a dog's clicking claws. That must mean Adam was here as well.

She started to reach for the flowers, to get rid of them before Adam saw them, then stopped. Knowing Iris and her outgoing nature, she'd probably already mentioned them. The three of them walked into the kitchen, Adam saying, "Hey, Jazz."

Iris held up a brilliant yellow tennis ball. "Sheba and I are going to play fetch out back." She and Sheba disappeared out the back door.

Jazz resisted an urge to tell her to stay inside. That would be *so* over-the-top.

Adam looked at the flowers. "Ugly prank. Are you okay?"

"Where I come from this might be a warning rather than a prank. I'm trying not to let it get to me, but it is, a bit."

He nodded. "I read you. I doubt it was intended to be threatening, but I can see why you'd feel differently."

"Dead flowers," she said.

He pulled out a chair and faced her. "Flowers." He repeated the word but it wasn't questioning.

She tore her gaze from the awful gift and looked at him. "I can't help thinking...well..."

"You all have the names of flowers."

She swallowed hard. "Yeah. I've been trying to banish that notion."

He frowned, drumming his fingers. "They look like they come from one of the two groceries and they must be at least a few days old. Nobody would remember who bought them."

"No."

"I'm going to throw them in the trash. I'll be right back."

Even with the flowers gone, she didn't feel much better.

Adam returned quickly but didn't sit with her. "Flounder for dinner?"

"That's the idea. If I can shake this off. If I can remember how I intended to cook it."

"Let me take care of that."

Next thing she knew, he was washing his hands at the sink and looking at the fish. "That's quite a bit."

"Have you ever gone shopping with Iris? Well, if you're going to cook, you ought to stay for dinner."

He flashed a smile that wasn't quite a smile. "Will do. I like to cook sometimes. Better than loading up on cholesterol at Maude's diner, or Mahoney's Bar, or enjoying Hasty's grillmanship at the truck stop diner. Great food but I'm not in the market for an early heart attack."

She relaxed a little and watched him.

He headed for the pantry and soon emerged with a big container of instant potatoes. "Veggies in the freezer?"

"Yes."

"Nothing fancy, but we've got to fill up our athlete."

JAZZ STILL LOOKED DISTRACTED, disturbed. He couldn't blame her. He, too, had made the connection between flowers and that hideous bouquet.

Dead flowers. It *did* seem like a message, but that

had to be a coincidence. He couldn't imagine anyone in this town, including teens, who would even conceive of such a thing as a prank.

For Jazz's sake, he had to stick to the story that it was all a joke. While it felt threatening, it might not mean anything at all.

In order to make her feel better, he forced himself out of his morose mood and kept up a light patter while he cooked. When Iris came back in, his monologue became a conversation and grew funnier. She jokingly compared Adam to a famous TV cook, and he demanded to know where she was hiding his toque.

And bit by bit Jazz joined in. Exactly what he wanted. She simply *couldn't* worry about those flowers without other cause.

Brussels sprouts, lightly browned in butter, joined a mountain of mashed potatoes seasoned with chicken broth he'd found in the cupboard. Parmesan-encrusted flounder came out of the oven looking perfect.

Adam felt pleased with himself. Yeah, he could cook, but he didn't often and he was glad he hadn't lost his touch. His palate wasn't disappointed either. Both Iris and Jazz appeared to enjoy everything, too, and both complimented him.

Past the flowers, thank God.

He and Jazz finished eating long before Iris, who managed to polish off all the leftovers. Even the mashed potato bowl was cleaned.

"How does your mother afford you?" he asked Iris lightly.

"It's not easy but she loves me."

Adam looked at Jazz. "I can't argue with that."

Jazz smiled. "I'm learning. I never fed a football team before."

"Oh, come on," Iris said. "It's not that bad!"

"Absolutely not," Jazz said swiftly. Clearly, she didn't want Iris to take it to heart.

"You should see what I usually eat," Adam remarked. "Not as much as you, though. Weight lifting."

"That'll do it," Iris agreed. "I told you, Aunt Jazz, you need a dog to walk three times a day."

Jazz laughed. "Great try."

All this time, Sheba had been snoozing quietly near the cabinets, pretty much out of the way. Iris jumped up to take care of the dishes, most of which went into the dishwasher, and Sheba raised her head, wagging her tail.

Adam spoke. "Don't let Sheba talk you into giving her scraps."

Iris giggled. "There aren't any."

"Wonder how that happened," Jazz said dryly.

Adam was glad to see that Jazz had apparently let go of her initial concern about those flowers.

But then Iris did a typical teenage thing. She sat down at the table with a glass of milk and said, "Can you believe those flowers?"

Thud, Adam thought as he watched Jazz's face tighten. Crap, he'd been trying to distract her because the last thing he wanted to do was dismiss her feelings.

Nor could he blame her for them. The feeling she had been watched, added to the flowers, added to being in a strange place…well, most people would be disturbed.

He spoke. "Some guy you know probably thought it would be funny." He hoped for a *maybe*. He didn't get it.

Iris drank more milk then used a paper napkin to wipe away the mustache. "Actually no," she replied. "At least I don't think so. But who'd announce it if he was that type?"

"Most likely they fell from someone's trash and some-one else did it to tease you."

Iris considered it, then nodded. "Yeah, maybe. An idiotic impulse." Then she rinsed her glass and stuck it in the dishwasher. "A bunch of us are meeting at the church hall to play cards. Gotta run. Back by ten, Aunt Jazz. They throw us out."

She was out the door like a shot, leaving Adam to look across the table at Jazz. Her mood had fallen again.

She spoke. "Would you like to come into the living room? I've got a bad habit from home. I don't have a living room in my studio, so a table serves as the fill-in for everything. But there's no point being stuck in Lily's kitchen."

He'd been about to leave, to give her some space.

But then she said, "I almost didn't let Iris go."

Aww, hell.

Adam made coffee and carried it in a thermal carafe into the living room, along with a couple of mugs.

"What I really want," Jazz said, "is a beer."

"I can run to my place and get a couple of longnecks if you want."

She shook her head. "Thanks, Adam, you've been wonderful this evening. I should apologize for taking up so much of your time. You didn't have to do all this."

"No, I didn't. Returning to civilian life taught me one thing."

"Which is?"

"That there are a few guardrails I have to observe, but the rest?" He shook his head. "I don't have to do a damn thing I don't want to."

That drew a smile from her. "A sense of freedom?"

"Mostly." He sipped his hot coffee, waiting. He was sure she hadn't invited him into the living room because she wanted him to leave.

He knew the room well, with its two overstuffed taupe recliners and matching sofa, a colorful Persian-style rug lying on the floor in the center of the room. Photos of Iris covering the walls which were painted a medium blue. Curtains of a darker blue. And the big-screen TV that once had enthralled Iris and appeared to get little of her attention now. In all, a restful room.

But Jazz didn't look at all restful.

"Talk to me," he said after a few minutes. "You're still upset, aren't you?"

"And feeling like I'm overreacting. Being ridiculous."

"When you figure out how to successfully argue with a feeling, let me know. So, the flowers?"

"Not just them. That feeling of being watched. I *never* feel like that, and now I can't brush it aside. Then this. It's more than ugly. I can't escape the feeling that they were a threat."

She turned her head toward Adam, who occupied the recliner next to hers. Neither of them had raised their feet. "Did Iris say anything else to you about the flowers? Before you came over here?"

A thought struck him, that he'd been looking at this from the wrong direction. "You're more worried about Iris than about yourself."

"Why wouldn't I be?" Jazz shook her head. "Maybe you folks don't think the way I do, but I come from a different environment, unfortunately loaded with threats. Especially to women. I'm not talking about trouble on every street corner, but there's enough of it to make a woman cautious. Here everyone feels safe."

"Mostly," he agreed carefully.

"So I've got a beautiful teenage girl insisting on walking everywhere, even out to the college, often by herself. She's been doing it for years and doesn't see any possibility of danger in it."

"She's probably right," he said firmly.

"*Probably* isn't good enough." Jazz sighed, shaking her head. "Okay, I must be overreacting. As long as she didn't seem disturbed."

"She didn't. Not at all. She just told me it was weird and shrugged."

Jazz eyed him. "But then you came over."

"Well…" He drew the word out. "I guess I just wanted to see for myself."

She smiled lopsidedly. "Do tell."

"I've been in places where I had to be hypercautious. I wouldn't consider this town to be one of them, but some old habits die hard."

"Do you still think this was a prank?"

He snorted. "You know high school boys. They're probably snickering about it, hardly able to wait for Monday to hear Iris talk about it."

Tension let go of her face and shoulders. "Yeah," she murmured. Then she smiled. "When you put it that way…"

Fairly certain that Jazz was okay now, Adam departed with Sheba. He was okay, too. The event had proved to be enough distraction to pull him out of his solitary maunderings over memories he wished he could excise.

But neither of them knew that there *was* a real threat, and the danger lay in wait in the stack of mail on the hall table.

Chapter Five

Iris had returned home shortly after ten the night before and had collapsed in bed within twenty minutes.

Jazz remembered herself at that age, and how she was apt to stay up late most nights if she could. Iris loved her sleep, understandably, and on Sunday mornings wanted to sleep in.

Jazz enjoyed her coffee with the kitchen window open and birdsong to keep her company. She needed a sweater for this cooler climate but there was something to be said for that. It made her feel snuggly.

Last night's angst had departed, followed this morning by a calmer wait-and-see attitude. Adam's description of teen boys snickering about their prank made sense to her.

As for that feeling of being watched? One day meant nothing. Easy to imagine the whole thing. So she stretched, yawned, sipped more coffee and smiled at the happy bird right outside the window. Spring must feel great to it.

She sometimes wondered how birds handled the winter if they didn't fly south. What did they eat? How did they stay warm? Were there enough bird feeders in the world to keep them healthy? Maybe not, but they were still here.

"Coffee," a rusty voice said.

Jazz turned her attention from the window to see Iris enter the kitchen wearing emerald-green pajamas topped by a white robe that hung open. Her feet had already found their way into some black fuzzy slippers.

"It's there," Jazz answered, amused.

"Yeah," Iris mumbled as she pulled a mug from the cupboard. "I could smell it."

"Did it wake you up?"

"No, some dang bird did. Wouldn't shut up."

"And here I was enjoying it."

Iris glowered as she came to the table. "Not the same bird. Mine is loud. Obnoxious."

"Oh. Say, I was wondering, how do the birds here survive the winter?"

Iris's scowl was fading as she drank coffee. "You should visit some time. The window frames look like they've grown feathers."

A startled laugh escaped Jazz. "What?"

"They hunker around windows where heat escapes, all puffed up like balls. Periodically they attack the bird feeders. I swear Mom puts ten pounds or more of seed in her feeder every week. And they still can fly!"

Jazz giggled. "They sound like you."

"The food maybe, but not that squawking, trust me."

Iris fell silent while she drained her cup. "Okay," she announced, "I've reached first gear. French toast for breakfast? I'll make it."

"Between you and Adam, I'm going to feel like a princess."

"Nah, we both just like good food."

"What? I'm trying!"

Iris grinned. "And I'm kidding. It's a tradition. On Sunday morning, if I want French toast, I make it. Fair trade, especially when Mom can sit back and kibitz."

Jazz poured herself a second coffee. "Does Lily kibitz much?"

"I don't usually give her much reason, but she needs an excuse to be a mother sometimes."

Jazz burst into laughter.

A MAN OUT on the street paused, listening. His face darkened with rage. Laughing? He was going to strike that laughter out of Lily forever. Just as she'd stolen his laughter and his life. And his daughter.

Lily was alone a lot of the time, he'd noticed, which would make his task easier. But he wanted her to feel fear. Terror. All in good time. He'd had plenty of time in prison to stoke his anger and plot.

Only he hadn't plotted for this dinky town. Hadn't ever considered that he'd need to stay out of sight as much as possible. In Miami he could have blended in anywhere.

Conard City was a different matter, requiring a different plan. He had no doubt he'd figure it out and it wouldn't take ten years this time.

But no more laughter for that woman. Never again.

His mind began to roam over the ways he could ratchet up her fear until it turned to terror. There might be *some* advantages to a small town.

He'd liked the touch of the flowers, though. He hoped Lily was already uneasy.

Yeah, she probably was. In some ways Lily was a smart woman. But only some ways. She'd done a lot of stupid things with him, stupid things that meant she had to learn a lesson.

Satisfied about the flowers, he walked on, his mental wheels spinning.

IRIS AND JAZZ spent a fun morning together. Iris regaled her aunt with tales of her amazing victories at cards. Told her about this one boy, named Tony, who kept flirting with her.

"How do you feel about that?" Jazz asked.

Iris shrugged. "Kinda flattered but I'm not interested."

"Is something wrong with him?"

"Not that I know, but where would I fit him in?"

Jazz couldn't repress a grin. "I think that'll change."

"Not without me giving up something else important. Boyfriends can wait until later." She waved an airy hand.

For some reason, Jazz felt Iris wasn't being quite truthful. "I'm sure when you get around to it, you'll have your pick."

Iris screwed up her face. "Everybody's so certain."

"About what, sweetie?"

"That I'll want a boyfriend. Well, he's going to have to fit into my life, that's all I can say. Come on, let's take a walk, see some of the limited sights around here. There are some pretty houses that Mom always admired. A nice park. Ooh, maybe we'll see Edith Jasper."

"Who's she?"

Iris's smile broadened. "A tiny old lady with a very big Great Dane. The sight alone is worth the price of admission."

Jazz had to admit that would be something she'd like to see.

THE PARK WAS only four blocks away, and Jazz was instantly charmed. Kids were running around having fun on the playground equipment or sitting on the grass with cars and trucks. Moms and dads relaxed on benches in conversational knots while keeping an eye out. A few people walked dogs.

Paths rambled around, too, between trees and bushes and even some flowering shrubs. This would be a great place to relax and stretch her legs.

"Why did you never bring me here before?" Jazz asked her niece.

"Because you haven't been here that long, and I've been busy."

"Good point."

"Let's go this way," Iris said, turning them to one of the paths. "I like this one best because of the way it winds around. For some reason it makes me happy."

Amazing, thought Jazz, considering Iris seemed to be naturally happy most of the time.

But the creepy feeling came back as they strolled along the path. Jazz's neck prickled. Someone was staring.

Oh, hell, she told herself. It was a busy park. People all over the place. Any one of them might briefly stare. *Get a grip, girl.*

They never saw the famed Edith Jasper, however. Iris spied some friends and ran over to them when Jazz told her to go ahead, that she'd just walk home.

She didn't especially want to fall in with a bunch of teen girls who would probably burst with questions about her. But she also didn't want to leave Iris alone.

Damn, she thought. Iris was with friends in a busy

park and Jazz needed to get past this senseless uneasiness. She made herself wave, then walked out of the park.

It was a beautiful spring morning and that was exactly the thing she should focus on.

IRIS CAME HOME a couple of hours later. Like a fresh breeze, she wafted into the house and plopped herself at the kitchen table.

Jazz was sitting there with her laptop, trying to work but still finding it hard to concentrate. The different environment seemed to be causing some writer's block. Oh, well, she'd keep trying, and it wasn't as if she was in a time crunch. Yet.

"My friends and I splurged on lunch at Maude's diner. Am I bothering you, Aunt Jazz? Are you trying to write?"

"Trying is the operative word. Success not so much. So how was lunch?" Jazz closed her laptop.

"I loved every mouthful. We had a great time, too. That burger was yummy, but the fries were the best."

Jazz put her chin in her hand. "You actually eat fries?"

"Not often, which makes them better when I do. I am so stuffed now, though."

Jazz smiled. "I didn't know you could get there."

Iris giggled. "Just don't tell my coach about it. But you and I ought to go to Maude's sometime."

"Why is that?"

Iris wiggled her eyebrows. "Because you'd feel your arteries hardening, you'd want to walk more, and since you'd need help with that, you'd get a puppy."

Jazz just shook her head. "Dang, you're persistent."

"I wouldn't be on the swim team if I wasn't."

Jazz couldn't argue with that. "I'm not exactly sedentary."

"No, I see you using Mom's exercise bike. But it would feel so much better outdoors."

Jazz lifted her chin from her hand. "Next time Lily calls, you ask *her* for a dog."

Iris screwed up her face. "I know what she'll say."

"Exactly," Jazz replied feeling momentarily triumphant. Although she privately thought that Iris ought to have her dog. She was a great believer in pets, especially for young people, and if Lily had to bend herself a bit to take care of the animal, she had the benefit of working from home, too.

Besides, given Iris's energy level, she'd probably manage to fit in most of the care herself despite her already packed life.

There was a knock at the front door and Iris jumped up. "I'll bet it's Sheba."

"Sheba knocks?"

Iris's giggle trailed behind her.

It must be Adam, Jazz thought, suddenly wishing she was wearing something better than her frayed jeans and well-worn sweatshirt. And what a strange thought that was. Anyway, Adam was probably still concerned about her reaction yesterday over the flowers. A very considerate man.

The sound of Sheba's claws tapping the wood floor of the hallway proved Iris was right. Jazz almost laughed at the way Iris had believed it was Sheba. Evidently Adam took second place to his dog.

"I'm taking Sheba out back," Iris called as she raced down the hall.

Adam entered the kitchen, and he apparently shared Jazz's thought, saying wryly, "I'm the runner-up."

"That's a fact. Grab a seat. Do you want me to make coffee?"

"I'll make it, if you don't mind. I don't expect to be waited on. I often drop-in. Because of Sheba."

"Iris is really taken with her."

"And I'm willing to share. To a point." Adam moved comfortably around, starting the drip coffee pot, reaching for mugs. "You want some?"

"Please."

Two mugs descended to sit on the counter. These were blue and white, Lily's favorite color scheme. Many of the dishes had a Blue Willow pattern, or something reminiscent of Chinese designs. The motif carried through to the utensil jars which were Delft Blue pottery.

"It looks like you were working," he said as he brought coffee to the table.

"*Trying* to work. Writer's block R us."

"That must be frustrating."

"It will be, if it goes on too long. It seldom does, though."

He nodded. "What do you hear from Lily?"

"Not a whole lot, which isn't surprising. She's told me about these trips. Meetings all day and cocktails and dinner parties in the evening. She must have Iris's energy level."

"But you prefer a quieter life?"

"I'm sort of an introvert," Jazz admitted. "The bigger the group, the quieter I get. And sometimes I just need to find a quiet corner to recharge. I'm not the best guest."

"Friends?"

She smiled. "A small group of very good friends. I'm

comfortable with them, and they don't get bent if I go all quiet on them."

He sipped coffee, then asked, "Am I too much, dropping in like this?"

Jazz shook her head. "You're just one person, and I suspect you have a need for quiet sometimes, too."

He arched a brow. "Am I wearing a sign?"

She chuckled. "No. Just a feeling. You're an introvert, as well?"

"I wasn't always." But he didn't explain.

That heightened her curiosity, but there didn't seem to be a good way to ask why. She was always hesitant to pry into people's thoughts and feelings. They'd share what they wanted to, and she gleaned most of her understanding from observation.

They sat quietly for a few minutes. The sound of Iris playing with Sheba drifted in through open windows.

Then Adam asked, "Are you feeling any better today?"

"Pretty much." She bit her lower lip then said, "I had that feeling of being watched again, while we were at the park. It has to be my imagination."

She saw his stare grow piercing. He even stiffened almost invisibly. What the heck?

"Well," she added swiftly, "there are a lot of people in the park."

"True." But he spoke quietly, almost thoughtfully, then drummed his fingers on the table briefly. "That's not a good feeling to have."

"It makes my neck prickle. Which is overkill. I mean, what's there to fear from being stared at? Maybe it's somebody who has the feeling that I'm somehow different from Lily."

"Maybe." He sighed and sipped more coffee. "I'm liking that little scheme you and Iris have hatched about not telling people you're not Lily." One corner of his mouth hitched up.

"It's probably wrong of me."

"Why? It's likely that even if you told them they'd think you were funning them."

"I hadn't thought about that. I just don't want to keep correcting people." She smiled. "I told Iris, and maybe you, that if I messed up anything, Lily could do the apologizing."

He laughed, clearly enjoying the idea. "You'd better mess up something because I want to see Lily's confusion and then her stammered apology."

His response amused Jazz. "I don't think Lily has stammered since third grade."

"What about you?"

"I honestly don't recall. I *must* have been caught flat-footed a time or two. Or more. Or maybe I was just good at wriggling out of things."

Iris returned with Sheba. The dog was panting a bit, but still appeared to be grinning. Iris was, too.

"That was fun," she said, heading for a lower cupboard. She pulled out a large metal bowl and filled it with water, placing it on the floor for the dog. Sheba dove right in.

"It's okay, Aunt Jazz. We keep this bowl just for Sheba."

"Did I say anything?"

"Nope. Ooh, that coffee smells good." She poured herself a mugful and joined them at the table. "Sheba was getting too smart."

"How so?" Adam asked.

"Toward the end, she stopped chasing the tennis ball. She'd just watch it land, then walk over to get it."

"Hah!" said Jazz. "Now that's smart."

"I thought so."

Sheba, done with drinking, sat beside Adam and rested her wet snout on his denim-covered thigh. He began to pet her head, ignoring the dampness. "She's a good girl," he remarked. "But too tired right now to wag her tail."

"Give her a few minutes," Iris said knowledgably. "She's like me. It doesn't take her long to get up and go again."

"Do you ever stop?" Jazz asked.

"Well, I *do* sleep. Sometimes."

ADAM RETURNED TO his house as the afternoon began to wane. Shadows from the mountains had moved in, a false twilight beneath a brilliant sky.

He got the biggest kick out of Iris. She was almost always good for his mood, unless the mood was too black and too deep. On those days, except for his handyman jobs which at least kept him moving, he'd withdraw into his house beyond reach, often working out his dread, anxiety and memories by lifting weights.

Unfortunately, he couldn't bench press anything heavy enough to really work his upper body, not without a spotter. He could have gone to the gym at the college during public hours, but he didn't want to be with so many people. All the noise, the banging and clanging from every direction, could trigger him. Not always, but even occasionally was too much.

Nor was the cost worth it. He'd had to learn to avoid

triggers insofar as he knew what they were, and the meds the docs had tried hadn't helped him.

It was what it was, he told himself, the product of his own life choices. He honestly wasn't sure any longer about what had impelled him to join the Army. Not that it mattered. He'd done it and wasn't going to lay the blame for his problems at anyone else's door.

His hip had begun to ache mightily. His limp had grown more pronounced, throwing everything else in his body off balance until he started aching all over. Shaking his head, he gave up the idea of heading for the weights and instead headed for his fridge.

Frozen dinners filled the freezer, except for the ice machine on one side. He pulled out two and headed for that miracle, the microwave.

Except that he'd often thought of it as a time waster. How often did he do nothing else because the damn thing cooked so fast that he didn't have time to do anything else?

When both meals were heated, he carried them into his small living room and placed them on a wooden TV table. First, he popped some ibuprofen and sucked it down with cold beer.

It was going to be that kind of night.

Giving in to reality, he flipped on the big-screen TV to the news. Not that he wanted news. In fact, he mostly hated it, but it was always an easy go-to and prevented him from having to scroll through the guide looking for anything but reality TV. Which wasn't all that real, to his way of thinking. Just a cheap way to fill the slots for advertisers.

Gads, he was turning into a curmudgeon.

He scrolled anyway, because hearing about the latest

outrage didn't qualify as distraction. He stumbled on a show about Bigfoot, which might be entertaining. Some myths were fun.

But his thoughts drifted from the show to the women across the street. Those flowers bothered him. Jazz's sensation of being watched bothered him.

He'd felt watched, and the sense could seldom be safely ignored. Although this was a different place than a war zone it shouldn't be dismissed out of hand.

But the combination of the flowers and Jazz feeling watched unsettled him. Worried him. If someone was watching her, why? She hadn't been here long enough to have attracted any real attention.

Then there was Iris. What if the girl was really the one being watched?

His stomach tightened and the meatloaf in front of him lost his interest.

Maybe he was becoming paranoid. Given every other skew in his brain now, maybe he was.

Small comfort. He resumed eating meatloaf that now tasted like ash and trying to watch the pseudoscientific program that tucked bits of fact in around loads of speculation.

He actually kind of liked the idea of Bigfoot. Imagine a parallel hominid species living a stealthy, concealed life away from one of the world's biggest threats: mankind. Yeah, he could get into that for an hour or so.

The meatloaf regained its flavor, the tension eased out of him.

But he didn't forget. He needed to find some unobtrusive way to keep an eye on Iris and Jazz.

Although watching out for Iris would probably require

a whole team, given the way that young woman was always on the move. The thought made him smile faintly.

Just keep an eye out.

ANDY ROBBINS KEPT an eye out. He'd been keeping it out all day. Learning your prey's habits was essential to a good hunt.

Now he had to wonder if that big guy from across the street could turn into a problem. He'd spent a lot of time with Lily that afternoon. A lot.

Maybe a romance. The thought ratcheted Andy's anger to a whole new level. Lily was *his*, always had been even when she'd gotten him arrested and convicted. She was *still* his property to do with as he pleased and she needed to pay, not go waltzing off into the sunset with some brooding bear.

He ground his teeth as he stomped through dark back-streets to that lousy motel room. It was hardly better than his prison cell, although even he had to admit that was unfair to the motel and too complimentary to the prison.

He had time, he reminded himself. Time to plan and prepare, and he'd better do both or he wouldn't be successful. Another turn in prison would kill him.

Nor was he a fool. Some might think he was brain-less for getting himself in trouble with the law, but Andy didn't believe that. Betrayal had put him in prison, not his own actions.

If Lily had just behaved like a good wife, none of that would have happened. None of it.

And he was going to get her good.

Chapter Six

Monday morning brought gray skies and a misty rain. Iris grabbed her usual yogurt and apple for breakfast and an insulated lunchbox she had packed the night before.

She dashed out, calling, "See ya later, Aunt Jazz."

God, that girl was making her feel old, Jazz thought as she drooped sleepily over a cup of coffee. Such an impossible amount of energy.

And now she had the entire day ahead of her to beat herself against a search engine for a manageable recipe that involved a pork roast, or maybe some more fish, or…hey, wasn't there some ham? That ought to be easy. Especially since she seemed to remember seeing a box of instant potatoes au gratin on the pantry shelf. She could manage that.

But Iris wouldn't be home until just before dinner, and Jazz was beginning to feel the misery of her work refusing to budge and the solitude of not being able to meet a friend for lunch.

She guessed she wasn't *that* introverted. She certainly wasn't agoraphobic. Yesterday's walk in the park hadn't been enough outside time.

She yawned, freshened her coffee, then tried to decide her own breakfast. There was enough yogurt in there to feed an entire team, almost all of it mixed with granola. Good enough, although she would have preferred vanilla or blueberry. *Well, heck, girl, next time at the store buy something for yourself instead of being overwhelmed by Iris's needs.*

Then, drowsy or not, she laughed at herself. Iris was overwhelming, yes, but in a good way, and it was only her own customary solitude that kept her flat-footed through this experience.

Well, that and seeming to have lost the anchor of her work. Man, that was something she *seriously* needed to bang her head on. It was one reason she swam in a sea of personal tranquility. Frequent interruptions scattered her thoughts, distracted her from her work, and sometimes made it difficult to pick up the thread.

Writing also fulfilled her in a way nothing else could, even when she started muttering *damnbook* as all one word.

Carrying a notebook, even while away from the computer, had become nearly habitual so if an idea popped up when she was away, she could scribble it down. Lately no ideas had popped up, and her story was lost in limbo.

She ate her yogurt, trying to rattle her brain into some kind of gear. It seemed intent on drifting.

Maybe she ought to just resign herself to this being a vacation, because it appeared it wasn't going to be anything else.

She dumped her waste in the bin and her spoon into the dishwasher. Standing at the kitchen window, she considered opening it, but the mist held her back. Wyoming felt chilly to her Florida blood, and the dampness wouldn't help.

Then she heard the heat kick on. Well, there was a reason for feeling chilly if the heat turned on.

She sighed and headed to the bedroom to dress. Actually starting this day might help.

Jeans and a sweatshirt later, with her black hair caught up in a ponytail, she still didn't feel any more productive. Lost cause.

A brisk walk to the grocery might be in order. Maybe it would clear the fog from her head.

She found one of Lily's light jackets with a hood. It looked warm enough and rainproof, and perfect to cover one of Lily's heavy sweaters. Then she grabbed a couple of the reusable grocery bags and headed out.

The air felt a bit raw, as if winter were moving back in. Surely the wrong time of year? But what would she know?

She didn't encounter many people, but that hardly surprised her. It was a workday, and given the way the air felt, only someone as desperate as she would be out here.

She almost laughed at herself. Desperate? Maybe so, but not for any good reason. With the hood up, a bulky sweater under the jacket, she felt comfortable enough. Maybe she should borrow more of Lily's clothes. It had been a habit when they were younger and she'd bet her sister wouldn't mind now.

By the time she reached the store, her hands were reconsidering her decision not to hunt up gloves. Once inside, though, she began to warm up. A couple of people said hi, calling her Lily, and she just smiled back, returning the hellos. No one tried to stop for conversation, which was fine with her.

She wasn't quite sure why she was here, except to get out of the house for a stroll. The store made a good destination, and she decided to get some of the fruit yogurt she liked.

Wandering slowly, browsing, she eventually wound up with all she needed to make a large salad for her and the always-ravenous Iris. She even picked up a variety of dressings to pad out the limited selection Lily had.

She also began to have fun. She shopped for herself at home, but this was different, buying larger quantities, choosing items she loved that she felt Iris might love as well. Something different from Iris's choices and the foodstuffs already in the pantry.

Such as fresh broccoli. She made a decent cheese sauce for that. And, look, there were fresh mustard greens to add to her salad. She loved the zing in them.

But given that she had to walk home, she couldn't afford to get carried away.

Feeling better, she stepped out of the store with her two bags and immediately felt those eyes on her again.

This time it went beyond a sense of her scalp prickling to an ice that poured down her spine.

Too much. Too often. Striding along the sidewalk, her pace picked up as she felt as if someone was boring a hole into her back.

She couldn't help but look over her shoulder, but she saw a handful of people. Not one appeared interested in her.

"Hey, lady," a familiar voice called.

She looked to her left and saw Adam in a big white-paneled van. "Hey," she answered, feeling marginally better.

"Let me give you a ride home. I'm headed that way, and it's feeling like it's about to rain."

She was only too glad to accept. He leaned over to

throw open the door for her, and she slid in, putting her bags of groceries on the floorboards. He bent and lifted them by their handles, raising them over the seat to place them in back.

"I just finished a job," he said by way of explanation. "Did Iris eat you out of house and home?"

She managed a small laugh. "No, but nearly everything there is her choice. I decided I wanted a few of my own."

"Great idea. You count, too. You were walking kind of fast. Worried about rain?"

"I won't melt. No, I just had that feeling again."

He was silent as he pulled up in front of the house. "How bad?" he asked.

"I felt as if something was boring into my back."

"Damn."

"You think my imagination is running wild."

"Far from it."

The rain started, lightly. A perfectly dismal day, she thought.

"Let me help you get the groceries inside."

"I can do it," she said stoutly.

"Jazz."

It was all he said, so she let him get the bags as she climbed out. When they reached the front door, she saw it. A cry escaped her. "My God!"

"Step over it. Get inside *now*."

She didn't argue, the sight of the gutted squirrel was more than she could stand. He passed the bags to her, then closed the door firmly.

What he did she had no idea as she stood there shaking. A few minutes later, he entered, closing the door behind him.

"Let's get these into the kitchen," he said, taking the bags from her.

She followed, hoping the vision would fade away. It didn't, especially when he grabbed a bucket from the small mudroom and filled it with water from the sink. She heard the front door open and close again.

In a chair, she wrapped her arms around herself and began rocking. This was no joke. It was a threat. She could barely grasp that anyone would do something so cruel. She couldn't believe it was just a nauseating prank. No way.

Adam returned, taking the bucket to the mud porch before returning to sit across from her. "It's gone," he said flatly.

Her response was a whisper. "Thank you."

An eternity seemed to pass until Adam broke the silence.

"This was no joke," he said his voice threaded with steel.

"No," she agreed, her voice still near a whisper.

"I know there's an extra bedroom upstairs across from Iris's. I'm moving in."

Jazz's world reeled. He thought they needed protection.

ADAM WATCHED HER eyes close. She gripped the edge of the table, but there wasn't a damn thing he could do about her reaction. He simply waited while his mind ranged over possibilities. The only comfort he could find was that this clearly couldn't have been directed at Iris.

No, it was directed at Lily, because hardly a damn soul knew she was Jazz.

But what could Lily have done? As far as he knew she

was well-liked in this town. She certainly couldn't have done a thing to draw this kind of threat.

"Iris," Jazz said. "Oh my God, Iris."

"It wasn't directed at her."

"How can you be sure?" Her eyes had darkened with fright.

"Because it was done while you were out shopping. If it had been intended for your niece, it would have been there when she came home from school or swimming."

Jazz nodded jerkily. "But I haven't been here long, and no one knows…" Her voice trailed off. Then, "Lily."

"That would be my guess."

"But Adam, you've lived here for years. You'd know if someone had a grudge."

"Well, I don't." He drummed his fingers on the table. "You look cold. You need something hot. Soup? Coffee? Something else?"

"I don't know if I could stomach anything just now." Shrugging, she tugged off the jacket. "Maybe if I let people know who I am?"

He shook his head, his expression grim. "If you do that, it'll just push the threat down the road. Lily will face it when she gets home, and we have absolutely no idea what's going on. Maybe we can figure it out first."

"What if we can't?"

"Then I'll shout from the rooftops that you're Lily's twin and we'll deal with it then."

She nodded slowly. "I wouldn't want anything to happen to my sister." She appeared to be losing some of her tension. "What about the police? I guess I should call them."

Adam noted that she didn't seem to be worried about

herself, at least not as much as Iris and Lily. Interesting. They'd been the first of her concerns.

"That would probably be a good idea. They at least need to be aware, but I don't think they'll be able to do anything yet."

"Probably not. How do you trace some dead flowers and a dead squirrel?" She shuddered. "Maybe some coffee. Soup sounds too heavy."

He was happy to oblige, glad to have anything to do that might give her even a smidgeon of comfort. A deep anger was growing in him. What kind of creep would do this?

Combined with Jazz's feeling that she was being watched, he couldn't begin to minimize any of it. Not even to make her feel better. They were past that.

When she didn't reach for the phone, he did, getting straight through to dispatch. Velma's familiar croaky voice answered him. Sometimes he thought that woman was going to die at the console.

"Velma, this is Adam Ryder. I'm at Lily Robbins's house and we've got a problem with a threat. Can you send someone over when you have a chance? No rush."

When he hung up, he poured coffee for them both. Jazz rested her elbow on the table and cupped her chin in her hand.

"This is unreal, Adam."

"Couldn't agree more."

She sighed, and eventually raised the mug to her lips. "I don't know what you do, but this coffee is better than what I make."

"Probably because you don't have to make it yourself."

"Maybe." But her face still didn't have much color.

He wondered how to get some food in her. A shock like she'd just had was difficult for the body to handle.

"I'm still worried about Iris, Adam. She's out there so much on her own. Maybe I should drive her."

He understood, but in his gut he felt that was a step too far. The evidence, little as it was, didn't point to the girl. "She's rarely alone, Jazz. And you can't coop her up here like an unhappy bird. She'd hate it, probably never forgive you, and be trying to find ways to escape."

She nodded and sighed. "I'm here only because she didn't want to give up everything to go with Lily to Europe. Imagine that."

Adam managed a rusty laugh. "Your niece has been a world traveler for years. Any one of her friends might leap at a chance to go to Europe, but not Iris. She's been there, done that."

At least that drew a faint smile from Jazz. "True."

"Now let me put the groceries away. You supervise."

"I'd forgotten all about them!"

"Hardly surprising." He rose and began to empty bags, spreading the contents on the counter. "I'm reasonably sure the yogurt goes in the fridge. After that it may be a foray."

"I'm not sure where Lily keeps everything."

Adam glanced over his shoulder. "Organize it for *yourself.* Lily didn't leave you a map so she'll have to deal with it when she gets back."

Jazz snorted. "My sister has never been big on organization except in her job. She might never notice."

The threat hadn't vanished but Jazz's fear had settled down. Adam felt relief. "I don't know when Jake Madison is going to get here," he offered as he put the last item away. "I'll run over to my place and get what

I need for a few days. If I see the black-and-white out front, I'll hurry back."

She looked at him, her jaw dropping a bit. "You were serious about staying with us?"

"Hell, yeah. Get used to it."

JAZZ WAS MORE grateful than she would have believed. Honestly, she was now afraid of being alone. She couldn't forget the sense of eyes being on her, either. The two things felt inextricably linked now.

Someone *was* stalking her.

Worse, despite Adam's reassurance, she was more worried about Iris. In Miami she'd never let a girl Iris's age run about so much with so little supervision. Hell, it wasn't any safer for a grown woman. Places you didn't go, neighborhoods you avoided. Oh, a whole laundry list of things. A subtle form of repression, she supposed, but staying safe was paramount.

Here was different. Clearly. She didn't believe her sister would have allowed this much freedom if she didn't believe it was safe.

But Jazz remained uneasy. On the one hand, she wanted to protect Iris. On the other, she didn't want to frighten her niece. Rock meet hard place, she thought.

Wait and see appeared to be the only approach.

The police chief arrived just as Adam was carrying a large duffel bag across the street. Jazz opened the front door to greet both men, the sight of Adam so welcome she nearly sagged.

Chicken. No reason to be terrified of being alone. Not yet.

The cop greeted her, extending his hand. "Howdy,

Ms. Robbins. I'm Jake Madison, chief of police. I hear you had a little problem today?"

Jazz stepped back, opening the door wide. "Please come in, Chief. Oh, and you, too, Adam." Sheba, as always, was on Adam's heels.

Adam dropped his bag with a thud near the hall table.

Jazz led the way into the living room, and once everyone was seated the chief asked, "What happened?"

"First I need to explain something," Jazz said. "I'm not Lily Robbins. I'm her twin, Jasmine Nelson."

Madison nodded. "I'd never have guessed it."

"It's not obvious," Adam agreed.

"Anyway," Jazz continued, "I haven't been making a point of it. I'll only be here a few weeks and there's no reason to leave everyone scratching their heads about who is who."

"I can see that. Okay, so you're not Lily. Does that fit somehow with the threat?"

"It might," Jazz began. "The first thing was a bouquet of dead flowers on the porch. Iris found them."

Madison arched a brow. "Dead?"

"Very. All I could think was that it was intentional. I didn't want to, but with Iris, Lily and me, Jasmine… well, I couldn't quite shake it."

Chief Madison nodded. "I can see why."

"I had just started to believe it was a prank of some kind, but then today…" Jazz hesitated, her mind jumping back to what she'd seen with her stomach turning into a hollow pit.

She blurted it out. "There was a gutted squirrel on the front porch, right outside the door."

"Hell," said Madison. "Where is it?"

Adam spoke. "I put it in the trash, but you can see it if you want. I also washed the blood off the porch."

"Blood?" Both of the chief's eyebrows lifted.

"Blood," Adam repeated. "Enough of it."

Madison shook his head, his lower jaw thrusting forward as his lips compressed. "It was done out there."

"It had to have been."

Everything inside Jazz curdled and turned cold. Her voice dropped to a ragged whisper. "That was done *on* the porch? But how? Wouldn't someone have seen it?"

"On a morning like this?" Madison shook his head. "Wouldn't take long, either."

Jazz covered her mouth with her hand, a new wave of shock ripping through her.

"Doesn't sound good to me," Madison said. "But right now, without evidence of a useful kind, I don't see what we can do except keep a close eye out. And we'll do that, Ms. Nelson. Around here we're not so busy we can't look after a neighbor."

He rose, then offered something more. "We can ask around discreetly. See if anyone might have noticed anything. We'll let you know. Adam? Can you show me that squirrel?"

Jazz didn't feel a whole lot better as the two men went outside. On the front porch? Someone had done it right there while she was at the store?

Horror began to creep in with fear.

ANDY ROBBINS WAS fairly pleased with the result of his little present. So she'd gotten unnerved enough this time to call the cops. Victory for him.

He wanted her fear. Eventually he wanted to smell it,

to taste it, to see it on her face and in her eyes. But that had to wait. Later, he'd enjoy every minute of his revenge.

For now he had to be content to watch it unfold bit by bit.

Maybe it was getting time to ratchet up even more.

Smiling he wandered down the street after his obligatory gawk at the cop car. Had to act like everyone else.

Which was harder than he would have supposed after prison. Seeing the cop just made him want to run.

Chapter Seven

Iris appeared surprised to see Adam when she arrived home with her instrument case in her hand and a heavy backpack hanging from the other shoulder.

"Hey, what's up," she asked before dumping her load. "I'm not used to seeing Adam here making dinner."

"Get used to it," Adam answered. "I'm moving into the spare bedroom for a few days."

Iris's eyes widened. "How come?"

"I'm waiting for an exterminator. Whenever he gets done, Sheba and I won't be able to go back until the fumes dissipate."

Iris's eyes widened, then she giggled. "Adam has bugs!"

"It happens to the best of us."

Still grinning, Iris headed toward the dining room, followed by Sheba who had been quietly snoozing near the back door.

"Great save," Jazz said quietly. She'd been wondering how she was going to explain this.

"I hate lying, but sometimes it's necessary." He was working on some kind of casserole that was consuming diced chicken breasts, green beans and cream of chicken soup to which he'd added a half cup of white wine. Jazz had offered to help but he had reminded her of the old saying *too many cooks spoil the stew.* "You'll love this. One of my favorites from childhood."

"Did you *have* a childhood?" She meant to tease him but got a serious answer.

"Not one I care to talk about. According to Lily, yours was pretty good."

She felt bad for touching on something Adam apparently found painful After a moment, she answered him. "We were very lucky. Since growing up, I've learned just how lucky. Good parents are hard to come by but Grandma kept everyone in line."

He smiled over his shoulder. "Was there much keeping in line?"

"Well, as Grandma used to say, age had taught her patience with children. Of course, she wasn't raising us and trying to make us good little kids. She was willing to let us cut loose."

"Then Mom and Dad had to cope with the results?"

"There didn't seem to be many bad results. But how many parents would allow a kid to use an entire roll of clear tape on open boxes?"

"Not many, I'd think."

At last he popped the casserole in the preheated oven and set the timer. Then he surprised her by pouring her a glass of the Chardonnay he'd just used.

"Medicinal." He winked.

It was a great Chardonnay, a table wine. "You didn't use a cooking wine?"

"Rule—never cook with a wine you wouldn't drink."

He joined her at the table with some of the coffee he'd made just before he started dinner.

"How are you doing?" he asked seriously.

"Better. Over the shock. Just getting angry now."

"I'm not surprised. The worst part is wondering who is that cruel. Or maybe that Iris had been meant to find it."

"God, what a thought! You've been trying to tell me this isn't directed at Iris."

"Yeah." He sipped from his mug. "I'm inclined to think it wasn't. She always comes home late, and you *do* go out, like this morning. You may be an introvert, but you're not a hermit."

She nodded, tasting the wine again. "Then why?"

"If we knew that, we'd be half the way toward solving the mystery."

It was true, but the question kept bothering her. Why? *Why?*

Iris surprised them by clearing off half the dining room table and setting it with Lily's Blue Willow china. The casserole, served over egg noodles, tasted as good as Adam had promised. Sheba lay patiently at Adam's side.

"Does she need some exercise?" Iris asked about the dog.

"Always."

"Then I'll take her out back after supper." She wrinkled her nose. "No dessert?"

Adam lifted a brow. "I think you can read the directions on the brownie mix."

Iris laughed. "Caught."

"Homework?" Jazz gently reminded her, taking a stab at being a responsible adult.

"Not much tonight. Later this week it might get heavy. I'll take Sheba out now, and get the dishes when I come back in. You two ancients relax in the living room."

"The mouth on you!"

That drew more laughter from Iris. Sheba followed her instantly when Iris picked up the tennis ball from the foyer.

"It's miserable out there," Jazz remarked.

Adam shrugged. "At least we don't have to be out in it."

They moved into the living room, and this time Adam poured them both a glass of wine.

"I wouldn't have taken you for the wine type," Jazz remarked.

"Oh, I have a broad range of tastes. The bottle of beer you think I should be holding is in my fridge."

Jazz's spirits had begun to rise in part, she was sure, because of a delicious hot meal. And Iris would lift anyone's mood.

"I feel like I was such a chicken today."

Adam shook his head. "No, you weren't. That was a shocking discovery. It appeared threatening."

"Appeared?" She didn't know if she liked that word. It *had* been threatening. There was no other way to see it.

A few seconds passed before Adam spoke. "I wasn't dismissing it. Not at all. But right now all we have is the *appearance* of a threat."

"But the flowers!"

His expression grew grim. "Believe me, I haven't forgotten."

Jazz sighed, trying to shake the gloomy feelings and get back into the better mood she'd begun to develop at dinner. "I'm being a drag."

He put his wineglass on the side table and leaned forward, resting his elbows on his knees as he looked at her. "Sometimes the brain takes a while to process things. It keeps running them over and over until, hopefully, it's done with them."

She studied him, sensing a deeper meaning in his words. "You have experience with it?"

He grimaced. "War."

One word, and it shook her. She forgot everything else except a blooming ache for him. "Still?" she asked quietly.

"Yes."

Oh my God, she thought, unable to express the emotions that overwhelmed her. *Oh my God.* She couldn't think of a thing to say that wouldn't sound trite or maybe stupid.

He spoke again. "Everything in life has a price. Some worse than others."

"That's awfully philosophical!" She could scarcely believe he could toss off those words. The ache in her heart grew stronger. "How bad?"

"I learned to manage. Various activities."

Manage. That meant he was still dealing with all those memories. Now she felt small for freaking out over dead flowers and a mutilated squirrel. Yes, they were bad, even frightening, but nothing to compare to his life then and now.

Small as she felt, she didn't say anything about it. He'd only try to reassure her that her reaction was normal. Maybe it was. But for the first time she wondered how the sight of that squirrel had affected *Adam.*

He'd seemed so calm, so in charge. God knew what kind of gut-churning reaction it might have caused in him.

He hadn't dismissed her shock or fear. Instead he'd

taken charge again, moving into the spare bedroom. Mostly to make her feel safe, she guessed.

"You don't have to stay here," she said presently.

"Trying to get rid of me?"

"No. Oh, no! It's just that you have other things to do than ease my fears." Her probably exaggerated fears.

"No, I don't. Anyway, I have bugs and I still need a bed to sleep in."

At last he drew a laugh from her. She couldn't help it. "That was brilliant."

He flashed a smile. "I have my moments."

Iris returned, both she and the dog shedding water. "Sheba needs a rubdown," she announced. The weather had done its usual on her stubborn hair. It frizzed every which way. "Don't worry about towels, Aunt Jazz. Mom keeps a stack of microfiber towels for cleaning and for Sheba. Doesn't she, girl?"

Sheba appeared to grin.

"Come on, Sheba, into the kitchen with you before you decide to shake off any more water."

"It appears Sheba is a welcome guest here," Jazz remarked to Adam.

"As if Lily has any choice, given Iris's attachment."

"She wouldn't object. I know my sister."

"Besides, it probably calms Iris's pining for her own dog."

He had a point, Jazz thought. Then she realized that her earlier fear had given way to her appreciation of the handsome man who sat across from her. God, he was attractive.

Oh, not that. Please. She'd be leaving. He had his own life. He could become a complication she didn't want and a complication he probably didn't want for himself. And just for sex? Because that was all there could be.

She rose, needing to get control of all her runaway feelings. "I'm really tired. I'll see you in the morning." Not a single qualm about leaving him alone with Iris. She trusted him completely, she realized.

Oh, man, that was bad. Very bad.

He spoke. "I think I will, too, once I've stolen my dog back. Sleep well."

That didn't happen because she couldn't stop thinking about Adam in the room right above her head. Every time he took a step or two, she heard the floorboards creak.

What was going on? Was her brain playing games to distract her from the squirrel?

Yeah, she decided. That had to be it. No other reason.

ADAM WASN'T DOING much better at the whole sleep thing. He paced for a while in the small room, then realized he was probably disturbing Jazz. He sat on the edge of the single bed, listening to the springs creak.

That squirrel had stirred him up again. A small wedge that opened a door to bigger, grislier memories. Hell. He didn't want to wrestle with his demons tonight. Not tonight. They'd mostly given him a break for the last week or so, a time of peace he cherished.

But all it took was one trigger. Today had come close to triggering him. He'd managed to clamp the lid on it, but now the slime was trying to seep into the open.

He swore quietly. Sheba immediately jumped up onto the bed and laid her head on his thigh. He stroked her gently, grateful for her love and doggie kindness. Always there, always ready to let him know she cared. A companion who never abandoned him.

"You're the best girl, Sheba."

She nosed him in response.

There had been times when he hadn't been sure he'd make it except for her. Times when she'd been his lifeline, his last tether to the present.

The slime seeped away little by little, driven out by Sheba, by thoughts of the woman sleeping downstairs. It was odd, but he'd never felt this way about Lily.

At last he felt the touch of amusement. Yeah, it had plenty to do with something else about Jazz although he couldn't identify it.

But he was worried, more worried than he wanted to let on. Yeah, he'd called Jake Madison to come over, but that still hadn't told her how seriously concerned *he* was.

There was nothing random about what was going on. Jazz suspected it, but Adam knew it in his gut. Gut feelings had saved his life more than once and he never ignored them.

He had one now, and it was strong. He guessed that exterminator was going to have to take a while getting here, because he wasn't moving back to his place until he was sure this was over, or they found the creep. If this was supposed to be humorous, someone needed a shrink. If it wasn't, well the guy was still a sickening creep.

The worst was that creeps like that were too often unpredictable.

Chapter Eight

The morning dawned gray, promising another wet, drizzly day.

"We're usually dryer than this," Adam remarked.

Iris looked up from her oatmeal. "Climate change," she announced.

"Not global warming?"

Iris shook her head. "Climate change. The weather is all over the map."

Adam looked at Jazz who was smiling. She spoke. "She's right. I live in Miami and I'm closer to it. We're flooding more than ever, and hurricanes are growing stronger."

"Yup," said Iris. "And coming closer together." She jumped up, rinsed her bowl and spoon in the sink and put them in the dishwasher. Then she grabbed her backpack and headed for the front door. "I might be home early tonight."

"Why?" Jazz asked.

"Some of the swim team are sick. We may call off practice." Her voice trailed after her. "Bye!"

"Dang," Jazz said. "That girl is something else."

"Smart, too," Adam replied. "Global warming isn't a popular subject in these parts."

Jazz gave him a wry look. "Climate change," she reminded him. "And I'm not surprised. Few people want to think about it, let alone talk about it. It's too big to get a handle on."

"Understandably."

Jazz noticed that he didn't offer an opinion one way or another. Did he agree or disagree?

"Listen," he said, "if I don't take Sheba for her morning walk, she's going to bust. Come with us?"

Jazz hesitated, but only momentarily. Despite the chilly wet day, a walk sounded good. "I'd like that. Let me grab some warmer clothes."

"Do you have any?" he joked.

"Well..." Then she shrugged. "When I was in an urgent care office a few years ago, we were having a fifty-degree morning. There were four people chatting, and one of them said the office had told him to come early because the cold would keep a lot of people away until it warmed up some."

Adam nodded, encouraging her to continue.

"That's when I got a bit annoyed because he thought it was *funny* that anyone would think the weather was cold. He was laughing about it. And I'm sitting there thinking, *Damn Yankee, you try living down here full-time for a few years and you'll have a different idea of cold.*"

Adam laughed. "I didn't mean to be insulting, but *do* you have something warm to wear?"

"Lily has plenty. I'll find something."

"And I agree it's cold out there. Thirty-six degrees and drizzling. Nobody would be warm."

It was her turn to laugh as she hurried back to the bedroom. Adam was good company, she decided as she pawed through Lily's drawers and closet. She found a pair of blue wool pants and a thick sweater. Thirty-six degrees? Deeper in the closet she discovered a warm jacket that appeared to be waterproof. It even had a hood.

"Success!" she announced as she returned to the kitchen.

"You look ready," he agreed. He pulled on his own jacket, clipped a leash to the now-dancing Sheba, and they headed out. The only difference this time was that Jazz made sure she'd locked the door. Not that it would prevent another ugly present on the doorstep.

But she didn't want to think about that. The world smelled fresh, maybe because of the drizzle. She pulled up her hood and enjoyed watching Sheba explore her world. Judging by the amount of time she spent running her nose through grass that had barely started to green, everything must have changed for her overnight. She certainly seemed to be absorbed.

In between sniffs, Sheba pranced.

"That dog has the right idea," Jazz remarked.

"What do you mean?"

"She's loving life. Very much in the moment."

"Yeah," he answered. "Humans spend too much time living in *tomorrow*."

"I never thought about it that way, but you're right. Planning ahead. Even worrying ahead."

"Exactly. The worrying ahead is the part that perplexes me. Half the things we worry about, at least half the things, never happen anyway."

"Then there's that proverbial bus. How do we even know we'll be here tomorrow?"

"Sometimes we don't."

A bit of her joy in the morning dissipated. *War.* He would certainly know that tomorrow might never come.

Or even the next hour. She wondered how much of that lingered with him but felt she didn't have the right to ask.

In some ways, Adam struck her as a very private man. She supposed that was okay with her as she was running out of words anyway. An interesting comment for a writer to make, she thought wryly. Although lately she seemed to have run out of words for the page as well.

When Sheba had filled her nose, done her business and pranced for a while, she was the one who tugged the leash in the direction of home.

"She must be getting pretty cold," Adam remarked. "I'm surprised she didn't want to go back sooner."

Jazz, with her hands freezing even in her pockets, couldn't have agreed more with Sheba. "Maybe she was having too much fun to notice."

But maybe not only the dog. Jazz's nose felt nearly frozen, and her cheeks weren't doing much better, but she'd been having a good time walking anyway. This was evidently the Wyoming version of a Florida walk in the heat and humidity.

When they got home, Sheba started running throughout the house as fast as she could.

"The zoomies," Adam remarked. "As soon as she slows down, I'll towel her off. I think she's warming herself up, though."

"Wouldn't surprise me." Jazz hung her sister's jacket over the back of a kitchen chair to dry it off. The wool pants, however, kept her warm. She headed for the counter to brew some fresh coffee. Warm. Hot. She needed it now.

At least there had been no surprises at the door.

She was still troubled about why anyone would do such a thing, but troubled or not she also knew there was no answer. Human behavior often couldn't be explained, especially when it was outside the norm.

Sheba apparently loved being rubbed down, and Jazz smiled as she watched the dog grin and wiggle herself until she got toweled in the places she wanted.

Adam disappeared around the corner with a handful of small towels, then returned. "I laid them over the washer and dryer to dry out."

"Thanks."

The coffee was ready and he didn't wait for Jazz to hop up and serve it. He poured two mugs and brought them to the kitchen table.

"Okay," he said. "It was raw out there."

"Just a bit. I think my cheeks might be raw, too."

"They're certainly red, but I imagine mine are, too. Looks like a winter sunburn."

"Hah! Good one."

He glanced toward the kitchen window. "It's not getting any better. Two days of this crud. Misty, wet, cold. Tomorrow doesn't promise to be any better."

Then he lifted one corner of his mouth. "Discussing the weather. How boring. The kind of thing strangers and ranchers do."

"We *are* kind of strangers."

That widened his smile a bit. "I may be a relative stranger to you, but I don't feel like you're one to me. I've known Lily since she moved here, and we've talked a lot, including about you. No, I'm not getting confused by the similarity in appearance."

She believed him since he'd picked out a difference right from the beginning. "I hope she didn't tell you everything."

"I'm sure she didn't. Would you tell on her?"

"Never."

"See?" He shrugged slightly.

Jazz, not gregarious by nature, wondered what else she could say. He'd already made it clear that he didn't want to talk about his childhood, and she was sure Lily had hit all the high places in theirs.

In the silence, she heard the heat kick on again. About time.

"Listen," he said presently, "you need to work. I feel like I'm stealing your time, and Iris will be home early. Grab an apple or something and get to it. I've got some books to read."

Well, she could hardly argue with that. "Thanks." She left her coffee mug and went to the office. High time she put some words on her computer screen. Well past time. Maybe she'd write a man like Adam into her book. Just similar, because she didn't use real people in her novels. That would be a violation of trust. But loosely modeled? Very loosely modeled.

She felt good sitting down at her laptop for a change. Since arriving here it had looked too much like a chore.

Maybe her brain wasn't dead after all.

JAZZ HEARD IRIS come in early. She was immediately disturbed because her niece's stride was slow. She shut her laptop and hurried out to the hall in time to see Iris toss the mail on the hall table and drop her backpack. No smile from the girl, just a dragging step.

"Iris? What's wrong?"

"I think I caught the bug that hit the swim team. I don't feel good, Aunt Jazz."

Sheba came running from somewhere else in the house as she always did when Iris came home, but this time she drew up short, watching. Maybe she sensed something was wrong?

"You don't look good." Jazz crossed to her and laid a hand on Iris's forehead. "You feel warm, too. Go make yourself comfortable in the living room and I'll bring you some chicken soup. If that sounds good, anyway. And maybe the thermometer, if I can find it."

"The soup sounds good." Iris managed a tired smile. "I don't know where the thermometer is. Mom hasn't used it since I was in elementary school."

"Need a blanket?"

"I dunno yet."

Jazz immediately tried to help the girl out of her jacket, but Iris shrugged her hands away. "I'm not helpless. I just don't feel good. Sheesh, you don't have to hover."

Jazz didn't take offense. How could she? Besides, she'd never liked being hovered over herself. "I'll just get that soup."

There were only a couple of cans in the pantry, but she remembered a whole chicken in the freezer. Surely she could remember how to make homemade chicken soup. Well, and roast the darn thing as well. The chicken meat made a good meal, and the broth made from the carcass was wonderful.

She glanced at the clock and figured she didn't have enough time to get it ready for that night. Maybe tomorrow if Iris was still sick. If not, they could still eat roast chicken.

While the soup heated, she pulled out the chicken, putting it in a bowl of cold water.

She felt someone behind her and turned to see Adam. He'd been reading upstairs.

"Something wrong with Iris?"

"She seems to have caught the swim team bug, and I'm not allowed to hover."

"Sounds like Iris, all right. Got a TV table set up for her?"

She shook her head. "Didn't think of it yet."

He smiled crookedly. "Tell you what. You go set up the table and I'll bring the soup, okay?"

"Then we'll both be hovering."

"She'll have to deal with it."

Fair division of labor, Jazz decided. Fair division of Iris's objections.

Once they had Iris seated at her soup, Jazz suggested some TV to entertain her.

"At this time of day? All that's on is the news and the weather. I know what the weather is." Sheba had come to rest right beside Iris's chair, and Iris reached down to pet her briefly. The dog's tail wagged a couple of times.

Jazz's smile widened. "Cricket is on."

"Cricket?" Iris looked appalled. "That's boring."

"Not at all. Compared to a baseball game a T20 is faster. It requires real strategy. And what's more, there are no pinch hitters or substitute pitchers. Eleven players to a team, all of them have to be able to bat and field, and only five bowlers are chosen in each team."

"You're going to have to explain." But Iris looked interested.

"I'll sit here and explain if you want. Trust me, this makes baseball look slow."

"That's not hard to do," Adam remarked. "I'm game. Let's turn it on." He looked at Jazz. "How did you discover this?"

"Not exactly a discovery," she replied, picking up the

remote. "I have a friend from India and he got me intrigued. Then he insisted I go with him to the exhibition game played every year in Lauderdale by international players. I got very much hooked."

"What two teams play?" Iris asked as Jazz pulled up the guide on the screen.

"Not teams the way you think of them, at least not usually. Cricket is played all over the world, and except in international competitions where they represent their countries, teams are made up of players from everywhere."

Pale as she was looking, Iris appeared to approve of that idea. "Let's go, but you better be prepared to do a lot of explaining."

Jazz laughed. "Someone had to teach me, too. I'm not sure I get it all yet. But I'll give it a try." She turned on a game that had already begun and got ready to talk. It was going to require a lot of talking.

An hour later, as the Indian Premier League game reached a close, Jazz looked at the time. "Oh my gosh! I forgot all about dinner!"

"I've got it," Adam said, rising. He headed for the hallway.

Jazz followed as Iris attempted to watch the interviews after the game. Her niece was a quick study and seemed to have picked up quite a bit in the half of the match they had seen.

"Are you going out?" she asked Adam as he pulled his jacket on.

"Not for long. I'll pick up dinner at Maude's. But I better ask everyone what they want. Especially our sick girl."

Surprisingly for an ill young woman, Iris asked, "Can I eat something bad, Aunt Jazz?"

"I'm not your coach. Besides, you're not feeling well. Have whatever you want."

A few minutes later, Adam headed out the door after explaining some of the selections to Jazz. He'd written the choices on a scrap of paper.

"We're all going to eat the wrong things tonight," Iris said.

"I'm astonished that you'll break your training diet for anything."

"It won't be the first time." Iris closed her eyes. "I think I need a nap."

Jazz started for the kitchen when she spied the mail Iris had dumped unsorted on the hall table. She went to complete the task, peeling away all the sales flyers, offers of lower-rate mortgages, and reminders that it was about time someone had a dental checkup.

Then she came to the handwritten postcard and gasped. Her knees suddenly felt like water.

I'm watching you.

JAZZ SAID NOTHING about the postcard when Adam returned with dinner. With Iris in the house, it seemed like exactly the wrong time to bring up this mess.

Iris looked at the foam container on the TV table and remarked, "Foam is bad for the environment."

Adam regarded her. "Then *you* talk to Maude about it."

Iris gave a weary laugh. "I'm not brave enough."

"I don't think anyone would be."

Jazz spoke, trying to keep her mind off the postcard although discomfort filled her. "Is she a dragon?"

"Next best thing," Iris answered.

"But she still has customers?"

Iris shrugged. "We're all used to it."

"And the food is great," Adam reminded her. "The food more than makes up for service...which can be quite entertaining."

"It's a wonder she doesn't break more cups and plates," Iris remarked. "The way she bangs them down."

"Probably made of painted cast iron."

Iris laughed tiredly at the joke, then sighed. "I guess I'm not used to being sick."

"Do you feel too bad to eat?" Jazz asked.

Iris started to shake her head, then winced. "My head aches. My body aches. I feel so tired. But nothing's wrong with my stomach."

"Then go for it," Adam said.

Jazz spoke. "How about some dishes to eat off?"

"I won't be able to wash them, Aunt Jazz."

"And I'm incapable of popping things in the dishwasher? Puh-leeze."

Another weak laugh from Iris. "No plate necessary. The box is part of the fun."

As if the girl was going to have much fun eating from the look of her, Jazz thought. She wondered if she should do something more, like drag Iris to the doctor. She wasn't that familiar with illness herself.

But the thought of dragging Iris to a doctor was daunting. Her niece would have to feel a whole lot worse to agree.

Strike one for being a mere aunt.

"I'll be okay, Aunt Jazz," Iris said as if she read Jazz's face. "Really."

Jazz smiled faintly. "How'd I know you'd say that?"

"Because you're getting to know me. Now you guys go eat in the kitchen. The dining room table is a mess and using your laps won't be any fun."

Reluctantly Jazz followed Adam to the kitchen.

"I think she wants to be alone," Adam remarked. "No hovering, remember?"

"All too well."

Jazz slid her container onto the table and put the thawing chicken into the refrigerator while Adam went to make another pot of coffee. He really seemed to like it.

"It was nice of you to run out and pick up dinner."

"Like any of us was in a mood for cooking. The only thing I didn't like was leaving you guys alone. Maude probably never had such an impatient customer."

Jazz was about to tell him once again that he didn't have to disrupt his life, but there *was* that postcard, bright red in her mind for all it was just a basic white card. The third warning that something was happening. Threatening.

Before she opened her meal, she went to get the card. It sounded as if Iris was still watching cricket, but maybe she'd fallen asleep. She might need that more than food.

When she got back to the kitchen, she sat down with Adam who was just opening his meal.

"This came in the mail today."

He reached across the table and took the card. "It's addressed to Lily."

"Turn it over. The back side was up when I saw it."

He read the words printed on the back and frowned deeply. "This is no joke. Especially not when you've been feeling watched. I'll tell the Chief about this."

She nodded. "I'm wound so tight now I don't feel like eating."

"Eat anyway. Just a little. God almighty, what's going on here?"

Jazz doubted she could pick up a fork, let alone swallow anything. Her stomach felt as if a rock filled it.

"Come on, just one french fry," Adam coaxed. "Bland. Safe, soft. The meat probably looks like too much just now."

It certainly did. But he'd gone to all the trouble to get the food, and she hated to be rude. Just one fry. Maybe that would get her started.

Adam put the card on the table to one side and began to eat his own meal. "It's postmarked from Cheyenne."

Jazz gave him a hopeful look. "That's far away, isn't it?"

"Not that far. Just eat, Jazz. We can beat our heads on this later."

She reached for another fry, to please him, and discovered that a bit of her appetite had returned. Maybe he was right. Starving herself wouldn't help anyone, least of all Iris.

"This guy," she said, "is an SOB"

"Yeah."

Jazz looked at the food in front of her and decided it was time to dig in.

ANDY ROBBINS WAITED in Cheyenne. He had more postcards to send, increasingly frightening, he hoped. But right now he didn't want to hang around in Conard City too much.

What had persuaded Lily to move to such a small place? Iris must be bored to death. It wasn't Lily's kind of place either, as evidenced by her jetting all over the world now. And she'd always liked things to do from art museums to concerts to night clubs.

When he was willing to let her go, at least. Museums bored him and the concerts she chose rarely appealed to him.

But he smiled as he remembered the times he'd stopped her. Sometimes with a blow or two. Women had to be kept in line.

But mostly he wouldn't let her see her friends. She might have talked to them.

Not that Andy had done anything wrong. Just being a strong husband, doing his job. Anyway, he didn't like it when Lily screwed up. When she made him furious.

No woman had the right to do that to a man. *No* woman.

Well, now was the time to make her regret it.

Chapter Nine

Adam was seriously disturbed by this campaign of terror. It made him furious on Jazz's behalf and worried on behalf of Iris. His urge to violence had pretty much died in the war, but he was feeling it right then. He wanted to take someone out with his bare fists. Grab him by the throat.

But he was looking at a ghost enemy. Unknown. So far unknowable other than that he had some fixation on Lily. Or a grudge. But what could it be? Adam had known Lily during the years since she had moved to Conard City. A very pleasant, very smooth woman who clearly knew how *not* to offend. Part of her job, he supposed, but of one thing he was fairly certain: those who knew her in this town liked her.

While Lily might have been an alien species to the kind of folks who lived here, she had managed to fit herself in, globe-trotting or not. Iris had almost instantly fit right in.

Now this. An unmistakable threat. Judging by the squirrel, it was a threat of violence.

Adam had seen the worst of human nature so little surprised him. But Lily had been frank about choosing a small town so her daughter could live freely and without fear.

With a few exceptions in the past, that was true for all the kids here.

Now this.

He needed to get out and run a few miles. Or get to his personal gym. But he didn't want to leave Iris and Jazz alone. No way. And what about his vets support group tomorrow evening? He'd have to skip that along with his exercise.

Later, when he was alone upstairs, he swore. He wanted to pace his room but didn't want Jazz to hear. Downstairs was off-limits for making any real noise because Iris had fallen asleep in the living room, having eaten only a small part of her dinner. Continued pacing would likely disturb her.

Crap! Well, since he wasn't going to sleep, he might as well hunt up something to eat or drink. He could do that quietly and gnawing on some food was better than gnawing on his fists.

In stocking feet, he descended the stairs taking care to step near the wall to minimize any creaks. He carried his boots with him. Nobody who'd been a soldier wanted to be caught barefoot when action was required.

He saw light spilling from the kitchen as he descended, so he wasn't surprised when he discovered Jazz at the table, chin in her hand, her expression weary.

"Can't sleep?" he asked as she looked up.

"Hardly. You either?"

"Nope."

"There's a bottomless coffee pot," she told him. "Not to mention leftovers from dinner and a whole bunch of Iris-friendly snacks if you'd prefer fruit."

"Coffee won't help either of us sleep," he remarked as he chose an apple from a wire basket on the counter.

"At this point I don't care. I keep wondering what's next."

"Hard not to wonder." He bit into the apple as he sat facing her. It provided a satisfying crunch and a mouthful of juice. "Iris?"

"Still soundly asleep with the dog beside her. Nice of you to share Sheba with her."

Adam shrugged. "Sheba knows how to find me if I need her. That dog is half Iris's anyway."

"So it appears."

He noticed that Jazz didn't even try to smile. Too tired and worried to try to lift the corners of her mouth, he guessed. He couldn't blame her.

Here she was in a strange place with her niece dependent on her. Quite a load of responsibility when things were going wrong.

"You must have jobs you need to do," she remarked.

"Nothing on my schedule. Folks know how to reach my cell if they have an emergency." Although what the hell he'd do about it if someone truly needed him he couldn't imagine. No leaving these two on their own.

His hip had started aching again, and while he was usually able to bury the pain, tonight it bit him and refused to be ignored. Ibuprofen, maybe.

Perhaps he'd been trying too hard not to limp so Jazz wouldn't ask him about it. It was a bad reminder of Afghanistan, a subject he avoided.

Jazz spoke. "I wish I knew how to corral Iris more without letting her know how scared I am for her."

"I don't want to scare her either. And this threat seems to be directed at Lily."

"From the postcard, yes. From the other stuff I'm not so sure."

Neither was he, but he didn't want to say so. Jazz was already upset enough.

"Maybe I should call Lily."

Adam immediately shook his head. "She's half a world away. Nothing she can do about this. No reason to scare her."

"But she might have an idea who could be..." Then Jazz shook her head. "What would she do anyway? Answer questions on the phone then continue with her work? Not likely." She knew her sister too well. Lily would race home, race into town hell-for-leather, and probably be just as stymied as they were. Adam was right. No need to scare her.

She sighed and sipped the coffee she shouldn't be drinking at this hour. He decided to join her. What the hell. Sleep had decided to skip town, leaving them both wide awake.

Eventually she spoke. "We've got to do something."

"I don't know what at this point. We don't know who's doing this or why. We need more to go on. Any suggestions?"

Jazz had none, of course. How could she? That was the wall they were both up against.

The night passed slowly as they both dealt with their inner worries.

JAZZ WANTED TO crawl out of her skin. Drag herself and Iris into a dark hole for safety. But Adam had been right when he said that they needed to try to solve this before Lily came home. If they could before something terrible happened.

And that postcard, still sitting on the table, seemed to emphasize that someone meant to terrify Lily.

Not that Lily could be terrified easily, except probably when it came to Iris. Jazz had long admired Lily's strength, far more than her own. She had never been tested the way Lily had.

Thank God.

Now her sister was running around the world, a highly respected consultant to various entities, from the World Bank to the UN. She'd always had the smarts.

Not that Jazz thought poorly of herself. She'd never have been able to write books if she didn't have a measure of self-confidence. *Her* babies went out into the world to be liked or disliked, criticized or lauded. She'd long ago decided that critiques, positive or negative, were merely a single person's opinion. What really talked were sales numbers, the numbers her career rose or fell by.

She wanted to walk to the window, to look out at a normal world, but she had the curtains drawn against the night. Against the possibility than anyone could look in and see.

Against the threat that so far seemed to lie outside these walls. With Adam in here, she felt safer. He'd shaken up his entire life to come riding over here like the cavalry. She doubted many would do that.

He kept moving in his chair, not as if he were anxious, but as if he were uncomfortable.

"Is something wrong?" she asked.

"With me? Not really. My hip just hurts too much to ignore sometimes."

"I'm sorry. Old injury?"

"Not old enough, apparently. Putting it back together didn't make it much happier."

"That's awful." She bit her lip then asked, "How?"

"How did it happen? The war. Others have it a lot worse."

Which closed the discussion, Jazz decided. Maybe she'd walked into private places. Maybe she had reminded him of terrible things. If so, this situation had to be awful for him.

She knew he was a vet, but she'd never really considered how this might affect him. Now she felt awful about him, too.

"It's okay, Jazz," he said as if he could read her face.

Well, he probably could. She'd often been told her face was an open book. "It's not okay. How could it be? You shouldn't have to go through that. No one should."

"Well, I put on the uniform."

"Sure. As if you had any idea what you were getting into."

"Most people don't. It doesn't matter. I made a choice. I live with the consequences, like everyone else."

A remarkably strong and clear-eyed view. She wasn't sure she agreed with him, however, but she couldn't argue with him.

Silence fell again, echoed by the quiet night outside.

Eventually he spoke. "There'll be more postcards. Brace yourself."

She started. "How can you be sure of that?"

"Because this guy is a coward. If he wasn't, he'd come out in the open and do whatever it is he's fantasizing. He wants to scare, not to act. At least not yet."

"Yet?" She hated the sound of that word.

"He's ginning himself up bit by bit. Telling himself he's enjoying the fear he's engendering, but do you see him at the front door actually *doing* something? He's giving us time, whether he knows it or not. Time to prepare. Maybe time to find out who he is."

"Well that's hopeful," she said a bit sarcastically. "So far he's good at covering his tracks."

"So far. But I'm a great believer in people making mistakes even in threatening situations. I've seen enough of it. He'll make a mistake."

"I hope."

He went to get more coffee and another apple. "Want anything?"

"A huge piece of cheesecake or a cinnamon roll. The more sugar the better."

He smiled faintly. "Can't do anything about that right now, although I think you'll find some sugar in the pantry."

Miserable as she was, Jazz summoned her own smile. "Just a spoonful, right? Like that song."

"Oh, live a little and take two."

Out of context though it was, Adam was lifting her spirits. Just a bit. She was grateful to him.

"So," he said as he sat again, wincing slightly as if he were trying not to reveal his discomfort. "Here we sit, two people faced with a situation and no control. I hate it when I don't have control."

"I feel the same. But what's that saying? If you want to make God laugh, make a plan."

"Too true. But we can't even make a plan yet." His face hardened. "We'll get there, I swear."

She believed him, believed Adam would move heaven and earth to protect her and Iris. Mostly Iris, the main concern for both of them.

As if summoned, Sheba arrived to nuzzle Adam's arm, then rest her chin on his thigh.

"Good girl," he murmured as he stroked her head and back.

In that moment Jazz saw another side of Adam. A gentle, soft side.

Sheba will come when I need her.

Evidently he needed her now, and Jazz was surprised when he bent over to drop a kiss on the dog's head.

Sheba raised her head to look adoringly at Adam, then licked his face with a kiss of her own. He'd said she comforted him, and apparently that's what she was doing now.

He continued to pet her, fondling her ears a bit.

Jazz wondered what Sheba had sensed that she had not. Just a minute ago she'd been thinking that Adam would move heaven and earth for Iris and her, and now the dog sensed a need.

Memories brought on by this mess somehow. Jazz couldn't imagine what this situation had to do with war, unless it was the tension. Or that hip of his.

"Need some ibuprofen?" she asked.

Adam looked up from the dog. "I've been thinking about it since I got down here."

"Thinking is not the same as action. I'll get it for you."

Jazz brought him the bottle so he could decide how much to take. A doctor had once told her that she could take as many as four at a time for her migraines, as long as it didn't upset her stomach. "There's prescription ibuprofen that strong. Take what you need, just don't exceed four every six hours."

She saw Adam pop four tablets. She suspected he could have used something stronger, but who could get that now?

"How bad is it, Adam? And don't brush me off."

"Nerve damage," he said. "Joint damage. Maybe a hip replacement down the road." He shrugged. "I can still live with it."

That said a lot. *Still live with it.* "That's awful."

He shook his head. "As they say, it is what it is."

"You can say that about a lot of things, but it doesn't make them any easier to endure." Rising, she decided that sleep was a lost cause and went to get her own coffee. It had started to smell burnt, so she dumped it and began a new pot.

"We're both going to be useless tomorrow."

Still stroking Sheba, he nodded. "Except I'm used to functioning without sleep."

"I'm not. It's going to show."

"So sleep when you can. I'll hold the fort. And I'm going to stash that card so Iris doesn't see it until I can pass it to the law."

"I was thinking the same thing." She reached for the pot. "Want some fresh?"

"Oh, yeah. I got through a lot of nights on caffeine. Wasn't as good as this brewed stuff, though."

Jazz wrinkled her nose. "My dad used to drink instant. He traveled a lot so he had one of those heaters you could put in a mug to boil the water. I thought it was a horrible habit."

He smiled. "You get used to it."

"You can get used to a lot. Doesn't mean it's good."

He chuckled. "Got it in one."

Then the quiet fell again, the night seeming to creep into the room. Sheba finally lay down beside Adam's chair, still there in case she was needed.

Loyalty thy name is dog, Jazz thought.

The night would slip away soon, leaving dawn in its wake. Would it be gray and misty again? She didn't much care now, but it seemed apropos to the events. As if the sky shared their concerns.

It was a foolish thought, but it fit nicely into her writer's brain. Possibilities could be endless in her fantasy books.

In this world not so much.

Like right now. In one of her worlds, the trees would be whispering information. In another the very rocks might have an opinion. In this reality she and Adam were stuck waiting for a creep to make a misstep.

"Why don't you go try to lie down?" Adam said.

Which made her aware for the first time that her eyes were closing. Just a bit. Then anxiety would snap her awake again.

"I don't think so," she said after a minute. She wondered if she'd ever sleep again, not with anxiety slapping her every few minutes.

"Take some long, deep, slow breaths. It'll help relieve the tension."

She took his advice and soon realized that he was right. Physically she relaxed, although her mind didn't seem ready to slow down.

"We can't keep this up," she said.

"No we can't." He rose and brought them both fresh cups of brew. "I could use a beer right about now."

"Like you can find some any easier than I can get my cinnamon roll."

He winked. "There's a place just across the street, namely my house, which usually holds a six-pack."

"Then go get it."

He shook his head, and that was the end of that.

RARELY COULD EX-CONS find a job. Not that Andy had often held one. Lily's income had made it unnecessary and he didn't mind living off her earnings. They were pretty comfortable.

But something had happened to her. When he'd met Lily she'd been so ready to please him, quivering anytime he got annoyed with her. He hadn't needed to do much to keep her in line at first.

It pleased her to please him. A simple recipe for marital happiness. While he kept her from her friends, and mostly from her family such as it was, he didn't keep her from work. She was rising rapidly, proud of every new accomplishment.

He'd let her have that pride because it suited him. But then she got out of line a bit. Just before Iris. Damn, he'd hated that pregnancy. It meant there'd be a third person in their tightly controlled loop.

He'd tried to talk Lily into an abortion. Then he'd knocked her around to teach her to listen to him. Then it was too late and that kid was coming anyway.

Only after the brat was born had he realized he had a new method of controlling Lily. He'd told himself that he could make Lily behave in order to protect the baby because, as he knew too well, Lily was a selfish bitch.

Iris. Stupid name. That whole family had stupid ideas about names. Anyway, Iris had given him the excuse to threaten Lily into cutting away the remnants of her life: her family, her friends. A complete separation after that, keeping Lily from bad influences.

A threat to make Lily behave. Iris became a useful tool, often more useful than his fists. Although he still got a lot of pleasure out of hitting the woman every now and then. It was like a pressure relief valve.

But he'd had a lot of time in prison to reconstruct his images of the past. Lily had always been disobedient, treating him like crap. He'd been the injured party.

As for Iris, in his mind he'd built a loving relationship with her. *He'd* been the one to prevent Lily from having an abortion. He'd stood up for the kid, then protected her from Lily.

He believed he'd used every means he could to make Lily into a good wife.

She'd failed him and deserved everything that came her way.

As for Iris, he'd protect her as he always had.

Chapter Ten

Iris still felt ill in the morning. All she wanted for breakfast was toast with a bit of jam.

Jazz hated to admit that she was almost relieved that Iris would be home for another day. One day she needn't worry about her niece racketing around out there without any protection except her friends.

The sun had decided to wake that morning, and Iris seemed glad to have it brightening the world again. So was Jazz for that matter.

"I'm going to run across the street," Adam said while Jazz made toast. "I'll be quick, but I need a few things."

"The washer and dryer work," she said drily.

He laughed quietly. "I don't just need some clean clothes."

"Then don't forget the beer."

"I won't. If you feel okay about it, I may make a quick run downtown."

"I'll survive. We'll survive. Go."

"No more than half an hour," he said. He was going to do his best imitation of the winged god Mercury. "Lock up everything behind me. And Sheba can stay with Iris."

"You sure?" Jazz asked. She remembered his apparent need for the dog.

"Running helps. Trust me."

She wondered how it could possibly help his hip.

ADAM TOOK OFF as if the hounds of hell were on his heels. He didn't take his dirty clothes with him; Jazz was right that there was a washer and dryer over at Lily's house. He had a different errand in mind.

People waved as he dashed past, but no one gave him an odd look. Most folks around here were used to the sight of him running along the street at top speed. A mere jog wouldn't always help him. Now it wouldn't be fast enough to get back to his ladies.

He was starting to think of them as *his*. Oh man. He put it down to feeling so protective.

As fast as he was moving, he reached the bakery swiftly. Nearly a four-minute mile, he calculated. Not bad for a guy in his condition. He ignored the screaming of his hip.

He wasn't a frequent visitor to the bakery, but Melinda welcomed him with a warm smile and called him by name. Benefit of a small town.

She filled a couple of white bags for him, with Danish and cinnamon rolls and chocolate chip cookies.

"That enough?" she asked wryly.

"Ladies at home with a craving."

Melinda laughed. "That'll do it." Then she asked, "Are you running?"

"Yeah. Feels good."

"Then wait a sec."

Next thing he knew, she'd put the white bags in a larger paper bag with handles. "Now you can hang on to it."

"You're the best."

Then he was out the door at a full run, making a swing by the grocery where he bought plenty of chicken soup, subs for everyone—one a chicken salad out of deference to Iris's illness. If she wanted a meatier one with all the trimmings, he'd eat the chicken salad.

A six-pack of beer rounded out his purchases.

The lady at the register, Doris, eyed him. "You look like you're running again."

"Rumor has it."

She smiled and surprised him with large plastic-handled bags, doubled up. She even put the bakery bag safely on the top. "I don't know how you thought you were going to run all this home."

"Somehow," he answered, giving her a grin.

"Yeah. You soldiers, always biting off more than you can carry. Get going before you get stiff."

His hip really would have liked a heating pad, but he continued to ignore it. Jazz and Iris were home alone and the awareness gnawed at him.

So far, the creep who was sending messages struck him like a coward. The kind who would attack only those smaller and physically weaker. Adam was at least big enough to make him reconsider if he had more in mind than creating fear.

Just a little more than thirty minutes. Not bad. He used the key Lily had given him for emergencies to unlock the door.

Sheba appeared immediately, dancing around his legs with a rapidly wagging tail.

He heard Iris say, "My hair looks like a rat's nest."

"If that's your only worry," Jazz answered, "then you're doing pretty darn good."

"I don't want to miss the swim practice this afternoon."

"If you think the other sick girls are going to be in any better condition, I've got a bridge to sell you."

Adam smiled as he passed the living room and entered the kitchen. He began to unload the bags when he heard Jazz step through the door.

"What in the world did you do, Adam?"

"Went on a shopping spree. After a sleepless night, nobody's going to feel like cooking."

She joined him and helped with the groceries. "You got that right. If I didn't feel like I was getting an electric shock every few minutes, I'd be unconscious on the floor."

"The creep's got to you that much?" A stupid question considering he hadn't slept last night either.

He grabbed ibuprofen and settled at the table with a beer. Always five o'clock somewhere as the saying went. Although he didn't care with the jackhammer pain in his hip. "It's still chilly out there, especially for you Southerners."

Tossing him a tired smile, Jazz opened the bakery bags. "Oh my God, Adam! What did you do?"

"Somebody mentioned a craving last night." He shrugged, dismissing it, although her reaction pleased him.

"But this is so much! I can't eat it all. Nor will Iris since she seems to have remembered her training diet. Apples and oranges and bananas."

"Well, if she doesn't help you eat this, I'll take care of it."

"You think you're capable?" She sat facing him. "How were you so fast? I didn't see you drive away."

"I ran. I told you."

"But this fast?" she repeated. "When do you show up in the Olympics?"

"Never." He changed the subject. "How's Iris doing? If she's complaining about her hair, she has to be feeling better."

"I'm not sure about that. I think she's impatient to get over this bug. If her color was better, I'd agree with you. I keep wondering if I should take her to the doctor."

"So the doc can say there's a bug going around? Besides, you'd probably have to hog-tie that girl to get her to go."

"I was thinking of that."

He arched a brow. "You'd really hog-tie her?"

"Not hardly." She sighed. "I know nothing about this mother thing. I'm always worrying if I'm doing the wrong thing."

"Iris is still breathing, she hasn't needed a trip to the hospital, and she hasn't brought home a guy with a green Mohawk wearing chains and leather."

She cocked a brow at him. "He might be perfectly nice."

"Then ask yourself why he isn't advertising that. Now go have one of those pastries. You were jonesing last night. I'll go see if Iris wants one."

He tossed his beer bottle in the trash and Sheba followed him to the living room.

HER HEART ONLY half in it, Jazz looked through the pastry bags and decided on a cinnamon roll. A very big one. She was past caring about her weight. She poured some coffee to go with it, then sat again, thinking Adam was one heck of a nice guy.

Running all the way to the bakery? Because she'd

wished for a pastry in the middle of the night? Not many people would do that. Or would even remember her crazy wish, probably born of fatigue. Weariness could make people hungry, she'd heard. Regardless, she might not have tasted the roll at all except for the cinnamon.

The postcard was gone from the table, but not her memory of it. How could anyone have it in for Lily? Enough to go on a campaign of terror?

The only person she could think of was Lily's ex-husband, Andy, but he was still in prison. Safely locked away.

Jazz had been stunned when she'd found out what Lily had been enduring. She'd wondered why Lily had been growing more distant but had put it down to Lily's pre-occupation with her new family, especially Iris.

Then the horror had tumbled out once Andy was arrested. All of it. Sickening to the last detail. The only thing Jazz wanted to ask was why Lily had endured it for so long, but she never asked.

Instead she'd hit the books and learned just how corrosive living with an abuser could be. How damaging to self-esteem. How terrified of a man's anger. Then there was Iris, protecting Iris from the man.

Except the protection had finally run out and Iris had been hurt. Lily had snapped then and headed straight to the police. Jazz was convinced to this day that Andy had gotten his just desserts only because of Iris. That poor little girl. Enough to wring anyone's heart.

Jazz had been there for Lily and Iris from the moment she learned about the abuse, and all the way through the trial and sentencing. X-rays of broken bones, on both Lily and the child. No photos of bruising until it came to Iris.

Lily had explained her own injuries away, probably

from fear, but she hadn't explained Iris's away. No, from the first moment at the hospital she'd told the staff of Andy's physical abuse of the girl.

There'd been therapy, of course. Iris appeared to recover quickly. Lily had taken longer, but she'd gone back to work with a vengeance, rising high and rising quickly, as if she'd been held back during her marriage. Maybe she had.

Regardless, work had improved Lily's self-esteem immeasurably. Now years had passed and both she and Iris seemed to have recovered completely, although who knew what nightmares Lily might have in the dead of the night, nightmares she kept to herself.

She heard Iris and Adam talking, Iris sounding as upbeat as she could possibly manage when feeling ill. Then Adam returned.

"I turned Sheba over to Iris. That girl is going to steal her from me. Anyway, she said a cheese Danish sounds good."

"I'll take her one."

He gave her a crooked smile. "Hovering?"

"Checking in. Which I think I'm entitled to do." She realized she sounded snappish but felt no need to apologize. Lack of sleep, a horrendous level of anxiety, and not being able to close her eyes without seeing dead flowers, a gutted squirrel and that postcard. It would make anyone irritable—or worse.

Adam might be right that the guy was a coward, but that wasn't preventing him from inflicting fear.

She went to the living room only to find Iris sound asleep. That was good, she supposed. Rest could help almost anything.

Adam came in behind her and spoke in a hushed voice. "Try to nap. I'll be right here. You've got to sleep sometime."

"What about you?"

"If I sleep, I'm a very light sleeper. Any noise will wake me. Truly. Now go to bed. As tired as you are, I bet you fall asleep in two minutes. I'll stay on the couch in case *I* do."

She couldn't argue with him. Her eyes felt gritty and she wasn't at all sure she was thinking clearly.

Okay. She'd have to believe what he'd said about being a light sleeper, and given where he'd been, he was probably telling the truth.

The instant her head hit the pillow, she was out like a light.

ADAM SAT ON the other recliner, remaining upright. He'd probably doze some, but he hadn't been kidding. The slightest abnormal sound could wake him in an instant. And when it did, he'd become wide awake.

Lessons of war. War taught a lot of lessons, not often good ones.

So far he was pretty sure this creep wasn't likely to act. More postcards, probably. Maybe another ugly, gutted animal. Scare tactics. But why?

He couldn't imagine Lily having engendered that kind of hate in anyone. Just couldn't imagine it. There were people in this town who had enemies. But none of *them* would ever stoop to such heinous acts. They usually just ignored each other, had verbal fights and the occasional swinging of fists.

Pretty much normal reactions, the latter especially

when drunk. Occasionally Mahoney's bar enjoyed the inebriated results.

The cops would break up the fights if necessary, someone might spend a night in the holding cell above the sheriff's offices, but that was usually the extent of it. As long as no one got seriously hurt, why make a criminal case out of it?

Not necessary in this small town. People got drunk, threw a couple of punches, many of which missed their targets. He'd seen it happen more than once.

In a way, it amused him. Not a proper outlet for anger, but still amusing.

This was a whole different kettle of fish.

He sighed and looked over at Iris. She still slept but looked a bit flushed. Maybe because she was buried under a blanket. On the small side table a plate held an untouched cheese Danish.

He'd keep an eye on her, too, in case she worsened.

But Lily? This had to be a person from her past, someone she never mentioned. Deciding he needed to question Jazz, he dozed too, confident in his ability to wake.

Sleep needed its due sometimes.

JAZZ SLEPT LATER than she wanted, the late afternoon sun peeking through an edge of the curtain. She didn't practice her usual routine of allowing herself to wake slowly but sat bolt upright and scrambled for some clean clothes. To hell with a shower for now. She was sure she didn't stink yet.

She headed straight for the living room and there was Adam, wide awake. She then looked at Iris, who was sitting up too, and who hadn't touched the Danish.

Without preamble, Jazz said, "How are you feeling?"

"Awful," came the frank, tired answer.

"I should take you to the doctor."

"A waste of money," Iris argued.

Thus the fight began. "I'm worried about you."

"Oh, for heaven's sake! The swim team probably got it from someone at school, half the kids are sick and nobody's gone to the hospital. If they had I'd have heard about it." Iris waved her cell phone. "No alerts. No messages. Nada."

"Iris…"

"Nope. I'll live. I'll just be miserable for a while."

The mulish look on the girl's face told Jazz that Adam had been right: she'd have to hog-tie Iris.

All she could do was sigh. "You hungry?"

"Not really. Come on, Aunt Jazz. I'll live."

Then Iris leaned back in the chair, clearly fatigued.

Adam spoke. "Did she get that stubbornness from you?"

"And Lily," Jazz answered. "But I know when I'm beat."

Cricket reruns still ran across the TV screen. "I like this game," Iris remarked. "How come I never heard about it before?"

"I told you, Americans think it's boring."

Iris blew air between her lips. "Well, there was a time no one liked soccer because the scores were too low. It'll change."

"Want some chicken soup?" Jazz asked hopefully. "You need to keep up your energy to fight this bug."

"Sure," came a distracted answer as Iris returned to her fascination with the game on the TV.

Jazz headed for the kitchen. Adam joined her. "Coffee?" he asked.

"Yes, please." She found one of the cans of chicken soup Adam had bought that morning—had it been just the morning?—and started it on the stove.

"Are *you* feeling any better?" Adam asked.

"A whole lot. You?"

"I got some catnapping in. Although when I was young we had a cat who took her time about waking up, complete with half-open eyes and yawns. No catnaps for her. She slept like a log."

Jazz actually chuckled. "Unique."

"Definitely one of a kind."

"What was her name?"

"Tabby. I was a creative seven-year-old. Not."

"I think it's a cute name."

"You and eight million other people."

Jazz took the soup to Iris in a large cappuccino cup. Less likely to spill. "Want some company?"

"You go talk to Adam. And give Sheba back to him. Evidently I've monopolized her."

"The dog has two homes."

Iris managed a smile. "Yup."

Sheba was willing to follow when Jazz called her, and greeted Adam with adoring eyes and a tail that wagged fast enough to helicopter her from the ground.

"You've been babysitting today, haven't you, girl. I think it's time to take you out back." Adam looked at Jazz. "I'll scoop the backyard, so don't worry about it."

"I hadn't even considered it." Which was true.

Out the back window, she saw Adam and Sheba playing fetch with the tennis ball. Now that he thought he was unobserved, Adam limped visibly.

God, he probably shouldn't have been running around town today. Then she remembered the chicken in the fridge and hard on the thought's heels, she also remembered the subs Adam had bought. Plenty of pastry, too.

She helped herself to another cinnamon roll and poured her coffee.

When Adam returned, he fed the dog and filled a bowl with water. Then he grabbed a stack of cookies, a cup of coffee, and sat.

"Ibuprofen," she said.

He arched a brow.

"I saw you outside. Maybe you have to put up with some suffering, but whatever helps ease it."

"Orders?"

"You got it. In fact, I'll get the tablets and you stay put." She retrieved the bottle from the cupboard, got him a glass of water, then plopped both on the table beside him.

"Mothering me?"

"I doubt you need it." She waved at his water glass. "My great-grandmother used to keep a bottle of water in the fridge at all times. I loved it."

"But your parents didn't?"

Jazz snorted. "The refrigerator was always too full, according to Mom, but heaven forfend anyone took too much ice."

"Dang."

Jazz shrugged. "Just the way it was. I'm an ice fiend now."

"Living where you do? I'm hardly surprised." He hesitated visibly. "Jazz, I was wondering?"

She waited.

"Nobody around here has the least reason to do this kind of thing to Lily, so I was wondering if someone from her past might."

Jazz didn't want to get into this. It might be betraying Lily's confidence. And what if Adam didn't understand the psychology of an abused woman? Many people didn't, simply demanding to know why the woman hadn't left her abuser sooner. They didn't know how slowly it began, how it undermined the woman's confidence. How it left her feeling responsible for every blow. How it made her feel that she deserved it.

She decided to anyway, believing Adam could be made to understand if he didn't immediately.

"Her ex-husband," Jazz said hesitantly. "He's in prison for abusing her and Iris."

"Dear God in heaven!"

For the first time, Jazz saw Adam look shocked. Really shocked.

"Oh my God," he said after a few seconds. "The two of them?"

"I always thought the X-rays of Iris were the clincher for the jury. A lot of people don't understand why a woman doesn't walk out. But those X-rays were heart-wrenching. Apparently, Andy had been using Iris as a threat to keep Lily in line. Then he went too far."

Adam just shook his head. "I can't think what to say. But you're sure he's in prison?"

"Florida doesn't have early release. Except in a few exceptional cases where the state might decide a prisoner has been on enough good behavior to get out after eighty-five percent of his sentence is complete. Takes some heavy-powered legal assistance to manage it, though. Almost everyone serves a full sentence."

"Wouldn't they have to tell her if they released him?"

"I don't know."

He swore again, drumming his fingers on the table,

clearly thinking. He picked up a cookie and ate it. He drank coffee. Then he spoke. "It might explain a lot if he's out. Maybe I can get the sheriff to investigate. But abuse…isn't that all about control?"

"Control combined with a twisted mind."

He swore yet again, giving her a taste of an Army mouth. Quite a repertoire.

"Poor Lily. Poor Iris. God what a trial. You'd never guess now."

"They seem to have recovered," Jazz answered. "At least as well as they ever can."

He shook his head and ate another cookie. "I'm glad Lily isn't here."

"Me, too. I don't ever want to see her that terrified again. I feel awful that I never knew anything about it until she pressed charges."

"She was good at covering up, I take it. Even with her twin?"

"Clearly. I didn't see much of her at the time. She always had an excuse. The job, Iris, going out somewhere. I thought I understood. I guess not."

He shook his head and reached for another cookie. He stopped himself. "I have an eating disorder when I get really angry. Better than battering holes in walls."

"By far." She felt awful for telling him about Andy. Not so much for Lily's privacy but because it had so visibly upset Adam. He was being so protective of her and Iris. Wasn't that enough?

"Well," he said presently, we've definitely got to get to the root of this before Lily gets home. She's been through enough without fearing that some weirdo, any weirdo, might do that to her again."

Jazz agreed wholeheartedly. "But what can we do? We have no real clues. At least none that are useful."

"First thing is call the sheriff."

"Not the chief of police? What was his name?"

"Jake Madison. No, the sheriff. He's got more resources, and Jake would have to turn to him anyway. Might as well start at the top."

Now IN CASPER, Wyoming, Andy Robbins set himself up in a homeless shelter, jockeying with other men in ragged clothing and dealing with the stench of unwashed bodies. At least this place had a group shower.

Meals were served with prayers, which Andy hated, but for food he'd put up with it in order to save his pocket change. Hitchhiking around this state was easier than he would have believed, but he didn't want to rent a car again too soon. The credit cards in his pocket were probably hot by now, and he needed to get a new one soon.

In the meantime, he spent a few bucks on another postcard and a stamp. Postmarked from a different place, a place that suggested he was getting closer to her. Lily would tighten like a spring.

Then there was Iris. Maybe he could use her to control Lily again. He didn't want to kill Lily. Oh, no. He wanted the satisfaction of terrifying her and beating her into line once more. She needed to understand that she'd never escape him, never defy him again. She was *his.*

Plus, she had to pay for his prison sentence. And he'd learned some damn useful tricks in there.

Smiling, he dropped the card in the mailbox outside the post office, smiling with anticipation of her reaction.

Savoring her growing fear.

But if terror didn't kick her back into line…well, he might just kill her.

No one else was going to ever have her. Sure as hell.

Chapter Eleven

Iris began to feel better in the evening. She chose the chicken sub but asked Jazz to cut her just a quarter of it. "I'm not that hungry."

Being hungry at all was an improvement, Jazz thought. She began to feel relieved about that at least.

Unfortunately, the sheriff arrived while Iris was eating and there was no way to prevent Iris from knowing.

Gage Dalton presented an interesting figure, a visible hitch in his step, a burn scar covering his cheek that tugged up one corner of his mouth. There was a story there, Jazz thought, the writer in her trying to create one.

But Iris. She didn't want Iris to know about any of this unless it became unavoidable. Adam dealt with the problem.

"Got a sick young 'un here, Gage. Let's step outside. Jazz?"

She grabbed her jacket from the back of the kitchen chair and joined both men on the end of the porch farthest from the living room window.

Gage studied Jazz for a few seconds. "You're not Lily, but damned if I wouldn't have thought so. Twins?"

Jazz nodded. "I'm Jasmine."

"What's happening?" Gage trained his dark gaze on Adam.

"Did Jake Madison talk to you?"

"About the flowers and the squirrel. He mentioned it. I didn't like it at all. He and his men have been keeping an eye out. Well, so have mine. Nothing seems unusual."

"Then we got this." Adam pulled the card from the inside pocket on his jacket.

Gage accepted it. "Damn it all to hell. Really?" Then he looked at the two of them. "Can I keep this?"

"Help yourself," Jazz answered. "I sure don't want it."

"Probably no identifiable prints on it," Gage remarked. "To many people handled it, including you two." He frowned deeply. "I don't like this any more than you. The flowers…maybe a sick joke. The squirrel, plain sick. But there's no mistaking the threat now. No way to brush it aside."

Adam agreed.

"You said you needed something from me?"

Jazz spoke. "From the card, we know the threat is directed at Lily."

Gage nodded agreement. "Nobody around here has a problem with her."

"That's why Adam asked about people in her past. There's one. Her ex was an abuser. Abused both her and Iris. Lily sent him to prison. He should still be there in Florida."

Gage nodded again. "Florida doesn't have any early release worth talking about, but I'll check." Now he shook his head. "You'd be amazed how much you can do while you're still inside of a prison."

Jazz felt a trickle of ice run down her spine. Her voice came out a whisper. "Meaning?"

"You get a friend who finishes his time before you. A friend willing to do a little chore for you."

Jazz's hand flew to her mouth. Suddenly she felt as if she couldn't breathe. "That's possible?"

"Not only in the movies," was Gage's grim response. "Okay, I've got a lot of investigating to do. All from a G-D postcard. Hell. I'll keep you posted."

With that, he turned and limped to the official Suburban parked on the street.

"He's good people. You'd never guess that when he arrived here, folks called him Hell's Own Archangel. But that's a story for another time." Adam looked at Jazz. "Let's get inside before Iris's curiosity overcomes her. I'll explain this."

"Be my guest."

She realized she was shaking only when she stepped indoors into the warmth. She didn't want to see Iris, not when she was this upset. Iris wouldn't miss it.

Instead she went to the kitchen and stood looking out the window, arms wrapped around herself, shivering. Andy might have sent someone from the *prison*? The problem, big enough before, had just grown huge. Gigantic. Now there'd be no way at all to identify this sleaze.

She felt a nudge against her leg and looked down. Sheba was staring up at her with liquid brown eyes. Evidently Sheba felt Jazz needed comforting. Nothing like the caring of a dog, she thought.

Unwrapping her arms, she squatted down and hugged the dog. "We'll get through this," she murmured into Sheba's scruff as her eyes dampened. "We will."

She heard Adam's step behind her. "Good news, Iris wants more of her sandwich and a diet soda. I'll take care of it." Then he snorted. "The damn pooch is playing nurse."

A watery laugh escaped Jazz. "So she is."

"You keep her for a while. I'll get her back soon enough."

"Yeah, when you need her. Maybe. If she isn't too busy."

"At the rate things are going, she's on full-time duty."

After looking after Iris, Adam took the dog out back to play fetch. It wasn't the biggest yard in the world, but it was enough for Sheba who got to run, turn around sharply, snap at the air and mainly sniff around for new and interesting smells. A very doggy time.

When they came in, Sheba sat in front of Adam.

"Treat time, huh?"

She wagged her tail.

"Okay, let's go get a few biscuits."

IRIS WANTED TO sleep in her own bed that night. Jazz was happy about it but insisted on following the girl up the stairs to make sure she was okay.

"Hovering again, Aunt Jazz. I'm feeling a whole lot better. Maybe I can get back to school and the team tomorrow."

"We'll see."

Iris blew her a raspberry.

Once her niece was safely tucked in bed, Jazz headed downstairs to find Adam pacing like a restless lion.

"Is something wrong?"

"Only that my hands are tied right now. Only that I have to wait for another shoe to drop. I'm not built for this."

"Is anyone? Pace away. I'll just enjoy the view."

That stopped him in midstride and seemed to nearly choke him. He faced her. "What?"

"You heard me." She gave him a lopsided smile. "There has to be something to enjoy right now. Anyway, I won't embarrass you. I'm going to have a piece of those subs you bought."

ADAM STOOD FOR a while, pacing forgotten. He felt a bit stunned by what Jazz had said, wondering what she meant. Nobody had ever said anything like that to him before, and he didn't know what to make of it. She couldn't possibly have been flirting with him. No way. Hell, given her fears for her sister and Iris, sex had to be the last thing on her mind.

She'd probably just been trying to distract him. Having someone pacing endlessly the way he was could be damned annoying.

The need for action ran along his every nerve ending. Patience had been required at times when he was in the military. Sitting in camouflage, covered in brambles and brush, waiting for an enemy. But that was different. He knew what was coming and why he had to wait. This time he had nothing except some vague threats. No direction, no idea of outcome. Not a foggy clue about whether Iris might be in danger.

He was seriously worried about Iris. Jazz, too, of course, but after what she'd told him about this Andy guy hurting the girl... Hell.

They couldn't lock Iris up like a bird in a cage. Not only would she fight it like mad and probably risk breaking her neck climbing out of her upstairs window, but they'd have to explain. She just wouldn't stand for it. Given the girl's breezy attitude toward life in general, she probably wouldn't believe *she* was in any danger. Nope. Besides the postcard had been addressed to Lily.

Iris would undoubtedly worry about her aunt but wouldn't see how she herself might be in danger.

Maybe he was making a mountain out of one molehill, but there wasn't enough to go on to avoid considering the possibility.

At last he wandered into the kitchen where Jazz had begun to eat half of her sub. He got his own from the fridge and joined her.

"You like?" he asked.

"Exactly what I would have ordered."

"How are you doing?"

She shrugged one shoulder and finished swallowing before she said, "I was in a holding pattern once. Flying back from New York to Miami from a conference. Damn, more than two hours waiting for a landing slot. Possibly worse, they showed a map of where we were in flight on the screen in front of us. It didn't help. But I also hadn't realized just how far one of those circles takes a plane. Dang, we could have landed at any number of major airports."

He snorted, still unwrapping his sandwich. "That would have made the passengers *so* happy."

"Might have been fun to watch the fireworks. Anyway, this is like a holding pattern, only it's not going to be over in a couple of hours."

"Nope."

"I got worried about the idea of someone in prison acting on Andy's directions."

Adam studied her, wishing she looked better, as she had when he met her. Hardly to be wondered that stress was taking a toll on her.

She spoke again. "What did you tell Iris about why the sheriff was here?"

"Just that they were looking into some vandalism and wondered if I knew anything about it."

Jazz looked up. "You think she bought it?"

He shrugged. "That girl may think she's feeling better, and maybe she is a little, but not by that much. She didn't look any too steady going up those stairs."

"No, she didn't." Jazz sighed then ate another bite of her sandwich. "I should have told her she couldn't go upstairs because I'm not going to be her dumbwaiter."

He chuckled. "I didn't think of that. Well, I can ferry drinks and food up to her."

Jazz ate a little more. "I'm sure this tastes better than it seems to right now. Anyway, tomorrow I'm going back to some kind of normal. As in roasting that chicken I put in the fridge to thaw. Maybe even get some writing done. What about you?"

"I'm beginning to feel like a fifth wheel. Is my presence annoying you?" He braced himself.

She appeared startled. "No! Why would it? It's not like you're flopped on the couch demanding chips and dip and more beer."

"Still..." He needed to watch over these two, but he couldn't escape the possibility that he might be unwanted.

"Stop it," she said sharply. "You're helping. You're making me feel safer, especially about Iris. I'm sorry it's boring you to tears."

"It's not boring me at all, and I'd still have the same impatience and worry across the street. I'd be peering out the window round the clock and hoping nothing was going on in your backyard."

Sheba, who had quietly joined them to lie on the floor in her favorite corner, huffed. Adam looked at her immediately. He didn't hear that sound from her very often.

"Sheba? Is something wrong?"

The dog rose and stretched, then came over to the table, her tag jingling quietly. She sat and looked from one to the other.

"What is it, girl?"

A cocked head.

"Oh, crap," Adam said as he understood.

"What?"

He looked at Jazz. "I think she feels the pack broke up when Iris went upstairs. She wants us all together."

"Seriously?"

"Dogs can be like that." He returned his attention to the setter. "Go find Iris."

The dog took off like a shot and soon they heard the thud of her paws on the stairs.

Jazz laughed. "I guess you got that one right."

"I am not always stupid, although Sheba makes me feel like it sometimes."

He finished his sandwich, his mind running around like a hamster in a wheel, when finally he shook himself. *No.* This was a waste of time and energy.

"Let's get away from this damn table. There's got to be something on television. And Sheba will let us know if Iris needs something."

ANOTHER DAY DAWNED, once again chilly and rainy. Iris didn't even talk about going to school. "It's not that bad, Aunt Jazz, but I still don't feel good. Maybe by Monday?"

"I sure hope so, or I'm taking you to the doctor if I have to handcuff you."

"We'll see." Despite not feeling well, Iris managed to look stubborn.

"Ready to come downstairs and join the world for breakfast?"

"Yeah. But I'm not really hungry."

"You should eat a little unless you're sick to your stomach."

Jazz waited outside the bathroom while her niece took a shower. Iris changed into sloppy clothes that must make Lily shudder, but apparently Iris found them comfy. Socks on her feet, they headed downstairs.

Adam had beat Jazz to it. He was scrambling eggs with cheese and building a stack of buttered toast. "Sit down, ladies. This is one meal I can deal with."

Iris picked at her breakfast, but at least she ate. Then she looked at the two of them. "When are you going to tell me what's going on?"

Adam and Jazz both froze. Then Jazz cleared her throat.

"What do you mean, Iris?"

Iris shrugged. "Adam didn't move over here because he needs an exterminator. Aunt Jazz, you didn't know Adam long enough to be romancing at that point. Then the sheriff shows up. I don't believe he came to question Adam about some vandalism. The top guy doesn't do that, he sends one of his deputies. So try another lie."

Jazz looked at Adam. Adam looked at Jazz. Flummoxed, Jazz then looked at her niece. She didn't want to lie, but upon reflection she had decided she didn't want Iris to live in fear. The threat was clearly directed at Lily, not her.

"A postcard," Adam said, filling the awkward silence. "It was addressed to Lily but sounded kind of threatening. I suppose we should check to see if there were any more in the mail."

Iris shook her head. "I'd have noticed a postcard. I had to throw away enough of those glossy ones. Did you know you can get a free dental exam? In Casper? Sheesh."

Jazz tried to smile and thought she felt her mouth respond to the urge.

Iris frowned though. "Do you think Mom's in danger?"

"I think," Jazz said, choosing her words with care, "that we need to find out who this bully is so that your mom doesn't have to get cards like that when she gets home. But there might not ever be another one."

Iris seemed content with that. For now anyway. She ate a few more mouthfuls, then said, "I'm getting a headache. Can I have some ibuprofen?"

Jazz didn't see anything wrong with that. Adam beat her to the punch though, bringing the bottle to the table. "I'll join you. We can have a pill party."

Iris giggled at that. "But where's the beer?"

Adam arched his brows. "Have you looked at the clock?"

Another giggle from Iris. "You'd never let me have one. Mom wouldn't either, which is okay by me. It smells bad."

Jazz ate well, complimenting Adam on his scrambled eggs. "Light and fluffy. Not everyone can do that."

Iris spoke. "Can I go watch TV? Maybe cricket?"

A mere glance at Iris told Jazz the girl was looking worse again. "You really like it, huh?"

"Now that I understand better what's going on. T20 you called it?"

"Because there are only twenty overs, or 120 balls, in a game for each side. Fast."

"It seems like it."

They soon had Iris back in the recliner with a warm blanket and a can of chilled soda, which seemed a contradiction, but Jazz shrugged mentally, thinking, *Kids!*

She found a game on TV for Iris, warning her that it was a rerun and might be chopped up.

"That's okay. I like the highlights."

With Iris settled, Jazz and Adam returned to the kitchen table. Jazz decided she was going to hate that table, even though in her small studio at home she didn't have much better but she didn't spend as much time at it.

Sheba ran back and forth between the kitchen and the living room as if she couldn't decide where she wanted to be.

"Split pack?" Jazz asked.

"Maybe. Or she feels everyone needs her attention."

"That's entirely possible. Got any thoughts, Adam?"

"Yeah. This sucks. I guess we wait to see if there's another postcard."

"Or worse." Once again she was trying not to crawl out of her skin, trying to tell herself she was overreacting. "Don't you want to get back to your place? Back to your job?"

"Sometimes I go weeks without a broken water heater, backed up septic system, a leaking pipe, an oven that's not working, a blocked dryer vent. Amazing."

He made her want to laugh, and she decided to give in to it.

He smiled back. "Have you heard my cell phone quack?"

"Quack? Seriously?"

"It gets my attention." Dragging him away from places he didn't want to go, placing him firmly back in the present. He was all in favor of any trick that worked. The quack usually did, but not always.

The war haunted him, but it haunted many others. Like a dream, a repetitious nightmare that wouldn't go away. Except that it wasn't a nightmare. Sometimes it happened in the bright light of day. It was *real*.

Sometimes the past became the present, as real as the woman sitting at the table with him. Maybe things triggered him, but so far he hadn't found many of the triggers. If he had, he might have been able to avoid them.

Instead the memories hovered at the distant edge of consciousness and burst forth at the time of their choosing. He had to sit there and wonder if it would happen soon, happen in front of Jazz. The idea sickened him.

Not something he could afford to worry about. It was out of his control.

But hell, so was this maniac who was determined to frighten Lily. Maybe that's all he intended. Just to frighten her, but the squirrel really disturbed him. That took some kind of bent mind.

Just then, his phone quacked.

"Duty calls," Jazz remarked. She got up to get some coffee.

Adam answered his phone. "Hi Jess." Jess was rounding up the group for tonight. "Sorry, can't make the meeting tonight. See you next week, I hope. Yeah, okay. You, too."

She brought two cups to the table. "Meeting?"

"My vets group."

"You should go. You can't stay here *all* the time."

Annoyance rose in him. "Damn it, Jazz, if you want

me out of here, just say so." Instantly he wished he could take the words back. The expression on her face, a mixture of shock and hurt and something else he couldn't identify.

"Don't take it that way," she said quietly. "I'm not giving you an eviction notice. I'm just concerned because you must have other things to do. Better things than babysitting me and Iris."

His irritation remained despite his regret for his outburst. "Listen, lady. I ain't got one better thing to do than make sure Iris and you are safe. Period."

She bit her lip and leaned back against the counter, forgoing her chair. "But it seems like such a small thing…"

"Really?" he asked harshly. *"Really?"*

After a few seconds, she shook her head. "No. It doesn't." She closed her eyes. "Those flowers felt like a death wish. The squirrel like a serious threat. The postcard would be nothing without those things."

"Exactly. Maybe it *is* all nothing. Maybe some creep is just getting his jollies. But what if he isn't? That's why you're so uneasy all the time. That's why you wish you didn't have to let Iris out of your sight. And I don't think you're overreacting. The only good thing I can say is that this doesn't seem to be in any way directed at your niece."

"There *is* that." At last she came to sit and reach for her coffee. The mug was still warm, and the coffee felt good going down her throat. Heat. She needed heat. Maybe she should go borrow one of Lily's heavier sweaters.

The kitchen window revealed a gray, drizzly day. Cold and damp, at least to her Florida blood.

Adam rose. "I'm going to take Sheba for a walk. Will you be okay for twenty minutes or so?"

It seemed strange to even be asked. "Of course."

Five minutes later, Adam and his dog were out the door. Jazz sat with her hands wrapped around her mug wondering if she would ever feel warm again. Or completely unafraid.

BY THE TIME Adam and Sheba returned, Jazz had moved to the living room and was watching cricket with Iris, who was eating crackers with liver sausage and cheese.

Content to see her niece eating a larger amount, Jazz explained the finer points of the game while Iris got involved enough to have developed a favorite team, at least in this match. She quietly cheered a good hit, groaned when someone lost a wicket, and had even started paying attention to the bowlers' styles. She was going to have mastered the game before the weekend was over.

Then her phone rang and she answered. "Ooooh, school's out. Hi, Betsy! Yeah, I'm feeling a little better. Are you over it yet?"

School was out. Smiling, Jazz left Iris to her endless phone calls with friends and returned to the kitchen where Adam was wiping Sheba with a towel.

"I'm going to need to mop the floor," he remarked. "Sheba couldn't resist the puddles or the mud. Thank God she didn't roll around in it, but her paws!"

They were certainly muddy and had left prints all the way from the door. "Nothing that can't be fixed."

"This animal is going to tempt me to throw her in the bathtub."

But Sheba, oblivious to the threat, sat grinning and soaking up the rubdown.

"Let me get the dishpan," Jazz suggested. "You can save her the indignity of a bath."

"She'd love that," Adam agreed. "Despite how many she's had, she'll never like a bath."

Adam made Sheba sit while Jazz filled the dishpan with lukewarm water. "I don't want her running in to see Iris until she won't traipse mud everywhere."

Surprising Jazz, Sheba didn't seem to mind having her paws dipped in the water and gently rubbed by Adam. She lowered her nose a few times to sniff, then raised it, swiping Adam once with her tongue.

"I guess she likes that," Jazz remarked. She brought another towel so Adam could dry the dog's feet.

"She's an attention hog," Adam said fondly. When he was satisfied and sat back on his heels, Sheba ran in a few circles then raced to the living room.

"Zoomies," Adam remarked. He rose stiffly and picked up the wet towels.

"You cold and wet?" Jazz asked. Just then she heard Iris exclaim from the living room.

"Sheba! You never jump up!"

Adam waited, clearly listening, then Iris's giggle floated to them. No problem.

"I'm not too cold for a beer," Adam said, answering her question.

Jazz noticed he got himself some ibuprofen as well. Then he sagged onto a chair with a muffled curse. "Damp, cold weather."

"Makes you hurt worse?"

"I'm that old story about rheumatism making the knees ache. It'll pass. I should have asked if you want a beer."

"I know my way to the fridge. And soon I'm going to have to remember how to roast a chicken. I used to do it all the time, but now I'm hazy on details."

"I'm sure the internet can help. It's saved my bacon more than once."

She retrieved her laptop and opened it, remarking, "I bet there's at least ten different recipes for it."

He snorted. "Pick the one that looks simplest. The way you *would* have made it before everybody's recipe was online."

Iris's giggles reached them as Jazz pored through web pages and the laughter had an odd effect on her. She looked across the table at Adam.

"I'm not afraid anymore," she announced.

"No?" He arched a brow.

"No. What I am is angry and getting angrier." Indeed, it was burning inside her like a coal fire, growing steadily. Fear was evaporating in a determination to stop this creep before he made her sister's life into a living hell. "You're right about this guy being a coward. That same kind of coward Andy was, picking on smaller and weaker people."

She felt stupid for not having thought of Andy from the beginning, but in her mind he was off the table while he was still in prison. Jazz, however, was sure of one thing: this crap would stir those memories in Lily, and God knew how her sister would handle them.

And what if Andy had somehow obtained an early release? God, she'd seen the guy in court, she'd listened to and watched the images and stories that Lily had told. She'd known her sister, for the first and only time in her life, on the edge of a nervous breakdown.

Stuck here, unable to identify the creep behind this, or to know what he might do next, infuriated her. Adam was right. She needed to keep impersonating Lily in the hope this snake would emerge from under his rock before Lily came home.

"What made you angry?" Adam asked.

"Thinking about Lily. I was afraid before like some kind of chicken but I'm afraid now for Lily. Given what she's been through with her ex, how do you imagine this might hit her? That creep she was married to nearly broke her. I never, ever, want to see that again."

"I can hardly imagine."

"You don't want to. But I was with her through the endgame, from the time the police arrested that man to his sentencing. The day he was sentenced was the first time I saw her smile in ages. A *real* smile. I'd die before I'd let her lose that smile."

Adam finished his beer, then got himself another one. Facing her again, he said, "Tell me about it."

"Tell you what?"

"About exactly what got Lily to that point. I don't understand the abuse dynamic. You told me generally, but I still don't fully get it."

Jazz sighed. "Most people don't. The first they want to know is why didn't she just leave. I think I told you."

"But she didn't. From what I've seen of her, and you, it leads me to believe it's far from that simple."

"It is. Books helped me better understand, but it's basically simple. Lovebirds. Seemingly solid relationship. Eventual separation from friends and family because the guy just doesn't like them. Because he gets irritated when she sees them. Alongside this is steadily increasing abuse. At first he always apologizes. Brings flowers or gifts and swears he'll never do it again. He lets her know in no uncertain terms that he wouldn't have gotten mad except for something she said or did. So then she tries harder to become the perfect wife."

"God," Adam muttered.

"Natural reaction to want to make the person you love happy. But then it moves past that to *fear* of making him angry. And because you've distanced yourself from everyone you could trust, you're all alone with this guy. He's your only support. Or so you believe. From there the abuse just ratchets up, and because of your fear of him you'll lie even when he sends you to the hospital."

She heard Adam nearly growl.

"So, into this comes Iris, a baby he didn't want and got stuck with anyway. And Iris becomes his cudgel. Threats against her if Lily doesn't behave."

He swore forcefully. "Then the bastard hurt Iris."

"Yeah. That yanked Lily out of the whole cycle. Sliced through her fear of him and her fear of failing him." She paused and closed her eyes briefly. "Sometimes, for some people, that's not enough to make them get out. The terror is overwhelming, the feeling of no escape is controlling."

"But there are safe houses, aren't there?"

"Sure. But a lot a victims can no longer believe in safety. Often for good reason. He'll find them, they're sure."

Adam wiped one hand over his face. "What an ugly, ugly picture."

Jazz looked down. "Imagine living with the guilt afterward. The shame. Anyway, counseling seemed to help them both, like I said, and Lily picked up her career and made huge strides from the place where Andy had kept her stuck. But I don't want this to take her back there. No way. We've got to prevent that."

"I can't agree more. But we're stymied now. We need him to make a mistake."

She nodded. "At least this creep doesn't seem interested in Iris." As soon as she spoke the words, a shiver ran down her spine.

Not Iris. But how could they be sure?

Dread filled her. A dark, deep dread.

ANDY HAD DEVELOPED a well of patience in prison, but that well wasn't very deep. He was reaching the bottom of it now and he could barely stand the waiting any longer.

He decided it might be a good time to return to Conard City. Just for a look around. A way to plan what he wanted to do, not just think about it.

Imagining it had been good enough during nearly ten years in prison. It had carried him through the rocky weeks after his early discharge. He'd left that damn prison without anything except the clothes and wallet he'd arrived with. Essentially no money at all.

But he'd managed anyway. A day labor job here and there, money good enough for a man who was now used to nearly nothing. Even meals were better at homeless shelters than at the prison.

Dumpster diving had become his friend. Hitchhiking worked if he avoided cops.

But now he needed to be in total control of his journey. Control was massively important to him. He hadn't had any for years now.

He hungered for it, and that bitch had stolen every bit of control he'd had. He wanted it back. All of it. Most especially of Lily. He'd never forgotten how he'd savored treating her like a dog and having her scramble to follow his every command.

That beautiful, supposedly powerful, woman had held no power when it came to him. He'd held it all.

Hell, except for her job that supported him, he'd have dressed her in rags just to prove his point.

Time to get going, he decided. He needed to smell her fear again, to see it in her eyes, and playing his little games wasn't enough. While he enjoyed the idea of her receiving his most recent postcard, it didn't satisfy him. Yeah, he was edging her back into a pliable state, but maybe he could find a faster way to do it.

His financial situation, as he thought of it, didn't allow him to get a car, so late at night he borrowed one from a used car lot just beyond the outskirts of Laramie. Then he helped himself to plates from a truck elsewhere in town. He mailed one last postcard from there, checked his money and the credit card he'd heisted from a guy's wallet in Casper, and left town.

The credit card would work for a tank of gas, but not much beyond that, he figured. He chose to head east for gas when Conard County was west. Muddying his trail. He wasn't stupid.

Then he would set out for Conard County. He'd been away for a few days, and nobody had seemed interested in him when he was there. This time he'd stay farther away. Maybe keep this well-used pickup mostly out of sight.

Maybe heist an ATV somewhere along the way. You never knew, but it was good to plan for possibilities.

Smiling, he gassed the truck then turned toward Conard City. Oh, this was going to be good.

Chapter Twelve

Monday morning brought cheerier weather, and Iris headed back to school with one caveat from Jazz.

"Take it easy with the swimming today. You don't want to make yourself sick again."

Iris breezed off, smiling happily, and Adam looked at Jazz.

"You think she'll listen?" he asked.

"No, but I had to say it."

He laughed. "What about you? Anything you'd like to do today?"

Well, she didn't have to worry about Iris while she was in school and with her friends. "Get out of this house. Take a walk in the fresh air. Maybe go to the grocery."

"That chicken you made was pretty good."

Jazz smiled. "I managed okay. Now I want to try something else. I've given up on writing until I get home."

"Do you feel bad about it?"

"My editor will probably feel worse. I think I'm already scheduled for publication. Regardless, life happens, and it's happening right now. In ways I don't like." She shook herself. "No use thinking about that now. I'll wait until it's time for the mail. Then I can get uptight wondering if there's another postcard. Or worse."

Adam studied her, then spoke. "If you don't mind, I'll walk with you."

"I'd like that." Very much. Maybe too much. But what was the point? Much as she liked Adam, as attractive as she found him, she'd be going back to Miami.

But some nights in bed, when she could shake her worries, she thought about him. Lasciviously. Sometimes she even ached to know what it would be like to make love with him.

Egad, this was going nowhere except into trouble. And she had enough trouble right now.

"Then," he said, unaware of her thoughts and continuing the conversation, "I want to go over to my place and bring over some of my workout equipment. Maybe some weights and a mat. I'll put them in the basement."

Once again, guilt struck her. "I'm messing up your life."

"*You're* not messing up anything, and I'm doing exactly what I want to, okay? Now get your jacket. I'd call it spring out there, but you'd probably call it winter."

That called a needed laugh out of her. She hurried to get her lightweight jacket and joined him on the porch.

"The coast is clear," he said in a conspiratorial voice.

She had to grin. "You're good for me," she announced. "Ditto."

They climbed down the porch steps then stood on the sidewalk. "Which way?" Adam asked.

"The prettiest route to the grocery."

He led her a few blocks over to a wider avenue. The leaves were new, the light green that came before the darker color of summer. Still a little feathery in places.

Branches overhung the street, making it almost tunnel-like except for the dappled sun that spilled through.

Large gracious houses lined the street on both sides, ornamented with Victorian gingerbread, boasting wide, deep front porches. Some even featured hanging bench swings; many were decorated with window boxes, flowers just beginning to bloom.

"This place is enchanted," Jazz said.

"Another era." He pointed to a gray-painted clapboard house with darker gray trim. "Sheriff Dalton lives there with his wife, the librarian. Miss Emma."

She tilted her face toward him. "Miss Emma? Really?"

"Seems outdated, doesn't it? But evidently she's been called that since she became librarian in her early twenties. No one seems to know why. Maybe it was kids being taught to be respectful back then. Regardless, she'll always be Miss Emma."

"I like that."

"Well, that's her family house. Her father was Judge Conard, and the Conards were one of the founding families here. As if the name wouldn't tell you. Word is that she's collected the history of this area going back as far as possible. And, I hear, she's still collecting stuff. There's no escape from history around here. Best behave."

Jazz laughed again. The world was lightening, for however long it might last, and she was happy to take the gift.

She felt bad when she realized Adam's limp had grown more obvious, but he didn't say anything and she kept her mouth shut. It must be awful living with continuous pain but it wasn't her place to draw attention to his limp unless he said something. They continued their circuitous route to the store through residential streets.

ADAM'S HIP WAS killing him, more than usual. He wanted to suppress his pain but couldn't. And he didn't want to see pity in Jazz's eyes.

She kept on drawing him the way Lily never had, even though they looked as if they'd sprung from the same mold. Both were confident women, successful in their careers. Lily had never appeared to be interested in men anyway, and now he understood why. He simply couldn't imagine the hell she'd lived through.

Maybe that was the difference he sensed. At times he thought he caught a spark of sexual interest in Jazz's gaze, but then it flitted away.

Naturally it would. She would be leaving in a few weeks, going back to her own life and friends. Besides, what would she want with a battered vet who still struggled with PTSD?

Anyway, they both had more important things to think about, like the threat to Lily. Given Lily's background, he agreed with the need to put this all to bed before she returned.

At the grocery, Jazz mulled over the available food. She appeared to be considering what she might cook that night. There had to be at least one recipe in her head the way she was looking around. Or maybe she was mentally assembling one.

After a bit, she'd filled her cart. "Okay," he said, "what's the menu?"

"Fruit for Iris of course. I believe she keeps an entire fruit farm in business. Apples, oranges, bananas. Orange juice. Gads, she doesn't have to worry about sugar, either. I'm totally envious of that girl."

He laughed.

"Cereal. Oats. Crackers, whole wheat. Bread, multigrain. She'll settle for rye, though."

"Okay, okay, I get it."

"Well, she *did* ask if I thought she could eat that delicious meal you brought home from the diner. French fries? Never will they pass her lips."

"I think I saw her snag a couple."

"I never saw. She's safe."

Now he was grinning.

"And the rest of the stuff?" The ingredients were making little sense to him except for the lasagna noodles and jar of high-class marinara. Cheese, a few pounds of hamburger.

"I'll make meatloaf tonight. Lasagna tomorrow when I have more time."

"Ambitious." Meatloaf? He hated it.

She cocked an eye at him as she added golden mushroom soup and A-1 sauce to the cart. "I know what you're thinking. Meatloaf is dry." She winked. "Mine is not. In fact, it's famous with my friends."

"Okay. Just don't say tuna casserole."

"Maybe I'll make tuna salad one of these days."

"Now that I like. In fact, I'll make it."

"I may definitely put you on it."

As she checked out, he looked at the growing stack of groceries. The bagger, however, was packing the bags pretty full. "I should have brought my truck. It's a good thing we can carry all this between us."

She smiled. A sweet expression always. He'd like to keep it on her face. "I was counting on you."

He took the heaviest doubled bags, leaving her the lighter ones. He knew for sure he had the muscle strength.

The walk home was good, despite his hip. He just enjoyed Jazz's company.

Back at the house he helped her unload everything. When he started to put away the soda crackers, onions and A-1 sauce, she said, "Not those."

"Really?"

"I put all my ingredients in my cooking space so I don't forget something or have to run around looking for it."

He nodded. "Good idea."

"You may get the dishwashing detail as I prepare, though."

"Not a problem, lady. I'm really experienced at that. I'm going to run across the street to bring some of my workout equipment over and put it in the basement, if you're okay with that."

He saw the fear return briefly to her gaze, but she said nothing except, "Go get it."

ADAM LIMITED HIMSELF to dumbbells and the exercise mat. He could do a lot on that mat to keep himself going for a while. He put it all in the basement. He returned to the top of the stairs in time to hear Iris come home. Early.

Then he heard the door bang. He looked in that direction, discovering this was no breezy, happy Iris. Instead she threw today's mail at the hall table, knocking the carefully stacked letters onto the floor.

"Sorry," she said pettishly, then stomped into the living room.

Adam turned a bit and saw Jazz in the kitchen doorway. "What's going on?"

"I guess I need to find out. I've never seen her in this mood."

"At her age she ought to be having more of them."

He remained in the hallway so he could eavesdrop, even though he knew he shouldn't. Still, he was concerned about Iris. If she had moods like this, he'd certainly never seen them or heard about them.

Jazz spoke gently. "What's wrong, Iris?"

"Sally!"

Silence. Adam waited, knowing that Sally was Iris's best friend. Now his curiosity was truly piqued.

"What about Sally?" Jazz asked.

"She stole my boyfriend! My best friend stole my boyfriend! I'm not going to swim today. Maybe never again 'cuz she's on the team!"

"Wow," Jazz said.

Wow, Adam thought.

"I didn't know you had a boyfriend. You said you didn't have time for one."

"It was mostly at school and we talked a lot on the phone at night. We even made plans for the summer. But he was holding hands with Sally today, and neither of them would look at me. So I asked her. Yeah, she stole him! She even knew about him and me, but she went ahead and did it anyway. And he's been calling her for a while. She didn't even tell me. He didn't tell me."

"That's pretty awful," Jazz said sympathetically.

What sounded like a sob issued from the living room. "I'm quitting the swim team."

"Because of Sally?"

"Because I don't ever want to see her again. Because I

don't have time to go anywhere after school. The most I could do was a movie on the weekend, but we never did that. Homework! But Sally doesn't have any more time than I do, so it can't be that." Another sob. "He didn't like me as much as he said he did!"

"That's terrible." Jazz fell silent for a brief time. Then she said, "You probably don't want my opinion but you might want to look at this another way."

"There is no other way!"

"Yes," Jazz said firmly. "There is. Think about it. He didn't break up with you before he went wandering. Who needs a guy like that? What if he came back to you? Could you ever trust him?"

Iris sniffled for a while. "Maybe not."

"Basically, he cheated on you. And Sally has snagged a guy who is cheater."

More sniffling. "I should pick up the mail." Clearly trying to change the subject.

"I'll do it." Again Jazz fell silent for a minute or so. "You probably don't want to hear this, but here goes. Go to the swim practice tomorrow and act like you don't care. It won't be easy, but you'll keep your pride."

Iris sniffled again. "Maybe. Darn it, Aunt Jazz, you've got a whole different idea about this."

"Maybe because I've walked in your shoes. Just make yourself look like the better person. Of course, you don't have to listen to me. All your decision."

Adam heard Jazz stir, then she came out of the living room. He guessed she knew he'd been eavesdropping by the way she gave him a crooked smile.

"I'll pick up the mail," he offered.

"Leave it. It's a good comment on this day. Let's go make meatloaf."

Suddenly Iris's voice reached them, still sounding like she was on the edge of tears. "Not meatloaf! You've got be kidding!"

"Mine is famous," Jazz called back. "It's better than most."

In the kitchen, Adam headed straight to the fridge and pulled out a longneck. "Want one?"

"What I need is a stiff bourbon. But yes please."

They sat at the table, which seemed to have become their favorite gathering place.

"Like some help with that meatloaf?" he asked, not wanting to discuss the issue at hand for fear Iris might hear.

"What I want to do is dress down Sally and this boyfriend in a way they'll never forget. But that won't do any good at all and it would only embarrass Iris."

"An urge to violence." He smiled crookedly. He liked her fire. Good to see it. Talk about getting overwhelmed on a simple visit to her niece. But he also felt a great deal of sympathy for Iris. Being scorned like that seriously hurt.

"Sucks," he said.

"More than sucks. It's hurtful. Agonizingly hurtful at that age. And humiliating."

"That, too. So, the meatloaf?"

"Just finish that beer and go do your workout. *I* want to take out my anger on the damn hamburger. I suppose the workout makes you feel better."

"In more than one way," he confessed. "It's a great way to deal with memories I don't want."

She tilted her head. "The war?"

"Yup." He turned his bottle up and drained it.

"And how's your hip after that walk to the grocery?"

"Grinding along as usual."

"Grinding?"

"No better way to describe it." But that was more than he wanted to say. "I'll go do the workout. You need anything at all, holler down the stairs."

"I will."

He detested the look of sympathy on her face. He didn't need sympathy. Not even a little of it. Should have kept his mouth shut.

He rinsed the bottle and threw it in the trash before limping toward the basement stairs. "I won't be long."

"Don't hurry on my account. That hamburger is going to get it."

He nearly chuckled. "Beat it to death." Then he climbed down the stairs.

DINNER WAS A subdued affair. Iris insisted on cleaning off half the dining room table and setting it. Then she said, "I'll pick up that mail. My fault."

"Leave it," said Jazz. "It suits my mood."

Iris struggled for a red-eyed smile. "Mine too, honestly. I hate to say it, but that meatloaf smells good."

"Oh, wonder of wonders. I told you it was famous. I'll make some broccoli and mashed potatoes in a little while. I should have baked a cake but your mom doesn't keep any boxed mixes around and it's the only kind I know how to make."

"I couldn't eat it anyway."

"Screw your training diet. I wouldn't mind if you broke it out of frustration anyway. You need chocolate but that's one other thing I don't have. I wasn't planning on a breakup."

Iris sniffled. "Neither was I, but next time I'll plan better."

"Keep a quart of chocolate ice cream at the back of the freezer for emergencies. Not that you'll probably have another one like this."

"Damn," said Iris. "I should have guessed. He's a jock."

"And you aren't?"

Another weak smile from the girl. But that was the end of her attempt to be sociable, and Jazz went to work on side dishes. The meatloaf was approaching done.

THEY SAT AT the table with Blue Willow plates, sliced meatloaf and sides. Each of them served themselves, Adam heaping his plate.

"Dang, this is a fantastic meatloaf," Adam said after tasting it. "I can see why it's famous."

Iris, who had been slowly forking it, finally tried a mouthful. Her eyes widened. "You weren't kidding. Okay I'll eat this again. But only yours."

Then conversation lagged. Iris ate with heavy sighs, and Adam and Jazz were both disinclined to converse in the face of all that misery.

After dinner, Iris wanted to do the dishes and Jazz insisted on helping her.

Girl time, Adam thought. He left them to it and went to the hallway to clean up the spilled mail. It might suit Jazz's mood to leave it, but he had a concern: another postcard. Maybe that was why Jazz didn't want Iris to straighten up the mess, and maybe she wanted the mess left because she feared what she might find.

So he bent to the task, lifting and stacking until he uncovered a post card.

I'm coming and you'll never know when.

Adam's heart slammed, then rage filled him. Another threat, this one stronger. He tucked the card inside his shirt pocket. He didn't want to show it to Jazz, but it would be wrong to keep her in the dark. She had a right to know and she wasn't a child.

He started stacking the remaining mail when he saw an official envelope. "Holy Mary," he murmured. "Damn it all."

He looked up, staring into space, then straightened and put the envelope under others to conceal it. He decided to place the postcard there as well. After Iris went up for the night, he'd talk with Jazz.

Chapter Thirteen

Andy arrived in Conard County that same night. He parked his stolen truck out of sight under some low-hanging trees in the middle of nowhere.

He'd snagged a sleeping bag earlier from an empty tent in a rustic campground, and when he'd bought gas on the credit card—which would soon be smoking hot—he'd picked up enough food and beer to keep him going for days. The bed of the truck, with its camper shell, made a perfect bedroom and dining room for him.

Tomorrow he'd go looking for Lily and an opportunity. Although he was beginning to think Iris might provide that opportunity. He'd spotted his daughter on his last visit to this ink spot town and had felt slammed. He identified her easily because she was almost a carbon copy of Lily except for that hair.

Talk about getting even! To torture Lily once again with their kid. Yeah, he liked the symmetry of that.

Pleased with himself, he ate a stale turkey sandwich and a larger bag of potato chips.

Not that he'd ever hurt the kid. No, that was the single time he'd lost control. He was sure he could control himself when he needed to. Anger didn't rule him, and he was all about control.

What he never realized was that he'd never controlled himself to any meaningful extent except in prison. There, punishment and retribution came swiftly.

He'd never realized that his love of control was about controlling everyone except himself.

He listened to the murmur of the trees above, feeling very satisfied with himself.

IRIS WENT UPSTAIRS at her usual time, maybe to talk to girlfriends. Except for Sally.

Jazz had moved into the living room with Adam. "Good workout?" she asked. "And the hip?"

"I took more ibuprofen." He rose. "I know it's late, but I need a cup of coffee. You?"

She hesitated. "Something's going on. Tell me."

"When we've both got coffee. We're going to want to talk for a while, not sleep."

"Oh, God," she said quietly. "Another postcard?"

"In a minute, Jazz. In a minute."

He went to the kitchen to make coffee, leaving her nearly on the edge of her seat with anxiety. She'd never been a nail chewer, but she was considering it just then. Her fingers dug into the arms of the recliner. She knew something awful was coming just by the way he wasn't tossing out information.

Adam brought her coffee.

"All right," he said. "Well, it's not all right, but wait while I get the necessary mail."

"A postcard," she murmured, her mind rebelling, her anger returning. Whoever this was, he was playing cat and mouse with her and her sister. An ugly game to anyone who'd ever seen a cat play with a mouse. For a cat, it was a matter of survival, and the play wearied the prey until it would no longer retaliate. Which didn't make it any prettier. This guy was no cat but he seemed to be trying to tire his prey.

Adam returned with a postcard and an envelope. He sat while she scanned the postcard. Her stomach clenched into a painful knot.

"Dear God!" She tried to keep her voice low because of Iris, although she probably wouldn't hear anything except the friend's voice on the other end of her phone. "Dear God."

"Exactly. And this. It appears to have been in the stack since shortly after you arrived. No reason for Iris to pick it out."

This time her stomach flipped and nausea filled it. "No, she's observing her mother's privacy."

But written in hard black ink in the upper left-hand corner were the terrifying words:

State of Florida.
Department of Corrections.

"Adam…"

"Open it."

She lifted her head slowly, looking at him. "But it's addressed to Lily."

"Do you really think she'd complain to the post office that you opened her mail? Especially *that* mail?"

He was right, but she honestly didn't want to open it. She was positive it couldn't contain good news, such as that Andy had been shivved by another prisoner. Or that his sentence had been extended by ten years for some other misdeed.

She reluctantly, slowly, opened the top of the envelope, then pulled out the one-page letter. Her roller-coaster took another dive then rose to the height of fury.

"It's him," she said, her voice tight. "It's him." Then she passed the letter to Adam.

Adam scanned the page quickly. "I figured."

Andy Robins had been released early from prison on gain time. Something that almost never happened, not in Florida.

FOR A WHILE there didn't seem to be anything to say. Adam hated that he had no comfort to offer Jazz. Her eyes had gone almost hollow, but fury flared in their depths.

"We'll deal with it somehow," he said eventually. "We'll deal together. You're not alone."

The faintest smile whispered across her face. "Thanks."

"No need. Now let's go to our favorite perch in the kitchen and have a beer or more coffee." The beverage in their cups had grown cold. "I wish I'd dashed out earlier and gotten you some bourbon."

"Beer is fine. Maybe it'll help peel me off the ceiling."

"The ceiling isn't my favorite hangout," he agreed. Rising, he offered his hand to help her up.

She gripped him tightly, more tightly than necessary. He didn't mind, but it gave him a sense of her emotional state, more than anything she'd said.

In the kitchen, she dumped her coffee in the sink and left the cup on the counter, indicating she'd rather have a beer. He put his cup beside hers and switched off the pot. Focusing on ordinary tasks while his mind absorbed the enormity of this latest installment of *Terrifying Lily.* A horror show.

Yeah, he'd suspected this. Jazz probably had, too. The difference was that she had a very clear idea of what

Andy Robbins could do. He was now no amorphous sleaze who'd just be content to spark fear. This was a man capable of serious violence.

Why couldn't the bastard have just gone elsewhere? Why this need to make Lily's life into a living hell?

Adam got the beers, glad he'd bought another six-pack at the store earlier. Had that been today? He was familiar from war with the way time could stretch, how mornings could seem so far in the past that they felt like another day. He just hadn't realized this was going to turn into one of *those* days.

Now it had.

He joined Jazz at the table, opening the longneck for her. Then he opened his own. The minutiae of detail seemed important now. Something to focus on besides the murderous fury inside himself.

Something to focus on besides the wish that he could sweep away this entire problem to make all the ladies safe. At least Iris had so far been sheltered from this, but could that continue?

When he thought of that innocent girl, his rage ramped up even more. She didn't need the trauma, the knowledge that someone wanted to hurt her mother. Memories of what her father had done to her had probably faded, maybe even been forgotten the way traumas sometimes were, as if the mind could wall them off. Plus she'd been so young.

He had to protect Iris from all of that.

But how? His hand tightened around the cold bottle he held. For him, the worst of this was not knowing exactly how this guy would carry through. How far he would go. How to stop him if he couldn't be found. How he could put an end to this.

Not being able to plan except in the most general way.

Jazz spoke. "I'll get a gun," she said. "A shotgun because I won't need much of an aim. If that bastard shows up anywhere near this house, I'll kill him and I don't care if I spend the rest of my life in prison."

He didn't tell her how killing a person, even a person who was threatening you, could haunt your days and nights forever. Why bother? He was prepared to do the same, and he was already haunted by faces he would never forget. By the internal graveyard he carried.

"I'll teach you how to use it," he said. And he would. Everyone deserved self-defense. "He's a cockroach."

"A snake."

"Aww, don't get hard on snakes. They only act against us in self-defense."

Jazz's face had hardened until it was unreadable, then the faintest of smiles flickered over her lips. "You're right. He's *human*."

"Kind of the worst of it. I heard somewhere that out of all our primate cousins, the only ones who fight wars and kill each other are chimpanzees. I don't think we've improved much."

She sighed, finally drinking some beer and letting her face relax. "I'm not going to sleep tonight."

"Me neither. Maybe we'll catch a few Z's tomorrow while Iris is safe at school."

"How am I going to let her racket around by herself?"

"I don't think she's ever alone, Jazz. The guy's after Lily, but even so if he tried to snatch Iris her friends would raise hell, too. Not an easy nab."

"No." Again she sighed. "Damn it, Adam. Damn it. That monster deserved more than he got, and he should still be in prison. Hell, he should have been sent up for life."

Adam frowned. "Didn't they charge him with multiple crimes?"

"You bet. I don't remember them all. What I *do* remember was the judge running the sentences concurrently instead of stacking them. He could have done that. I'm not one to think people ought to spend all their lives in prison, but when they're violent like that? Over the span of years? Does anyone really expect them to learn a lesson?"

"Lily's ex probably didn't. If this is her ex. No way to be sure, but the timing is suspicious."

"Oh, it's Andy all right. Lily was terrified of him for good reason."

Adam drank more beer. Nearly ready for a second. "You know, I never would have guessed that Lily had been through such a hell. Nothing about her suggests it."

"She's overcome it, but I think she's putting on a brave face sometimes." Jazz rested her chin in her hand. "What a nightmare. I'm so glad Lily isn't here."

So was he, but he was wishing Jazz wasn't here either. Nor Iris. But how would that help? The creep would find another time to do this, assuming it *was* Lily's ex.

He reached across the table and covered Jazz's free hand with his own. Her bones felt so small and delicate. All of her appeared delicate. "Go lie down, Jazz. I'm here."

"Lie down and be all alone with my imagination? I don't think so."

"You don't have to be alone."

He heard her draw a sharp breath. He hadn't meant that the way she was probably taking it, but he didn't rephrase himself. Instead he stood up. "Come on. You can lie down and I'll be nearby. Talk if you need to. But if you don't get out of that damn chair your butt is going to hurt and you're going to freeze in that position."

He persuaded her to stretch out on her bed. She removed her shoes, her only concession, and covered herself with a blue Sherpa throw.

"Oh, for Pete's sake," she said irritably as he sat in the corner chair. "Lie down, too. You must need to stretch some."

So he did, but he left his boots on, and he didn't need a blanket to keep him warm. Being near Jazz was doing a good enough job of that.

DESPITE HERSELF, JAZZ fell into a restless slumber. When eventually she stirred, it was still dark outside but she hardly noticed.

Sometime while she slept, she had become wrapped in Adam's arms. She knew she had crawled into them because she had moved away from the edge of the bed toward him.

His embrace was welcoming, holding her close, a hug that felt so good she wanted it never to stop.

Daringly, she snuggled in a little closer and felt his arms tighten. God, she ached for this comfort. Ached for him.

Then, to her embarrassment, she realized he was awake. "I'm sorry," she said, her voice still cracking from sleep.

"For what?"

"Umm, for crowding you?"

"You haven't. We both needed some relaxation and I guess we got it."

She pulled away, still embarrassed, but with anxiety beginning to creep in again. She sat up and yawned, hating how much she missed his arms. She had to remind herself once again that she was going back to Miami. "I need a shower."

He stood up. "Take it. I'll meet you in our favorite kitchen."

The shower eased some of the tension from her and she was tempted to remain longer, but remembering that Iris would probably need some hot water soon, she made sure to leave some.

Fresh clothes felt good, too, making her feel almost like her old self. Since arriving here, she *had* become a new woman, a changed woman. Ugliness was touching her in ways it seldom did.

Tempting smells were emerging from the kitchen. With her hair wrapped in a towel and her shoulders wrapped in Lily's wooly burgundy shawl, she stepped into the room to find Adam at the stove.

"Bacon," he said. "To be followed by toast and eggs. I make a mean scrambled egg as I'm sure you've noticed. Coffee's ready."

"Anything I can do?"

"Grab a cup and take a seat. I don't work well with others."

A snort escaped her. "I *so* believe that."

A sound from above caught Jazz's attention. "Iris is waking up."

"I made enough bacon for her, too, but I bet she doesn't eat it. Toast and eggs though, maybe."

"She hasn't exactly been following her training diet the last few days."

"I wouldn't always either, without a multimillion-dollar contract."

Casual conversation that was helping the morning feel normal. Except it wasn't normal.

She spoke to Adam's back as he stood at the stove. "You always live here?"

"Born and raised. My dad was a hired hand out at the Stiller spread. Then he got too old to work, my mom died of heart failure and Dad killed himself."

"Oh my God! I'm so sorry, Adam."

He turned to place a platter of bacon on the counter nearby. "They had a decent life. It wasn't easy but as far as I know they were happy. I'm sure of one thing. My dad wouldn't have offed himself if he'd been able to live without my mother."

"Hard on you, though."

"I was in the Army by then, kinda focused on my own survival. It hurt, sure, but it took a while for it to sink in. And by then the grief had already softened. How many eggs?"

"Two please." She felt ravenous.

"I'll make two for Iris. So seven eggs."

There went most of the carton. Not that Jazz minded. She simply added it to her mental list for the next trip to the grocery. And there *would* be another trip out, she vowed. Staying in this house all the time would drive her crazy.

But when Iris was safely at school, why not leave the house unattended…as long as Adam was willing to come with her.

Going out alone didn't seem like a smart thing to do right now.

Iris appeared, hair a bit damp. She evidently still

hadn't recovered from her betrayal by Sally and the "boyfriend." Not that she was likely to anytime soon. Life's hard knocks hurt.

Iris hesitated over the bacon, then took two strips along with her plate of eggs and four pieces of toast.

"Swimming today?" Jazz asked.

Iris's expression became determined. "You bet. I'll show them I don't give a gosh darn."

Adam spoke. "Way to go."

ANDY ROBBINS WATCHED Iris emerge from the house with her school backpack and a small duffel. He'd already learned that she swam every day from the guy at the gas station who was only too willing to talk when Andy said he knew Lily from college. Today he'd follow her to discover her route and if she'd ever be alone.

Iris would be the best tool to get at Lily, he had decided. The very best. Either way, with Lily or Iris, he'd use the chloroform he'd made.

Amazing what you could learn how to do in prison.

Satisfied with his decision, he needed only to figure out what he'd do with one or both of them, depending. If Iris became his lever against Lily, he might have to handle this a whole different way.

Digesting all this, he headed back to his campsite with a few items from the convenience store at the gas station. Wonder of wonders, the credit card still worked, but he should find another one soon before this one blew up in his face.

Another problem to consider. He sure didn't want to draw attention in this town.

He cooked himself a little Spam over a small fire and downed it with beer.

Lily must be afraid by now. He considered all he had done so far and nodded approvingly. It could be anyone who'd done those things.

She'd probably have heard from the Department of Corrections that he was out now, too.

But she'd never, ever, think that after all these years he would follow her over this huge distance. Nope.

Lily had never been *that* bright.

IRIS TRUDGED TO swim practice alone. Once she had walked this way with Sally, but no more. Never again.

But she was going to have her revenge by acting as if she didn't care at all. Aunt Jazz was right about that.

She barely noticed the creaky old pickup that drove past. Plenty of those around here. Plenty.

Instead she focused on the wild land that filled the road on both sides. The college still hadn't reached out and gobbled it all up. Better for the environment if they didn't. Besides, she loved the wildflowers, a few hardy ones blossoming despite the cold weather they'd had a few times this spring.

She loved it here, but she still hoped she wouldn't be around to see that land developed. She'd lived here long enough to know this place was on a boom and bust cycle through the years. It was in a bust cycle now, but that would change.

Things always changed.

ADAM WENT TO do his workout midafternoon. The basement was dark but illuminated well enough by overhead bulbs that he could manage his equipment. The long fluorescent light above the washer and dryer added to the fight against darkness.

The space was occupied, of course, by the washer and dryer, as well as the water heater and the furnace, but all of that left him plenty of room.

When he'd worked as many muscles as he could without some of his equipment, he headed upstairs, pleasantly sweaty. A shower next, if Jazz was okay.

Boy, had she stepped into a mess when she agreed to watch Iris. It had probably sounded like an easy job and it would have been except for some creep with ugly things on his mind.

Now this breakup. Adam really felt sorry for the girl and she was too young yet to believe that someone better would come along. In the days ahead, she'd get past this betrayal. Because it *had* been a betrayal, the kind that tended to leave scars.

He would know. He'd had a relationship like that. Cindy Lou Brown. Big mistake, but it would have been easier if he hadn't discovered her cheating. Lots of cheating. No one man was good enough for Cindy Lou.

But she sure did like presents, especially expensive ones.

He shook off the memory and looked for Jazz, finding her in that little office room to the back.

"Working?" he asked.

"Trying to."

"Mind if I go take a shower?"

She swiveled her chair around. "Now why would I mind?"

"Oh, I can think of a reason or two. I'm off, back shortly."

She turned back to her laptop and he headed upstairs, wondering if he'd interrupted her work. Maybe he should just leave her alone when she was staring at that machine. Not say a word, rude as it would feel.

He still needed to tell Gage Dalton about that letter. Maybe Gage could dredge up a mug shot of Lily's ex and give it out to his deputies. That would make both him and Jazz feel better. Marginally.

Hot showers were a luxury he still enjoyed fully. Years in the Army had exposed him to enough cold showers to last a lifetime.

His hip had begun to shriek again, so the next thing on his list was that ibuprofen bottle. He toweled off quickly, dressed just as quickly in a flannel shirt and jeans, then headed downstairs on a hip that wondered if it should support his weight.

God, he hated it when it got like this. Pain was one thing, weakness another.

When he reached the foot of the stairs, Jazz came out of the office. "I give up!" she said.

"Did I break your concentration?"

"As if I had any." She marched toward the kitchen. "I thought escaping into my fantasy world would make me feel better. It usually does. I'm beginning to think nothing will make me feel better until we get rid of this creep, and I don't care anymore *how* we do it. He needs to be erased just for all this anxiety and aggravation."

Wow, that was a statement, coming from Jazz. "Did you call the sheriff about that letter?"

"What good will that do?"

"Maybe he can pull up this guy's mug shot. Share it with all the cops."

She paused just as she reached the coffee maker. "I didn't think of that."

"I didn't exactly hop all over it, either."

"We're getting too tired and worn out. Which is why I'm making more coffee. I may never want to see any caffeine again after this."

"I wouldn't blame you." He grabbed the ibuprofen and swallowed them dry before easing into the chair. Well, that didn't help.

"Pain again?" she asked.

"There's no *again* about it."

She sighed, looking sad, but didn't speak. She headed for the pantry.

When she did speak, it was to say, "God knows what I'm going to make for dinner tonight."

"Let me take a peek."

"You stay in that chair until the ibuprofen hits. There's got to be something in here that I recognize."

He could have laughed if they weren't both feeling so unhappy and edgy.

"Well, I found some granola bars, Adam. Want a couple?"

"Please."

She emerged holding the box in her hand, then placed it in front of him. "I'll have one, too, while I try to figure out dinner."

That sent her straight to the freezer. "Fish. More fish. I should have succumbed and bought a beef roast. Or another chicken. Or some pork chops."

"I have some pork chops at my place. Let me run over and get them. It's one thing I cook often enough."

She smiled faintly. "That would be nice."

So he hiked himself out before the coffee was ready, before he ate one of the granola bars. He returned a few minutes later with frozen chops and a six-pack.

Jazz eyed the beer. "You weren't kidding about beer in your fridge."

"Occasionally some of the guys from my group show up. It's all about hospitality."

She gave him the *yeah, right* look and he wondered if he should bother telling her he wasn't hooked on the beer, then decided *why bother?* They poured some coffee, then tried the granola bars.

"Do you think," Jazz asked, "that being made with yogurt makes a granola bar any healthier?"

"I dunno. I think of them as energy. Sugar."

She bit into hers. "Yup. I suppose there are enough good things in this to salve Iris's conscience."

He chuckled. "Jazz, she's an athlete. Lots of carbs required."

"That's true," she admitted. "I guess I'm thinking about my waistline and not hers."

He thought her waistline was just perfect but didn't embarrass her by saying so. One of those things better left unsaid unless a relationship became intimate. He switched tack.

"I've heard Iris mention her grandmother a few times, but I've never met her."

"You won't." Jazz sighed. "She's in a nursing home with full-blown Alzheimer's. She doesn't recognize Iris at all, and barely does any better with Lily or me."

"Now that is sad." His sympathy surged. "Not only sad, but awful."

"It is. My mind is so important to me that I can't imagine losing it. I'd hate it. Anyway, Mom is lost somewhere in her early life. She keeps asking for our dad who died ten years ago. She remembers Lily and me as small children and doesn't believe we're grown up now. She likes listening to the music of her era, and I visit as often as I can so she doesn't feel lonely."

"That's gotta be hard."

"It is, but with time I've gotten more used to it and just pretend I'm a friend. She can accept that."

"Ouch." Nothing to do, nothing to fix. Life's nastiest problems.

"Life can take some awful turns but I don't need to tell you that."

"I've got some buddies who suffered traumatic brain injuries." There he went, sharing again. "They're not much better off than your mom. And no, I'm not minimizing what's happening to you. Just saying I kinda know what it's like from the outside looking in."

"I'm sure that's horrid, too. You still see the men and women they used to be."

"That's it."

After a minute or so, Jazz shook herself visibly. "God, when did I get morose? I'm not usually like this."

"The times aren't usual and I apologize for asking about your parents."

"Perfectly natural question." She waved a dismissive hand. "How long will it take those chops to thaw?"

"Not very. They're thin. Got any fresh brussels sprouts?"

"As a matter of fact, I do. Iris likes to eat them raw. Why?"

"I'll sauté them in butter. Scrumptious."

"That leaves her carbs." Jazz rested her chin in her hand. "Brown rice. For Iris, no other kind. Okay?"

He nodded. Distraction. This was all distraction, but she needed it. Come to that, so did he.

"I'll call the sheriff now," he announced. "A mug shot of the ex could be very helpful."

She nodded, her gaze still distant.

Gage reached for his cell, thinking he wouldn't blame Jazz if she wished she were back in Miami. A long, long way from this. Lily would no sooner have let her know this was going on than Jazz was telling Lily, even though Jazz had mentioned calling her sister a time or two.

But caught right in the middle was Iris which, given that Jazz was just her aunt, meant that Jazz was burdened with the question whether to tell Lily.

"Nothing's going to happen to Iris," Jazz announced firmly. "I'm not going to let it. I don't care about myself. I'll kill the bastard first anyway."

"That's obvious." Part of the conundrum, too. His heart squeezed as he thought of these two ladies who meant so much to him. But he had to let Jazz know. "Jazz, killing a man changes you forever. Don't do it if there's any way to avoid it."

Then he punched in the sheriff's number.

GAGE DALTON ARRIVED sooner than Jazz would have expected. She managed a smile and invited him in for coffee or a beer.

"I'll take that beer," he said. "Won't put me over the limit." He limped down the hall to the kitchen.

Two battle-scarred veterans, Jazz thought, even though she didn't know Gage's story.

"I heard you," Adam said, handing Gage a beer after he sat. "Welcome to the war room."

Gage lifted one brow. "The war room?"

"We're practically camped in here," Jazz answered. "We could go to the living room, though."

Gage shook his head. "Better with an upright back." He took a swig of beer. "Okay, you said something about a letter when you called?"

"I'll get it," Jazz said and jumped up. Any action, however small, felt necessary. She went into the office to pull down the envelope from the high shelf in the closet. The postcard was inside it.

Mutely she handed it to Gage, then leaned back against the counter, waiting.

"Department of Corrections," Gage read. "Oh, hell, don't tell me."

He pulled out the postcard first and read it aloud. "'I'm coming but you'll never know when.' Okay, that's taking the cake. This creep wants to keep Lily on tenterhooks."

Then he pulled the letter out of the envelope and scanned it. "Well, knock me down. This is almost impossible. I was checking into it, and even though Florida offers gain time to inmates who behave, it almost never gets applied. Some kind of crummy setup. I wonder how the hell this guy managed it?"

Jazz spoke. "I met Andy only a couple of times but the guy's a really smooth talker. I bet he got on the right person's good side."

"Must be." Gage ruminated briefly, then took another swig of beer. "Okay, I'll get a hold of this guy's booking photo or prison photo. I'll give it to every cop around. If he gets anywhere near here, someone should see him."

Adam spoke. "Only if they're looking in the right direction at the right time."

"Yeah, there is always that. And my people are spread pretty thin. So are the city police. They were just a sop to the egos of the city council. Not enough of them, really, to do all the policing in town."

He tapped the envelope on the desk. "I'll make this a priority. Mind if I take this letter? I'll return it, but there's information on it I need so there's no screwup on my end."

"Take it," Jazz said. "I'm not sure Lily will ever want to see it, but I guess she should."

"That's up to you, but I *will* return it."

Gage finished his beer and the two men hobbled to the front door. Jazz stayed put, hoping that at last they'd make some progress instead of spinning their wheels waiting for the next shoe to drop.

IN THE FIELD alongside the road, Andy Robbins hunkered down in the tall grasses waiting for Iris. In his hands he held an expensive camera, good cover for him. He'd found it in the truck and wondered if it was stolen, given the age and condition of that truck.

Probably. The idea amused him. Anyway, if anyone happened to stumble on him, he'd just say he was taking photos of the mountains.

Days lasted longer here, he noticed, than in Florida. The change in the lengths of the days wasn't hugely noticeable like it was here. Interesting and he wondered why but didn't care enough to find out.

Just as twilight took over from the brightness of day, he saw Iris come out of the community college gym. At first she was among a group of girls, but then she struck out on her own. That seemed odd, but he was glad of it.

He'd watch one more night after thinking about it, after finding a good place on that damn mountain. He wasn't used to mountains, and he didn't like the way they seemed to steal his breath.

He'd live. And he'd get what he wanted.

Smiling, he headed back to his camp, knowledge tucked away like seeds in a pinecone.

Chapter Fourteen

Jazz waited for Iris to come home, nervous as always
since the mess started. She couldn't help but worry about
her niece, but agreed there was no point in trying to hem
the girl in. She'd have plenty of reasons why that would
be both awful and foolish, and Jazz didn't want to scare
her. Clearly the threat was being directed at Lily.

Adam suggested they sit on the porch for a change
of venue. "Nobody's going to come after you while I'm
sitting right beside you."

She hesitated. "Gun?"

"I doubt it. This guy is more into scaring than shooting."

"Andy," she said. "Andy was like that."

"My guess is that prison didn't change him one bit."

"If it's him, then apparently not. But he did beat up
Iris that one time."

As they moved to the porch with some instant lemonade, mainly because Jazz couldn't face any more coffee,
Adam didn't reply.

But once they were seated in the wooden rocking
chairs out front with the ever-gentle Sheba beside Adam,
he spoke.

"Sometimes I don't think prison changes anyone.

Maybe it makes them worse. Regardless, he only attacked Iris that once, right?"

"Just the once."

"Then I doubt he wants to do it a second time. Mainly, from what you said, he wants control of Lily again, to put her in the same state of fear that he used during their marriage. Hurting Iris that first time only got him a trip to prison, not control of Lily."

She thought about it as she rocked, wishing the lemonade tasted as good as her mother's fresh-made. "You may be right," she allowed finally.

"Patterns. People always have patterns."

That was true. In her observation of people, used in her books, she had noted it but hadn't thought of it that way. People seldom changed. Change was hard, difficult. Ways of viewing things didn't much alter, either, though some would claim that they had. Usually, however, they just found a better reason for what they said and thought.

She sipped more lemonade, waving to a couple with a toddler who passed by on the sidewalk. This town felt so friendly to her and she hoped it wasn't an illusion.

"Twilight lasts so long here," she remarked. "It's shorter in Florida."

"We're farther north," he replied.

"I know, but the difference still surprises me. Longer evenings. Pleasant." But cool, too. She set her glass on the wooden table between them and pulled the gray cardigan closer around her front. Maybe she should have added another layer.

Boy, was she giving Lily's wardrobe a workout.

A man passed by, waving and calling a greeting to them by name. "Evening, Adam. Evening, Lily." He was truly dressed as a cowboy, Jazz noted with amusement.

Common enough around here, she supposed, but she hadn't been out enough to notice.

She spoke. "Adam? You ever wear cowboy boots?"

"Only when I'm going to ride a horse, which isn't often. Dang things weren't designed for walking, although I suppose you could get used to them."

"What bothers you?"

"The heel. It's high and angled, designed to grip a stirrup. But when I'm walking, it shoves my feet down into the narrow toe box. Which is pointed to make it easier to slide into the stirrup."

She nearly laughed. "That's quite an analysis."

"I tried walking in them when I was younger. I figured out what was bothering me, that's all." He turned to look at her. "Now ropers are different, lower heel, rounder toes, tighter ankle. Better for roping cattle. Easier to walk in for long periods."

"That's the whole encyclopedia, I guess."

"Not hardly. There are different kinds of cowboy boots, too, but I don't want to bore you."

She doubted she would be bored, but why press him? Her concern about Iris was tightening around her, and she kept peering down the street hoping to see her niece.

"It's getting late. Iris should be home by now."

"Not that late," Adam answered. "We'll call out the cavalry if she doesn't appear soon."

How soon, she wondered. But just as she was considering calling for help, she saw Iris turn a corner and head toward them. Alone. Where were all the friends? she wondered as relief flooded her.

Iris waved, then trotted toward them. When she arrived at the porch steps, she grinned at Jazz. "Just can't stop worrying about me, Aunt Jazz?" Sheba jumped up to greet her and Iris rubbed her ears.

"I'm not used to being responsible for a girl your age," Jazz replied.

"Get used to it or you'll go crazy before Mom gets home. I'm gonna drop my bag inside then come join you guys. That's lemonade, right? No hidden shot of vermouth?"

"Iris!" But Jazz laughed. "It's not much of a lemonade, but it passes. The pitcher is on the counter."

"Be right back. Just don't start a romantic conversation. I'm not going to be long enough."

Romantic conversation? Jazz nearly blushed as she looked at Adam. He shrugged. "Not a bad idea, frankly."

Not a bad idea? Deep inside she thrilled to the words. Oh, God, no. She'd been trying to avoid these feelings almost since the outset, and now they were flooding her. She quickly looked away from Adam, fearing he might read her response in her eyes.

Iris returned in a couple of minutes. "Just flyers in the mail today. I ditched them," she remarked. "There's better lemonade than this?"

"Your grandmother used to make it. I tried a couple of times but I wasn't happy with the results. This is the best you'll get from me."

"Good enough." Iris drank half her glass. "Sally's avoiding me. Good."

"And the ex?"

"He doesn't matter to me anymore. He's a sleaze."

"Yup," was Jazz's only response. "Are you late home tonight?"

"Only because I dropped my backpack. I forgot to zip

it. Papers everywhere, and it didn't help that it's breezy. The dog ate my homework ain't gonna fly."

Sheba nuzzled her then returned to Adam's side. Was Adam feeling bad? Jazz wondered. Nothing about him would indicate it, but he wasn't exactly smiling, either. And Sheba, who often seemed willing to abandon Adam for Iris, was almost clinging to him.

Maybe he was struggling with the memories he so rarely mentioned. The thought saddened her and she wished she could help even though she was sure that there was no way. A man left in his own private hell, one which had no escape.

She had no idea how to reach out and get him to talk about it, either. As an introvert, starting a conversation, especially about difficult subjects, often eluded her. It was a good thing she didn't face the same problem in her books, she thought wryly. Or at least not often. Her characters were often splashed in bold colors, and when they weren't talking she could delve into their internal lives.

Not so in the real world.

She smothered a sigh at her own inadequacies. A sigh would have caused someone to ask her what was wrong, but what could she say? That she wished Adam would open up more, share his moody feelings?

Yeah, right.

At times she felt she knew him very well. At others he was a stranger. It would probably always be so.

As the twilight began to deepen, she shivered. It sure got cold quickly at this altitude. She rose, her nearly empty glass in hand. "This hothouse Florida girl is going inside to get warm."

Iris laughed at her. "Toughen up, Aunt Jazz."

"Not enough time to do that, kiddo. Don't give me

a hard time. You two go ahead and enjoy yourselves out here."

Iris, Adam and Sheba followed her, however.

"Your dinner is in the microwave," Jazz told Iris. "I slaved all day over frozen ziti."

God, she loved to hear Iris laugh.

It wasn't long, however, before Iris cleaned up a large heap of the ziti and four pieces of garlic bread. She put her dishes in the dishwasher. "Bet that bread was frozen, too. I'm off!"

Then she ran upstairs presumably to phone and text friends.

Jazz arched a brow at Adam. "No homework?"

He'd pulled a longneck from the fridge and now sat at the table sipping the beer. "She's pretty diligent. I doubt she'd let that slide."

"You're right. She's an amazing girl."

"Not to put too fine a point on it." He stirred, shifting his weight on the chair.

She was immediately reminded of his pain and sympathy welled in her. "Would the living room be more comfortable?"

"Right now nothing would be."

"That's awful."

He shrugged.

She leaned forward. "Are you always so stoic?"

"What good would it do not to be? I'm lucky."

He'd said something like that before, but she wondered how often he didn't feel lucky at all. Not that he'd ever say.

But Sheba was plastered to his side, often looking up into his face. He petted her with his free hand, especially her long silky ears. Then he looked down at the dog. "Time for a walk?" he asked.

Sheba wagged her tail.

Adam looked at Jazz. "Just out back. Not a long one."

With those words he brought back the tension that had fled for just a little while when Iris returned safely home.

"I know," he said gently, as if he could read her face. "Nothing like walking down a narrow defile not knowing if the threat is above or below. Or even if it's there at all."

She nodded, wishing she could be braver. Sturdier. One thing for sure, she was getting angrier by the day. The taunting alone was cruel.

But if this did indeed turn out to be Lily's ex, she had a whole lot more to be angry about than that. She'd sat in court while her sister sat at the prosecutor's table and had listened to all of it. *All* of it.

She still couldn't imagine how hard it must have been for Lily to strip herself bare in court, talking about those matters. Admitting she had endured such things. Talking about the way she had been snared then terrified.

And the defense attorney! He was just doing his job, but trying to paint Lily as a liar? In the face of those X-rays and hospital reports? She wondered how anyone could stomach defending such a man.

Andy should just have pled guilty, but not Andy. As the trial progressed, she saw just how smarmy he was. Became certain that he believed he could charm his way out of anything.

But not that time.

Now, somehow, he must have charmed and smarmed his way into an early release. *Oh, I was the victim. That woman cheated on me, hated me and lied about me.* Or some such crap.

Sure.

Sighing, she put her head in her hands and stared at the tabletop. Now he was out there again, somewhere. Was he still a threat even after all this time?

But who else could it be? And how could he be found?

A shiver ran through her, but not from the cold. It wasn't a shiver of fear but felt more like her body was trying to release the unending tension. When Iris was around, Jazz played a role, as if everything was okay.

But nothing was okay, and she was certain she was taking another major shift in her world view. The biggest had been during the trial. This was a close second.

She hoped this bugger continued to mistake her for Lily and took his swipe at her. Anything to protect Lily and Iris. Anything.

"Please God," she murmured. "Let us finish this before Lily gets home. Before she has to become frightened, too."

At the moment, though, she wondered if God was even listening.

WALKING AROUND THE backyard with Sheba helped Adam as much as the dog. The grinding pain in his hip lessened a bit, and he enjoyed watching her sniff around. A dog's view must be so very different, and sometimes he wished he could experience that amazing sense of smell. It must paint the world in ways he couldn't imagine.

But at last Sheba finished her rounds. He cleaned up after her and carried the small bag to the trash bin.

He hadn't been this wound up in quite a while. He hated not being able to get a good grip on this threat, this man. All the guy had to do was make one mistake. Just one. So far he hadn't made a useful one if he'd made any at all.

If it *was* Andy Robbins seeking vengeance, he had to be a damn fool to come back for a second helping of Lily. People who allowed themselves to be driven by such things often screwed up. Got themselves into serious trouble. Made themselves too easy to identify.

He took Sheba back indoors and joined Jazz in the kitchen. How could he explain that the softness of the living room furniture aggravated his hip by bending it into different positions. He didn't like to talk about it, didn't want to seem like a complainer. But maybe, if Jazz asked again, he should tell her something about it.

Holding back all the time seemed stupid considering how much he liked her, how strongly he craved her. God, what a mess this had turned into.

He filled Sheba's bowl with fresh water, then asked, "Coffee? I need the caffeine to wash out the beer." Not strictly true but he needed to be on high alert.

"Sure," she answered, raising her head from her hands. "I feel like a tightly coiled spring anyway."

He studied her, his concern growing considerably. "You should skip the coffee and get some sleep."

"Nothing's going to let me sleep. Not yet. I'll just be alone in the dark worrying. It's nice to share that worry and have you buck me up."

Nice compliment, but overstated. "I haven't been doing much of that." When the coffee was ready, he poured two mugs and joined her at the table, easing into the chair. "This is like shadow boxing. Not nearly as satisfying as a punching bag."

She gave him a half smile. "I want to punch someone."

"Me, too."

"I can just hear Andy talking himself into an early release. He's so damned charming. Maintaining his innocence with sincerity. Blaming it all on Lily. I wonder if he believes that, too. But he *did* beat up Iris. For God's sake, Adam, she was just four."

He nodded and sipped his coffee. "A monster."

"At least."

"But none of these threats seem directed at Iris."

"Except maybe the flowers. *She* found them."

He didn't answer that one. There was no answer.

They fell silent for a while.

Then Jazz jumped up. "I've got some of those frozen cinnamon buns. Whatever we don't eat will fuel Iris in the morning."

"Thanks. Sounds good with this coffee."

"I'm apt to put on ten pounds at this rate."

That wouldn't make her any less attractive. He believed nothing could do that.

More silence.

Then Jazz popped the question. "Tell me about your hip, *please.*"

"I already told you the basics." But Adam knew that wasn't what she meant. He braced himself. He owed it to her, especially with what he was feeling about her. Besides, she'd take his secrets away with her when she flew home.

"War," he said after a few minutes. "Obviously. A rocket-propelled grenade from the cliffs above. Even though we were armored up, it blew a big hole in the transport. Those of us who could piled out to escape the fire. Then came the gunshots. American guns, stolen, or maybe some leftover Russian equipment. Armor-piercing bullets. They got a few of us, me included."

She paled, although clearly she couldn't imagine it. Who could unless they had been there?

"Oh my God," she murmured. "Sheer hell."

He couldn't deny that. But memories had begun to surface, making his skin crawl, his mind try to run into the past.

He decided to double down. If she couldn't handle it, then he needed to know before he dug himself in any deeper with her.

She pushed for it. "And now? It follows you?"

"Like too many people. It doesn't go away, Jazz. Apparently never. I carry a graveyard of faces inside me. The enemy, my buddies, they're all there."

He saw her eyes glisten with unshed tears.

"Don't ever kill anyone," he said slowly, for the second time. "It changes you forever."

She stared angrily at him. "Right now I'd like to."

"I imagine so."

"And the rest of it, Adam? Surely that's not all of it."

"It's not." He hesitated but remained determined to get through all of this. To learn her reaction even if it killed him inside.

He went to get more coffee, knowing he was trying to deflect the moment. *No go.*

Back at the table, he plunged in. "It haunts me all the time. It's always bubbling beneath the surface, trying to emerge. Sometimes it succeeds. I get angry, viciously angry, not fit to be around other people. I can withdraw entirely, facing it, reliving it. I run and work out trying to contain it, and most of the time that works. But not always. Talking about it at group can help, talking with others who have been there. But the issues never resolve. I'll be driving down the road, suddenly afraid of a roadside bomb. I wish I could find all my triggers, but I can't so I don't know how to avoid getting set off." He paused. "I can't ask anyone else to go through this with me."

She came around the table, wrapping her arm around his shoulders. "I'm so sorry, Adam. So sorry. But maybe instead of making that assumption you should ask, should try. Few of us are meant to go through life alone."

"I'm not alone," he answered stubbornly. But emotional intimacy? He was living without that all right.

Then he raised his head and looked up at her. In an instant everything clicked.

JAZZ FELT THE MOMENT. Something wild rose in her in answering the fire in his eyes. She wanted. She needed, and as everything else slipped away into the background, Adam rose and took her in his arms.

"Now," he said roughly.

"Now," she agreed.

Moments later they were in her bedroom, stripping wildly as if a hunger too long denied erupted into an explosion that blew them both away.

They tumbled onto the bed, hands seeking and exploring. Jazz felt as if there wasn't enough air in the entire universe as she silently begged for completion.

She reached down, surrounding his hardened staff with her fingers. The conflagration became consuming and she got her wish as he filled her, filled every corner of her body and soul.

She whispered his name, some part of her remembering Iris upstairs—that she didn't want to shock her niece. Then she climbed the roller coaster to the very top, and when she plunged over, her stomach feeling as if it had grown weightless, Adam followed her over the edge.

LATER IN A tangle of sheets and comforters, they lay tightly entwined. Jazz felt as if the glow that suffused her was brighter than the stars.

Adam spoke hoarsely. "I'm usually a better lover."

"Shh. It was great. No complaints."

"Someday…" He left the thought unfinished.

She didn't want to say the word. Her glow was fading, and as it seeped away, reality began to intrude. There would never be a someday. Their worlds were too far apart.

But reality also brought their biggest concern back to the forefront. Reluctantly they eased apart and reached for their clothes. Jazz didn't want even to risk a shower.

Danger lurked and it was growing closer.

THE NEXT EVENING, Andy Robbins snatched Iris. It was incredibly easy. She was alone, the twilight had begun to take over the world. He called her over to his truck saying he needed directions.

Iris came over as if she had nothing to fear in this world.

"Hey," he said when she reached his open window, "there's a fork ahead. Which way do I turn to reach the downtown?"

She smiled and opened her mouth to answer.

He grabbed her arm and at the same moment slapped the chloroformed rag over her mouth. Almost instantly she sagged.

He had her. Pushing her to one side, he slipped out of

his truck, lifted her and hoisted her into the bed beneath the camper shell.

Nobody had seen. No one was around.

Satisfied by his own brilliance, he headed for the mountain nearby. Thunder Mountain he'd heard it called.

Now he really had something to hang over Lily's head. Something to terrify her once again into submission.

Behind him on the road lay Iris's backpack and sports duffel. No kind of trail for anyone to follow.

He began to whistle a jaunty tune.

Chapter Fifteen

As the twilight eased toward night, Jazz was pacing, pacing until it was a wonder she hadn't worn a hole in Lily's rugs.

Adam had gone out to look for Iris, but the terror creeping along Jazz's spine worsened by the minute.

This was no case of an unzipped backpack. She tried to tell herself that Iris had fallen, sprained an ankle. Something so ordinary they could laugh about it later.

But she didn't believe it.

Then the landline phone rang. Her heart climbed into her throat.

"Hello?" Her voice shook.

A creepy voice came back, a voice Jazz had never forgotten, only this time it wasn't smarmy.

"I have my daughter," Andy Robbins said. "Don't call the police. I'd hate to have to hurt her like you made me do before. I'll call with instructions tomorrow morning. You'd better follow them to the letter, Lily, or you'll never see Iris again."

A click. The sound of an empty line.

She stood frozen, phone in hand, barely aware that Adam's truck had pulled up out front.

He nearly burst through the door, Sheba on his heels, carrying Jazz's backpack and duffel.

"Has she showed up?" he demanded.

Jazz shook her head. Violent tremors began to tear through her.

"I'm calling the police."

"No! Adam, no!"

He stopped, dropping Iris's things to the floor. "We've got to…"

"If we call the police Andy will hurt Iris."

His face darkened like a violent thunderstorm. "That bastard. That bastard!"

"He'll do it, Adam. He's done it before."

That froze him. His face darkened even more if that was possible. "I take it he called."

She nodded and her tremors worsened. She felt on the verge of collapse. Her mind rebelled but the sound of Andy's voice in her head wouldn't let her escape. The worst nightmare had become real.

Adam came to her and wrapped her tightly in his arms. "We're going to get through this. We'll get Iris back safely."

She shook her head and tried to back out of his embrace. "You can't know that."

He didn't argue. "I suppose he'll call with instructions? When?"

She spoke, her voice shaking. "Morning? He said he'd call but I'm not sure when. I don't know if I can stand the waiting. All I can think of is Iris out there, terrified, in the grip of a maniac."

The image was too vivid.

ADAM KNEW HIS own capabilities. Capabilities this animal wasn't considering. Reluctantly, he released Jazz.

She hugged herself instead. He'd have cut off his own head to save her and Iris, but she didn't need to hear that. It wouldn't help.

"Let's go to our command center," he said.

"Our what?"

"The kitchen. Where we do everything."

He'd hoped for even a small smile but didn't get it.

"I don't know if I can hold still," she answered.

"Try it. We need to clear our heads."

As if that was going to be easy for either of them.

He made the inevitable coffee, forgoing a beer because he didn't want his head even the tiniest bit clouded.

But clear thought wouldn't come immediately. They were both too worried, preoccupied by their fears for Iris.

"I'm so upset about Iris," Jazz said presently. "So worried. My God, if we get her back safely, how is this going to affect her? She won't be the same bubbly girl anymore."

He wanted to disagree but couldn't. An experience like this had to have an impact, even if she and Lily and Jazz were all unharmed. Maybe that was the thing that made him angriest of all: what this would do to all of them even with the best outcome.

Sheba nudged his thigh, then laid her head on it. He absently stroked her silky ears and fought back the memories that this tension summoned. Not the time for that. Not now.

He and Jazz were stuck waiting for the next move.

ANDY ROBBINS FELT extremely proud of himself. No one had seen him grab the girl, although by now they'd found her backpack and duffel, which would only heighten Lily's fear. Good. Let her stew in it.

Equally pleasing was the way Iris had given him no trouble. The chloroform had steadily worn off while she was in the back of his truck and, though she was still woozy, she'd followed his every direction as they climbed the mountain after leaving his truck behind. The way Lily once had. The way Lily would do again.

He carried a backpack of additional supplies for the girl. He didn't want her to go hungry or become dehydrated and he didn't know for sure how long this might take. He was a good father, after all, despite what Lily had claimed in court.

Well, he'd make sure Iris was safe in the cave he'd found just for her. It wasn't big, but he'd tie her so she could get around and move when she needed to. He'd already stashed some food and blankets up there.

Yeah, he was a good dad.

He didn't whistle on the way up the mountain. The climb left him somewhat breathless, as it would Lily. He smiled at the thought.

And behind him, the girl walked obediently. Not even teenage mouthiness. She'd figured out who was boss and didn't argue.

Lily would figure it out, too. The only question was how long he would make her suffer.

THE NIGHT WAS ENDLESS, swamped with terrible fear and anguish. Jazz's head filled with horrific ideas of what that man might do to Iris. Another, worse, beating? Rape? Leaving her alone somewhere cold and frightened in the dark, hungry and thirsty?

Andy was capable of all that. Andy was capable of just about anything. His desire to inflict suffering knew no bounds and while he had said he wouldn't hurt Iris if

Lily followed his directions, she feared he'd been lying about that as he'd lied about everything in his life.

She paced endlessly, cold to the bone. No sweater could ease this aching chill.

Every time she looked at Adam, she saw her fears reflected, although in a different way. The man looked hard, his face almost like stone and his eyes...those kind brown eyes were almost black. He'd kill. She knew he'd kill Andy.

Good riddance to scum, she thought. Good riddance.

Until she recalled how Adam had said that killing someone changed you forever. Oh, God, don't let it come to that. He was carrying enough ghosts for an entire army.

But she sure as hell wouldn't blame him.

At last she got herself another cup of coffee. Maybe it would help warm her, and Adam had kept the pot fresh all night.

God, when had mere minutes become so endless?

At last she sagged at the table across from him. He shifted, easing his hip. Sheba slept in a corner by the cupboards but every time something moved, her eyes opened. A very light sleep. The tension in this house must be troubling her, but what could Jazz do about it?

"I feel like a coiled spring," she said.

Adam nodded. "That's one description. I'm feeling murderous."

She had guessed it. How uncomfortable that must be making him feel. How many bad memories this must be dredging out of him.

She ached for him, too. Andy was messing them all up.

"We'll get through this," he said, his voice as tight as stretched steel. "Swear to God."

She shivered, thinking that no one should want to cross this man. No one.

IRIS TREMBLED IN the cave when she'd been left, tied to a nearby tree with sturdy climbing rope. Her father—God, her own *father*—was doing this. Yeah, she knew who he was. Recognition had exploded within her out of the nearly forgotten past. *Her father.*

Something about that man had made her reluctant to fight, choosing patience instead, seeking any kind of opportunity to escape. She hadn't found one.

When the creep left her in the dark cave, she wasn't at all impressed by the water he'd left her, or the packages of power bars. They didn't reassure her.

Instead she felt around hoping to find a rock sharp enough to cut the rope that bound her. She had no idea where she could go if she escaped. Wandering around on this mountain without guidance could kill people.

He'd left her a musty, filthy blanket. She pulled it around herself against the night's cold, her mind whirling with useless ideas.

He'd promised he wouldn't hurt her. He just wanted her mother. She didn't believe him.

Iris started praying for Lily more than herself. For Jazz who was facing all of this.

Hoping that Adam would find a way to get to her. Her only real hope.

Maybe in the morning, with some light, she'd have better ideas. Then her mind drifted into happier places, so many wonderful times with her mother, so many good ones with Aunt Jazz. Great times with her friends.

She'd been blessed. Only now did she realize just how blessed.

WITH DAWN THE horror remained. Jazz felt as if she were stretched to breaking, but snapping would help nothing. Sleep might have helped, but she was well past that. Adrenaline would keep her going until she collapsed.

She tried to tell herself she was being ridiculous, that when the phone rang she'd instantly emerge from the deepest sleep, that she couldn't do anything until Andy told her what he wanted.

That didn't help. Worry crawled through her and all over her skin like a million stinging ants.

It was after ten when the phone finally rang. Adam was right there with her. She picked up the handset and heard the line crackling.

Andy was on a cell phone, the signal poor in the mountains. From that she knew he had Iris in the rugged, higher terrain, a terribly vast space, impossible to search in any timely fashion.

Her heart and stomach sank until she wondered if she might vomit.

"Lily."

She'd never forgotten that voice, not after the trial. "I'm here. If you hurt my daughter—"

"She's my daughter, too."

That oily voice sickened her even more. As if Iris's relationship to him had ever mattered to Andy.

"Now listen," he said.

"I'm listening."

"You drive up the dirt road leading to the old mining

town. Then hike northwest and start climbing. On foot. I'll see you. I'll let you know where I want you to go. But hear me, and don't mistake me. If you call the cops, if you bring anyone along on the hike, I may just forget Iris is my daughter. God, what a stupid name."

Then he disconnected, leaving nothing but the hum of an empty line.

Jazz looked at Adam, her torment reaching new levels.

"I heard," he said coldly.

"He'll kill me," Jazz said quietly. "Worse, he might kill Iris."

"I know. I'll come anyway."

Anger burst in her, a white-hot heat. "Don't you dare. I mean it. I'm not risking Iris, not for your male ego."

He looked as if she'd slapped him but then the icy expression returned. "I get it."

"I mean it," she repeated. "There's nothing you can do to help now."

"I can fill a light backpack for you. You'll probably need some water, maybe even some trail mix. Climbing in the mountains can wear you out quickly, make you easy prey."

She shuddered but let him help her fill a pack she had seen in Lily's bedroom. Those water bottles would be heavy, but she didn't care. If she could have shaken the mountains, she would have.

She let Adam drive her to the mining camp, then set out alone, wrapped in a thicker jacket of Lily's, carrying gloves in her pockets along with a small canister in one, and a compass in her hand.

Northwest. Even that was a huge area.

Adam gave her a tight hug before he drove away, leaving her all alone to face the unimaginable.

EXCEPT ADAM DIDN'T leave her alone. He had no intention of doing that. The situation was too unstable, too dangerous, to leave Jazz out there on her own. Or to rely on Andy Robbins to reveal Iris's whereabouts in any useful way to rescue the girl.

And if there was one certainty in the middle of this mess, it was that Andy Robbins didn't have Adam's ability to track stealthily from a distance.

He drove off a side road that headed south not much below the remains of the small mining town. He had a survival pack in the rear of his truck, an army habit he hadn't been able to break. Thank God.

Shortly he was outfitted in camo, a pair of high-powered thermal binoculars hanging around his neck and his rifle slung over his right shoulder.

He had a decent idea of where Andy had put Iris. The compass direction given to Jazz had been a big clue to Adam.

Thunder Mountain protected a wolf den, a small cave that had somehow escaped the crushing weight above it. Andy would have chosen that, not an unprotected open space where Iris might be more easily found. A place where he could pretend that he was protecting his daughter. As if.

Adam wasn't worried about the small pack of wolves up there. They were shy creatures and if their pups weren't inside, they'd stay back, watching. Waiting to take their home back. The den was essential to the pack's survival as a group, but not essential enough to risk a battle with a human predator. *Their* larger prey were mostly grazing animals that offered a threat only with their heels. Wolves were far smarter than the humans they dodged. Never fighting a battle that wasn't essential, never starting a war.

The climb over rough ground was riddled with the cuts and gorges created by runoff from the winter snows and the remaining glaciers above. He climbed through obstacles as much as he moved through gentler ground.

He ignored the agonizing pain in his hip that was growing almost with each step. And frequently he paused, seeking Jazz's heat signature between trees.

He still had her in his sights, but no sign of Andy. How far was that bastard going to make her climb? How many risks would he put her through, maybe hoping she'd hurt herself and he'd have her under his full control?

From time to time, Adam searched other directions, taking no chance the monster would come at her from the side.

Not that he believed that bastard was capable of that kind of caution. If the fool had possessed a brain, he'd have known that you don't threaten a mama bear's cub.

Adam had even managed to press a can of pepper spray in Jazz's pocket. She'd looked at it, then nodded.

Adam was sure she'd burn out Andy's eyes if she got the chance. He just hoped she'd be upwind if she used that stuff.

But she would be too furious to think about it. He hadn't offered a caution because he knew that if the opportunity came Jazz wouldn't consider any such thing. She'd gone long past protecting herself.

Gritting his teeth against pain, he continued his trek. He knew where Jazz was. He just wished he knew Andy's position.

ANDY LAY CONCEALED behind a boulder, watching Lily's hike through binoculars. He'd seen that guy drop her off and head back home. Good.

The only question on his mind now was just how much he was going to make that woman suffer for all she'd done to him. Because she *was* going to suffer. His payback for all the pain she had caused him. He deserved it, just as she deserved the hell he intended to put her through.

She'd be on her knees begging before he was done. She'd be promising him anything at all if he would let Iris go. He liked that picture and began to grow impatient.

As for Iris, he planned to take her with him. He was her father, dammit. He needed to raise her right: obedient, wanting to please him. A *true* woman. She was still young enough to be molded into what Lily should have been.

Savoring the images that had begun to grow in his mind's eye, he counseled himself to patience.

Look at Lily now, he thought. Climbing as ordered. Being a good woman at last.

JAZZ DEVELOPED A new worry as she climbed along a narrow game trail. Hours now and no sign of Andy. Did he intend to take Iris away and begin his own form of in-home schooling? If she'd had the strength left to shiver, she would have. Instead she kept putting one foot in front of the other.

Two hours. She'd been climbing for over two hours now. Physical fatigue began to overwhelm her. She'd have to sit, wasting precious minutes drinking water, eating one of those power bars Adam had tucked in her pack. No choice.

At last she found a deadfall with one trunk about the

right size to sit on. If she didn't keep her strength up, she might never climb high enough.

She wasn't used to this new altitude and she could feel her lungs protesting, her cells kicking her with their need for more oxygen. Too bad. She *had* to keep going. Every minute she rested was causing Iris more terror, more suffering.

But life in the gentler landscape of Florida hadn't prepared her for this treacherous terrain. So much of it, so endless.

She wished she'd brought a pistol because she'd delight in shooting Andy, but she also knew she probably wouldn't have had the chance to use it. Or maybe even the will.

But what he was doing to Iris…

She rose, grabbing the backpack. She *had* to get going again.

ADAM SAW JAZZ SIT, saw her get up after a few minutes. He swept the entire area around her once again. Nothing, dammit. Nothing.

Then he caught a heat signature a few hundred yards above Jazz. His quarry. He set out, trusting the duff to cover his sounds, moving as lightly as he ever had in a battle zone. Creeping up on the enemy. It was in his blood.

The shrieking in his hip acted as a goad.

Nothing would stop him now.

ANDY ENJOYED WATCHING Lily struggle up the mountain. The woman was soft, too used to a desk job. He'd used his prison time to get into the best shape of his life.

Poor little woman. She had no idea of the hell that

was coming her way. No real idea. If she thought he'd been hard on her before, she had no idea how hard he could get. He'd practically been a pussycat before prison. No more.

Unable to wait any longer, sure that Lily was alone, he got going. It was high time. He'd waited ten long years for this.

ADAM WAS SWINGING around behind Andy. The element of surprise couldn't be overrated. Andy would be focused on Lily and not expecting a rear attack. The coming moves were already clear in Adam's mind. He just needed to be able to protect Jazz before the creep could harm her.

He'd make it.

JAZZ HEARD ANDY COMING. He didn't even try to be quiet about it. Confident brute.

But maybe he had every right to be. He'd kidnapped Iris. He'd forced Jazz to come up alone into these mountains. But she had to find Iris. Get that man to take her to her niece. Whatever the cost to herself.

She just had to hope that some opportunity would come to kick the guy in his package or scratch his eyes out. Or get that pepper spray out of her pocket and use it.

Andy's voice, smarmy again said, "Hello, Lily. Ready to fall back in line?"

"I loved you once," Jazz said.

"You'll love me again. Drop that backpack."

She did as ordered, then said, "If you want me you're going to have to take me to Iris."

"All in good time. Don't move. I didn't come to this party unarmed. I can gut you like I did to that squirrel."

Fury and fear both filling her, she stood still. He came around behind her, grabbed her hands and began to tie them together.

She thought of snapping her head back to hit him in the mouth or chin but stopped herself. That wouldn't get her to Iris.

Then she caught sight of the slightest movement in the brush above.

Adam! Oh my God, Adam.

ADAM HAD TO alter his tactic. Andy was now behind Jazz. To come from behind, he'd have to swing around a bit.

Easy enough. Plans were made to be adjusted.

He moved, taking care not to dislodge anything with his boots, creeping as silently as he'd ever crept in the 'Stan.

ANDY SPOKE, FOR once not trying to charm. "My knife is right against your back. You might not feel it with that jacket on, but that doesn't make any difference. It'll slice through and get you in the spine. Now *climb!*"

Jazz did as directed, just as she was sure Iris had. Some risks were foolhardy, and with her wrists bound the chance of getting at Andy seemed impossible.

She thought of Iris being forced up here the same way, and she coiled with anger, hating her helplessness.

But Adam was out there somewhere. He hadn't listened to her, and so far Andy seemed to suspect nothing. Her only hope now. Iris's only hope. She clung to it as her weary legs continued to climb. Prayed Adam wouldn't do a thing that might endanger Iris.

ADAM HAD NEARLY reached the best position, grateful for the brush that concealed his movements. The undergrowth had begun to green with spring, making it quieter when he moved through it.

Andy and Jazz passed him. He waited another minute for his best opportunity. Bound like that, a knife behind her, meant Jazz couldn't do a damn thing to help.

And he had to get to Andy before he cut her.

His breathing slowed. The pain in his hip seemed to vanish. He was as still and silent inside as he'd been on any covert operation.

He saw his opportunity and got ready to spring with his rifle in his hands. He'd have just liked to shoot the SOB but couldn't risk the possibility that he might be wrong about where Iris was stashed.

Then his moment came and he leaped onto the game trail right behind Andy.

JAZZ HEARD THE wonderful voice say, "I've got the business end of this rifle on your back, Robbins. Stop or I'll shoot you now."

Andy started to turn. "You'll shoot Lily, too."

"My aim is better than that. Stop now. Let Jazz get ahead of you or you'll take your last breath."

JAZZ? CONFOUNDED, ANDY let Lily go ahead. There was no mistaking the rifle pressed hard into his back. Jazz? Lily's sister?

The rifle prodded him. "Drop that knife. Then get facedown. Now."

Not even Andy was stupid enough to try to argue with a rifle. He valued his hide more than revenge, and the steadiness of the icy voice behind him warned him that this man knew what he was doing.

He dropped the knife, watched a tan boot kick it beyond reach.

"Facedown," the steely voice said. "I know a hundred ways to disable or kill a man."

Andy didn't doubt it. Beaten, he lay down, his face full of dirt. A heavy boot landed on his back and he let his wrists be bound tightly.

"Jazz? Come over here."

She obeyed. Andy heard a knife saw through the rope around her wrists.

"Take us to Iris now." A hand gripped Andy beneath his shoulder, pulling him to his feet as if he weighed nothing. "*Now* or you're going to look like something that the butcher has ground for sausage."

JAZZ WATCHED ALL this with amazement. Adam had spoken those words and she never doubted he'd meant them. Would Andy really take them to Iris? He'd certainly looked cowed.

The trail resumed its steady upward march. Her legs burned and started to feel weak, but thoughts of Iris kept her going.

Then at last they emerged into a small clearing and found Iris trying to cut through a rope with a sharp rock.

When Jazz saw her she collapsed with relief. And Iris cried, "I've never been so happy to see anyone in my life!"

Hugging each other, she and Iris stumbled after Andy and Adam, back down toward the mining camp.

"Try your cell," Adam said to Jazz. "Dial 911 and keep at it until you get a signal."

Finally she found one, about the time they reached the decrepit mining town. They sat at last and the two women started to cry.

"We'll wait for rescue," Adam said. "Best day of my life."

"Mine, too," Iris and Jazz sobbed in unison.

The best day indeed.

After a sheriff's deputy arrived and carted Andy away in cuffs, Adam led the way to his truck.

He stashed their gear in the back, thrilled they had Iris back. And sorry Jazz had seen the worst side of him. The pain pierced his heart.

Chapter Sixteen

Jazz didn't call her sister. She figured Lily didn't need to get upset until she was home in a few days, able to see Iris safe.

Iris huddled in the recliner, wrapped in a blanket, still trying to process the horror she's experienced, accepting endless cups of cocoa, her appetite otherwise diminished.

How was her niece going to deal with this, Jazz wondered. Another psychologist? Probably.

Andy resided safely in the county jail. He'd probably face federal charges as well as state and county. She hoped that would make Iris and Lily safe for much longer than ten years.

But Adam had not reappeared. He'd turned his truck into his own driveway after helping Iris and Jazz inside and hadn't been to see them since.

Jazz hated to imagine the memories this event had stirred in him, turning him into a man who had stalked a killer and had made dire threats.

A man who had once again turned into the very thing he'd been trying to escape.

Her heart bled for him and she shed tears for him.

After two days, she decided it was enough. Risking

everything, risking seeing him caught up in PTSD, she asked Iris if she'd be all right for an hour or so.

Iris nodded. "Sure."

Sure. Not very comforting.

Then Jazz screwed up her determination and marched across the street. She had to knock several times before Adam answered the door.

He looked awful, unshaven, wearing his rumpled camo as if he hadn't changed clothes. His face was drawn into harsh lines, his color faded to gray. Sheba looked saddened.

He let her in reluctantly, but said, "Go home, Jazz. Iris needs you."

"She's not the only one."

"Ms. Mercy marching across the street, huh? Go home. You've seen some of the worst in me. I don't want you to see any more."

She stared at him, wondering what the hell she could do. Then she did the only thing she could think of.

Closing the space between them, she wrapped her arms around him and hugged him as tight as she could. He stiffened.

"Jazz..."

"Shut up, Adam. I'll love you any way you come."

He froze. "You don't know."

"I know now, and I was never so grateful for a warrior. I've got a good idea what you might have done out there. I don't care. I still love you. Will always love you. Get as angry as you want. Hide away when you need to. Run on that lousy hip for hours. I've also seen the best in you."

His stiffness began to ease. "You can't know."

"Maybe not all of it, but I'll deal with it as it comes. Because I love you."

He moved back just enough to look into her face. "You really mean that?" He sounded tentative now.

"I really mean that. I wouldn't say it if I didn't."

"God, Jazz!"

"How many times do I have to say it to get it through that thick skull of yours? If you can tell me you don't feel the same, that you just want me to go back to Miami, tell me now. Send me away into the loneliness without you. It'll practically kill me, but you don't need to worry about that."

His face at last softened completely. "I can't send you back to Miami."

"Well, good. We can sort everything else out later. I love you," she repeated for the umpteenth time.

A frown flickered across his features. "You've got to promise me you'll hang around to see more of this, and I don't mean a week or two. And that you'll leave anytime you can't take it."

Her heart began to take wing as he spoke, however indirectly, about a future. "I promise."

Then he smiled, like the sun rising on a gray day. "I love you, too. But give it time. Now let's take Sheba back to Iris. She needs the dog more than I do now. But not as much as I need you."

The usually silent Sheba woofed.

It was settled, Jazz thought as Adam's arms cradled her gently. So good. It would always be good even on the darkest of days.

Because she trusted him completely. Because he now owned her heart.

Then she began to smile, too.

* * * * *

HELD HOSTAGE AT WHISKEY GULCH

ELLE JAMES

This book is dedicated to my children, whom I love dearly. When life gets me down, they rally around me and lift me up. I can always count on them to be there for me, and they can count on me to be there for them. I love them so very much and feel blessed that they are mine.

For you, Courtney, Adam and Megan.
With love,
Mom

Chapter One

Tessa Bolton retied the shoestring on her running shoe and straightened. Though the sun had yet to rise completely, the day promised to be clear and beautiful.

She inhaled deeply, raised her hands above her head and released the air out of her lungs. After a few stretches, she was ready to follow the trail along the river's edge, her usual morning jog that got her day off to a good start.

A figure appeared in the gray light of dawn, coming toward her as she started down the path.

She tensed for a second before she realized who it was. A smile curled the corners of her lips and she raised a hand in greeting.

"Good morning," Tessa called out.

Joseph "Irish" Monahan slowed his jog to a walk as he approached. "We have to quit meeting like this," he said with a wink. "You'll start thinking I'm stalking you."

She laughed. "If anything, you'll think I'm stalking you. You're always here well before me."

"I like to run before the sun comes up. Always did in the army. That way I can beat the heat."

Droplets of sweat dripped off his forehead and his naked chest and shoulders glistened in the soft haze of morning. He always ran without a shirt, the sweat en-

hancing his muscular physique. The man was one-hundred-percent eye candy.

Tessa swallowed hard to force back her desire to run
her fingers across his chest to test the hardness of his
muscles. "You're not in the army now," she pointed out,

"No, but I work for someone else, and I like to get
there early." He shrugged his broad shoulders. "You
know, lots of mouths to feed."

She chuckled. "As in horses, cows and chickens?"

He nodded, a grin spreading across his face. "I rarely
hear a complaint about the chow served in the mess hall."

"I would think the country life would be boring after
all those years in the Special Forces." She tilted her head.
"You were Delta Force, right?"

He dipped his head. "I was. Best years of my life."

Tessa's brow furrowed. "If they were the best years,
why did you leave the army?"

His gaze shifted from hers to somewhere over her
shoulder. "I was ready to get on with my life. When
you're Delta, you tend to put the rest of your life on hold."

She frowned. "I don't understand."

His gaze returned to hers. "It's hard to have any kind
of relationship outside your team when you're never
home. I didn't risk getting married, only to be divorced
within a year." He shrugged. "I saw too many of my buddies go through that."

"So, you gave up the military and came to Whiskey
Gulch to get married?" Her lips twitched as she fought
to hide her smile.

His forehead creased. "I wouldn't say that. I left the
military to discover what real life is all about. And I was
getting too old to hold up under the physical demands
of the job."

Her gaze swept him from head to toe, finding him perfectly fit. "I doubt you had any trouble keeping up with the younger guys."

"Yeah, but it was only a matter of time before my luck ran out. A stray bullet, flipped vehicle, or shrapnel from an IED or mortar round would have put me out of commission and the army. As it was, I left on my own terms."

Tessa grabbed her ankle and pulled it up behind her, stretching her leg. "And working with the animals will keep you satisfied with life?"

His lips curved. "Among other things. The boss, Trace, has other activities in mind for us and he's bringing on other men like me to handle them."

"Really?" She dropped her ankle and reached for the other, pulling it up behind her. "What kind of activities?"

He lifted a shoulder. "Some kind of security service. We're all trained soldiers, we have skills not usually found in the civilian world. He has an idea that we can use our training to help others."

"Sounds admirable. Whiskey Gulch is a small town. Will you find enough of that kind of work here? I'd think you'd have to be in a more populated area to warrant starting a security service."

"Trace thinks if we start it, word will get out. People will find us." Irish shrugged. "In the meantime, I have animals to feed and care for. They're therapeutic."

"And after all you've been through as a Delta Force operative, you could use some downtime." Tessa smiled. "Thank you for your service."

His cheeks reddened. "I'd better get going." He frowned, his gaze going to the river trail. "You all right to run alone?"

Tessa lifted her chin. "I've done it every morning for the past few months. I'll be fine."

"Same route every day?"

She nodded. "I'm trying to improve my time."

"You should really alter your route. Never do the same one twice. Be a little more random."

She laughed. "What could happen out here? We're in the middle of nowhere."

Irish's eyes narrowed. "I make it a habit to never say what could happen. It's like tempting fate to throw something in your path. Something bad."

She planted her hands on her hips. "Are you telling me this tough Delta Force soldier is superstitious?"

He crossed his arms over his chest. "Damn right I am. Intuition saved my butt more times than I can remember."

"I don't believe in luck, fate or intuition. Knowledge is what you have to bank on."

"You're a nurse, right?"

Her brow dipped. "Yes. So?"

"Don't you base some of your work on instinct?"

She shook her head. "I don't call it instinct. I call it experience. I don't leave my patients' lives up to fate or hunches."

Irish tipped his head. "Believe what you will. I still think luck and intuition play a major part in our lives and the paths we choose or are chosen for us." He glanced toward the trail along the river's edge. "Sure you don't want me to run with you?"

Tessa shook her head. "No. You have hungry subjects to feed. I'll be fine." She turned to leave.

"Tessa?" Irish called out to her.

She glanced over her shoulder. "Yes?"

He opened his mouth, must have thought better of it,

and closed it again. He gave her a crooked smile. "Nothing. Have a good run." He turned, climbed into his truck and drove away.

For a long moment, she stared after him. If she wasn't mistaken, he'd been about to...what? Ask her out? See if she wanted to get coffee? Tell her he was ready to start working toward that life after the army, and he wanted to test the waters with her?

Tessa shook her head. Sure, she found Irish attractive. If he asked her out, she probably would say yes. But that didn't mean they were headed down the path of happily-ever-after. She had too much baggage of her own to waltz down that lane.

Once bitten, twice shy?

That was Tessa to a tee. Her ex-husband had ruined her for other men. His abuse had left her little more than a shell of herself. Over the past few months, she'd worked to regain her self-esteem and rebuild her confidence. She'd be damned if she let another man drag her down again.

Not that Irish would do that.

Tessa rolled her shoulders to ease the tension that always came with memories of Randy. He'd sucker punched her with his fists and words on more than one occasion.

She'd indulged in comfort food until she was fifty pounds overweight.

Randy Hudson, being the jerk he was, had ridiculed her over her weight, along with all her other perceived faults, which had only made her sink deeper into depression.

One day, she'd looked at herself in the mirror and found a stranger looking back. That day, she'd decided enough was enough. She'd thrown out the brand-new carton of Rocky Road ice cream, put on her sneakers and gone for a walk.

Walking became running and she only ate to fuel her body, not to feed her depression.

When Randy criticized her, she stood up to him, telling him that she wasn't going to take it anymore. He either had to quit disrespecting her or she would leave.

Well, she'd ended up in Whiskey Gulch where she'd grown up, and Randy had remained in San Antonio.

Leaving him, getting the divorce, starting over, had been the best decision of Tessa's life. She'd shed the fifty pounds plus an extra ten. Never in her life had she felt better physically and been more content with her life.

But she had to admit, she missed having someone in her life. Tessa hadn't dated since her divorce. She wasn't confident about her choice in men. When she'd met and married Randy, she'd been certain he was the perfect man for her.

Boy had she been wrong.

How could she be certain the next man she decided to date wouldn't be another Randy?

For weeks, she and Irish had bumped into each other, crossing paths at the river trail. She'd be lying to herself if she didn't admit that she found him attractive.

Randy had been good-looking as well. Good looks weren't everything. The next man in Tessa's life had to be kind-hearted and nonjudgmental. Supportive, not destructive.

So far, Irish had been nothing but a gentleman. She'd been tempted.

Shrugging off her thoughts about the former Delta Force operative, Tessa slipped her earbuds in her ears, set her music to her running playlist and took off down the river path.

Her feet hit the ground in time to the songs, the playlist motivating. She'd had the same music now for a couple of months. The familiarity with the different songs let her know where she was in her workout. When she heard the strains of "Born to Run" by Bruce Springsteen, she knew she was halfway, and it was time to turn around for the jog back.

She'd been running for twenty minutes when she passed through a wooded area with weeping willow trees hanging low overhead. With Duran Duran in her ear, she didn't hear the sound of footsteps or the rustle of leaves until a figure burst out of the willow branches, dressed in dark clothes with a black ski mask over his face, and blocked the path.

Tessa let out a sharp squeal and dodged to the left to avoid running into the man.

He moved faster, grabbing her arm with hands encased in the kind of gloves used for good grip in sports.

Tessa dug her feet into the dirt, twisted and pulled to free herself from his grasp, to no avail.

He punched her in the side of her face, yanked her around and caught her in a headlock, clamping his arm around her neck.

Her pulse raced and her vision blurred. Tessa fought for her life. When her struggles didn't free her, she stilled, trying to remember the self-defense lessons she'd taken before she'd left San Antonio. It all came back to her.

Tessa went limp in the man's arms.

He fumbled to hold her upright.

As the man bent over to steady her, Tessa bunched

her legs beneath her and pushed against the earth, rising up so fast, he didn't have time to move out of her way.

Tessa's head hit the man beneath his jaw, whipping his head up and back. His arm loosened around her neck.

Tessa shoved his elbow upward and ducked beneath it, slipping behind him. Planting a foot on his backside, she kicked hard, sending him flying into the willow tree.

Before her attacker could regain his balance, Tessa ran as fast as she could to get back to where she'd parked her car by the road.

She'd only gotten halfway there when he slammed into her from behind.

Tessa hit the ground on her hands and knees, oblivious to the pain of gravel scraping against her skin. The man on her back grabbed her by her ponytail and pulled her head back.

"You'll pay for that," he said, his voice low and threatening, his breath hot against her ear.

On her belly, pinned to the ground, Tessa flailed her arms and legs. Nothing she did could shake him from her back.

He grabbed her arm, shifted to one side and attempted to roll her onto her back.

As she rolled onto her side, she cocked her arm and slammed her elbow into the man's face.

He cried out, clutched his face with both hands and rocked on his haunches.

Tessa shoved him hard, sending him flying to land flat on his back.

With only seconds to spare, she scrambled to her feet and ran, refusing to look around. She could hear the sound of his footsteps on the gravel behind her as she reached her vehicle where she'd left it what seemed like hours ago.

Her heart pounding, she pulled the key fob from the tiny pocket in her shorts, hit the unlock button, yanked open the door and flung herself inside.

With her hand shaking, she fumbled to get the key into the ignition.

Out of the corner of her eye, she saw movement. He was almost to her.

Her heart leaped into her throat as she slammed her hand down on the button that locked the doors.

The man in the ski mask grabbed her door handle and yanked hard. When it didn't open, he pounded his fists against the window.

Terrified, Tessa shoved her shift into drive.

Her attacker flung himself onto her hood and pounded the front windshield with his fists.

Tessa hit the accelerator, jerked the steering wheel right then left and spun in the gravel.

The guy on her hood slid from side to side, holding on, refusing to let go.

Tessa gunned the accelerator shooting the vehicle forward. Then she slammed on her brakes.

The man on the hood slid off onto the ground.

Tessa pushed the shift into Reverse and backed away as fast as the vehicle would go. She made it to the paved road and kept going in reverse, heading toward town. When she'd gotten far enough away from her attacker, she spun the steering wheel, shifted into Drive and raced toward Whiskey Gulch. Her cell phone would have been little use with reception spotty that far from town and the transmission tower.

Tessa didn't slow until she saw the first houses on the

outskirts of town. Even then, she flew down Main Street, coming to a skidding stop in front of the sheriff's office.

The sheriff and another man were standing out front when she stumbled out of the SUV and ran up the steps.

The other man was Irish, now dressed in lightweight workout pants. He turned, a frown pressing his eyebrows together. "Tessa?"

"Help," she cried and threw herself at the unsuspecting man.

Chapter Two

Irish wrapped his arms around Tessa and held her tight. "Hey, what's wrong? What happened?"

The sheriff reached out and touched Tessa's arm. "Are you all right, Miss Bolton?"

She shook her head, burrowing her face against Irish's chest. "He grabbed me."

Irish stiffened. "Who grabbed you?"

Tessa shook her head. "I don't know. He wore a mask. He grabbed me in a chokehold. I…almost…didn't get away." Her body shook as she sobbed in Irish's arms.

He tipped her head up and stared down into her watery eyes. "Where was this? On the river trail?"

She nodded. "I've never…had this…happen," she said between gulps of air and sobs.

"Do I need to get an ambulance?"

Tessa dismissed his question. "No. I got myself here. I can get myself home."

Sheriff Barron shook his head and reached for the radio mic on his shoulder. "I'll send a unit out to the trail now."

"Please," Tessa said. "You have to catch him."

"We'll do our best," the sheriff said as he ducked back inside the office, calling out orders as he went.

"Where are you hurt?" Irish asked, staring at her face, his thumb tracing a red mark near her temple.

Tessa winced and captured his hand. "He hit me in the side of the head. Then he wrapped his arm around my neck." She raised her other hand to her throat.

"How did you get away?" he asked.

Tessa shook her head. "I went limp. When he loosened his hold, I came up fast and head-butted his chin."

Irish gave her a gentle smile. "You're smart."

"I took self-defense training in San Antonio before I moved back here." She snorted. "I almost forgot everything I'd learned."

"Apparently, you didn't." His hand squeezed hers.

Tessa's eyes rounded. "Or I wouldn't be here now."

"Thank God." Irish gently touched the top of her head. "We should have you checked out."

When he tried to set her at arm's length, she clung to him, her body trembling. "I've never been more frightened in my life," she whispered.

Irish smoothed a hand over her burnished red hair no longer contained in the ever-present, tight ponytail she'd worn earlier. "All the more reason to get you to a hospital and have them check you out for concussion."

"No," she said. "I'm okay."

Uncertain, he held her away from him. "At the very least, you need those scrapes on your knees taken care of."

She tipped her head toward the building. "I'm sure the sheriff's got a first-aid kit."

Irish's eyes narrowed. "I'd rather have a doc take a look." When her brow furrowed, he held up his hands. "But if a first-aid kit is what you want, by all means, let's get that." He held open the door for her and guided her through with a hand at the small of her back.

The woman manning the front desk hurried around the partition wall. "Oh, Tessa, sweetie. I heard what happened to you." She moved aside and gestured toward her seat. "Here, take my seat."

"No, Ramona. I'm okay." Tessa smiled. "Besides, you're working."

"It's fine," Ramona said, pointing to her headset with the mic next to her mouth. "Bluetooth is amazing." She headed to a closet at the far side of the room. "We have a first-aid kit in here somewhere." She opened the door to find the kit secured to the other side. "We don't use it that often. But it's here for just such an occasion. What do you need?"

Irish led Tessa to Ramona's seat and urged her to sit. "We could use something to clean the wounds and bandages to cover them."

Tessa collapsed into the padded chair, shaking. She clasped her hands in front of her as if to still them.

The sheriff strode back through the office, heading for the door. He stopped in front of Tessa. "I'm on my way out to the river road to see if we can find anything to lead us to your attacker. Think you can show us where he attacked you?" He held up his hand. "If it's too traumatic, I don't expect you to go, but it would help to know exactly where it happened. We might find some evidence that could lead us to the perpetrator."

Tessa pushed to her feet, her back stiffening. "Anything I can do to help catch the guy." She shuddered. "I hate to think of him attacking another woman who might not get away."

Irish frowned. "After we take care of those scrapes."

He opened an alcohol packet, knelt in front of her and looked up into her eyes. "This might sting."

"Just do it," she said, and sank back into Ramona's chair.

He swiped the pad over her skinned knee.

Tessa sucked in a sharp breath but didn't cry out.

It had to be stinging. Irish admired her even more. She refused to show weakness.

After applying a bandage to the knee, he treated the other. Then he took her hands in his. "Any scrapes here?"

She pulled them free. "Nothing I can't live with," she said. "The sooner we get out to the river road, the better chance we have of catching that guy."

"More than likely, he's long gone," the sheriff said. "But we might find some clues as to who it was. And brace yourself, I'll be asking some pointed questions. In many cases, victims know their attackers."

Irish clenched his fists. "All the more reason to wear a ski mask. We need to find the bastard."

The sheriff nodded toward Tessa and then the door. "Are you following me in your own vehicle?"

Tessa opened her mouth.

Before she could speak, Irish answered for her. "She'll ride with me." He glanced at her. "If that's okay with you?"

She gave him a shaky smile. "Thanks. I got myself here, but I'm not so sure I could drive back out to where it happened without falling apart."

He took her hand in his and squeezed gently. "Hang in there. You're not alone now."

She dipped her head. "And I'm glad. I've never felt more vulnerable. Even when…"

Irish's eyes narrowed. "Even when what?"

"Oh, nothing." Tessa squared her shoulders. "Let's do this. That man can't be allowed to run free. Since he didn't get me, he might go after some other lone female." She drew in a deep breath and led the way out the front of the building. "I couldn't live with myself if he hurt someone else."

"He's the one with the problem. You aren't responsible for his actions," Irish said, following her to the parking lot. He waved toward his pickup. "Leave your car here, for now. I'll bring you back."

"Aren't you supposed to be at work out at Whiskey Gulch Ranch?" she asked.

"Trace will understand. I'll call him as soon as we're in the pickup. This is just the kind of thing he'd want to help with."

Tessa paused at the door to his truck and looked up into his eyes, her brow creasing. "What do you mean? Trace owns a ranch. Why would he think this is something he could work?"

"Trace Travis inherited his father's ranch, yes, but he still feels the need to protect and serve." Irish grinned. "And to use the skills he acquired and mastered as a Delta Force operative in the army. He's set up a security business."

"Is that why he hired you?"

Irish nodded. "There are three of us now, counting Trace. But we have more coming on board as they separate from the service."

"It's nice that our men in uniform have a place to work outside of the military," Tessa said as she climbed into the passenger seat of Irish's truck. "I worked with veterans coming home from war, getting out of the military. The struggle to find themselves in the civilian world is real."

"No kidding." Irish slid into the driver's seat and pulled out of the parking lot, following the sheriff down the highway that led out of Whiskey Gulch. "But all that aside, I'm worried about you."

Tessa sighed. "I'm okay. He didn't get me."

"He almost did."

"My self-defense training saved me."

"This time," Irish said.

Tessa shot a frown toward Irish. "Surely, after failing to capture me, he won't try again. Will he? I mean, he didn't get me. Will he go after an easier target?"

Irish shrugged. "We can only guess about his motivation and intention. He could have chosen you as a crime of opportunity."

Tessa nodded. "That's what I was thinking."

"Or he could have targeted you specifically." Irish glanced her direction in time to see her swallow hard.

"But why?" she whispered.

"I don't know." Irish paused before asking, "Have you made an enemy out of one of your patients?"

Tessa shook her head. "My patients love me."

Irish grinned. "That, I could believe." He reached out and bussed her under her chin with his knuckles. "What's not to love?"

She snorted. "A lot. I'm sure I've pissed off someone along the way. I just can't remember who." Her brow dipped low. "Really. Not one person comes to mind."

"Because you're such a nice person. How could anyone be mad at you?" As he navigated through town, he reached out and took her hand in his. "Do me a favor and don't go running along the river without a buddy."

"I need to exercise," she said, staring down at her hand in his. "It's what helped me through a rough time."

"Yeah?" he prompted, hoping she'd open up about her rough time, but giving her the option of ignoring his prompt.

She sat silent for several seconds. "My ex-husband gave me hell when I left him."

Irish's hand tightened around hers. "How so?"

"He didn't want the divorce."

"Why did you divorce him?" Irish started to let go of her hand. "You don't have to answer. It's none of my business."

Tessa's fingers curled around his, holding tightly. "No. It's okay. I guess I'd had enough." She stared through the window, her jaw hardening. "The last time he broke my ribs, I realized he wasn't going to change. He couldn't control his anger, and I wouldn't survive the next time he lost it."

Irish swore softly, his hand on the steering wheel squeezing hard. Any man who hit a woman was not a man in Irish's books. "I'm sorry," he said softly.

"Why? You didn't hit me. I stayed in the situation too long. I should have left sooner."

"I'm sorry you had to endure it," Irish said softly. "Is that why you took self-defense classes?"

Tessa nodded. "Randy ignored the restraining order all too often. He didn't like losing. Even if he didn't love me, he didn't like the fact that I'd left *him*. He took it as if he'd lost a game." She grunted. "I just wanted to be free of fear. I moved home from San Antonio to get away from Randy."

"You think he might have come here to seek revenge?" Irish asked.

Tessa paused. "I don't know, but I don't think it was him. I mean it's been a while since I left my ex. Why would he seek revenge now? Besides, the man on the trail was a taller than my ex. And maybe stronger?" She shrugged. "It all happened so fast, I can't recall everything about him. The whole attack was such a blur."

"So, you're not exactly sure of his height and build?"

Her mouth twisted. "No. I just didn't feel like it was Randy."

"It might not hurt to check on his whereabouts," Irish stated. "Let the sheriff know."

She nodded. "I will." Tessa shivered as they pulled off the road onto the gravel parking area beside the river where Irish usually found Tessa's vehicle parked after his run.

Irish turned to her. "You don't have to do this, you know."

She drew in a deep breath and let it go. Then, squaring her shoulders, she gave a brief nod. "I need to show him where it went down. If they can find anything that would lead to catching my attacker, it would be worth the effort."

"True." The trail along the river was bordered by brush, tall grass and trees. She didn't expect it to be easy to find evidence, but she wanted to do whatever she could to help.

Irish shifted into Park and climbed down from his pickup.

Before he could round the front of the truck, Tessa had pushed open her door. Yet she sat in the passenger seat, staring at the trail along the river where it disappeared into the stand of trees lining each side. Her body tense and her eyes wide, her breathing came in short, rapid spasms.

Irish touched her arm.

She jumped, her gaze shooting to him.

"Sorry," he said. "I didn't mean to startle you."

She shook her head. "No, it's not you. I'm just jumpy."

"You have every right to be." He held out his hand.

She laid her fingers in his palm. "Let's do this."

"You don't have to be afraid. The sheriff and I will make sure you're protected."

"I know. It's just…so soon after…" She stepped onto the running board and dropped to the ground. When she tipped forward, off balance, Irish wrapped an arm around her waist to steady her.

"Are you okay?" he asked.

"I am," she nodded. "Just incredibly clumsy."

"Can't say that I mind." His voice came out low and rich, his arm tightening around her. The scent of her hair curled around his nostrils and made him drag in a deep breath. She smelled so good.

Irish's jeans tightened. Now was not the time to be so attracted to this woman. She'd been attacked. For all they knew, the perpetrator had been about to rape or kill her.

THE SHERIFF WAITED at the beginning of the trail.

When Tessa and Irish joined him, he turned and fell into step with them. "Do you remember about where the attack occurred?" the sheriff asked.

She nodded. "It's where the weeping willows hang over the trail." The muscles in her belly tightened. An inordinate amount of fear welled up inside. Even when her husband beat her, she hadn't felt this anxious. Probably because she'd known it was coming.

With the attack this morning, she'd been taken off guard. And it had all happened so quickly. Her breaths became shorter and her chest tightened. If she wasn't careful, she'd have a full-on panic attack before they reached the spot.

A large warm hand reached for hers, gently wrapping around her cold fingers. That little bit of connection was enough to slow her pulse and bring her back from the edge.

Tessa glanced up at Irish.

He gave her an almost imperceptible nod and then focused on the trail ahead.

That's what she needed to do. Focus.

Her footsteps faltered as they approached the willows bending toward the trail, not quite touching. What once had provided a welcome respite from the hot Texas sun now represented a more sinister place.

A shiver rippled down the back of Tessa's neck.

The sheriff bent to examine the ground, pointing at the dusty trail. "We have a good shoe print here. It's a lot bigger than yours. It could belong to your attacker.

Irish's hand squeezed hers. "I was out here earlier, but those treads don't match my running shoes."

"No. They look more like some kind of hiking boots." The sheriff pulled his cell phone out of his pocket and snapped pictures of the print. "Did either of you see any others while you were jogging?"

Tessa stared at the boot print. "I rarely see anyone, except Irish."

"Same," Irish said. "We've been passing each other most mornings and I haven't seen anyone else on the trail at the time we come."

"You keep the same schedule every day?" the sheriff asked.

Irish and Tessa nodded simultaneously.

"I actually should know better," Irish said. "When deployed to a foreign country, we have to vary our schedules and break up habits to keep from becoming targets."

Tessa shook her head. "But we're not in a foreign country. We're in Texas."

"But the same precautions should be taken."

"Things like this aren't supposed to happen in small towns," Tessa said.

"They happen more often than you'd think," the sheriff said, his tone serious.

Tessa shivered. "I moved home to get away from the big city and the crime that goes along with it. But mostly to get away from my ex-husband."

The sheriff's mouth twisted. "We do the best we can. However, we can't read the minds of criminals. Our jobs would be a lot easier if we could."

"I know." Tessa touched the sheriff's arm. "It's just frightening to know that this type of evil is free and walking among us. Who will he attack next?"

"I don't have much to go on, other than your account and description. I'll poke around here and see if I can find anything else that could lead us to the perp."

"Thanks, Sheriff." Irish pulled Tessa's hand through the crook of his elbow. "I'll take Miss Bolton back to Whiskey Gulch."

"I'll let you know if I discover anything," the sheriff offered.

"Thank you," Tessa murmured. *Just find him.*

Irish walked her back to his truck and helped her into the cab. He paused and looked up at her before closing the door. "Are you going to be okay?"

She nodded, a sob rising her throat. Tessa swallowed hard to push it back down. Irish was just being nice. "Thank you."

He climbed into the truck and started the engine. "For what?"

"For believing me and for bringing me back here so that I didn't have to face it alone."

Irish pulled out onto the highway and drove to Whiskey Gulch, a frown tugging his brow downward. When he pulled up in front of the sheriff's office next to her vehicle, he shifted into Park, climbed out and hurried to the passenger side.

Tessa fumbled with her seat belt.

"Here, let me," he said and reached around her to unsnap the buckle, leaning close to her in the process.

Tessa inhaled the scent of him, all warm and woodsy from having jogged along the same trail that morning. She wanted to reach out and smooth a hand over his taut muscles. Were they as hard as they appeared?

The thought came on so swiftly, her hand rose from her lap before she could think straight.

"Are you sure you're all right?" he asked. Still inside the cab with her, he was so close, Tessa could have leaned forward ever so slightly and kissed him.

Her eyes rounded and her breaths came in shallow, constricted gulps. "Yes. Yes, of course."

Irish leaned back out of the truck and offered her his hand. "I could stay with you today, if you like," he offered.

Tessa took his hand and let him help her down. "That won't be necessary. I work all day and I'm surrounded by people." She gave him a weak smile. "I'll be fine."

"What about tonight?" he asked, his tone softening.

"I'll be fine. I get home before sunset and I'll be sure to check all dark corners to make sure there isn't anyone lurking."

"Is your house near others?" Irish asked.

Tessa shrugged. "Somewhat. I'm at the end of a street, if that's what you mean."

"That doesn't mean you're surrounded by other houses."

"I have a house on one side," she said.

"And across the street?" he prompted.

Her lips pressed together. "Empty lot."

Irish's brows knit. "I'll come over and check your house when you get off work."

She shook her head. Since divorcing her husband, she'd been determined to make it on her own, guarding her independence with a vengeance. Though it would be nice to have some backup in this case.

Tessa exhaled the deep breath she'd taken at his words. "That's not necessary. I've lived on my own. I know the drill. Have my key ready before I get out of the car. Look in all directions before leaving the relative safety of the vehicle. I even have a small can of Mace on my keychain."

Irish crossed his arms over his chest. "How long have you had the Mace?"

"About three years. I bought it in Houston."

"That stuff might have a limited shelf life."

"If it makes you feel better, I'll check the date on it." She touched his arm. "I'll be fine."

His eyes narrowing, Irish stared at her for a long time. Then he held out his hand. "Let me have your cell phone."

"My cell phone?" Tessa frowned.

With a nod, Irish wiggled his fingers. "Your cell phone."

Tessa reached into her SUV and pulled her cell out of the cup holder, then she gave it to Irish.

He held it out. "Unlock it."

She entered her code and pushed the phone back to him.

Irish added himself to her contacts and passed it back to her. "Now you have my phone number. If for any reason you're scared, bored or lonely, call me." He curled her fingers around the phone and squeezed gently. "I'm not just saying that to be nice. I really mean it. If you hear something go bump in the night, call me. I'll be there." He scowled. "I don't like the idea of you being alone in your house after what happened."

She touched his arm. "You don't have to worry about me. I'm not your responsibility."

His scowl deepened. "I know that, but I also know what happened to you today. I'm worried about you."

"I'll be okay."

"At least let me follow you home and make sure no one is lurking around your place."

Her lips twisted for a brief moment and then she sighed. "Okay. If it will make you feel better."

Irish nodded. "It would."

Tessa didn't want to admit she was relieved that someone would follow her to her house. Though she tried to sound tough, she wasn't feeling at all safe. She'd been attacked in broad daylight. It could happen again.

A shiver rippled down the center of her spine. "Do you have time to follow me now?" she asked. "I need to get to my house, change and go to work."

Irish nodded. "I'll be right behind you." He held her door for her as she slid behind the steering wheel of her vehicle. Once he'd closed the door, he hurried for his truck and climbed into the driver's seat.

Tessa waited for him to back out of his parking space

before she pulled out onto Main Street and headed toward her house.

Her attacker had gotten away. What if he came after her again?

She checked her rearview mirror several times during the few blocks to her house. Still shaken, she was glad Irish was behind her.

Chapter Three

Irish pulled into the driveway beside Tessa's SUV and stared at the little quaint and homey sky-blue cottage with the white shutters.

He quickly shifted into Park and shut off the engine. Jumping out, he came around to her driver's-side door as she pushed it open. "Key?"

Before exiting the vehicle, Tessa stared hard at her home. "Do you really think he might come looking for me here?"

"Since you don't know who he is, or why he attacked you, it pays to be overly cautious. Let me check things out before you go inside."

She nodded and laid the keys across his open palm.

When her fingers touched his skin, he felt a jolt of awareness blast through him. She wasn't the usual kind of woman he found himself dating. She was far too serious and had that girl-next-door thing going on with her strawberry-blond hair and blue-gray eyes.

"Stay here and lock the doors."

Tessa shivered. "What about you? What if there is someone inside? You could be hurt."

He gave her a tight smile. "I'm a trained combatant. I've done this before."

"That's right. You were Special Forces." She shrugged. "I'll stay here." She pulled her cell phone out of her purse. "I'll be ready to call 9-1-1 if you're not back in less than three minutes."

He chuckled. "Good thinking. If the house is empty, I'll be back in less time." He leaned in and kissed her cheek.

Tessa touched the spot he'd kissed, her eyes wide. "Why did you do that?"

"For luck." He winked. "If it bothered you, I won't do it again."

"No. It's okay." She looked down at her hands "It just surprised me."

"Sorry." He tipped his head toward her steering wheel. "If you have to, leave and go back to the sheriff's office." Irish closed her door. "Lock it."

After she did, he climbed the steps to the front porch and checked the doorknob.

Locked. That was good.

He inserted the key into the lock and opened the door, slowly. He hadn't brought his handgun with him. Hopefully, he wouldn't need it.

Pushing the door open, he peered inside. The front entry was shaded from the morning sun. Stepping in, he stood for a moment, listening for sounds, waiting until his vision adjusted to the dim lighting.

One by one, he moved from room to room, checking in closets, underneath beds, behind the shower curtain and in the pantry. There wasn't a basement or garage, so he was done in under three minutes and back out on the porch. "All clear."

Before he could get to her SUV, Tessa had the door open and was getting out.

Irish cupped her elbow. "Sure you're feeling okay?"

She nodded. "I'm fine. Just a little shaky. I didn't expect to get attacked on my morning run."

"No one expects that. You should really have a running buddy, never go on your own."

"I don't know many avid runners. Most people are too busy with young families to get out that early in the morning."

"I'll run with you," Irish said. "There is such a thing as safety in numbers."

The corners of Tessa's mouth dropped. "I hate that I have to rely on anyone. I fought hard for my independence. I feel like it's being stripped away from me."

He held up his hands. "I have no intention of taking away your independence. But it would be unwise to run alone. Especially after what happened today."

She agreed. "I know that, now." Her frown deepened. "I don't like it. But I know it." She sighed. "Thank you. I can start earlier to match your usual time."

"Fair enough. And having you with me will keep me safe," he said with a crooked grin.

Tessa snorted softly. "Like you need someone to keep you safe."

"Despite popular belief, I'm not indestructible. Neither are you." He stuck out his hand. "Promise you won't stand me up tomorrow morning?"

Tessa placed her hand in his. "I promise."

He smiled. "That wasn't so hard, was it?"

"Harder than you think," she muttered.

He let go of her hand and took her other one in his, holding it firmly. "Ready?"

She drew in a deep breath and let it out slowly. "My knees are shaking," she confessed.

He laughed and squeezed her hand. "Mine do that after a good hard run. It goes away."

"I know that feeling. But this is different."

"I'm sure it is," he said.

She shook her head and stood staring at the house. "What's wrong with me? I've entered this house alone many times. This is my home. I shouldn't be afraid to go inside."

Irish hated seeing the fear in her face. He let go of her hand and slipped his arm around her waist. "I'm with you every step of the way. The house is clear. No one inside to jump out at you."

"I trust you," she admitted. "I'm just a bit punchy, is all."

"One step at a time is all you need." He waited for her to take that first step.

And she did. Followed by another and another. Soon, they had climbed the steps to the front porch.

Irish had left the front door open. "You want me to go first?" he asked.

She nodded. "Please."

He took her hand again and led the way inside. "I'll stay as long as you like. Or you can tell me to leave and I'll wait outside."

"I really thought I could handle this on my own. But now I'm not so sure." She squeezed his hand. "Stay."

"I checked all the closets, under the bed and in the pantry. No bogeymen hiding anywhere in the house." He smiled down at her. "You'll be all right."

"I know," Tessa said.

He hated seeing her so afraid of walking into her home. Irish wanted to find the bastard who'd done this to Tessa. The attack had stripped her of any kind of feeling of safety, even in her own home.

He'd talk with Trace. Maybe there was something they could do to help. At the very least, Irish planned to be with her as much as possible to ensure the attacker didn't get a second chance.

TESSA STARED AT the interior of her little cottage. Everything looked just like it had when she'd left it that morning to go jog. Everything inside the house was the same, except for the woman standing in the doorway with a man she barely knew.

Irish stood beside her. "I'll leave you here." His fingers loosened around hers.

Tessa tightened her hold on his hand, suddenly reluctant to let go of his warmth and strength.

"Or not." He chuckled. "Take your time, but I can't hold your hand while you dress for work." A teasing grin tipped his lips. "Unless you want me to." He shook his head. "At the very least, I'll be here until you're ready to go to work. Then I'll follow you there."

She let go of his hand. "Are you sure?"

He nodded.

"You need to get to work, too."

He chortled. "The horses can wait. While you're getting dressed, I'll call Trace and let him know what's going on."

Tessa rubbed her arms as if chilled. "I don't know what's wrong with me. I've walked through my front door a hundred times and never felt like this."

Irish touched her arm. "You've never been attacked like that before. You have a right to feel nervous. But I'm here. I've got your six. You can do this."

"You're right. I can do this." Tessa squared her shoulders and marched toward her bedroom door. As she reached the threshold, she glanced over her shoulder at the man standing in the entryway.

He gave her a nod.

Tessa entered her bedroom, closed the door behind her and leaned against the cool wood panel. A rush of emotions washed over her. Allowing herself a couple minutes to fall apart, she shook from head to toe. Then she stood tall, willed steel into her spine, gathered her scrubs and underwear and headed into the adjoining bathroom. Maybe if she washed away the dirt from the trail, she'd feel more like herself—the cool, confident nurse who had it together.

Inside the bathroom, she grabbed the shower curtain, her heart hammering against the wall of her chest. Then she released the curtain and let go of a strangled laugh. As Irish had promised, no one was hiding in the shower or anywhere else in the house.

Feeling a bit ridiculous, Tessa stripped out of her workout clothes and stepped beneath the spray, letting the warm water wash away the grit and grime she'd acquired from rolling in the gravel along the river road. The bandage Irish had applied to her knee soaked off, allowing water to clean the scrape. It stung, reminding Tessa that she was alive, not left to die beside the river. She'd used her skills and brain to get herself out of the situation.

Squirting shampoo into her hands, she rubbed it into her scalp and rinsed. Then she put dab of bodywash on her loofa and scrubbed every inch of skin, erasing the feel of her attacker's hands on her body.

As the dirt from the trail washed down the drain,

Tessa thought about the man standing outside her bedroom door, waiting for her to finish dressing for work.

She'd thought about him on a number of days as he'd jogged by her. Tessa had wondered who he was and what his story was. At the very least, she knew he was honorable and that he would never do what the attacker had done. Call it a gut feeling, she knew Irish was a good man.

Determined not to take any more time than she had to, she rinsed off, applied conditioner to her hair and rinsed all over. After switching off the water, she climbed out of the shower and toweled dry.

She ran a brush through her wet hair then slipped into her undergarments and scrubs. The woman staring back at her from the mirror was the Tessa she knew and was familiar with, not the scared woman who'd entered the bathroom a few minutes before.

With little time to spare to get to work, and not wanting to keep Irish any longer than she had to, she pulled her hair back into a tight ponytail and wrapped the tail into a bun at the nape of her neck.

It was still wet, but that was okay. With the warm Texas weather, her hair would dry quickly.

She cast another glance at her reflection. With her hair pulled back from her face, the bruise on her temple was more apparent. She thought about applying concealer to the bruise, but that would take too much time.

She didn't care if people saw the bruise. Someone had attacked her. Wasn't it best for folks to know an attacker was out there so they could take precautions and not suffer her same fate or worse?

Tessa slipped into her shoes and left her bedroom. Irish had his back to her, staring out the front window of her cottage. He turned to see her standing there staring at him.

Heat rose up her neck, flooding her cheeks.

"Ready?" he asked.

She nodded. "Almost. I'd like to make a sandwich to take for lunch."

"Take your time. I called Trace. He said he'd get started feeding the animals."

Tessa grabbed her purse. "I can skip the sandwich. Let's get on the road. I've already taken up too much of your time. I don't want to hold you up any longer."

Irish smiled. "You're not holding me up. I promise." He tilted his head toward her kitchen. "Come on, let's make your sandwich. What do you usually have?"

She followed him into the kitchen. "I throw a bit of deli turkey, tomato and lettuce on a couple slices of bread. But peanut butter and jelly will hold me over a twelve-hour shift."

Irish shook his head. "No way. Come on, I'll make your sandwich." He headed for the refrigerator. "Everything in all the usual places?"

She nodded. "Yes. But I can make my own sandwich. You don't have to."

"Allow me." He opened the refrigerator and fished out the lettuce, tomatoes, turkey and mayonnaise.

Tessa tore off a paper towel and laid two slices of bread on top of it.

Irish quickly assembled the sandwich.

"I really am quite capable of making my own lunch," she said.

Irish grinned. "I get that. This gives me something to do and keeps me out of trouble."

"Can I get you some coffee?" she asked. "I'm making some for myself."

"Sure," he said. "I'd like that."

While she made coffee, he wrapped her sandwich in cellophane. They worked side by side in the small kitchen.

Tessa was surprised at how naturally they moved around each other. Her ex-husband would never have helped her make a sandwich for himself, much less her.

He'd never bothered to do anything around the house. The kitchen, especially, was woman's work and her responsibility. She'd been happy to work there. Randy rarely entered it, if only to grab a beer from the refrigerator.

Her husband had always found fault in everything Tessa did. Cooking had been one of Tessa's escapes, the kitchen a sanctuary from his criticism.

By the time Tessa had two steaming cups of coffee ready, Irish had the sandwich wrapped and tucked into her insulated lunch bad along with a package of potato chips.

She snapped lids on top of the travel mugs of coffee and handed Irish one of them.

He held out the lunch bag. "Ready?"

Tessa nodded. "Ready."

"Let's go," he said. "I'll follow you to the hospital."

"Really, you don't have to follow me. I can get there on my own. Nobody is going to attack me in a moving vehicle."

"Call me overly cautious," Irish said. "I want to see you all the way to the hospital and inside the door before I turn you loose." He frowned. "Humor me."

She gave him a weak smile. "I really do appreciate what you're doing for me. I should get my act together."

"Lady," Irish said, "your act is together. You're holding up better than any female I've known—or male, for that matter—after being attacked like you were."

They left the cottage together.

Irish locked the door and handed her the keys.

Irish escorted her to her SUV, opened the door and inspected the inside before he allowed her to get in.

Maybe it was overkill, but it made Tessa feel better, knowing there wasn't someone waiting to pounce on her. Eventually, she'd have to check her house and car on her own.

Tessa valued her independence and guarded it fiercely after she'd left Randy, knowing she'd be on her own. Now that she was safe from the man who'd verbally and physically abused her, she was exposed to others who might harm her, such as the one person who'd attacked her on the trail.

For six months, she'd lived in the bubble of the little town of Whiskey Gulch, going about her life, lulled into a sense of peace and belonging. Small towns were supposed to be safe, weren't they? After this morning, Tessa wasn't sure.

She slipped in behind the wheel of her SUV.

"Lock the door," Irish commanded from outside her window.

Tessa clicked the button. The lock snapped into place. She pulled the seat belt around her and clicked the buckle.

Had it really been only that morning since she'd been attacked? It felt like a day ago, or maybe a week...so much had happened in between. Now she was on her way to work, like any other day.

Tessa backed out of her driveway and pulled out onto the street.

Irish followed close behind, all the way to the hospital.

She pulled into her usual spot and waited while Irish parked his truck in the space next to hers and got out.

He came around his vehicle to open the door to her SUV.

"I think I can take it from here," she insisted.

He held out his hand. "Once you're inside the doors."

She sighed. "I hate that I feel like a toddler being dropped off at the day care."

He chuckled. "Not even close." Irish held out his arm for her and waited while she decided how far she was willing to take his protector side.

"I have to do this by myself," she said. "It's daylight. The parking lot is populated. I can get myself from my car to the building without any problem."

"Again," he said with a twist to his lips, "humor me. I feel better knowing that you're inside the hospital and safe."

Tessa clamped her lips shut to keep from arguing about his insistent involvement.

When they reached the entrance to the emergency room, the automatic doors opened and her coworker, Allison Wade, spotted her from where she sat at the administration desk.

"Tessa, sweetie." Allison hurried over, grabbed Tessa's arm and drew her through the entrance and into the ER lobby. "I heard about what happened." She scanned her from head to toe. "Are you all right?"

Tessa glanced over her shoulder at Irish and gave him a little wave. "How many people know?"

"We all heard." Allison led Tessa through the restricted doors and into the tiny break room. "Brian was on duty at the fire station when the call came out over the police scanner. He called me as soon as he knew it was you." Allison glanced toward the other nurses and doctors coming through the door.

"And Allison let us all know," said Dr. Slade, the ER doctor on duty.

Tessa guffawed. "Good news travels fast, doesn't it?"

"Good news?" Allison shook her head. "I was terrified for you."

Dr. Slade pulled out his pen light and shone it into Tessa's eyes. "That's a nasty bruise you have."

"I'm fine," Tessa said. "He hit me there."

The doctor winced. "We should do a thorough once-over to make sure you aren't missing anything."

"No, really, Dr. Slade. Everything is where it should be." Tessa held up her hands. "Other than the bruise and a few scrapes on my knees, I'm okay. I got away before he did any real damage."

"At least let me get an ice pack for that bruise." Allison headed for the supply cabinet.

"No, Allison," Tessa said, pushing through the crush of staff members. "We have work to do."

"Work, schmerk," Allison said. "I'm getting that ice pack." She led Tessa to the supply cabinet, grabbed a cool pack and pressed it to Tessa's face. "Here, hold that against your temple while I take care of a patient."

"Look," Tessa said. "I'm here to work. I'm perfectly capable of manning my shift. This little bruise on the side of my face is nothing."

"Yeah," Allison said. "And being attacked on a lonely road is nothing. I don't think so. I'd be terrified to leave my house."

Tessa couldn't refute Allison's words when she'd been afraid to go into her house, much less come back out. If it hadn't been for Irish, she might have been more hesitant to get back out…but she would have. Life went on. "Really," she said. "I'm okay." Her statement was as much for herself as for Allison.

Allison nodded. "Okay. But at least tell me who the hunk was who brought you to work. Tell me you got his number."

Tessa's cheeks heated. "That's Irish. He works out at Whiskey Gulch Ranch and runs every morning along the river, a little earlier than I do."

Allison grinned. "Do they have more hunks like him out at the ranch? Is Irish single? Tell me all."

"You have a boyfriend." Tessa shook her head. "What about Brian?"

Allison's grin widened. "Brian and I have been together so long, we could stand a little competition."

Tessa shrugged. "I really don't know much about Irish, other than he likes to jog in the morning."

"How did he end up following you to work?" Allison asked.

"He was at the sheriff's office when I came skidding in sideways after the attack. He's been with me ever since, just to make sure I'm okay."

Allison scrunched her nose. "He runs when you run? Are you sure he wasn't the one who attacked you?"

Tessa shook her head. "No way. He was already in town when I was still out jogging. Besides, the man who attacked me was heavier set than Irish and bigger around the middle."

Allison tipped her head. "I don't know. Irish is pretty tall and broad-shouldered."

Tessa's heart fluttered. "Yes, he is."

Allison took Tessa's hands. "If you need a place to stay for a few days, you can stay in my apartment. I have a spare bedroom you can sleep in until the guy is caught."

"Not necessary," Tessa said. "I have a can of Mace in my purse and a handgun in my nightstand."

Allison cocked an eyebrow. "And you know how to use both?"

"Damn right I do," Tessa responded.

"That's my girl." Allison hugged Tessa.

"All right," Tessa said. "Let's get to work."

Working helped settle her nerves…some. All day long, she looked over her shoulder and jumped when someone touched her arm. She studied every man she came into contact with, wondering if the attacker was walking among them.

Physically and emotionally exhausted by the end of her shift, she wasn't surprised her head throbbed and her back ached. She hadn't taken a break, afraid she'd think too much if she didn't stay busy.

"Hey, Tessa," Allison called out behind her as she organized another drawer of supplies.

Tessa turned. "Shouldn't you be on your way home?"

Allison glanced at the clock on the wall. "Yes. And so should you. The offer still stands. You can come home with me and stay until they catch your attacker."

Tessa shook her head. "I can't do that. We don't know when or if they'll find the guy. I'm sure you don't want me moving in with you indefinitely."

Allison shrugged. "I'm okay with that. Or I could move in with you. As long as you don't mind Brian coming over every night." She winked.

"Really, I'm all right. I'll be fine," Tessa said and closed the drawer she'd finished.

Allison stood with one fist perched on her hip. "Then why haven't you left yet?" She cocked an eyebrow.

Tessa sighed. "I needed to fix the supply cabinet and drawers. They were a mess."

"They're always a mess." Allison took her arm. "I'll follow you home, if it will make you feel better." She walked with her to the exit.

As the glass door slid open, a familiar face appeared on the other side.

Tessa's heart fluttered.

"Never mind," Allison murmured. "Your bodyguard has arrived."

Irish stood on the sidewalk outside the hospital, a grin on his face.

Tessa's cheeks filled with heat. "What are you doing here?"

His grin twisted. "Not a '*Gee, Irish, I'm so glad to see you*'?" He nodded toward Allison. "I'll take her from here."

Allison batted her eyes and smiled. "I'm sure she's in good hands." She let go of Tessa's arm and waved. "See you in the morning." And she left Tessa standing in front of Irish, feeling very much like she'd been cast adrift in a riptide.

Irish held out his hand. "Do you want to ride with me, or will you be driving your own car?"

She had to think before she could respond. The man made her head spin. Or was that the residual bump on her temple or the headache that had been nagging her all day? Whatever… "I'll drive mine," she told him. "But you don't—"

He held up his hand. "You might want to save it. I'm following you, either way."

Tessa let out a breath. She wouldn't admit aloud that she was glad to see him and going home wasn't nearly as scary with Irish watching her six.

So much for being an independent divorcée.

Chapter Four

Irish had spent the day worrying about Tessa. He hadn't liked leaving her side, even though she'd been at the hospital all day, surrounded by people.

With her attacker at large, Tessa wasn't safe. He might already be plotting his next opportunity to surprise her when she least expected it.

He escorted Tessa to her SUV and held the door for her.

"Thank you," she said as she slid into the driver's seat.

He grinned. "My pleasure."

After he closed her door, he hurried to his truck and waited for her to pull out onto the street.

The drive to her house didn't take long. His plan was to stay with her as long as she'd let him. The woman was hardheaded and determined to handle the situation on her own. He'd brought reinforcements to help his cause.

Dinner.

Tessa pulled into her driveway and parked.

He wished her little cottage had a garage she could park in and close the door before she got out of her vehicle. Then again, anyone determined enough could slip into the garage as she closed the door. Then she'd be trapped in the garage with him, and no one would know.

Irish studied the location, not liking it at all. Hers was the last house on the street with an empty lot across from her. The one house on the other side appeared to be closed up and the one diagonal from hers had a For Sale sign out front.

From what he could tell, she was alone on her street. If she screamed for help, no one would hear.

All the more reason to stay, Irish told himself.

Not that she'd let him.

Thus the pizza he'd ordered before he left the Whiskey Gulch Ranch and picked up on the way through town. Who could resist a pizza with all the best toppings?

His mouth watered at the scent of cheese, tomato sauce and pepperoni. If she didn't like all the fixin's, he had the backup. A chicken salad with several choices of dressings—chicken on the side in case she was vegan.

He'd borrowed a chick flick from Rosalyn Travis, his boss's mother.

The longer he could convince Tessa to let him stay, the better he'd feel. The thought of leaving her alone made his skin crawl.

Irish climbed out of his truck, grabbed the pizza, salad and video, and met Tessa as she exited her vehicle. "I don't suppose you like pizza and salad?"

She lifted her nose and sniffed. "Pepperoni?"

He nodded. "And everything else but anchovies."

She closed her eyes and her lips slipped into a smile. "Sounds amazing."

"Rosalyn Travis sent a romantic comedy movie. Said something about cheering you up." So, it was a little lie. The movie had been Irish's idea. He'd asked Mrs. Travis for a funny chick flick that would help take Tessa's mind off the attack.

"That was very thoughtful of her." Tessa closed her SUV door and pressed the lock button on her key fob. The locks clicked in place. "Please tell her thank you. She's always so kind when I run into her in town."

"I think she's adopted all of us as her children. Her husband's death was pretty hard on her."

"Having Trace home from the military seems to have made a difference."

Irish nodded. "He's a good guy. Always had our backs when we deployed."

Tessa walked toward the cottage, her key in hand. "Everyone in town was surprised to learn that Matt Hennessy was Mr. Travis's son from a previous relationship before he married Rosalyn."

"No more surprised than Matt and Trace."

"How's that co-ownership of the Whiskey Gulch Ranch going?"

"Matt and Trace are great to work for." Irish shook his head. "They couldn't be more different, and yet have the same philosophies and values." He balanced the pizza box in one hand. "If you'll unlock the door, I'll clear the interior before you go in."

Thankfully, she didn't argue this time. The dark circles beneath her eyes told the story. She was too tired to argue.

Carrying the pizza, salad and movie, Irish entered the cottage, senses on alert. In minutes, he'd checked the premises and was back at the front door for Tessa. "All clear."

"Good, because I'm starving and my mouth is watering for that pizza."

Irish held the door as Tessa entered and set her purse on the table in the small foyer.

"I put the pizza on the counter in the kitchen. You can have the whole thing by yourself. If you feel all right with me staying for a bit, I'd love to join you." He smiled. "Your choice. I don't want to crowd you."

"It's your pizza," she said. "You should stay and eat it. Unless you need to leave, in which case, I'd love to grab a slice before you go."

"I'm kind of new in town. I don't have anywhere else I have to be." He closed and locked the door. "Point me to the paper plates."

"All the animals are fed?" Tessa entered the kitchen and pulled plates from the cabinet.

"All fed. The stalls have been mucked and I even had time to shower." He winked. "I hear some women love the earthy scent of horse manure." He shrugged. "I don't get it. But whatever melts their butter."

Tessa laughed. "Thank you for showering. I, for one, prefer to eat without the earthy scent of horse manure mixing with the delicious aroma of pizza sauce and cheese."

Irish opened the pizza box and stood back for her to choose first. "Then I made a wise choice and we have something else in common."

"And what do we have in common?" she asked as she selected a slice of pizza.

"We like pepperoni and jogging in the morning."

Her hand holding the pizza stopped halfway to her mouth.

Irish could have kicked himself for bringing up the subject of jogging. He was there to help her *forget* about the incident, not to remind her. At least for a little while. "I'm sorry. I shouldn't—"

She shook her head. "No. Don't. I have to get back out

there and jog again. I don't want my running to be the trigger that makes me afraid to get outside. I worked too hard to get to the point I am to let the…assault…set me back." She squared her shoulders and took a bite of the pizza. "Mmm." Her eyes closed for a moment and her face appeared euphoric. "So good."

Irish almost choked on the bite of pizza he'd taken at the same time.

Her moans and the way her chest rose and fell made him think of other things that could make a woman moan and breath heavily besides eating pizza.

His groin tightened and he fought to swallow the wad of pizza at the back of his throat. When it caught instead, he coughed.

Tessa set her pizza on a plate and pounded his back. "Do I need to perform the Heimlich maneuver?"

Tears ran from his eyes as he shook his head. "Wrong pipe," he managed to choke out.

She pulled a beer from the refrigerator, twisted off the top and handed it to him. "Wash it down."

He took the bottle and upended it, sluicing the pizza down his throat. When he could breathe again, he sighed. "Thank you." He checked the bottle and grinned. "We have another thing in common…we like the same beer."

She smiled. "Good." Tessa got another beer from the fridge, opened it and took a long swallow. "I don't like drinking alone."

"That's why you have me here," Irish said. "With pizza, salad and a movie guaranteed to make you laugh, what more could you ask for?"

"Peace of mind. Never being attacked again. Never having to worry whether I'll live to see another day?"

She carried her plate and beer into the living room and sat on one end of the sofa.

Irish shoved the salad into the refrigerator and followed Tessa into the living room with his plate of pizza and the movie. "That's pretty heavy thinking."

"Which could lead to some pretty heavy drinking." She took another sip of her beer and stared at the bottle. "But I need a relatively clear head in case he comes back to finish what he started." Tessa set the bottle on the coffee table and took another bite of pizza.

Irish held up the movie. "Ready for some entertainment to get your mind off less pleasant musings?"

Tessa nodded. "Sure." She rose and took the movie from him.

When their hands touched, a spark of electricity zipped through Irish.

A soft gasp escaped Tessa's lips.

Irish glanced up.

Tessa's eyes flared. She jerked the movie from his grasp and clutched it to her breast. Without uttering a word, she spun, darted to the television, and fumbled to open the movie's case.

Once she had the disc in the player, she grabbed her plate and carried it to the kitchen.

"You're not done, are you?" Irish asked.

"No," she said. "I'm going back for more."

More.

That's exactly what Irish wanted. More.

But not pizza.

Music poured from the speaker and the movie introductions flashed on the screen.

Tessa, with her plate and a second slice of pizza, settled on the other end of the couch. Just out of Irish's reach.

That was probably for the best. If Tessa sat too close, Irish would be tempted to put his arm around her and pull her close. He blamed the urge to hold her on his need to protect her, nothing else.

But that wasn't the truth. He'd been drawn to this woman with the athletic build, strawberry-blond hair and gray-blue eyes since the first day he'd come across her jogging the river trail. She'd flashed him a shy smile and kept running.

That smile had made his day when he'd been so new in town. She'd warmed him with the simple gesture and made him think of Whiskey Gulch as home.

Which was what he'd wanted all along. A place to call home. He'd left the military to start a new life. Actually, to start living a normal life, where he wasn't gone from home the majority of the year and he could come home to dinner most nights.

Granted, he came home to an empty apartment and frozen dinners unless Rosalyn Travis invited him to eat with their family. Rosalyn, with her son's fiancée could cook up a helluva a meal, enough to feed an army, if needed.

And Irish repaid them by volunteering to wash dishes and occasionally grill steaks in the backyard.

Tessa adjusted the volume on the movie to a low, steady hum they could hear without being blasted out of the small living room.

Irish found himself watching Tessa more than the movie, wanting to know more about this woman who'd fought her way free of an attacker. He was impressed.

Irish's lips quirked. "Your self-defense lessons really paid off."

She glanced his way and nodded.

"Why did you think Whiskey Gulch would be such a rough place to live you'd need lessons on how to defend yourself in order to live here?"

Tessa's gaze shifted from him to the wall and she shrugged. "I had my reasons."

"Were you worried about anyone besides your ex-husband?" Irish leaned forward. "Perhaps we should start by questioning him."

Tessa disagreed, telling him, "No, I wasn't worried about anyone here. Otherwise, I would have been more aware and watchful during my morning runs."

"A woman can't be too careful these days," Irish said.

"Especially when the one hitting her is someone she knows," Tessa murmured.

"Sadly, that's true." Irish's hands clenched into fists, anger burning deep in his chest.

"It's not important." Tessa didn't look his way. Her gaze remained firmly on the romantic comedy neither one of them had been watching.

"It sure as hell is!" Irish exclaimed. "If your ex-husband did this, he needs to be stopped. Did you tell the sheriff about him? He might be the one who attacked you today."

"I doubt it," Tessa said. "He works and lives in San Antonio."

"And you know he's in San Antonio? It's only a couple of hours away by road. Faster if he flies."

She waved her hand. "He wouldn't take the time to come after me. And I have a restraining order against him. He only hit me when it was convenient for him to do so."

Irish snorted. "When is it ever convenient to hit a woman?"

"When you're married to her?" Tessa chose that moment to look at Irish. "He was my husband. He thought he had every right to hit me."

Irish's hands clenched into fists. "No man has the right to hit any woman," he said through gritted teeth.

Tessa's lips formed a firm line and she lifted her chin. "I came to the same conclusion. After he put me in the hospital, I filed for divorce, took self-defense classes and then moved home to Whiskey Gulch. I couldn't get far enough, fast enough."

"Oh, Tessa…" Irish reached across the gap between them and took her hand. "I'm sorry."

"For what?" She stared down at his hand holding hers but didn't pull it free. "You didn't hit me."

"I'm sorry that you went through that and then had it happen to you again this morning." He lifted her hand and pressed his lips to the backs of her knuckles. "I wish I'd been there for you. If I'd been a few minutes later…"

"Or if I'd been a few minutes earlier." She curled her fingers around his. "He might have waited for another day, another time and caught me just as unaware." Tessa squeezed his hand and let go. "The point is… I'm okay. Now, I'm aware and it won't happen again." She pushed to her feet. "I'm tired and need to get some sleep before my shift tomorrow."

Irish rose. "And our jog before that?"

"And our jog before that," she agreed with a smile.

"I don't like leaving you alone."

"I've been alone since I got back to Whiskey Gulch. I know what to do to stay safe."

"I get that you need your independence, but I'm worried that jerk will come back."

"I'll leave all the lights on, have my gun beneath my pillow and my Mace with me as well." She gave him a tight smile. "I've got this."

"And you want me to get out of your hair." He dipped his chin. "Gotcha. You have my phone number. If you hear anything go bump in the night, call me. I don't care if it's a cat dumping over your trash can…call me." He glanced around the small living room. "Do you mind if I check all the window and door locks?"

Tessa waved a hand. "Knock yourself out."

Irish made quick work of testing all the locks on the windows and the back door. He stopped in the front entryway. "You're all set. If you want me to stay, I can camp out on the couch. I've slept in worse places."

She shook her head. "I'm going to be fine. I'm prepared."

"I'd feel better if you had a dog," he said. "A big dog. With sharp teeth."

She chuckled. "I'd be more afraid the dog would attack me than a person breaking and entering." Tessa smiled. "I'd hate to shoot the dog. I wouldn't hesitate to shoot the person."

"Okay, then. If you really don't need me…"

"I don't." Tessa opened the front door.

Irish had no other choice but to leave. He couldn't help someone who didn't want to be helped. "I'll see you in the morning." He leaned forward and brushed her forehead with his lips. "I hope you sleep. You can call me if you just want company."

"Thanks. I appreciate all you've done for me today. I can't keep taking advantage of you."

"I wouldn't offer if I didn't care." He backed out the front door. "I'll stay until I hear the lock click," he said.

She nodded. "Good night, Irish."

"Good night." He stood on the front porch while she closed and locked the door.

For a long moment, he continued to stand there, not wanting to leave her alone.

The darkness surrounding the cottage seemed to hold infinite possibilities, none of which Irish liked. Tessa's attacker could be in the shadows at that very moment, waiting for Irish to leave so that he could make his next move. He'd get motion-sensor floodlights and install them the next day.

Irish forced himself to turn, walk down the steps and climb into his truck. He checked his cell phone to make sure it was on and the volume was turned up in case it rang and Tessa had changed her mind and invited him to come in and stay the night.

The phone didn't ring and Tessa hadn't changed her mind.

For several minutes, Irish remained in his truck in Tessa's driveway, letting his vision adjust to the darkness. Nothing moved, not even a neighborhood cat.

He could stay in her driveway and sleep in the truck. Tessa wouldn't be happy. She'd been adamant about preserving her independence. After what her husband had done to her, he didn't blame her for wanting to take care of herself. Her ex hadn't done it for her. Why should she trust another man to keep her safe?

He started the engine and backed out of her driveway, his gut knotting the farther away from her he went.

He hoped and prayed she'd be all right. Driving back to the Whiskey Gulch Ranch, he second-guessed leaving her at least a dozen times. She had his number and there was always 9-1-1. She'd be all right.

Then why did Irish have that bad feeling he always got when something awful was about to happen?

Chapter Five

After Irish left, Tessa leaned against the door and drew in a deep breath. Had it really only been that morning that she'd been attacked? Her forehead still tingled over Irish's kiss. A fleeting thought whisked through her mind that she wished he'd kissed her lips instead.

Tessa pressed her fingers to her mouth. What would that have felt like? Why did she care? She wasn't in the market to find a husband replacement for the defective one she'd fought so hard to be done with.

Irish was different. He took the time to make sure she was all right. Randy never would have followed her from her home to work and back. He'd have expected her to get over whatever was bothering her so that she didn't inconvenience him in any way.

Not Irish. He was a gentleman. He'd brought pizza with no expectation of repayment in any form. The kiss on her forehead had been anything but passionate. Nevertheless, the gesture had sent heat rushing through her body, pooling low in her belly.

How she'd wanted him to kiss her lips.

Tessa moaned and pushed away from the door. The shine of his headlights through the front window announced Irish's departure.

For the first few months she'd been back in Whiskey Gulch, Tessa had struggled with loneliness. Her parents had been older when they'd had her and had passed away while she'd lived in San Antonio with Randy. Tessa was glad they hadn't known what Randy was doing to their only child. Everyone from Whiskey Gulch had assumed their marriage was a match made in heaven. The homecoming king and queen belonged together. They were perfect for each other.

Fortunately, her parents had insisted Tessa go to college. She had and majored in nursing. When she'd returned home, Randy had finished his finance degree from Texas A&M and come back to propose to her.

Fairy tale, right?

Wrong.

Her reality couldn't have been farther from the truth. From the day Tessa had said *I do*, Randy had considered her his property to do with as he pleased.

The honeymoon phase lasted a total of one month. They both got jobs and went to work. Tessa went to work for the ICU department of a major hospital. As the new nurse, she was assigned the night shift.

Randy worked during the day and expected her to have supper ready when he came home. He didn't care if she'd pulled a double shift. Dinner had to be ready or he'd shout at her, belittle her work and hit her if she talked back.

Yeah. Marriage hadn't been the happiest time of her life. She'd stuck with it because they hadn't seen each other much; she'd even volunteered for the night shift to avoid being at home with Randy as much as possible.

Even though Irish had gone around the house checking all the locks, doors and windows, Tessa made another pass once again checking all the latches on the windows, testing the doors to make sure nobody could get in. At each window, she stared out into the night. Every shadow that moved made her jump. The wind ruffling the branches of the trees became specters in the darkness.

She doubted she'd get much sleep that night. If she wasn't so afraid of actually going to sleep, she might consider taking a sleep aid. That wouldn't be good. All she needed was to be sound asleep because of a highly effective sleep aid and have somebody break into her house. She wouldn't wake in time to defend herself. Before morning, she could be raped and dead.

Not for the first time, she thought she needed a dog. A big dog. Or better yet, a bodyguard. One like Irish. Wasn't that what he'd said Travis was setting up? A security business. As in security of persons like her?

Tessa wondered what it would cost to hire a bodyguard. She snorted. As a one-income household, she could barely afford her mortgage payment and utilities. There was no way she had the funds to pay for a bodyguard. Not to mention, Irish hadn't asked to be her bodyguard. He had just assigned himself. For which Tessa was grateful.

When she was satisfied that all the doors and windows were secured, she headed for the bathroom, stripped out of her clothes and pulled on her favorite pajamas. No nightgown for her. If she needed to make a fast getaway, she wanted to make sure she was sufficiently covered.

Anger blossomed in her chest. She shouldn't have to worry about things like this. What kind of animal attacked a defenseless female?

The worst.

Tessa stretched out on her bed, fluffed her pillow and closed her eyes. As soon as she did, flashbacks of the man in the ski mask lunging out of the willow trees whipped through her brain. Her eyes popped open. Maybe she could fall asleep with them open. Yes, that's what she'd do, she'd fall asleep with her eyes open. For the next thirty minutes, she stared at the ceiling, straining to hear every noise. Every creak, every sound, in the house seemed amplified. When she couldn't take it anymore, she picked up her cell phone and dialed Irish's number.

He answered on the second ring. "Hey, beautiful. Miss me already?" he asked.

His warm tones washed over Tessa like a comforting blanket.

"No, I…" she stammered. "I must have accidently dialed you." She hated that she was lying. She hated worse that she felt she'd needed to.

"Having trouble going to sleep?" he asked.

"A little," she admitted.

"I can stay on the line until you go to sleep. I don't mind."

"Are you sure?" she asked.

"I wouldn't offer if I didn't mean it," he said.

"Thank you," she said, and lay there. She allowed her eyes to close. This time she didn't have a flash of her attacker but of Irish jogging toward her on the river trail.

"What shall we talk about?" he asked, his tone deep and rich.

She smiled. "I don't care. Anything."

"How 'bout what's your favorite football team?"

She laughed. "That's easy, the Texas Longhorns."

"No, no, no," he moaned. "You can't be a Longhorn fan."

"Why not?" she asked.

"We can't be together if you're a Longhorn fan, not when I'm an Aggie's supporter."

"That's too bad. And here I thought we were on to something between us. What about the NFL?" she countered.

"Okay, what's your favorite team on the NFL?" he asked.

"Denver Broncos."

He moaned again. "No, no, no, you're from Texas. You're supposed to like the Dallas Cowboys."

"You follow the Cowboys?" she asked.

He chuckled. "Yes, I do. Though they haven't been doing so well this season."

For the next thirty minutes, he talked about his favorite games, the different players, and the best commercials from the past five Super Bowl games.

None of it mattered in the grand scheme of things to Tessa. But just the fact that he was talking to her did. Before long, she was yawning and she must have been loud enough for Irish to hear.

"Are you ready to go to sleep?" he asked.

She nodded even though he couldn't see her. "Yes," she said.

"Sweet dreams, pretty lady," he said.

She smiled with her eyes closed. "Thanks for talking to me."

After the call ended, Tessa lay against the sheets, warm and comfortable, more from the tone of his voice than from the blankets covering her. Soon she drifted into a deep, dreamless sleep.

Seemingly seconds after she'd gone to sleep, the sudden sound of breaking glass jerked her awake. Tessa sat up straight in bed and reached for the gun she'd left lying on the nightstand. Her hands shaking, she flipped the safety switch off and aimed it toward the door. The crunch of broken glass in her kitchen made her slide out of her bed onto the floor on her knees, with the bed between her and the door. She fumbled in the dark for her cell on the nightstand and redialed Irish's number. She didn't know how long she'd been asleep. She prayed that he hadn't gone to sleep himself.

"Please answer," she muttered, "please answer."

Seconds later his voice came on the line. "Tessa, what's wrong?"

"Someone's in my house," she said, her voice low and shaky.

"I'm calling 9-1-1," Irish said. "I'll be there in two minutes. Stay on the line. I'm putting you on hold."

Her hand on the phone shook as she held it to her ear. In her dominant hand, she held her gun, aiming it toward the wooden panel of the door. Sure she knew how to fire the weapon, but normally she went to a gun range and her hands were steady. Right now, she was shaking so badly, she doubted she'd hit anything. Footsteps in the hallway alerted her to the fact that her intruder was headed toward her bedroom.

Two minutes was too long. This guy could get to her before Irish or the sheriff. Summoning enough courage, Tessa shouted, "I know you're there. I have a gun. I will shoot to kill!" The footsteps stopped in the hallway. "The sheriff's on his way."

The doorknob jiggled. Thanking God she'd thought to lock it before she'd gone to bed, Tessa did the only thing she could think to do.

She fired a shot.

It hit square in the middle of the door, going straight through and leaving a small hole.

The wail of sirens sounded in the distance, muffled by the walls of her house.

Again, the doorknob rattled and whoever was in her house kicked the door. By now she could hear the sirens much louder and getting closer. Where was Irish? He said two minutes. Hadn't it been five already? A horn blared over and over and over again. Getting closer and closer to her house. Footsteps in the hallway sounded, racing toward the kitchen. The intruder was on his way out the back. Tessa thought to go after him but thought again. All she needed was to confuse whoever was coming to help her. She might get herself shot by going after the intruder. She hunkered low behind the bed, the gun resting on top of the mattress in case the intruder returned. Her back door slammed open and the footsteps disappeared into the night. Seconds later, she heard pounding on the door.

"Tessa!" Irish's voice called out. "Tessa, open up and let me in."

She hesitated to answer. What if the intruder was waiting for whomever had come to her rescue? What if the intruder shot Irish? Tessa lurched to her feet and ran for her bedroom door, unlocked it and threw it open.

"Look out, Irish! He might still be out there," Tessa shouted. She ran down her hallway, holding her gun in front of her, ready to shoot anyone who stood in her way or who threatened to shoot Irish. When she reached the kitchen, her bare feet landed on a shard of glass and she cried out. A silhouette emerged in the open doorway to her kitchen. Ignoring the sharp pain in her foot, she leveled her gun at the chest of the man standing there in the darkness, her finger resting on the trigger.

"Don't shoot," Irish called out, holding up his hands.

"Oh, thank God." Tessa lowered her gun, a sob rising in her throat.

He flipped on the light switch. "Are you all right?"

She shook her head.

Irish glanced at the kitchen floor and cursed. In seconds, he started across the space between them, glass crunching beneath his boots. "Don't move," he said, his gaze going to her feet on the floor where blood pooled around her heel.

With a shaky laugh, she remained where she stood. "Don't worry. I'm not going anywhere."

When he reached her, he swept her into his arms and carried her into the living room, settling her on the couch. He laid his gun on the coffee table.

"Don't put your gun down. You've got my back," he said. "If anyone comes through that back door, shoot him."

She nodded and held her handgun in her hands, aimed toward the back door. The wail of sirens grew much louder as a sheriff's vehicle pulled into the yard, the lights flashing through the windows.

"I'm going to unlock the front door for the sheriff," he said. "You going to be okay right here?"

She nodded. Just having him in the same room was a relief.

Irish unlocked the front door, threw on the porch light and raised his hands. "Don't shoot," he called out. "I'm the one who called the sheriff's department. Search the perimeter, the intruder might still be around."

"Is Tessa okay?" a female voice called out. Tessa knew that voice. Deputy Dallas Jones, the only female deputy. She was almost as new to Whiskey Gulch as Tessa.

"We might need an ambulance," Irish told Dallas.

"No," Tessa said. "I'm okay. It's just a little cut. I can get to the hospital for stitches if I need them. But I don't need an ambulance."

"Are you sure?" Irish looked at her, his brow furrowed. "It's an awful lot of blood."

"I just need a pair of tweezers and a Band-Aid out of the bathroom in my bedroom. I'm a nurse. This is what I do."

"For other people," Irish pointed out. "You might have a hard time finding the glass in your own foot."

"Okay, I'll let you. If you don't mind? The tweezers are in a drawer in my bathroom. There's a first-aid kit under the sink. If you'll get those, I'd appreciate it."

Irish hurried through her bedroom and into her bathroom and was back in seconds, carrying the first-aid kit, tweezers, a damp washcloth, and a towel. He sat beside her on the couch, turned her to face him and lifted her foot to his lap. He bent over, studying her foot. With the tweezers, he gently extracted the piece of glass lodged in her skin.

"Sorry," he said.

"For what?" she asked.

"If I hurt you."

"I've been hurt worse," she said. "It's just a little cut. Put a Band-Aid on it. I'll be all right."

He washed her foot, gently removing all the blood, and applied a square of gauze and some medical adhesive tape to hold the gauze in place. "When it stops bleeding, I'll put a regular bandage on it. For now, you need a little extra pressure to stem the flow of blood."

"Now who's the nurse?" she asked with a smile.

He looked up into her eyes. "I've done this a time or two."

Her smile faded. "As Delta Force, I can imagine you did."

"We're trained in self-aid buddy care. If one of our guys gets hurt, we gotta be ready to assist until the medical staff gets there. We do have a medic on the team, too. Sometimes he's not close enough to stop the bleeding quick enough. And when you're in a battle, you just have to patch and go as quickly as possible."

She touched his hand on her foot. "Sounds intense, like something nightmares are made of."

He nodded. "I've had a few nightmares. I can imagine you're having a few of your own." He turned his hand over and captured hers in his.

Deputy Jones entered through the front door, a German shepherd at her side. "We searched the area. Whoever it is, is long gone. My dog didn't even pick up his scent. He must have got into a vehicle and driven away. We lost his scent pretty abruptly."

Once again, her attacker had gotten away. Tessa should have shot him when she'd had the chance. "Thank you for checking," she said.

The sheriff came through the door behind her. "Ms. Bolton, are you all right?"

She nodded. "Irish is taking care of me."

The sheriff grinned. "Then you're in good hands."

She squeezed Irish's fingers. "Yes, sir. I am." But how long could she rely on him to protect her? She couldn't afford a bodyguard and the man had a job at the Whiskey Gulch Ranch.

The sheriff had questions. While he asked them, Irish left the couch and went into the kitchen.

The sound of broken glass being cleaned up reached Tessa in the living room. "You don't have to do that," she called out.

Irish responded, "Yes I do. My mother taught me better."

The sheriff shook his head. "Let the man clean. How often do you get a man to clean your kitchen?"

Tessa almost said *never*. But that was her ex-husband Randy. Irish was a completely different man. And right then she was glad that it was Irish who'd come to help her. She valued her independence, but there was a limit to how independent she could be when somebody was breaking into her house.

For it to take Irish only two minutes to get to her, he could not have gone out to Whiskey Gulch Ranch. He must have stayed somewhere close by. For that, she was grateful. She didn't know what she would have done had that intruder broken through her bedroom door. She'd never shot someone before, but she wouldn't hesitate to do it if her life depended on it.

Chapter Six

As Irish cleaned up the glass in the kitchen, his chest tightened. The blood on the floor was only a fraction of what it could have been had her attacker gotten to her. He swept the glass into a dustpan and dumped it into the trash receptacle. With a damp mop, he cleaned the blood off the floor. The sheriff warned Irish not to touch the back doorknob or anything around the door so that they could dust for prints.

The sound of Tessa's voice in the other room as she spoke with the sheriff and the deputy reassured him she was going to be all right. The glass on the back door of the kitchen would have to be replaced. Or, better still, Irish would recommend that instead of glass she replace the door with something more solid.

Irish thanked his lucky stars that he hadn't gone back to Whiskey Gulch Ranch like he'd told her he would. He'd made it all the way to the other side of town before he'd applied the brakes and turned around. Instead of heading out to the ranch, he'd pulled into the parking lot of the local watering hole, Stew & Brew, figuring he could stay there until they closed somewhere around two in the morning.

Out at the ranch, he would have worried that cell phone

reception was spotty. If Tessa had tried to get hold of him out there, the call might not have gone through until it was too late for him to help. The distance to the ranch would have been detrimental as well. It would have taken him more than fifteen minutes to get to her house. As it was, he'd just stepped out of the bar, debating whether or not to bed down in his truck and sleep the night away in the parking lot, when he'd received her call. He'd driven like a bat out of hell to get to her before the attacker did, all the while dialing 9-1-1 to get the sheriff's deputies out there as well.

Once he'd arrived, he found her front door locked. When Tessa had screamed, Irish had nearly lost his mind. His heart had leaped into his throat and he'd run for the back door. When he'd come through the open door of the house to find her standing barefoot in the kitchen with a gun pointed at his chest, he couldn't help the relief he'd felt. Sure, she could have put a bullet through him, but she was alive.

He made quick work of the kitchen cleanup. Once he was finished, he got a glass out of the cabinet, filled it with ice and water and carried it into the living room where Tessa was still talking with the sheriff and deputy.

"We've done all that we can do here," the sheriff was saying. "Do you want me to leave Deputy Jones positioned outside your house for the night?"

"That won' be necessary," Irish said. "I'll be positioned outside the house for the remainder of the night, and every night until her attacker is apprehended." He turned to Tessa. "Unless Ms. Bolton would prefer to have two people watching her house through the rest of the night, one should do."

Tessa's gaze met his. She turned to the sheriff. "Irish

is right, having Deputy Jones here won't be necessary if Irish is staying. I won't need somebody else standing guard. Besides, I'm sure Deputy Jones has plenty of other areas that she needs to patrol tonight."

The sheriff nodded. "As you wish. We'll be back in the daylight to see if we can find any evidence that your intruder might have left behind."

"Thank you, Sheriff Barron. And thank you, Deputy Jones. I appreciate you coming out so quickly."

The sheriff shook his head. "I wish we had more to go on. One thing's for sure, you're definitely being targeted. This was his second attempt to get you."

Irish had had the same thought. The attack on River Road could have been an attack of convenience. But he was almost sure the break-in tonight had been committed by the same perp. It was personal. He wanted Tessa. No one else.

"I'm worried about you being out here all by yourself," the sheriff said.

Tessa shook her head. "I'll be fine."

Irish said, "I'll make sure she's protected."

"Then we'll be going," the sheriff said. "I'm glad you're okay, Ms. Bolton." He and Deputy Jones left the house.

Irish stood at the door waiting for the sheriff and the deputy's vehicle lights to disappear down the end of the road. Then he turned to Tessa. "Do you have a sheet of plywood or something that I could use to cover the back window on the door in the kitchen?" he asked.

She shrugged. "The house came with a shed in the back. I'm not sure exactly what's out there other than the lawn mower. There might be some spare wood."

His lips twisted. "You wouldn't happen to have a hammer and some nails as well, would you?"

Again she shrugged. "I really don't know. I haven't had to do any repairs since I've been here, and I haven't been here that long. I bought this house from a retired couple who moved back to San Antonio to be closer to their daughter. I don't think Mr. Fellows took everything out of his shed when he and his wife moved out. You might find some tools and supplies in there. Let me get a flashlight." Tessa pushed to her feet and winced when her foot hit the floor.

Irish's lips pressed into a thin line. "You stay put. I'll take care of this."

She shook her head. "I have to get used to walking on that foot 'cause I have to work tomorrow."

Irish frowned. "Can't you call in sick?"

"No," Tessa said. "They're already shorthanded. I need to be there, even if I'm limping."

"Well, you don't have to be on your feet now. Just sit there. I'll take care of this. And have your gun ready." He moved her handgun closer to her on the coffee table.

"I'm not sure where my flashlight is," Tessa said. "I think it's in one of the drawers in the kitchen. The one closest to the refrigerator."

Irish went to the kitchen and rummaged through the drawer next to the refrigerator, finding a small flashlight that would do little to help him locate any of the supplies he needed. Leaving the kitchen, he went back through the living room and out the front door.

"Where are you going?" Tessa asked.

"Out to get a real flashlight," he said.

He located his large flashlight behind the seat of his

truck. He kept it there in case he broke down along the side of the road.

Flashlight in hand, he rounded the side of the house and hurried to where the shed sat in the far corner of the yard.

Inside the shed, Irish didn't find plywood, but he found a couple of boards and a container of nails. And he was lucky enough to locate a hammer in one of the drawers. He carried the boards, the nails and hammer back to the house and went to work covering the hole left on the back door, hammering away to accomplish the task. When he was done, he went inside, locked the door, and walked through to the living room area where Tessa sat on the couch.

"It's not pretty, but it will do for the night," he said. "Tomorrow, I will go to the hardware store and look for a new door."

"Thank you," Tessa said. "I'd do it myself but I'm gonna be at work." She tipped her head to the side. "But won't that make you late for your job?"

Irish shook his head. "I spoke with Trace. He's all for me sticking with you until we figure out who's attacking you. I told you, he has a security business startup and this is right up his alley as far as what he had in mind for us to do."

Tessa frowned. "I don't have the kind of money it takes to hire a personal bodyguard," she said. "I barely have enough money to make the payments on this house and the utilities."

Irish held up his hands. "Don't worry about it. Trace inherited enough money to allow him to take all cases, whether they could pay or not."

Tessa drew in a breath and let it out. "I hate this."

Irish nodded. "I do, too."

"I went from feeling safe and secure in my own home, to not having a place I can go and feel safe."

"I get that," Irish said. "If it makes you feel any better, I'll be right outside in my truck. If you need me, all you have to do is yell. I'll hear you. Do you want help getting back to your bedroom?"

She shook her head and stood, trying not to put too much weight on her injured foot. "I think I'll be all right. If I just put my weight on the ball of my foot, I won't hit the spot where the glass cut my heel."

"In that case, follow me to the door, if you can, and lock it behind me when I go out," he said. He started for the front entrance.

Tessa followed. "Are you sure you're going to stay all night in your truck?"

He chuckled. "Trust me. It's a lot more comfortable than a foxhole." He cupped her face. "I'm sorry this is happening to you. But I'll do my best to take care of you and make sure that nothing else happens again."

She leaned into the palm of his hand. "It's not your fault," she said. "You weren't the one who attacked me," Tessa said.

Still," he said, "no one deserves this."

"True. It shouldn't happen. But it does all too often," Tessa said. "Thank you for being here for me."

Irish brushed his lips across her forehead. "Don't forget to lock the door behind me," he said and stepped out onto the porch.

"Irish," she called out.

He turned. His gaze captured hers. "I'll only be a few steps away. All you have to do is call my name, yell, whistle—anything to get my attention."

She shook her head. "You can't sleep in your truck. You're a big guy. You'd be too uncomfortable."

"I'll be fine. Just being close will ease my mind." He turned again. "Don't forget to lock the door."

"Irish," she said with a sigh. "Come back inside. You can sleep on the couch."

He turned to face her. "I don't want to make you uncomfortable. I'm only here to make sure that you're safe. The truck will be fine for me."

"I would feel more comfortable having you inside the house rather than out in your truck," Tessa said. "Please, come back inside."

Irish entered the house, closed the door and locked it. "If at any time you feel uncomfortable with me being inside the house with you, let me know. That truck is just fine with me."

Tessa smiled. "After all you've done for me? I'm not afraid of you, Irish. Everything you've done has been to help not, hurt me. Besides, I would feel really bad if you got a crick in your neck or threw your back out because you slept in your truck. The couch is surprisingly comfortable. I think you'll be all right on it. And I'll feel safer knowing you're just a few steps away." She limped into the hallway and came back out with a blanket and a pillow.

"Help yourself to anything in the kitchen. I have deli meat in the refrigerator and bread in the pantry. You can make a sandwich. I even have some leftover spaghetti, if you're hungry for more of a meal."

"Thanks," he said. "I had a hamburger at the bar. But if you feel like having a sandwich or some spaghetti, I'd be happy to fix it for you."

She shook her head. "No, I'm ready to get some sleep.

I have an early morning and its almost that time now. Thanks for being here. Good night."

"Good night, Tessa," Irish said.

Tessa limped into her bedroom and closed the door behind her. A moment later, she cracked it open just a bit.

Irish stretched out on the couch and leaned back against the pillow. He could see Tessa's door from where he lay and took comfort knowing that nobody would get past him to her without him putting up a fight first. He linked his hands behind his neck and closed his eyes.

Sleep didn't come until the wee hours of the morning, and he was up again at sunrise. Until they caught the attacker, he would be with Tessa every minute of the day except for when she was at the hospital working. Even then, he considered asking the hospital staff if he could follow her around to make sure she wouldn't be ambushed in some dark corner.

He suspected Tessa would be resistant to him intruding on her work. *Baby steps,* he told himself. He'd take baby steps to make sure that she would be all right.

Irish had coffee ready and scrambled eggs cooking in a small skillet when Tessa limped into the kitchen dressed in scrubs. He hoped that this day would be a lot better for her than the day before.

"Good morning, sunshine," he said.

She inhaled deeply, closing her eyes. "Is that coffee I smell?"

He nodded. "Sure is. Wanna cup?"

"I'd love a cup." She pinched the bridge of her nose. "I feel like my eyelids are sandpaper today."

"That's understandable," he said. "You maybe got three hours of sleep last night."

"I'm sure you didn't get much more than that," she said.

"I got enough." He poured coffee into a mug and handed it to her. "I'm sure you know where the sugar and milk are, if you need it."

"Black's good for me," she said. "Anything to wake me up. It's gonna be a long day at the hospital."

Irish scraped the scrambled eggs out of the pan onto a plate. "I wish you'd really consider calling in sick. That foot's going to make it a miserable day for you."

She sighed. "I can't. I'm too new at this job. I have to be there. Besides, I can put a little bit of weight on it today. It's tender, but I can do this."

"You are one determined lady," Irish said.

"I have to be to make it in this world," she said. "There's no such thing as a free ride."

He laid the plate of scrambled eggs on the table. "Have a seat. Your eggs are ready." The toast popped up and he removed the two slices. He laid once piece on her plate and one on the plate he had for himself on the counter. He went back to work cracking eggs into the pan.

Tessa sat at the table. "So, you're good with animals. You're good with a gun. And now you're proving to be good in the kitchen. What else I know about you, Irish?"

"My mom and dad both had full-time jobs when I was growing up, and I'm the oldest and have two younger sisters I had to take care of. Getting them ready to go to school, getting them off the bus and watching them after school was my job. I'm handy in the kitchen out of necessity. I can braid hair, and I make a good guest at a tea party." He gave her a side-eyed glance. "I trust you won't tell the guys. I'd never hear the end of it."

She grinned and held up her hand as if swearing in court. "Your secret is safe with me."

"Glad to hear it." He scraped eggs onto his plate, carried the plate over to the table and sat down across from her.

"I'm surprised some woman hasn't snapped you up. With those qualifications, you're a great catch." Tessa took a bite out of her eggs and looked over her plate at him.

Irish shook his head. "The timing was never right. As long as I was with Delta Force, the army owned me. My first allegiance was to the military. Any relationship with a woman would have taken second place. It wouldn't have been fair." He looked across the table at her. "But you were married. No children?"

She pushed her eggs around the plate with her fork. "I wanted children," she said. "My ex didn't. The world seemed to revolve around him. He couldn't have handled the competition a child would bring into a relationship." She lifted one shoulder. "It's just as well. When he started hitting me, I knew that would be no way to raise a child. I'm really glad we didn't have children."

"Have you given up on the idea of children?" Irish asked.

Tessa's gaze shifted to the window. "I don't know. I'm not anxious to get back into a relationship. Apparently, I have bad taste in men. Who's to say I wouldn't choose unwisely again? And I couldn't bring a child into a world where his father is an abuser."

Irish reached across the table and took her hand. "Not

all men are like your ex-husband," he said. "And you were young when you married him. You couldn't have known that he was an abuser until he actually started hitting you."

"I should have known," Tessa said. "He was always very self-centered. He got a big head from being the captain of the football team and homecoming king. He could do no wrong. I was a cheerleader. He was a quarterback. It was a foregone conclusion that we would marry, even though we went our separate ways in college. We knew we'd end up married when we graduated. And we did."

Irish squeezed her hand. "What happened?"

She stared down at where their hands were linked. "I think the stress of his job made him angry. And he took that anger out on the only person he had available. Me. I know all men aren't the same. But having survived a bad relationship, I'm not eager to get into another anytime soon." Tessa released his hand, finished her eggs and carried her plate to the sink, limping all the way. "I'll be at the hospital all day, so I won't need you to protect me. I'll have people all around me and I promise not to leave the hospital until I get off work."

"Are you sure you'll be all right by yourself? Even in the hospital?" he asked.

"I'm usually very busy, and rarely alone. There are always people around me." She smiled. "Besides, I'm sure the horses miss you and want you to be there to feed them."

"I have backup at Whiskey Gulch Ranch. They're not completely reliant on me to take care of the animals."

Tessa held up a hand. "I promise I'll be okay. You can spend the day out there."

He finished his breakfast and carried his plate to the

sink, rinsing it and putting it in the dishwasher along with hers. "I would like to take care of that back door for you. But I can do that after I take care of the animals out at the ranch."

She smiled. "Good. I didn't want to disrupt your day any more than I have to."

He took her hands in his. "You are not disrupting my day. When I'm not with you, I'm worried about you. I'll be there when you get off work. You get off at the same time every day, don't you?"

She nodded. "I do. As long as there's not anything major going on in the hospital. Sometimes I have to pull a second shift. I'll let you know with a phone call or text message if that happens."

"Fair enough. I'll be there when you come out of the hospital to ensure you make it safely to your car and then to your home."

She smiled. "Thanks. All I have to do now is brush my teeth and I'll be ready to go. I have an extra toothbrush in the guest bathroom if you care to use it."

"Thanks, and when I'm out at the ranch, I'll be sure to grab my shaving kit. Until they catch that guy, I prefer to stay here with you. I hope you don't mind."

She shook her head. "After last night? No, not at all. I'm glad you're here."

"Good. I thought I was going to have to fight you again today."

She grinned. "Not today."

They went to their separate bathrooms. Irish found the spare toothbrush package and a small tube of toothpaste. He brushed his teeth and washed his face. Afterward, he rubbed his hand across the roughness of his beard and studied his reflection in the mirror. It would have to do for now. When he got out to the ranch, he'd grab what he needed and bring it back with him. In the meantime, he had to get Tessa to work on time.

She came out of her bedroom slinging her purse over her shoulder. "Ready?"

He nodded. "You could ride with me, you know. If I'm following you home from work, it just doesn't make sense that we ride in separate vehicles."

She shook her head. "If it's all the same to you, I'd prefer to drive my own car. Just in case something comes up and you don't get there on time."

He gave her a stern look. "I'm serious about not leaving the hospital without me there."

She drew in a deep breath. "I really like having my own vehicle."

"Fair enough. I'll follow you. You lead the way."

With her key in hand, she stepped through the door and waited for him to come out and close it behind him. She locked the door behind both of them and handed him the key. "You'll need that to work on the back door."

Irish pocketed the key and followed her out to her SUV. He checked the back seat before she got in. Once he was sure that there was nobody in it, she got in, cranked her vehicle, and he got in his truck and followed her to the hospital. Once there, he escorted her inside like the he'd done the day before.

She turned and waved. "I can handle it from here."

He stepped back, letting the sliding glass doors close. He didn't like leaving her, even for a moment. But she was right. There were a lot of people around her in the hospital. And she wouldn't be alone at any time during the day.

Irish went back to his truck and sat there for a few

moments watching the vehicles in the parking lot. The people going in and out. Suspicious of everyone. No one looked like a murderer as far as he could tell. When he could sit there no longer, he started the engine. He had work to do, so he headed out to the ranch, hoping that Tessa would be okay that day. When he came back into town, he would stop at the sheriff's office and see if they'd made any headway on finding out who had attacked Tessa.

Chapter Seven

Tessa entered the ER that morning like any other day, except that she was limping. And she'd barely slept because she'd had an intruder in her house. Yeah, it wasn't like every other day. She made it past the admissions desk and into the restricted area before being accosted by her coworker.

Allison was emerging from an examination room when she spotted her. "Tessa! Girl. That's it. You *have* to come stay with me."

Tessa grimaced. "I take it you've heard."

"Heard? Hell!" she exclaimed. "Everyone in the hospital has heard." Allison frowned. "And you're limping. What the hell? He hurt you, didn't he?"

Tessa shook her head. "Not actually. I was chasing him out the back door when I stepped on the glass from the broken window in my kitchen."

Allison winced. "Ouch. Come here, let's have a look at that foot." She led Tessa into an empty exam room and made her sit on the bed.

"I'm really okay," Tessa said. "We cleaned the wound, applied some antibiotic ointment and put a pressure dressing on it. It should be okay."

"I'll be the judge of that," Allison said and removed

Tessa's shoe and sock. "Nice dressing," she said. "The EMT do this?"

"No." Heat rushed up Tessa's neck into her cheeks. "Irish did."

Allison glanced up from Tessa's foot. Her eyebrows rising.

Tessa groaned. "Now don't go reading anything into that. He was the first on the scene. I called him as soon as the intruder broke the glass in my kitchen door."

Allison smirked. "So you called Irish first instead of 9-1-1?"

"It was the last number keyed into my phone. What can I say? It was easiest just to hit Redial."

Allison nodded with a quirky lift to the corner of one side of her mouth. "Uh-huh. You sure it wasn't that he was staying the night there?"

Tessa shook her head. "Contrary to what you might think, I'm not ready for that kind of a relationship."

Allison sighed. "You really do need to get out and date. Not all men are like your ex."

"I know," Tessa said. "And Irish is nothing like Randy. It's just that I'm trying to get used to liking myself. I need to learn to trust my own judgment again. I thought Randy was perfect for me, until I married him."

"High school relationships aren't always an indicator of a lifetime relationship," Allison said.

Tessa snorted. "Like you're an example? You and Brian have been together for how long now?"

Allison grinned. "Since eighth grade. But he's the exception to the rule," she said. "He's always been and always will be a gentleman. He never forgets my birthday and never forgets Valentine's Day. He never forgets the first day we kissed. Even when he was deployed for fourteen months, he managed to get a box of chocolates and flowers to me for Valentine's Day. He'd arranged with one of the florists in the town where we were stationed to have them delivered so I wouldn't miss out."

"Now why couldn't Randy have been like that? Although, gifts aren't what count. What really mattered was that he never displayed any of the little things that indicated true love."

Allison gave a gentle smile. "Like reaching for your hand for no reason at all?"

Tessa nodded.

Allison sighed and pressed her hands to her chest. "Or opening the door for you when your hands are full of groceries?" She grinned. "Or insisting that that he bring in all the groceries since you did all the shopping."

"No," Tessa said. "He doesn't have to. A good man shows his love in everything he does for his woman."

Allison gave Tessa a secret little smile. "Like sticking around town when he doesn't have to? Or being there as soon as he can when your house is broken in to? And dressing your wound like a professional?"

Tessa rolled her eyes. "And we're back to Irish, I take it?"

Allison nodded. "He is rather a hunk."

Tessa couldn't deny that. The man had broad shoulders, thickly muscled arms, a narrow waist and hips, and tight thighs. She would never forget the sculptured thighs. She'd admired him on more than one occasion. Tessa shook her head. "He was just being nice, and now I understand that he has also been assigned to me by his friend Trace Travis to be my personal bodyguard."

Allison's eyebrows shot up. "Seriously?"

Tessa nodded. "Trace Travis is setting up some kind

of security firm and hiring some of his military buddies to man it."

Allison removed the bandage on Tessa's foot. "And here I thought Irish was a simple ranch hand."

Tessa chuckled. "Irish is anything but simple. You know the man was Delta Force, right?"

"I had heard that he was prior military," Allison said. "But Delta Force? Wow. Those guys are the best of the best, aren't they?" Allison looked down at the bandage she had pulled away. "I guess that explains why he is so good at dressing a wound. Those guys have to be able to do that kind of thing out in the field." Allison glanced around. "So, if he's your bodyguard, where is he?"

"I told him I didn't need him while I was at the hospital. I have plenty of people around me to keep me safe."

"I hope you're right," Allison cautioned. "Just make sure that you're around folks all of the time. No darting into janitor's closets or dark rooms by yourself."

"I'll be all right. The people at the front desk don't let just anybody back here in the restricted area," Tessa said.

Allison shook her head. "True. However, someone who has the nerve to break into your house to attack you might consider that a challenge he can't resist."

Tessa's mouth formed a thin line. "Trust me. Now that I know he is specifically after me, I will remain ultra-aware of everything around me."

Allison studied Tessa's heel. "Looks like your wound is going to be all right. There's no swelling or redness." She swiped alcohol across it, let it dry and then applied a fresh bandage. One that wasn't quite as thick, since it had quit bleeding. "I'd advise you to stay off your feet, but since you're here at work, that's not a possibility. At least limit the number of hours that you're standing on the injured area, if you can."

"I'll do my best," Tessa said. "Thanks."

She went to work, balancing on the ball of her foot when treating patients and entering data into the computer system. Though her lunch break was short, she managed to put her throbbing foot up. During her shift, she had little relief from being on her feet. That was okay by Tessa. Sitting still during the lulls between patients gave her too much time to think about the attack. And about Irish. An unwelcome thrill of excitement fluttered through her the closer she came to the end of the day. Irish would be staying at her house again tonight. Sleeping on her couch. She'd see him when she got off work because he'd be there in the parking lot waiting for her.

Thirty minutes before the end of her shift, her relief nurse called in to say that she would be late by at least two hours. Could someone fill in for her?

"I can do it," Allison said. "No, wait. I have to be at my apartment immediately after work for the service technician to fix my air conditioner." She pressed her lips together. "I'd call and reschedule, but this was the company's first available appointment."

Tessa shook her head. "It's okay. I can stay."

Allison frowned. "You've been limping through this day like a trooper. I'll just call and have the maintenance guy come another day."

Tessa held up her hands. "It's okay. Things are getting kind of slow. I can sit down a few times and put my foot up. Sleeping at night without an air conditioner in this heat is insane. You need to go."

"I would have Brian do it, but he doesn't get off duty until seven tomorrow morning."

"I've got this," Tessa said. "You go take care of your AC."

Allison left at five o'clock.

Tessa texted Irish and told him she wouldn't be off until seven and not to come any earlier. He replied, "Okay."

As soon as Allison left, an ambulance rolled in with a teenager who'd been in a motorcycle accident. Tessa and the on-call doctor worked to stabilize him and then prepared him for transport to a bigger hospital in San Antonio more equipped to work with head injuries. By the time they had him loaded into the ambulance for transport, an elderly man entered the ER suffering with chest pains. He was followed by a child with a ruptured eardrum, a cowboy who'd stepped on a nail, a snake bite victim, and a case of pneumonia.

Tessa felt a hand on her shoulder. The nurse who had called in had arrived. It had only been an hour and a half of the two hours she had said she would be.

"Sorry I was late," she said. "I'll take over from here. You go home. Get some rest."

Tessa nodded. Her foot throbbed, a headache was forming behind her eyes, and she was exhausted. After thirteen and a half hours on her feet, she was ready to jump in the shower and hit the bed. Grabbing her purse from the locker room, she left the hospital and trudged out to her SUV in the parking lot. Clouds had moved in, making it dark even sooner than normal. She hadn't realized that she hadn't parked under a light. Before she reached her vehicle, she stopped, remembering she'd told Irish she'd wait for him.

A noise behind her made her look back. A large, shadowy figure ran toward her. Tessa's heart leaped as she couldn't make out the face of the person heading straight for her. Gut instinct told her to run. Headlights flashed in the parking lot and an engine revved. Caught between the man rushing at her and headlights now racing toward her, Tessa screamed. The man grabbed her arm, jerked her backward and wrapped his arms around her waist, trapping her against his chest. Then he dragged her behind a car.

The vehicle speeding through the parking lot made a sharp turn, its tires squealing against the pavement.

Tessa fought to break free of the man who held her tightly against his body.

"Let me go!" she yelled.

The vehicle spun in a circle and headed back toward Tessa and her captor. When it was clear that the vehicle was coming straight for her, Tessa worked with the man holding her around the middle to get out of the way of the oncoming car. Before she could guess his intentions, her captor threw her over the hood of the car they were standing beside and slid across after her.

The vehicle charging toward them smashed into the side of the car where they had been standing moments before, pushing the vehicle toward where Tessa had landed on the ground.

A hand grabbed hers. She was yanked to her feet and dragged away from the car that was sliding sideways.

"Run, Tessa!" a familiar voice shouted. "Run!"

A sob rose up Tessa's throat. The man who had grabbed her was Irish. The attacking vehicle backed away from the one it had crushed, drove around it and started toward Irish and Tessa. Irish pulled his handgun from a holster beneath his jacket and pointed it at the driver.

"Run, Tessa," he said.

Tessa couldn't make her feet move. She stood, gripped in horror at what was happening.

Irish would be crushed beneath the wheels of the vehicle barreling at him.

Irish fired a shot. The vehicle swerved and raced out of the parking lot onto the street, tires screeching against pavement once again.

Tessa ran to Irish, threw her arms around his waist and clung to him. "I thought he would run you over," she said, a sob choking her words.

"I would have moved out of the way in time," he said, smoothing a hand over her hair.

"He was coming at you so fast, I didn't think you would get away."

He chuckled. "So, does that mean you care?"

"Yes, I care." Tessa buried her face against his shirt and murmured, "Who else would be my bodyguard?"

"Why did you run from me?" he asked.

She shook her head. "I didn't know it was you. I thought it was somebody trying to abduct me. I did the only thing I could and ran. Then the car and…and…you threw me over the other car."

"I did. I had to get you out of the driver's path." He set her at arm's length. "Were you hurt?"

She shook her head. "I'm okay. Maybe a little bruised, but that's better than crushed between the grill of that lunatic's vehicle and the car he hit."

Irish's jaw tightened. "Exactly. I figured throwing you over the hood would do less damage." He took her hand. "Come on. Let's get you home. You can ride with me this time. We don't know where that guy went or if he's waiting to run into your car next."

Tessa didn't argue. She let Irish lead her toward his truck in the dark.

As they walked, Irish pulled his cell phone from his pocket and dialed 9-1-1. He gave a description of the vehicle and explained the incident. "I'd give you a license plate, but it had been removed," Irish said.

Tessa had been more worried about surviving either a man's attack or being crushed be two tons of metal. She hadn't even had the time to get a description of the vehicle, much less a license plate number. She was impressed by Irish's ability to observe in a time of stress.

Irish opened the door to his truck for Tessa to climb in. When she stumbled on the step, he gripped her around the waist and lifted her up and into the seat. His hands remained on her waist for a long moment as he stared up into her eyes. "Why didn't you wait for me to get here?"

She sighed. "I know I should have. But it was such a busy day, and I was so tired when I got off work, I didn't think. I was in go-home mode."

Irish chuckled. "Like a horse headed for the barn."

She laughed. "You're comparing me to a horse?"

He grinned. "I have the highest respect for horses."

"I guess that's okay then," she said.

"Buckle up, sweetheart." He closed the door, rounded the front of the truck and slid into the driver's seat. "Maybe I should stay with you all day while you're at work."

"I might consider it, if this situation goes on much longer," Tessa said. "But not tomorrow."

"Why not tomorrow?" Irish asked.

She smiled and leaned her head back against the head-rest. "I'm off for the next three days."

"Good," Irish said. "I'll spend the next three days strictly with you."

Tessa frowned. "You have to have better things to do than follow around behind me like a babysitter."

He shook his head. "Nope. Trace has me covered. This is my assignment. *You* are officially my assignment."

Her eyes still closed, she sighed. "That sounds so im-personal. Which is just as well."

"Why do you say that?" Irish asked.

She leaned her head to the side and opened her eyes to look at him. "As cute as you are in your jogging shorts, I don't need to get into another relationship."

Irish grinned. "So, you think I'm cute in my jogging shorts?"

Heat climbed up Tessa's neck into her cheeks. Why did she have to say that? "I must be really tired to have said that. But, yes, you do have a really nice physique. I'd be blind if I didn't notice. But don't think that that means anything."

He drove toward her house with a grin on his face.

Tessa couldn't help but smile herself. After the past two days, his cheerfulness made a difference in her life. She really needed to smile and laugh more. "I'm not sure what I have in my refrigerator, but you are welcome to stay and have dinner with me."

He shook his head. "I took the liberty of stocking your refrigerator, since I'll be staying with you for an unknown amount of time. And while I did that, I took care of that back door and replaced it with a solid one."

Tessa sat up straight and turned toward him. "You got all that done in just one day?"

He shrugged. "I can be pretty handy when I want to be. The door needs a coat of paint, but we can do that tomorrow while we're there."

"Why are you doing this for me?" she asked. "Surely that can't be part of the job of a bodyguard?"

"Gotta take care of my jogging buddy," he said. "You're the high point of my day when I jog the river trail."

Tessa didn't say it out loud, but Irish was the high point of her day as well. She always looked forward to seeing him run toward her and say hello.

"How do grilled steaks and baked potatoes sound for dinner tonight?" Irish asked.

Tessa snorted. "That would sound wonderful, if I had a grill."

"Then how does broiled steaks and baked potatoes sound?" Irish shot a glance her way.

"Perfect." She grinned. "I take it you're doing the cooking?" she asked.

He nodded. "I am. Have to keep the little woman off her feet. Speaking of which, how is your foot today?"

It throbbed now that she had the weight off it, like it was getting more blood to the injured area. "Achy, but I'll survive."

He pulled into her driveway, parked the truck and came around to her side to open the door. When she started to get out of the truck, he scooped her up and carried her to the front steps.

She wrapped her arm around his shoulders and held on until he reached the top of the steps. "My foot might ache a little, but I'm perfectly capable of walking on it," she said.

"I know." He winked and set her down long enough to unlock the front door. "Stay here. I'll be right back."

Tessa leaned against the wall and waited, her breath lodged in her throat, her pulse pounding.

A minute later, he was back. "All clear."

She let go of the breath she'd been holding. "How do people live like this?"

"Like what?" he asked.

She shook her head. "In fear of walking into their own home?"

"We'll catch that guy. He's got to slip up soon. Hopefully they'll locate the vehicle that he used as a battering ram and trace him through that."

"Unless he stole it," Tessa suggested.

"If he was smart, that's what he did," Irish said.

He led her into the house, turned, closed and locked the door behind them. "The question is, what did you do to piss him off?"

"I only wish I knew," Tessa said. As she set her purse on the counter, her cell phone rang. She glanced down at the caller ID and frowned. "Why is he calling?" she asked aloud.

"He who?" Irish asked.

"My ex-husband." She stared at the phone without picking it up. "Question is, should I answer it?"

"You say that you don't think that it was him who attacked you, but what if it was? Or what if he had hired somebody to do the job?"

Tessa shook her head. "Why would he do that? I gave him everything in the divorce—the house, the car, the bank account…everything but my clothes. All I wanted was away from him."

"Who initiated the divorce?" Irish asked.

Tessa's lips formed a thin line. "I did."

Irish shrugged. "Some men don't take rejection very well."

The phone rang again.

"Maybe you should answer it," Irish said. "Maybe he's calling to confess."

Tessa's jaw hardened as she pressed the button to answer the call.

"Tessa." Randy's voice came over the line, making her belly knot.

"What do you want, Randy?" Tessa asked tersely.

"I'll be in Whiskey Gulch tomorrow night and would like to meet with you, if I could?"

"Tomorrow night?" Tessa challenged. "Or are you already in Whiskey Gulch?"

"I don't know what you mean." He sounded confused. But then Randy was good at acting. He'd pretended to love her for all the years they were married. "No, I'm in San Antonio, but I'm headed to Whiskey Gulch tomorrow night and I'd like to meet with you. Would you consider having dinner with me?"

Her first inclination was to say no. But if he was responsible for the attacks, meeting with him might help to get a confession out of him. "Okay," she said. "I'll meet you for dinner tomorrow night, but somewhere public."

"That would be fine," Randy said. "Name the place."

"The diner on Main Street at six o'clock." Tessa's gaze met Irish's.

"I'll be there," Randy said.

Tessa ended the call without saying goodbye.

"Sounds like you have a date with your ex-husband," Irish said.

She nodded. "I wouldn't call it a date. I agreed to meet

with him. And if he's the one who's causing all these attacks…" Her lips pursed. "I'll take him down."

Irish reached out to take her hand. "And I'll be with you tomorrow night when you have that meeting with him."

Tessa frowned. "He might not confess if you're sitting with me. He's really good at bullying women when he's alone with them—or with me. When he's with other men, it's like he's a completely different person."

"I admit, I don't like the idea of you being anywhere close to him," Irish said.

"Me, either," Tessa said. "It took a lot for me to get away from him to begin with."

"Then call him back and cancel. You shouldn't have to deal with him," Irish said.

"I'm not the same person I was when I was married to him." Tessa lifted her chin. "I won't let him bully me anymore." She gave him a quick smile. "But if you could be somewhere nearby, that would make me feel a little better about being in the same building with him."

"Deal," Irish said. "I'll be in the booth next to yours. If he even hints at raising a hand to you, I'll be there to stop him."

"Okay, then—" Tessa squeezed his hand "—I'll meet with him."

She wasn't looking forward to meeting with Randy. He hadn't taken their divorce very well. But if he had anything to do with the attacks, she would find out. And meeting with him might be the only way.

Chapter Eight

Irish wasn't happy about the proposed dinner Tessa had planned with her ex-husband. If there was another way to get him to Whiskey Gulch for questioning, he'd do it in a heartbeat. Having him in town would give the sheriff's department a chance to interrogate him.

He lifted his cell to make the call to the sheriff when his phone rang. He glanced at the caller ID.

It was Trace Travis.

"Hey, boss," Irish answered.

"I'm at the sheriff's office right now with Deputy Jones. Do you mind if we come by and speak with Ms. Bolton?"

He glanced across at Tessa. "I don't mind, but let me check with her."

"I called you because I wanted to make sure she was up to it," Trace said. "I heard she was attacked again out in the parking lot of the hospital."

"If you have any news whatsoever about who the attacker might be, I'm sure she would love to hear." He lifted his chin toward Tessa. "Are you up to a visit from Trace and Deputy Jones?"

She stepped toward him, nodding. "Like you just said,

if it has anything to do with my attacker, I'm more than ready. Bring him on."

"How soon can you be here?" Irish asked.

"Give us five minutes," Trace said.

Irish ended the call. "Are you sure you're up to company?"

"Absolutely, as long as it has something to do with solving this case. I've racked my brain trying to figure out who could be mad enough to want to hurt me. Other than my ex-husband, I can't come up with a single clue."

"It's just as well then that your ex-husband is coming to town tomorrow…if he hasn't been here all along. None of your patients come to mind?" Irish asked. "You haven't recommended anyone for the psych ward?"

She shook her head. "Not one."

"Any old boyfriends coming out of the woodwork?" Irish tilted his head to one side. "I mean, you did move back from San Antonio. And this is your hometown. You're attractive and bound to be popular."

She smiled. "No, I dated my ex all throughout high school. He was the only person I dated." Her smile faded. "Everybody knew I was Randy's girl."

"Has anybody asked you out while you've been here?" He persisted. "Somebody you might have turned down?"

She shook her head. "I've pretty much kept to myself. I didn't want anybody to ask me out."

"You say your ex-husband was really angry when you hit him up with the divorce papers."

Tessa nodded.

Irish hesitated before asking, "Angry enough to want to kill you?"

She shrugged. "I don't know. Maybe." Her face was pale and she had dark circles beneath her eyes.

Irish cupped her cheek, his voice softening. "Do you want to get a shower while I make dinner?"

She leaned into his palm. "You're supposed to be my bodyguard. Not my personal chef and housekeeper."

"I've already had my shower and, as pretty as you are in scrubs, I'm sure you're covered in all kinds of hospital germs." He winked.

She nodded. "I do like to get out of my scrubs and take a shower as soon as I get home."

"Then go." He tuned her and gave her a gentle shove. "I'll hold off the sheriff's deputy and Trace until you get out."

"Thanks." Tessa entered her bedroom and closed the door.

With just a few minutes to spare, Irish hurried to the kitchen, pulled the steaks, which he'd had marinating for several hours, from the refrigerator, put them on a broiler pan. He then removed the potatoes from the pantry and scrubbed them. He didn't have time to bake the potatoes in the oven with the steak, so he poked holes in them and stuck them in the microwave for six minutes. He wouldn't start the steaks until after Trace and Deputy Jones's visit.

With everything ready, he left the kitchen and returned to the living room just in time to hear a knock at the door. As he walked across the living room floor, he could hear the water in the shower turning off. He opened the door to find Trace and Deputy Jones standing there. "Come in," he said, standing back. "Tessa's just finishing up in the shower. She'll be out in a moment."

"Good." Deputy Jones entered. "We have news."

"Good news, I hope," Irish said.

"I don't know about good news," Trace said. "But it's news."

Once they were inside, Irish closed the door. "Can I get you some coffee?"

"I'll pass," Trace said.

"I'd love some," Deputy Jones said. "I've got the night shift tonight, and I've been up most of the day searching through databases."

"It's gonna be a long night for you," Irish said.

"Did you get the door hung?" Trace asked.

Irish nodded. "Come see."

Trace, Irish and Deputy Jones entered the kitchen.

While Irish poured a cup of coffee for the deputy, Trace inspected the door. "Looks good. I'll bet Ms. Bolton will be glad that it's solid versus the one with the window in it. That makes it way too easy for a burglar to break in. All they have to do is reach through the broken window and turn the knob."

"That's exactly what he did. Thank goodness Tessa heard him break the glass and had the foresight to have her gun close by. I still need to patch the bullet hole she blew through the door to her bedroom." He handed the cup of coffee to Deputy Jones. "Milk or sugar?"

"I'll take a little sugar," she said, and set the mug on the counter.

Irish handed her a bowl and spoon. Deputy Jones scooped sugar into her mug and stirred.

"I hope you have good news for me," Tessa said as she entered the kitchen. She wore gray athletic pants and a loose T-shirt. Her hair was still wet and was combed straight back from her forehead. On her feet she wore slippers and limped, favoring her injured heel.

Irish's jaw tightened. "The sooner they find the bastard, the better."

"I don't know about good news," Deputy Jones said.

"Mr. Travis and I have been combing through databases this afternoon, searching for similar crimes against women."

"I didn't think there was a whole lot of crime here in this area," Tessa said.

"Normally there's not. Here, lately, we've had a few incidences of human trafficking," the deputy said, casting a glance at Trace. "Mr. Travis and Matt Hennessey have helped in solving some of those cases, which we have been really grateful for."

"That's pretty scary," Tessa said. "Human trafficking, here in Whiskey Gulch?"

"That's right," Deputy Jones conceded, her face set in grim lines.

"Do you think whoever attacked me is after me to sell me into some sex trade or something?" Tessa asked.

Irish's hands clenched into fists. "If that were the case, why then did he try to run you over in the parking lot of the hospital? Seems to me he wouldn't want to damage the goods."

"You're right," Deputy Jones said. "That wouldn't make sense. But then, this may not be a case of human trafficking."

"Then what do you think it is?" Tessa asked.

"I wasn't finding a whole lot of crimes against women in this area, so I expanded my search through all of Texas. The search was too broad. So I limited it to female victims in South Central Texas. Again, the search was too broad. I played with different parameters, including hair color of the victims, age, and even tried the occupation of nurse." Deputy Jones tipped her head toward Trace. "Mr. Travis picked it up from there."

"I went at it from a little different angle. In many

cases, the victim usually knows his or her attacker. If this guy had murdered, raped or accosted anybody else, it might have been somebody in or from this town. So I searched through the records from the sheriff's office, looking for similar cases. Only one in this county stood out to me. She was born the same year as you were and died on her high school graduation night."

"Penny." Tessa's face turned white. "You're talking about Penny Stevens. She was murdered on graduation night."

Trace nodded. "That's right. Penny Stevens, age eighteen."

Irish went to stand beside Tessa and slipped his arm around her waist.

"That was thirteen years ago. What could that have to do with what's happening to me now?"

"On a hunch," Trace said, "I searched a list of your classmates. She wasn't the only one who has died."

Tessa gasped. "Who else?" she asked.

Deputy Jones jumped in. "Between the yearbook and the obituaries for the town, Mr. Travis and I searched the crime databases looking for more of your classmates."

"And we found them," Trace said. "Five years ago, Kitty Kitterman disappeared out of her home in Kerrville. They found her body three days later in a ditch off Interstate 30, fifty miles west of Kerrville."

Deputy Jones added, "Three years ago, Bethany York, who'd become a teacher in San Antonio, went missing from her home one night. They found her body a month later in a ditch beside Interstate 30, within five miles of where they'd found the Kitterman woman's body."

Tessa pressed a hand to her mouth. "Were those the only others from my class?"

"Yes," Jones said. "And now the attack on you."

"Did these three women and you have something in common besides coming from the same high school graduation class?" Trace asked.

Tears sprang into Tessa's eyes. "Yes. We were all cheerleaders. The four of us were the seniors on the squad the year we graduated."

Jones's gaze shot to Trace. "Wow. We should have seen that. I guess we can now go through the list of the other classmates to figure out who had it in for the cheerleaders."

"Given the fact the victims were all in the same class and were cheerleaders, we have to believe that whoever murdered them knew them." Jones pinned Tessa with her gaze. "And he knows you."

Trace's brow furrowed. "And you'll know him."

Tessa leaned against Irish.

He tightened his hold around her waist.

She shook her head. "But who? Ours wasn't a large school. Which one of my classmates would want to kill us?"

Deputy Jones sighed. "We haven't nailed that down yet. We hoped you might have insight into your classmates."

Trace paced across the floor of the kitchen and turned to face Tessa. "Can you recall any incidents that may have happened in high school between the cheerleaders of the senior class and any of the guys in that class or any of the classes below?"

"I can't remember anything that would have caused someone to be so upset that they would murder the cheerleaders. I was too busy cheering at football games and organizing fundraisers. We all were."

Deputy Jones's lips twisted and she tapped her chin. "Was there a bad breakup between a cheerleader and one of the guys in your school?"

Tessa shook her head. "Not me. I was dating the quarterback from ninth grade on. Everybody knew I was Randy's girl."

Irish shifted next to her, retaining his hold around her waist. "What about the other cheerleaders?"

"They bounced around between different boyfriends. It could have happened." Tessa shook her head. "It's not like I can ask them now. They're dead." Tears streamed down her face. "Why did I not know this?"

"Kitty Kitterman had married a guy named Pearson," Trace said. "I talked with my mother. She and Kitty's mother were friends. She said the Kittermans left Whiskey Gulch after Kitty graduated high school. The York family had the same situation. They moved to Boerne, just outside San Antonio, after Bethany graduated. Penny Stevens's notice was the only that showed up in the Whiskey Gulch obituaries because she was the only one who still lived here."

"I can't believe we lost touch," Tessa whispered. "I should have been a better friend."

"People lose touch after high school." Irish pulled a chair out at the kitchen table and pressed her into it. He hated seeing Tessa so sad. Her tears ripped at his heart. He wanted to make her world right again.

"They were my friends," Tessa said. "My teammates."

"And you were busy surviving an abusive relationship with your husband. You can't beat yourself up about it," Irish said.

"Your husband was one of your classmates?" Deputy Jones asked.

Tessa nodded. "He was the quarterback of the football team. I was the head cheerleader."

"What were you saying about an abusive relationship?" Trace asked.

Tessa buried her face in her hands. "I divorced him after he'd beat me once too often."

Irish laid a hand on Tessa's shoulder, the anger he felt for Tessa's ex-husband burning like a blowtorch in his chest.

"Could he have been the one who attacked you?" Deputy Jones asked.

Tessa shook her head. "I didn't think so. I swear the guy who attacked me was bigger than my ex-husband. But then I haven't seen my ex in six months."

"She is, however, seeing him tomorrow night," Irish noted.

Tessa wiped the tears from her cheeks and looked up. "I am. We're meeting at the diner at six o'clock."

"I'll be there with her," Irish said.

"We can have a patrol car stationed close by. We can also have a plainclothes officer inside the diner," Deputy Jones said.

Trace gave Irish a chin lift. "Matt Hennessey and I can be there as well."

Tessa laughed, the sound catching on a sob. "I don't suppose you can position a metal detector at the door as well?"

Deputy Jones gave her half a smile. "I could ask the high school principal to borrow theirs for the evening."

Tessa glanced at the new back door. "Wow, this is all crazy." She shrugged. "But if Randy's the one doing this, we have to catch him. And we have to stop him from killing anybody else."

"Were there only four seniors on the cheer squad?" Deputy Jones asked.

Tessa nodded.

"That doesn't mean he won't start into the next grades," the deputy acknowleged. "Ones above or below. Kind of sounds like he has a gripe, though, with the senior class cheerleaders."

Trace crossed his arms over his chest. "Is there anyone left that you could ask about potential incidents that could have occurred?"

"Between now and tomorrow night," Deputy Jones said, "I'll start running some background checks on some of the guys in your class. Are there any you can think of that we should look at first?"

"Seriously, I must have walked around in a bubble my whole senior year. I thought everyone was happy. And everyone was working toward graduation. We planned a big campout by the bluffs for the night of graduation." Tessa drew in a deep, shaky breath and let it out slowly. "Being teenagers like we were, we knew there would be alcohol. So we collected everybody's keys. Nobody could leave until they'd sobered up in the morning."

Trace nodded. "Smart."

"That's what we thought," Tessa said softly. "We had a bonfire, music and dancing. It was a great party. Alcohol did flow freely. Nobody noticed that Penny was gone. So many of the young couples had gone off into the brush to make out. No one was keeping track."

Irish's lips quirked upward. "Sounds about right."

"We had a lot of pregnancies out of that party. It wasn't until the next afternoon that we heard about Penny. Her parents had alerted the sheriff when she didn't come home that morning."

"Where did they find her?" Irish asked.

"They sent a search party out to the bluff and found her body at the base of a cliff. At first, they assumed she'd wandered off drunk and fallen over the edge." Tessa's voice caught. "Until the autopsy report came in. She had strangulation marks around her neck. We were all shocked. The sheriff's department asked for help from the state crime lab. People came out and questioned every one of the students in the class. No one saw anything. After that night, many of us went on to college. We left Whiskey Gulch for four years. Those who stayed took up a trade, became receptionists in doctor's offices, or married and had children."

"Penny didn't get that opportunity," Irish concluded, his heart hurting for Tessa and the good folks of Whiskey Gulch.

Tessa shook her head.

"Hopefully, doing a background check on the guys in your class, we'll find something. Maybe one of them will have a police record," Deputy Jones said. "Maybe some jail time."

"I know Martha Stevens, Penny's mother. She and my mother were friends," Trace said. "I'll ask Martha if she knew of anything that happened that Penny might have told her. Something that's not already in the police records."

"There's a Josh Kitterman that works at the building supply store. Is he any relation to Kitty Kitterman?" Deputy Jones asked.

Tessa gaze momentarily held the deputy's. "That's her older brother. He joined the military after high school."

"We can stop by the lumber store tomorrow. I need to

get supplies to either repair or replace the door to Tessa's bedroom," Irish said.

"I'll spend some time looking through my yearbook, try to remember who might have had a gripe with the cheerleaders," Tessa offered.

"And we'll get everybody in place thirty minutes prior to your meeting with your ex," Trace said. "In the meantime, try to get some rest."

Tessa nodded. "I will. I hope you find something. I feel like I'm living on the edge and that my number will soon be up." She reached up and clasped Irish's hand on her shoulder, then tipped her head toward Trace. "Thank you for loaning Irish to me. I don't know what I would've done without him. I'd probably be dead by now."

"Irish and I served together. He's good at what he does," Trace said. "I've told him he's to stick with you until this is over."

Tessa laughed without mirth. "I just hope it's not over with my death."

"It won't be," Irish said.

Trace shook hands with Irish. "Stay with her."

Irish smiled. "You don't have to tell me twice."

"We'll leave you guys to your evening," Deputy Jones said. "If you remember anything, don't hesitate to call. I don't care what time of day or night."

"I will," Tessa promised.

Trace and Deputy Jones left. Irish followed them to the door and locked it behind them. He returned to the kitchen where he'd left Tessa seated at the table.

Silent tears slipped from her eyes. "I can't believe I didn't know this. Three women who were my friends in high school, and I didn't know they were dead."

"And now you're the target," Irish said. "I guess you know what that means, don't you?"

"I'm in danger?" Tessa asked. "We already know that."

"It means I'm going to stick to you like a fly on fly-paper." His mouth spread wide in a grin.

Her lips twitched. "Sounds uncomfortable, but I'm game."

"I just need to pop these steaks into the oven for a few minutes and chop up a salad. Think you won't starve in the next fifteen minutes?"

"Leave my steak in a little longer. I don't like it to moo."

"One steak well done coming up."

Tessa rose from her chair. "And I can help you cut up the salad."

"You've been on your feet all day. Just sit."

She shook her head and remained standing. "No, I need to move. This is all too much." More tears welled in her eyes and she swiped at them. "I don't know why I keep crying. It doesn't make anything better."

Irish wrapped his arms around her and pulled her against his chest.

"I shouldn't cry," she sobbed.

"Yes, you should," he countered. "They were your friends.

She buried her face against his shirt. "I'm sorry I'm soaking your shirt."

"It's okay. I have another."

For a long moment, they stood together. He stroked her hair and just let her cry. It ripped his heart out to see her so upset. And made him even angrier at the man who'd caused all this. He leaned toward her ex-husband being the one behind the attacks and murders.

The man hadn't been averse to beating his wife. He could harbor enough anger to kill other women. And maybe he hadn't killed his ex-wife because, at the time, they were married. But now that they weren't, he might be targeting her. And since he hadn't been successful so far, setting up a public meeting would draw her out. They'd have to be ready in case he tried to pull a fast one. The more Irish thought about it, the more Irish liked the idea of the metal detector at the door to the diner.

When her tears subsided, he moved her to arm's length and stared down into her red puffy eyes. Even with puffy eyes, she was a beautiful woman. "Come on. Let's get something to eat."

She nodded. "Thank you."

Before he could think better of it, he tipped her chin up and brushed his lips across hers.

Her eyes widened. "Why did you do that?"

"I don't know," Irish said. "It just seemed like the thing to do. And I have been wanting to do it all day."

Her gaze met his. "Would you do it again?" she asked so softly he wasn't sure he'd heard right.

He smiled down at her gently. "Only if you want me to."

Her tongue shot out and swept across her lips.

Irish's pulse quickened. "Do you want me to?"

She gave him a silent nod and lifted up on her toes.

He shook his head. "I shouldn't. You're in a very emotional state. Kissing you would be taking advantage of you. But, hell, I can't resist." He lowered his mouth onto hers and crushed her body against his. At first, his kiss was gentle, but when she opened her mouth to him, he swept in to claim her. For a long time, they remained locked in each other's arms.

When reason returned, Irish lifted his head and drew in a deep breath. "I'm sorry," he said. "I shouldn't have let that happen."

She shook her head. "You didn't let it happen. I asked for it."

"I shouldn't let it happen again," he said.

"Why?" she questioned. "We're both mature adults who can make our own decisions."

"Yeah, but you distract me, woman," he said. "And if I'm distracted, I might miss something. Something that could cost you your life." He set her away from his body and then dropped his hands to his sides. "I have to keep focused."

She smoothed her hands over her T-shirt. "Okay, then. Let's focus on supper."

Irish put the steaks in the oven, and got the lettuce, tomatoes, and other fixings out of the refrigerator. They stood side by side, cutting up vegetables for the salad. All the while he wanted to throw down the knife, take her in his arms and carry her into the bedroom to make passionate love to her. He couldn't keep her safe if he couldn't stay focused. And he couldn't stay focused when he was standing right next to her. Perhaps he should have Trace assign someone else to be her bodyguard.

Tessa tossed the cut tomatoes into the lettuce, glanced up at him and smiled.

In that one look, Irish knew that he was doomed. He couldn't let somebody else take charge of her safety. It was up to him to keep her alive. And he would. Or die trying.

Chapter Nine

Once the steaks were broiled and the potatoes were out of the microwave, Tessa loaded plates with salad, steak, and steaming potatoes, and carried them to the table.

Irish followed her with iced glasses full of tea.

"Doesn't seem right to be eating steaks without candlelight. Hold on." She set her plate down, went back to one of the cabinets, pulled out two candlestick holders and stuck two white tapers in them. She dug in a drawer for a box of matches and handed them over to Irish. "Will you do the honors?"

"It would be my pleasure." He struck a match on the side of the box and lit the two candles. Then he went to the switch on the wall and turned off the lights in the kitchen.

Tessa smiled. "That's better."

"It's almost like a date," Irish commented.

"Except you're my bodyguard, not my date. But it is nice to have some ambience." Tessa handed him a steak knife.

"Yeah, and if it were a date," Irish said, "I would have sprung for the filet mignon instead of the top sirloin."

Tessa puffed out her chest. "Actually, you're in luck

here because I prefer the top sirloin to the filet. They're not quite as thick and I can get it cooked all the way through."

Irish grinned. "I'd call that lucky."

"If this were a real date, where would you take me?" Tessa asked.

"Actually, I kind of like it right here. But since it's your place and I'm living in the bunkhouse, I would probably take you to a nice little restaurant with cozy atmosphere. Some place we can be alone but not alone. Not some place that's loud with a lot of music. I like music, but I like more to get to know the woman I take out on a date. And you can't do that when you have to talk over music. I'm not saying that after dinner I wouldn't take her dancing. I've been known to have a mean two-step on the dance floor."

"I take it you mean that you would be going to a dance hall," Tessa said.

"I can dance to rock or pop music," Irish said. "But I prefer country-western because I get to hold the woman in my arms."

A shiver of awareness caught Tessa off guard. She knew what it was like to have Irish's arms around her when she was scared. But dancing? Dancing could be a prelude to something more. Heat coiled at her core.

"Did your ex ever take you dancing?"

She gave a crooked smile. "Only to the prom. And only because he was going to be crowned the homecoming king. We danced one dance and that was it. It was the obligatory royal dance."

"And let me guess," Irish said. "You love to dance, don't you?"

She nodded. "As a cheerleader we choreographed tumbling and dance routines, but that's dancing by yourself or with the team. It's not as intimate."

Irish nodded. "That's what I'm talking about. A date should be intimate. What did you do on your dates with Randy?" He held up his hands. "You don't have to answer that. That's too personal and none of my business."

"It's okay." Tessa laughed. "Seems like we were always out with groups—other members of the football team…cheerleaders. Randy liked an audience. Granted, as a cheerleader, so did I. But after high school, I learned that relationships were more important than audiences. I had to work hard to make the grades I needed to get into nursing school. My study group became my family. My friends were very important to me. They helped me get through it. I wasn't a cheerleader in college. I didn't stand in front of everybody. I didn't have an audience."

"You said Randy went to different colleges," Irish said.

"He did. On a football scholarship. He was right back into the same situation he'd had in high school. He had an audience and he played for it. Up until his junior year when he injured his rotator cuff and he couldn't throw the football anymore."

Irish shook his head. "That had to set him back."

"His folks hired a tutor to get him through the rest of his studies to graduate with a business degree. They had friends in San Antonio who hired him as a manager. After he lost his position on the football team—"

"He lost his audience," Irish finished.

Tessa nodded. "I think he came back to Whiskey Gulch to marry me in some misguided attempt to reclaim some of his past fame."

"Or he knew you were a good catch."

"I'd concentrated on making good grades. While going

to college, I didn't have time for relationships. When I came back to Whiskey Gulch, it just seemed like the thing to do, to marry my high school sweetheart. I'd accomplished my educational goals. It was time to start my life goals of having a family and raising children. I thought Randy had the same goals. I didn't realize it was important to actually talk through life goals with your potential spouse before you marry."

"What were his goals?" Irish asked.

Tessa snorted. "Well, it sure wasn't having children. To him, life was always a competition. In football, it was a competition to be the best. In track, it was competition to be the best. In the business that he was hired into, he strove to be the best. He learned to play golf so that he could play with the bigwigs. He moved up the corporate ladder pretty quickly."

"In the meantime, what did you do?" Irish asked.

"I went to work in a clinic so that I could be home in the evening to make dinner for him or to go out as his pretty little wife—his arm-candy—to all the functions where the executive officers would notice him. Once again, he liked being the center of attention.

"And he was good at it, until his immediate boss realized that he was jockeying for his position. He had him transferred to a dark corner of the building, calling it a growth experience that he needed in order to move up the ladder. Every time he tried to get the attention of his boss's superior, his boss found a way to get in between them and stop him. Randy came home angrier and angrier, and he took it out on me."

"He became violent," Irish said.

"It started by him criticizing everything I did from what I cooked for dinner to what I wore. He didn't like how I fixed my hair or my makeup. He blamed me for the demotion saying that it reflected poorly on him because I didn't go to as many of the functions as I should have. I hadn't supported him in his profession. Never mind that I had a job of my own where I was on my feet most of the day and was tired when I got home. The man really should have been a lawyer. He was good at making me believe the garbage he fed me. It was all my fault. I believed it. I thought it was my fault that he didn't want to have children. I wasn't pretty enough. I wasn't good in bed."

"How do you figure?" Irish said.

She laughed. "He told me I was an ice queen. I would go to sleep before he even got to the bed. I wasn't passionate enough."

"Couldn't he see that you were exhausted?" Irish asked.

Tessa stared down at her untouched food. "I was exhausted, and I thought it was my fault that I was exhausted. I went to the doctor I worked for and asked him to run a CBC panel to see if I had low iron, or low something, that was causing me to always be so tired. All of that came back normal. I was healthy. He suggested I go see a marriage counselor.

"When I brought that up with Randy, he blew his top. That's when he hit me the first time. He said he didn't need a counselor. If anybody needed it, it was me. I was the one who was at fault. Again, I believed him. I believed all of his brainwashing. I deserved to be hit."

Irish shook his head. "No woman deserves to be hit."

She smiled. "I know that now. I should have seen the signs. Randy's boss was determined to get rid of him. When it finally happened, and they eliminated his position, Randy was so angry. He came home, picked a fight with me over the dinner I'd made, drank too much bourbon and then used me as a punching bag. He left me unconscious on the kitchen floor." Tessa glanced up.

Irish's face was as hard as a rock. His jaw was so tight, it twitched.

"I'm not telling you all this so you'll feel sorry for me. I want you to understand why I don't want to see him. I also want you to understand why I don't want you to do anything violent against him, even though he might deserve it."

Irish's fists clenched so tightly, the knuckles turned white.

Her eyes narrowed. "Promise me."

That twitch in his jaw kept jerking. He didn't say anything for a few moments. Then he let out a breath. "Okay, I promise. But I won't let him hurt you."

"Thank you. I learned something else from Randy. That violence for the sake of violence is never the answer. It's taken these past six months and lots of therapy sessions to come to the conclusion that I was not the one at fault. And it's taken me that long not to flinch when a man touches me."

Irish's eyes widened. "I've touched you."

She smiled. "Yes, you have. And I didn't flinch."

"Geez, Tessa. If I ever do anything that makes you cringe or feel uncomfortable, tell me. I'll stop doing it immediately, and I won't blame you. What you went through, what you're going through, is a form of PTSD. It is not unlike what some soldiers who've been captured and tortured by the enemy have gone through. It can take years before the nightmares fade."

Tessa nodded. "That's what my therapist told me." She

lifted her fork and cut into her steak. "But enough about me. What about you? What was it like in the war?" She popped the bite of steak into her mouth.

"That's a pretty broad question," he said, and stared across the table at her.

"If you could sum it up in one word, what would that one word be?" She gave him a crooked smile. "My therapist used that one on me."

He continued chewing and swallowed before he answered. "Intense."

Tessa looked back down at her plate, shook her head and laughed. "While my ex was stressing over a management position, you and your teammates were more worried about living through the night. That's real stress. But, really, what was it like? Being a part of Delta Force?"

As his gaze held hers across the table in the candlelight, he spoke one word, "Family."

Tessa's hand curled around her napkin.

"Those men, my team, were my brothers," Irish said. "I would have done anything for them."

"But you left Delta Force?" Tessa challenged.

He nodded. "I did. And not a day goes by that I don't second-guess myself. Should I have stayed? If I had stayed, would it have made a difference between life and death for someone? Does my team feel abandoned? Could I have saved more lives out in the field?"

He stared at the flame burning on the end of the candle. "I'm sitting here in the candlelight with a beautiful woman, while my team could be out in some hellhole, fighting against an enemy they may or may not be able to see. All because I wanted a chance to start the rest of my life. I didn't want to wait until I retired. Hell, I might be too old," he laughed. "I almost waited too long."

Tessa frowned. "What do you mean?"

"A week before I was supposed to deploy back to the States to process out, we had to go on a mission. We make jokes about short-timers, but it's true. More often than not, when a soldier or a unit has to perform a mission close to the date they're supposed to ship home, you're almost guaranteed that something bad will happen."

Tessa's frown deepened. "And did it?"

Irish nodded. "I was injured and almost didn't make it out. If it hadn't been for my teammates, I wouldn't have. They didn't give up on me. And to top it off, when we got back to our base, there was an MP waiting for us. He was there to deliver news to Trace Travis that his father had been murdered."

"I heard about that. What an awful tragedy. Mr. Travis was a good man." Tessa's gaze dropped to her hand. "And the rest of your team?"

"They survived the mission. And they've gone on without the two of us. To them, it's just another day in the life of a Delta Force soldier. Two fresh, green, Delta Force soldiers would join the team and take our place."

Tessa covered his hand with hers. "You may feel like you're letting them down by not being with them, but you're needed here. I need you. If you hadn't had my back, I would be dead now."

He turned his hand over and gripped hers. "Whatever happens tomorrow night, I'll be there. I won't let anyone hurt you."

"I believe that. And not because you're saying it." Tessa squeezed his hand. "Randy said a lot of things he didn't mean. And I believed his words. But I learned that actions speak a lot louder than words, and your actions have been honorable. And, by the way, this steak is delicious. We should finish before it gets cold."

His lips twisted. "You're right. We should eat."

Tessa ate a few more bites of her baked potato, her salad, and her steak before she gave up and set her fork beside her plate.

"Not tender enough for you?" Irish asked.

She shook her head. "I'm exhausted."

"Then I'll take care of the dishes, you go on to bed."

She yawned, covering her mouth with her hand. "I'm going to take you up on that. A man who will do the dishes is priceless. You sure know how to sweep a girl off her feet on a first date."

"You should see me on a second date. I might even scrub the bathrooms. I'm quite good at cleaning latrines. The army taught me that particular skill."

"Thank you for sharing your experience with me," Tessa said. "It puts my life in perspective."

He stood, held out his hand, and waited for her to place hers in his. "I'm so sorry for what you went through."

She stepped closer. "I know."

He cupped her cheek and brushed his thumb across her lips. "I can't imagine anyone wanting to hit this beautiful face."

"And I can't imagine the horrors you must have faced in battle." Tessa raised her free hand to cover his on her face. And she turned to press a kiss to his palm.

Irish tensed. "Your lips were meant for kissing."

She smiled shyly. "I'd be amenable to that idea."

He shook his head. "I can't."

Tessa frowned. "Can't?"

"If I were to kiss you, I'd lose all focus," he said. "I

need to retain my focus, or I might miss something that could mean the difference between life and death."

For a long moment, Tessa stared up at Irish's face, wanting so much more but not willing to push him into something he might not want as badly.

"Okay, then." She stepped back until his hand dropped to his side, turned, and hobbled out of the room. Her cheeks burned. She felt foolish for throwing herself at the man. If he'd really wanted to kiss her, he would have. Now she'd have to be content to go to bed and dream about a kiss that she'd never have.

IRISH'S GAZE FOLLOWED Tessa until she disappeared down the hallway. It had taken every ounce of determination not to kiss her, when every fiber of his being wanted to. The woman needed a protector. Not a man taking advantage of her distress. She'd been physically and emotionally abused by her ex. She didn't need a man confusing her while she was still working through her issues.

He went to work on cleaning the dishes and putting food away. When he was done, he stepped outside the house and stared up at the stars.

This was the perfect night to take a woman out on a date. A clear, Texas night with an infinite amount of stars. And the ones he would stare at the most would be the ones reflected in her eyes.

Maybe after this was over, after her attacker was caught, he might ask Tessa out on a real date. He'd take it slowly, make sure she was comfortable and that she knew without a doubt that he would never hurt her like her ex-husband had. Until then, he'd be strictly hands-off. He made a pass around the house, checking that everything was secure on the outside, even testing the back door to make sure that it was locked before he came back through the main entrance.

He paused in front of her bedroom door.

"Tessa?" When she didn't answer, he pushed the door open. A light burned on her nightstand and she lay against the sheets, her cheek resting in the palm of her hand. Her eyes were closed and she was breathing deeply. She was asleep.

Irish returned to the living room, sat on the couch and then stretched out, laying his head on the pillow. He hadn't felt too exhausted, but as soon as he closed his eyes, he was out.

He wasn't sure how long he slept, but a soft sound woke him in the middle of the night. It sounded suspiciously like someone sobbing. And then it stopped. He lay there for a moment, waiting for it to start again so that he could figure out where it was coming from.

A moment later Tessa appeared in her doorway, carrying her pillow and a blanket.

"Are you okay?" he asked.

She shook her head.

He patted the couch beside him. "Come here."

She limped across the living room and sat on the edge of the cushion.

"Bad dream?"

Again, she nodded. "I was back in the willow trees. Instead of a man attacking me, the willow branches wrapped around me." She shivered. "They pulled me in, suffocating me."

"Sounds creepy," Irish said. He turned on his side and scooted as far back as he could against the couch cushions. "You're welcome to join me." He lifted his head while she positioned her pillow next to his and then they both laid down. Her back to him. Her hand resting beneath her cheek.

"I'm not asking you to kiss me," she said. "But would you put your arm around me? I feel safer when you do."

He draped his arm across her middle and pulled her close. With her nestled against him, sleep was the furthest thing from his mind. He fought to control his body's natural reaction to hers pressed to his. It took a great amount of effort, but somehow he managed.

"Irish?" Tessa asked.

"Mmm," he responded.

"Have you ever been in love?"

He chuckled. Her question was unexpected and he wasn't sure how to answer. "I thought I was once."

"What was she like?" Tessa asked.

"She had curly red hair and green eyes."

"Oh," Tessa said. "Are you partial to red hair and green eyes?"

"I was back then."

"What happened?"

He laughed again. "When I tried to kiss her, she slapped my face and told me boys were weird. I got sent home from school that day. And I never tried to kiss a girl on the playground again."

"How old were you?" Tessa giggled.

He laughed. "I was in first grade. I swear that incident scarred me for life."

"Surely not." She turned to look over her shoulder. "You can't tell me you've been celibate all of this time."

"No, I can't tell you that." He swept her hair back from her temple. "I've dated other women. And I've kissed a few. But I've never been in love. I was afraid to let myself get that attached while I was with Delta Force."

"Afraid?" she whispered. "I can't imagine you being afraid of anything."

"I've had a few close calls where I've been afraid," he said. "I'm only human."

"In battle or in relationships?"

"Both."

Tessa laid her arm over his around her middle. "Now that you're not in Delta Force, do you think you'll let yourself fall in love?"

Not only did he think he would, he k*new* he would. He wanted to start the rest of his life. He wanted a family. He wanted children. He wanted a wife to come home to.

"Eventually," he said.

"Irish…" Tessa started.

"Go to sleep Tessa."

"Sorry," Tessa said, "sometimes I talk too much."

By morning, he would be exhausted. But for now, he reveled in the opportunity to hold her. To smell the fragrance of her hair. To feel the softness of her body against his. In the morning, he'd put some distance between them again.

Chapter Ten

Tessa slept better than she'd slept since she'd left San Antonio. She awoke to a warm arm around her midsection and lay for a moment, basking in a feeling of well-being. And something more. She'd asked Irish if he'd ever been in love, mostly because she had wondered what it felt like. She'd thought herself in love with Randy, but what she'd had with Randy had been high school infatuation that lasted into college, only because she hadn't had time to pursue another relationship. Yes, she felt warm and safe with Irish. And yes, she wanted to kiss him. Heck, she wanted more than just to kiss him.

An electric current rippled throughout her body.

Was it just physical attraction, or was it love? Could someone fall in love in just a couple of days? She'd heard of love at first sight, but she'd never been convinced that it really existed.

She wasn't sure what she was feeling for Irish. But it felt good. She lay for a few minutes longer as the sun peeked its way through the blinds in the front window. Irish had said he'd wanted to keep his distance so that he could retain his focus. Was it more than that? Was he not as attracted to her as she was to him? He'd said that he'd wanted to kiss her. A strong virile man like Irish would follow his instincts, wouldn't he?

Tessa sighed. All she knew was she couldn't keep throwing herself at him. She needed to give him the space he desired. And she wasn't doing that by lying next to him on the couch.

Moving slowly, she slipped out from beneath his arm and rolled quietly off the couch onto her hands and knees. She turned to note that Irish's eyes were still closed and his chest was moving in slow, steady breaths. Afraid she'd wake him, she crawled away from the couch before she stood and hurried to her bedroom, closing the door softly behind her. Tessa dressed quickly in jeans and a soft white T-shirt. Then she entered the bathroom, brushed her teeth, combed her hair straight and pulled it into a loose ponytail at the back of her neck. She applied a little blush to her pale cheeks, and some mascara to her eyelashes, and just a touch of rose-colored lipstick to her lips. Satisfied that she didn't look pale and pasty, she applied a fresh Band-Aid to her heel, and slipped on a pair of socks and shoes. When she was finished, she eased open her bedroom door and looked out at an empty couch.

So much for not waking him. The scent of coffee drifted to her and she followed it to its source.

Irish stood in the kitchen barefoot, his T-shirt untucked, and a five-o'clock shadow on his chin. Tessa took a moment to appreciate the view. The man had no clue how attractive he was. He made her heart flutter every time she saw him.

He turned and smiled when he saw her. "Do you want your eggs scrambled or fried this time?"

"Why don't you let me cook?" she said.

"Tired of my cooking already?" he asked.

"Far from it," she said. "But I like to pull my weight. I think we have enough ingredients to make omelets. How would you like that?" she asked.

"Sounds good. I can chop, while you man the skillet."

She smiled. "Deal."

Once again, they worked side by side, preparing a meal together. To Tessa, it felt as natural as breathing. They seemed to anticipate each other's needs, moving in unison to make two golden, fluffy omelets full of tasty vegetables.

While Tessa scooped the omelets out of the frying pan onto the plates, Irish filled glasses with orange juice and set them on the table, along with forks and knives. Tessa carried their plates to the table and set them across the table from each other.

When she started to take her seat, Irish held her chair for her, something Randy never did, unless others were watching.

"I could get used to having you around," she said. "It's a lot more fun to cook when you have help."

"I like to cook," Irish said. "It beats the heck out of chow hall food."

"I can only imagine," Tessa said.

They ate their breakfast talking about football teams and the livestock out at the Whiskey Gulch Ranch. Irish made her laugh when he discussed the different personalities of the horses in the barn and pastures. He made each one sound human, like friends. Some were gentle and others were full of sass. And he smiled a lot when he talked about them.

"You really like working with the livestock out at the ranch, don't you?" Tessa asked.

He nodded. "I'm living the dream. I promised myself

when I left active duty that I'd go to work with animals for a while before I pursued my other dream of home and family."

"Sounds like you landed in the right spot then," Tessa said.

"I don't think it would have happened if Trace's father hadn't been murdered. When I knew Trace on active duty, he talked about staying the full twenty or more. He never mentioned home. He didn't talk about his family, except for maybe his mother. From what he's said, there were bad feelings between him and his father. I think he regrets that he didn't have a chance to clear those feelings before his father was murdered."

"That is too bad," Tessa said. "I remember Mr. Travis did a lot for the community. He was well respected by so many."

"Trace had the option of going back on active duty, but he chose to stay and run the ranch. I wouldn't be here now if he hadn't made that decision to remain in Whiskey Gulch and set up his security business. He knew how hard it was for folks coming off active duty. After living in a war zone, the transition can be pretty rough. He wanted to give people separating from the military a purpose, utilizing some of the skills they had learned while in the military."

"It's a good thing that he came back to stay," Tessa said.

"He's giving his brothers-in-arms a place to work, helping people like me. And he's carrying on his father's legacy in his own way. Trace Travis is a good man, and his security business concept is admirable. Now, if we could just surface some clues, figure out who's after you and neutralize him, we can prove out the business concept."

Tessa's eyes narrowed. "Speaking of clues, I think I have an old yearbook. Let me get it out."

Irish nodded toward her plate. "Finish your omelet first, while it's hot. You need food to fuel your body. We don't know what we might face today."

She quickly cleaned her plate and carried it to the sink. Then she left Irish in the kitchen to go into the hallway where a bookshelf held old photo albums and yearbooks.

Tessa returned to the kitchen with a yearbook. She opened the book to the seniors and ran her fingers across the photographs. She pointed to a picture of a smiling brunette. "That's Penny." She turned the page and pointed to Kitty Kitterman. Turning the page once more, she pointed to an image of a pretty girl with blond hair. "And this is Bethany York."

Irish turned the pages back to the first one. "And there you are. You haven't changed much since high school."

"I have a few more crow's feet, and I've lost some of the muscle mass I acquired with all the gymnastics we did."

"But you still look the same," Irish said. "Your hair's a little shorter. That's really the only difference."

One by one, Tessa pointed out each of the guys in her senior class. Her finger paused on Randy. "He was the most handsome boy in the senior class," she muttered. "Not that looks mean anything, it's what's inside that counts." She laughed. "I learned that about Randy as well as myself."

"I understand about Randy, but what do you mean that you learned that about yourself?"

"I relied on my looks in high school." She glanced up with a twisted smile. "My looks didn't save me from the beatings in my marriage. I had to find the strength from within to leave him."

ANGER BURNED IN Irish's gut. If he didn't control it, he might break his promise to Tessa—not to hurt Randy that night when he saw him. He pulled himself back to the task of looking through her yearbook.

"You say Randy was a football player," Irish said.

She nodded. "The quarterback."

"And the guy that attacked you—" Irish frowned "—was bigger than Randy?"

"I could swear he was bigger than Randy," she said. "Even after college and losing his football scholarship, Randy liked to stay in shape. He had no tolerance for people who let themselves go."

Irish shook his head. "Is that why you jog? Did he badger you into working out so you wouldn't get fat?"

"Partly," she admitted. "But mostly because, when I'm jogging, I'm staying active. I don't have time to dwell on the failures in my life. And it generates endorphins and helps to cheer me when I'm down."

"Exercise has that added bonus." He glanced at the yearbook. "Which of the guys in your class were big guys?"

Tessa moved through the senior class pictures alphabetically. "Mike Bradley was one of the tallest guys on the team. He was on the offensive line. At six-four, he weighed over two hundred pounds, and he was hard to get around. He protected the quarterback."

Irish grimaced. "Is he still in Whiskey Gulch?"

Tessa smiled. "He is. He became the coach at the middle school. And he teaches history. He married while he was in college. His wife teaches at the elementary school. They have two small children."

A wife and kids didn't mean he wasn't capable of hurting someone else. "Did he ever have anger issues?"

Again, Tessa smiled. "Mike is a big teddy bear of a guy and one of the nicest human beings you'll ever meet."

Unconvinced, Irish shook his head. "You never know. Sometimes those nice guys are hiding things, even from their families."

"Not Mike, he was always an open book. And would do anything for anybody. He and his wife make the cutest couple. He's so big. She's so small. And they look genuinely happy. Mike isn't our guy." Tessa moved her finger to the next guy. "This is Connor Daniels. He was a football player as well. Not nearly as tall as Mike Bradley, though. He, too, was on the offensive line, and sometimes he played the position of running back. He was fast, on the field and with the girls."

"Still in town?" Irish asked.

Tessa nodded. "And he seems to have straightened out a lot. He trained to become a firefighter, and now he works for the town of Whiskey Gulch as one of the few full-time firefighters. One of the ladies I work with at the hospital, Allison, is dating a firefighter who works with Connor. He only has good things to say about him. I think he's dating Sadie Green, who works as a waitress at the truck stop along the interstate."

"It might be worth our time to talk to his girlfriend. She might feel differently than his coworker."

"Maybe."

"How do you know so much about all these people if you've been away for a while?" Irish asked.

With a slight grin, Tessa shrugged. "Hospital gossip

and it's a small town." She moved on to the next guy. "That's Nathan Harris, also a football player. A linebacker. He worked on defensive line."

Irish studied the man in the picture. Harris had a big face, brown hair, brown eyes, heavy eyebrows and a square jaw. "How tall was he?" Irish asked.

"Over six feet, and he was big-boned. And surprisingly fast for as big as he was. He made amazing tackles in some of our games."

"Does he still live in Whiskey Gulch?" Irish asked.

"I'm not sure about him, but his mother still lives here. I think he's a truck driver. He's got to be on the road more often than not."

"What was he like in high school?"

Tessa shrugged. "I don't remember much about him. Seems like he was there, on the fringe of the popular group, and kind of quiet. I don't remember him saying much." She slid her finger to the right, landing on a teen with dirty-blond hair and gray eyes. "That's Eddy Knowlton. About the same height as Nathan. He got hit hard in the last football game of the season. He had a concussion and I think it scrambled his brain a little bit. He's never been quite the same."

"Where is he now?" Irish asked.

"He works as a janitor at the hospital where I work."

Irish didn't like the sound of that. If he was the one behind the attacks, he had easy access to Tessa at work. "Do you think he's capable of attacking a woman?"

"I don't know," Tessa said. "Every time I see him in the hallway he's moving slowly, pushing a mop or a broom. He always keeps his head down and never smiles. I feel bad for him. He had so much going for him until that injury."

Irish knew head injuries did funny things to some people. He'd seen it in soldiers with Traumatic Brain Injuries. "Was he at the party the night of graduation?"

Tessa nodded. "Yeah, everybody was." Tessa turned the page and pointed to another male. "That's Wayne Payton. Talk about a guy that had anger issues." The young man had black hair, brown eyes, and appeared heavyset. "He was another offensive lineman, who occasionally played dirty and hurt the members of other teams. He's still in town, but he's working as a cable guy. He runs internet and TV lines around here."

"Which means he has access to people's houses."

Tessa nodded. "Yeah, but only when they let him in. He doesn't have keys to people's houses."

"Is he married?"

She shook her head. "No. He was married to Marcie Williamson, but that didn't last. They married right after she graduated high school. She divorced him within a year. She supports herself on the tips she makes as a waitress at the diner. She and Penny were good friends, and Penny's murder almost did her in."

"We should talk to her," Irish said.

"I know the police questioned her at length after Penny's death. They spoke to a lot of us that were at the party. Marcie was a year younger than us, also on the cheer squad, but a junior. She came to the party the night of the graduation with Wayne. I guess she got pretty drunk, because she doesn't remember when Penny wandered off or went missing. I never got the whole story from her."

Tessa's finger moved to the next image of a guy with light brown hair and brown eyes. "That's Hayden Severs. He was our receiver and our best running back. The guy was not that big, but he could run fast. And if Randy got the ball anywhere close to them, you could be guaranteed that Hayden would catch it."

"How tall was he?"

"Mmm, probably about five-ten. He was lean then and still is. He works for an autobody shop in town. And drives a tow truck."

"What about this guy?" Irish pointed to a young man with glasses.

Tessa smiled. "That's Wally, or Richard Wallace. He was the class geek. He ran the computer lab." She frowned. "He had the biggest crush on Penny. I remember the sheriff grilled him with questions. But he had a rock-solid alibi. He was not at the party that night. He was celebrating graduation with some of his geek friends, playing that retro game—Dungeons and Dragons—at the local church. There were at least three witnesses who attested to the fact that they played through the night."

"Who else in your class, or maybe a lower class, was big enough to be the man who attacked you?"

Tessa pointed to a few pictures of some of the guys in the junior class. After a while, she looked up. "I don't know what to tell you. It's been years since I've seen some of these people. Some of them I see every day. None of the men I know stand out as potential attackers. I tend to see the good in most people. But then, I thought Randy was a nice guy…until I married him. You see why I don't trust my own judgement?"

Irish smiled at her. "It's not a bad thing to see the good in most people."

"No, it's not." Tessa sighed. "But it leaves me open to be taken advantage of."

"Yes, it does." He glanced at the clock on the wall.

"Let's go to the lumber store and see if we can find Josh Kitterman and ask him about his sister."

She thumbed through a few pages. "Let's do it. All these months I've been living in Whiskey Gulch, I've seen Josh maybe three or four times. I haven't really stopped to talk to him. I didn't realize his sister had been murdered. I thought she was happily living somewhere else. Happily married, unlike me. I feel bad that I haven't said anything to him. I've been wallowing in my own misery of a failed marriage when others have had it worse."

"Yours wasn't a case of a failed marriage," Irish said. "It was a case of a successful escape."

She gave him a crooked grin. "When you put it that way, you're right. Let's go see Josh." She closed the year-book and stood.

"How's that foot?" Irish asked.

"It only hurts a little bit," she admitted. "I'm able to get around a lot better. Thanks to a certain Delta Force guy who's good at treating wounds."

"Glad I could be of assistance," he said with a bow. "It just puts me one step closer to achieving my status of knight in shining armor. I hope soon I'll be qualified to rescue damsels in distress."

She laughed. "You're already there. This damsel is quite satisfied with your work."

He held out his hand and she placed hers in his. Together, they walked to the front door. Tessa grabbed her purse on the way through the living room. Irish took the keys from her and locked the cottage.

Chapter Eleven

Irish insisted on taking his truck, reasoning that it was bigger, and if there was somebody that wanted to ram into them, it would hold up better than her SUV. The drive to the hardware store took less than five minutes. Irish could appreciate the benefits of living in a small town. It didn't take long to get where he needed go.

Irish pulled into the parking lot, shifted into Park, and climbed down, hurrying around the front of the vehicle to open the door for Tessa. He helped her down from the truck. She took his hand as they walked into the store. It was the first time that she'd reached for him. It made him feel strangely warm and content.

Once inside, Tessa leaned toward Irish. "That's Josh, behind the counter."

Three people stood in line, waiting their turn to check out in front of the man she'd indicated was Josh.

Irish tipped his head toward the rows of hardware and paint supplies. "While we wait for the line to clear, let's get something to repair that hole in the door. Unless you'd rather replace it?"

She shook her head. "I still owe you for the back door. If we can repair the bedroom door, I'm fine with that."

"Should be able to with a little putty and paint. And I

found the hole where the bullet actually hit the wall and embedded in it. We could use a little toothpaste or plaster to fill that hole and then just a little touchup paint should cover it completely."

They were standing in the aisle with the wood putty when Tessa whispered, "That's Wayne Payton."

"The cable guy?" Irish studied the guy. He was big, maybe a couple inches taller than Irish himself. And heavyset. "He was the one who dated Marcie, Penny's friend, who was a cheerleader in the class below yours?"

Tessa smiled. "That's the one. He was at the party with Marcie the night Penny died."

"Did he have an alibi?"

"Marcie." Tessa glanced up at Irish. "Should we go question him?"

"Why not? We're here."

What were the chances he'd up and confess to three murders and some attacks on Tessa? Irish thought. He could tell a lot from a person's expression. Maybe the man wouldn't confess in words, but his face might show some of his guilt if he was, indeed, the culprit.

Tessa squared her shoulders and walked with Irish toward Marcie's ex. "Hey, Wayne," Tessa said. "It's been a long time."

The man's eyes narrowed as he stared at her. "I heard you were back in town." He dipped his head at Irish. "This your new boyfriend, since you dumped Randy?"

Tessa's brow twisted. "Is that what he told you?"

Wayne shrugged. "Not actually. Randy said that he dumped you."

Tessa's lips turned up in the corners. "Sounds like Randy," she muttered beneath her breath.

"I figured it was probably you dumping him," Wayne

said. "That's what women seem to do. Marriage vows don't mean squat nowadays."

"I lived up to my side of the union," Tessa said, "until he stopped living up to his. That part about *cherish*? Randy had no clue. And he was well on his way to fulfilling the *'til death do us part*, with me being the one to die."

"That's not what he said. He said you were cheating on him." His gaze shifted to Irish.

"Believe what you want," Tessa said, a hand on Irish's arm to keep him from stepping toward Wayne. His fist clenched. "I heard you and Marcie split up," Tessa said, deflecting Wayne's attack on hers and Randy's marriage.

Wayne snarled.

"Were you of the same line of thought that Randy was?" she asked. "That a wife should be beaten regularly to keep her in line?"

Wayne squared his broad shoulders. "I never laid a hand on Marcie. She was the one who asked for the divorce. She never got over her best friend's death. After Penny was murdered, she was never the same. I married her anyway, hoping that we could make a life together. She felt guilty that Penny died that night, and she blamed me."

Tessa stiffened beside Irish. "Did you kill Penny?"

"No," Wayne said. "But you would have thought I did. I insisted that Marcie and I make out during the party. And because of that, she left Penny alone. If Marcie and I had not been making out, Penny wouldn't be dead. Therefore, I'm at fault. I might as well have killed Penny, based on the way Marcie was thinking."

"But she married you," Tessa said.

"Yeah. I thought that it would work out. That she'd

eventually get over it, and that the wedding would take her mind off Penny's death. And it did for a while. For that whole year that she was a senior, while I was waiting for her to graduate, she stayed busy planning our wedding." Wayne shoved a hand through his hair. "But after we married and settled into our own home, she had too much time on her hands to think about Penny. Our marriage fell apart. I even offered to go see a marriage counselor with her. She refused. Eventually, she filed for divorce."

His shoulders slumped. "The sad thing is, I still love her. I had every intention of living the rest of my life with her. Growing old, having grandchildren, the whole works. All that ended when Penny was murdered." He inhaled a deep breath and let it out. "Look, I don't know what happened between you and Randy, but I know he could be a real jerk when he wanted to be. And you were never anything but nice to me. I'm sorry about what I said. I'm sure you had good reasons for your divorce." He glanced at the watch on his wrist. "I've said enough. Now, I have to go. I'm supposed to be at work." Wayne walked away. He set the items he had in his hands on a shelf and left the store, his shoulders still slumped.

"Do you believe what he said?" Irish asked.

Tessa nodded. "I do. He appears to really regret having lost Marcie. And Marcie vouched for him that night. It wouldn't hurt to talk to Marcie again," Tessa said. "We could stop by the diner at lunch and see if she's working."

"Sounds like a plan." Irish glanced at the counter. Josh was still busy with two other customers.

Tessa touched his arm. "Hey, there's Nathan Harris."

Irish chuckled. "Is that all we have to do is come to

the hardware store to run into every male classmate? Is it the social Mecca of Whiskey Gulch?"

"Apparently." Tessa chewed on her bottom lip. "I have no idea how to approach Nathan. He was never easy to talk to and I have nothing in common with him."

"Let me handle it," Irish said.

He approached Nathan. "Excuse me. You from around here?"

Nathan frowned. "Yeah."

Irish smiled. "I don't suppose you know someone who can do some minor repairs around a house, do you?"

Nathan turned to fully face Irish. "Maybe." He looked past Irish to where Tessa stood and nodded. "Tessa."

"Nathan." Tessa gave him a tight smile. "I didn't know you still lived here."

"Never moved," he said. "Once Dad passed, I stayed around the house to help Mom out."

Tessa nodded. "I bet she's glad to have you around."

He nodded. "I don't hear any complaints. What about you? How long have you been back? Haven't seen you around much."

Tessa lifted a shoulder and let it fall. "Other than jogging, going to the grocery store and work, I pretty much stay close to my home."

Nathan lifted his chin. "Mom told me she heard through the grapevine that you ran into some trouble."

Tessa nodded. "Yes, I did."

"Someone attacked you out by the river?" Nathan shook his head. "Sorry to hear that," he said. "I just got back in town late last night."

"Have you been traveling?" Tessa asked.

He shook his head. "I drive a truck. That's probably

why you haven't seen me around much. I'm usually on the road."

"How's that working out for you?" Tessa asked.

Nathan shrugged. "It pays the bills, keeps me busy, and I come back often enough to help out Mom."

"Do you miss our high school days and playing football?" Tessa asked.

Nathan shook his head. "Not really. Football's a tough sport. It's hard on the body. And I don't miss all the drama of high school."

"Any drama in particular?" Tessa asked.

He shook his head. "Just all of it. I was never so glad to put a place behind me."

"You ever marry?" Tessa asked.

He shook his head. "Most women want a man who's home every night. I can't guarantee that in my line of work." He nodded at Irish. "This the new man in your life? I heard you ditched Randy. Can't say as I blame you."

Tessa's brow dipped and she stepped closer to Irish. "As a matter of fact, yes, this is the new man in my life. And why do you think that Randy deserved to be ditched?"

Nathan's lips curled back in a smirk. "He never did know how to treat a woman right. The man had everything. The best position on the football team, the prettiest girl in the school, and a college scholarship. Everything came easy to him and he took it all for granted."

"You could have gone on to college," Tessa said. "Why didn't you?"

"Not smart enough." Nathan's lips thinned. "Randy even had that going for him. He didn't have to work very hard to get good grades. He could do anything he put his mind to. I barely passed English, and I never could memorize all those dates in history. Only thing I was good at was math." He shook his head. "Yeah, Randy squandered his life. And then he lost you. Anyway, congratulations on the new man in your life. Glad to see you back in town. Don't be a stranger." Nathan turned to leave.

He'd gone two steps when Tessa called after him. "Hey, Nathan, you were there the night of our graduation party, weren't you?"

He turned, his eyes narrowing. "Yeah, why?"

"I just don't remember everyone who was there." She smiled. "I was just wondering."

"You probably don't remember because you were busy with Randy." He nodded. "I was there. I didn't stay long, though."

"Why not?" Tessa asked.

"Nothing there for me. Just a bunch of kids getting drunk. Why do you ask?"

"I just think about Penny every once in a while and wonder if anyone saw anything that would help us figure out what happened to her."

Nathan tilted his head to one side. "Like what?"

"Like if she left with somebody."

Nathan shook his head. "Nope, I didn't see her leave with anybody." He raised a hand. "Look, I need to go. I'm supposed to stop by the pharmacy for Mom's meds. See you around."

By the time Nathan left, Josh had freed up at the counter.

"Come on, let's go talk to Josh," Tessa said.

"Good morning," Josh Kitterman said from behind the counter. "What can I help you with?"

Irish set the tub of putty on the counter along with a small putty knife. "I'd like to purchase these."

"Hey, Josh," Tessa said. "Good to see you."

"Hey, Tessa," Josh acknowledged and rang up the items. "I've seen you around town, I just haven't had the chance to say hello."

"I wanted to say I'm sorry about what happened to Kitty. I can't believe I only just heard about it."

His eyes clouded and his mouth formed a thin line. "We were all pretty shocked."

"I was surprised there wasn't anything in the obituaries about her death."

Josh shook his head. "The folks had been gone so long that they only put the announcement in the Kerrville newspaper where Kitty lived."

"They ever catch the guy?" Tessa asked.

Josh shook his head. "Nope."

Tessa lowered her voice and spoke softly. "Do you mind me asking what happened?"

He sighed. "She was home with her two kids. One of them was two, the other was only eight months old. Her husband had gone out of town on a conference. He'd talked to her on the phone that morning, no problem. Everything was fine. When he got home that afternoon, he walked into the house, the door was unlocked. The two-year-old was sitting on the floor in the living room, crying. The baby was in her crib crying. Kitty was gone. He searched throughout the house, couldn't find her. Looked around the yard. She wasn't there. He called 9-1-1. The police searched the neighborhoods surrounding their house. Nothing."

"Was there forced entry on her house?" Irish asked.

Josh shook his head. "No. They think she must have

known who it was because she opened the door. Her husband was pretty broken up about it. Mom's been helping him out as much as she can with the kids. They found Kitty's body alongside the interstate, a couple of days later. The autopsy reported that she had been strangled. Someone had choked her to death with his hands." The more Josh spoke, the tighter his voice became. Finally, he looked away, as if to get a grip on his emotions. "It happened while I was in the military. I couldn't talk about it for a long time. I can't imagine what she went through." His voice faltered. "My poor sister."

"Did the police have any idea who it might have been?"

Josh shook his head. "None. And no one on her street saw anybody coming or going. In her subdivision, both the husband and wife have full-time jobs. Kitty was a schoolteacher. Since it was summertime, she was home with the kids."

Tessa reached across the counter and touched Josh's hand. "I really am sorry. Kitty and I were good friends. She was one of the nicest people I know. Hard to think anybody could do that to her."

Josh nodded. "And those poor kids will never know what a great mother she was. My wife and I get down there as often as we can. We bring the kids up here when we have time off. Kitty's husband just now started dating again. I really do hope he finds somebody who can love those children as much as she did."

"Me, too," Tessa said.

As Irish paid for his purchases, Josh looked across the counter at Tessa. "I heard you ran into some trouble here recently."

She half smiled. "Word gets around, doesn't it?"

Kitty's brother nodded. "Be careful. If Kitty knew

who attacked her, it could be somebody she knew from high school. Somebody from Whiskey Gulch. I mean, they never did find Penny's killer and Kitty's killer is still out there somewhere."

"Do you think they could be the same person?" Tessa asked. "The person who attacked me and the person who killed Kitty, Bethany and Penny?"

His eyes narrowed. "Deputy Jones came by earlier today and talked about the possibility. I also heard that Bethany York was murdered down in San Antonio. You were all cheerleaders and seniors in high school at the same time. It's not too far-fetched an idea."

"Did Kitty ever share her thoughts about the night that Penny died?" Tessa asked.

Josh shook his head. "I'd already left home. She'd written about it in a letter. But not her feelings about what had happened, other than she was sad that Penny was gone and that it was horrible that somebody had done that while they were all out partying. I guess she felt guilty that it happened so close and no one knew."

"I think we all felt bad for Penny," Tessa confessed.

"You know, if there's anything I can do to help you find the person who's attacking you, I'll do it. I know Kitty would have wanted me to help a friend."

"Thanks, Josh," Tessa said.

As they exited the hardware store, Tessa reached out and gripped Irish's hand. He closed his fingers around hers and squeezed gently.

"I'm sorry about your friends," he said. "This can't be easy, rehashing it." He knew what it was like to lose friends. Even though they knew the risks as a Delta Force operator, losing a brother always hit hard. "Wanna stop by the sheriff's office and then we'll go by the diner?" he asked.

She nodded. "Let's do it." She held his hand all the way out to the truck. Once there, she let him open the door and help her up inside.

He liked that she felt comfortable with him. And that she felt safe holding his hand. He wanted to find the guy that was doing this to her and take him out of her life so that she could live peacefully. Even knowing that when he did, his job here would be done. He didn't want to be done with Tessa.

Chapter Twelve

Irish drove to the sheriff's department and parked out front. Before Tessa was out of her seat, he was around the side and opening her door for her. Maybe it was part of his job to take care of her, but Tessa guessed that it was in his nature to open doors for women.

When he held out his hand, she placed hers in his and he helped her out of the truck.

"You do know I'm quite capable of opening my own doors, right?" she said.

He grinned. "Oh, yeah, I know that. Suffice it to say I enjoy opening the door for you. Please don't take that small pleasure away from me."

She smiled. "Okay. I'd hate to deprive you of your chivalrous deeds. You have to keep the shine on your knightly armor."

"That's right." He winked. "The armor has to shine."

Once inside, she spotted Deputy Jones sitting at a computer, with Matt Hennessey looking over her shoulder.

The deputy glanced up. "Oh, Ms. Bolton. Glad you showed up."

Tessa's pulse fluttered. "Have you found anything?"

Deputy Jones's lips pressed together. "Not much, but everything put together will count eventually."

"So, what's new?" Irish asked.

She pointed to the computer monitor. "We were able to get electronic copies of Bethany York's autopsy."

"And what did you learn from it?" Tessa asked.

"Like Mrs. Kitterman," Deputy Jones said, "Ms. York was also strangled. But there's something else."

Tessa stepped closer.

The deputy continued. "What was strange was that her fingers and toes showed signs of frostbite."

"Frostbite?" Tessa's forehead creased.

Deputy Jones nodded. "Frostbite."

"What time of year did you say she was murdered?" Irish asked.

Matt Hennessey turned to Tessa and Irish. "July."

"How?" Tessa queried.

"All we could figure was that maybe she'd been trapped in a freezer before her killer strangled her."

"And Kitty?" Tessa asked.

"We haven't gotten Kitty Kitterman's autopsy report yet. We'll let you know as soon as we do."

"Well, that's different than Penny's death. She was strangled and shoved off a cliff. No frostbite," Irish said.

"She was dead before she landed, according to her autopsy report," Matt Hennessey said. "Bethany York wasn't dead when she got frostbite."

"And she was found north of Kerrville off the interstate?" Irish asked.

"That's right," Deputy Jones said.

"Pretty close to where Kitty Kitterman was found. And Kerrville's not that far from San Antonio," Irish said.

"True," Deputy Jones said.

"It sounds like it's the same man who killed Kitty Kitterman and Bethany York," Matt said. "And based on the fact that Penny, Kitty and Bethany were all cheerleaders on the same squad, Penny could have been killed by the same guy. And that could be the same man who is now after Tessa."

"But what does that tell us about this man?" Irish asked.

"That he likes to strangle his victims, for one," the deputy said.

Tessa raised a hand to her throat and shivered. "And he nearly got away with it with me."

"Fortunately, he did not get away with it." Irish held out his hand. Tessa took it.

"How horrible for Bethany," Tessa said. "It's bad enough to be strangled to death, but to have to freeze before you're strangled. So cold that frostbite was on her fingertips, that's awful. He could have locked her in a restaurant refrigerator or freezer. Bethany was small. He could have put her in a chest freezer."

"In a chest freezer, she would have run out of air pretty quickly," Deputy Jones said. "Which means she would have died pretty quickly in a chest freezer. It had to be big enough for her to survive long enough for him to take her back out and strangle her. Her killer had access to a large refrigerator or freezer."

"Maybe he works in a restaurant?" Tessa suggested.

"Or a meat packing plant," Matt added.

"Is that all you have?" Tessa asked.

Deputy Jones nodded. "Told you it wasn't much, but every little clue adds up."

"We're going to find this guy, preferably before he gets to Tessa," Irish said.

"Where are you two headed now?" Matt asked.

"The diner for lunch," Irish answered.

"Is Trace holding down the fort at the ranch?" Matt grinned.

"Between his mother and Lilly, they've got everything under control."

Tessa started for the door and turned around. "Did you have any luck with your background checks on the male members of my high school class?"

Deputy Jones shook her head. "Nothing much. A few speeding tickets is all I've found so far. One DUI, but no felonies, domestic abuse or violent crimes." The deputy's gaze met Tessa's. "I understand that you left your husband because he was abusive. I didn't find anything in his background check about it." She raised her eyebrows. "You said he beat you?"

Tessa winced. "I didn't report it to the police or press charges. I just wanted out."

The deputy shook her head. "You know without a record, he could hurt someone else and the police would have nothing to go on. Abusive men are usually repeat offenders."

"I didn't think about that. I didn't want him to have a felony record. It would have made it harder for him to get work."

"It's not too late to file a report," Deputy Jones said. "You have the hospital records."

Tessa nodded. "I'll think about it." The thought of another woman suffering at the hands of her ex-husband made Tessa's stomach roil.

Deputy Jones turned back to the monitor. "We've got a few more of the guys to run through the background check and the other autopsy report to review. Should have that done before your meeting with Randy Hudson."

"Trace and I will be there for that meeting," Matt said.

"And I'll be nearby." Deputy Jones stood. "We didn't get the metal detector from the high school. The principal said it's out of commission and has a work order on it. The company that services it was supposed to be there today to get it working, but they got tied up on another job."

Irish frowned. "I'm not sure I like the idea of Tessa's ex getting anywhere close to her without running him through that metal detector first."

Tessa touched his arm. "I'll be okay. The killer likes to strangle his victims, not shoot them."

"Don't forget he tried to ram you with a vehicle," Irish reminded her.

She nodded. "I contend that Randy isn't the killer. We'll be in a public place, surrounded by people. The killer hasn't shown his face to anyone yet. I doubt it's Randy. But maybe he'll know something that could lead us in the right direction."

"Just be careful and don't get too close to him," the deputy said.

Tessa nodded. "I'll be on the alert for any signs of guns or knives. He'd never threatened me with either, but his feet and fists did enough damage."

Irish led Tessa out of the sheriff's office and helped her into his truck. The closer they got to the meeting between Tessa and her ex-husband, the tighter his gut clenched. He wanted to call it off.

WHILE IRISH DROVE to the diner, Tessa sat in her seat, her mind going over everything Deputy Jones and Matt Hennessey had said. Bethany had frostbite on her fingers. Her heart squeezed tightly in her chest. Bethany had suffered tremendously before she'd died.

The case for finding her own attacker had now become a journey for justice for her three friends. "We have to catch this guy," she said aloud.

"Yes, we do," Irish agreed.

Tessa drew in a deep breath and let it go. "What do you think about me setting myself up as bait to trap him?"

"No way in hell," Irish said.

"He's killed three women," Tessa pointed out.

"And if you set yourself up as bait, he could kill a fourth."

"Yeah, but if I set myself up as bait, it will lure him out into the open. We could capture him and keep him from doing this again."

"Would that be before or after he kills you?" Irish shot her a narrow-eyed glance. "Not an option."

"What if he gets anxious about killing another cheerleader and decides to go after someone besides me?" Tessa asked.

"We're not going to use you as bait. No discussion." Irish pulled into the parking lot of the diner, switched off the engine, and turned to face her. "This guy is playing for keeps. He won't stop until you're dead or he's dead. I prefer it to be that he's the one who dies. Not you."

Tessa smiled across at him. "Would that bother you as a strike against your record? I mean, you are trying to prove yourself to your new boss."

He leaned across the console and captured her face in the palms of his hands. "Record be damned. You don't deserve to die any more than those other three ladies deserved to die. This guy needs to be caught and stopped. Besides, I kind of like you."

She smiled at him. "You do?"

He nodded. "You're strong, you're brave, and you're beautiful where it counts." Irish laid a hand over his chest. "On the inside." He moved his hand back to her cheek.

"Are you going to kiss me?" Tessa whispered, her gaze sinking from his eyes to his lips.

"Do you want me to?" he asked.

She nodded.

"Then, yes. Against my better judgement." He leaned forward and pressed his lips to hers. It was a brief kiss in a public parking lot, but it warmed her to her very core. When he raised his head, he stared down into her eyes. "We won't use you as bait."

She nodded. "All right. Let's go in and see what Marcie has to say."

This time, when Irish came around to the other side of the truck to open her door and assist her, he gripped her around the waist and lifted her out of her seat, letting her body slide down his until her feet touched the ground. She rested her hands on his chest and looked up into his eyes.

"Losing focus yet?" she asked.

He groaned. "Yes, and that's not a good thing."

She gave him a sexy smile. "Maybe not, but that kiss sure was."

Inside the diner, Tessa waved to Marge, the waitress that she'd known since she could remember, and Barb a younger waitress. And she looked around for Marcie. "Hey, Marge, is Marcie working today?" Tessa called out.

Marge shouted toward the kitchen. "Marcie, you've

got company!" She glanced back at Tessa and Irish with a smile. "Are you two here to eat or to talk?"

"Both," Irish responded.

A pretty blonde exited the kitchen carrying a tray loaded with plates. "Hey, Tessa. Who's the cutie you have with you?"

"He's my…" Tessa hesitated.

Irish filled in. "Boyfriend."

Tessa didn't argue. It was easier to tell people that Irish was her boyfriend rather than her bodyguard. Although, given the number of attacks on her lately, people would probably understand why she had a bodyguard. What they wouldn't understand was how she could afford it. And, well, that would just take too much time to explain. It was easier to say that he was her boyfriend.

"Good to see you moving on," Marcie said. "Grab a table. I'll get some menus for you."

Irish chose a booth at the far end of the diner and guided her to the seat with her back up against the wall. He had her slide over and sat beside to her. It fit the role of boyfriend-girlfriend. And it felt good to have the warmth of his leg next to hers.

He put his hand out, and she laid hers in it. It was getting to be a habit to hold his hand. And he didn't ask for anything else, just to hold her hand. Randy hardly ever held her hand, even when they were dating. It was always a very possessive arm around her waist or shoulders. But never holding her hand. Tessa liked hand-holding. Tessa liked Irish. A little too much, considering she was just a job to him. She looked up at him. Or was she?

Marcie brought the menus to their table and laid them out in front of them. "Are you guys here to eat? Or do you just want coffee? Or are you going to question me like Deputy Jones did?" She gave Tessa half a smile. "I heard about what happened to you, and Deputy Jones explained how she thinks it could be related to what happened to Penny, Kitty and Bethany. Frankly, it scares the bejesus out of me."

"Could we get some coffee to start with?" Tessa asked. "And we would like to order something to eat for lunch. And then, if you have time, we'd love to talk to you." Tessa gave the waitress a gentle smile.

"Let me get that coffee and your order started, and I'll sit down." Marcie stepped back behind the counter, grabbed a tray, placed two cups on it and the coffee carafe. She came back, set the cups on the table and poured coffee into them, and then got out her pad and pencil. "What do you guys want to eat?"

Tessa ordered a club sandwich with potato chips.

"I'll have the same," Irish said.

"I'll be right back," Marcie said, and took the order to the kitchen. On her way back she called out to Marge, "Can you cover my tables?"

"Sure, go ahead," Marge said.

Marcie returned to their table carrying a glass of tea and sat in the seat across from them. "Okay, shoot. What do you want to know? Yes, I was there the night that Penny died. No, I didn't see if she left with anyone. I did walk her to her car, and stayed long enough to see her get in it. No, I didn't stay and see her drive away. As it was, they found her car exactly where it was when I left her."

"Why did you walk her to the car?" Tessa asked.

"She wanted to leave, and she wanted me to go with her."

Tessa frowned. "Why did she want to leave? It was our graduation celebration. We were there for the night."

"She wouldn't say, but I could tell that she'd been crying, and her hair was messed up."

Tessa frowned. "Penny's hair was never messed up."

"I know," Marcie said. "That was what was so strange. I would have gone with her, but I had already had a couple of beers, and Wayne was yelling at me to come back." Marcie stared down at her glass of tea. "You don't know how many times I wished I'd gone with her. If I had, she might still be here today."

"Or you might have died with her," Tessa pointed out.

"At least then I wouldn't have lived my life feeling guilty." Marcie heaved a sigh. "I let my friend down, and she died because of it. All for a stupid boy."

"And she didn't say why she was crying or why her hair was messed up?"

Marcie shook her head. "No, she didn't. I asked her, and she said it wasn't important. She told me to go back to Wayne and enjoy the rest of my evening, that she was going home. She never made it home. She never made it to Texas A&M where she got accepted to go to college. She never got to get married and have babies. Or become a teacher and coach gymnastics. She never got to do a lot of things because I didn't go with her that night."

Tessa reached across the table and touched Marcie's hand. "It wasn't your fault. You didn't kill her, somebody else did."

"I might as well have. Not going with her signed her death sentence."

"So, do you think somebody came on to her and that's why her hair was messed up and she wanted to leave?" Tessa asked.

"It was either that or she had a good make-out session and then got into an argument with whoever she was making out with," Marcie said. "I went over and over in my mind who that could be, but she had broken up with Connor a week before that party. And she'd said that she was really done with him, that she was going to college and didn't need that kind of commitment when she had college in front of her. Especially since he was going on to the fire academy. They wouldn't see each other for four years. She'd admitted that they'd grown apart over the last year of high school. And he was there that night with Angela Bates."

"Was she hanging out with anybody else?" Tessa asked.

"If she was, I wasn't aware of it. I was too busy sucking face with Wayne. You know we were married for a year, don't you?"

Tessa nodded. "I'd heard. I'm sorry about your breakup."

"He thinks I blamed him for Penny's death." Marcie shook her head. "I didn't blame him. I blamed myself. I couldn't get over the guilt, and I could see that it was bringing him down, too. He deserved someone better than me."

"So you ended it?" Tessa asked.

"I did." Marcie gave a half smile. "And the jerk hasn't moved on and found another woman to make his wife and raise his babies."

Tessa squeezed Marcie's hand. "Have you ever thought that maybe he hasn't gotten over you?"

"He should have. I wasn't good enough for him. Anyone who'd let a friend down like that…"

Tessa squeezed her hand. "You didn't let your friend down. You didn't kill Penny. Someone else did. You can't blame yourself."

"Yeah, well tell me that in the middle of the night when I wake up with nightmares. I see her face and then I see her lying at the bottom of that cliff."

"Do you remember seeing her at all that night other than when you walked her to her car?" Tessa asked.

Marcie bobbed her head. "I remember seeing her dancing in the firelight. She appeared happy then."

"Was there anyone else around her? Maybe dancing with her?"

Marcie stared out the window. "There were a lot of people dancing that night. And the fire cast shadows."

"Think about it," Tessa urged. "Any... Anyone big?"

"There were a couple of girls with her, and there were some guys as well. I remember because their shadows were bigger. But it was hard to tell. They were more or less just silhouettes in the darkness. Come to think of it, Eddy Knowlton might have been out dancing in that firelight. He was never really a good dancer, even in before his head injury. But there was at least one other who was equally as tall. And I can't place him right now. I can't see his face in my mind.

"But then, everybody was dancing, and if they weren't dancing, then they were in the bushes or truck beds making out. I'm sorry I can't be of more help. The night was a blur. Especially after the two beers I drank. I haven't had a beer since. I'm sorry this is happening to you, Tessa. You were always good to me. You worked with me to get the routines down right, and you always made me feel a part of the team. If I could think of anything else that I remember from that night, I'll let you know as soon as I remember it."

"Order up," the cook called from the kitchen.

Marcie pushed to her feet. "That might be your order. I'll get it."

"Marcie," Tessa called out after her.

Marcie turned.

"If you ever need someone to talk to or just want to hang out, come see me. I could use some friends." Tessa's lips quirked. "But you might want to wait until whoever's after me is caught. I don't want you to get caught in the crossfire."

She smiled. "Thanks, I appreciate that. I could use a friend, too."

Marcie brought their club sandwiches to them and, for a few short minutes, Irish and Tessa ate in silence.

"So, what do you think?" Irish finally asked.

"Sounds to me like somebody made a pass at Penny on graduation night, and she turned him down."

"And some men don't take rejection very well," Irish concluded, finishing his sandwich.

Tessa pushed her plate toward him. "Do you want the other half of mine?"

"No, but we can get it wrapped up and take it home. You might be hungry later."

"I have dinner with my ex later. I guarantee I won't be hungry."

"Maybe not while you're with him, but after you come back home, you might be hungry."

"Okay, you've convinced me." She asked Marcie to bring a to-go box for the other half of her club sandwich. Once Irish paid the bill, they left the restaurant and headed back to her home at the end of the street. Before Irish could turn off the engine, Tessa put her hand over his. "I don't feel like going in the house. How about we go out to the bluffs where this all started?"

"Are you sure?" Irish asked.

Tessa nodded. "I don't think there will be any clues out there as to who killed Penny, but I don't know, maybe some memories will come back if I just go out there. I haven't been there since that night."

"Okay, lead the way."

With Tessa's guidance, Irish drove out to the bluffs where the infamous graduation party had taken place. He parked the truck, and they got out and walked around.

"This used to be the favorite place for everybody to come make out with their boyfriend or girlfriend," Tessa said.

"And after Penny's death?" Irish asked.

"I doubt anybody comes out here anymore." Tessa walked to a spot far enough away from the edge of the cliff and pointed at the ground. "This is where the bonfire was. We stacked wood for days, and some of the parents even helped. I heard that after that night, all the graduation parties were held locked down in the gym at the high school with parents hovering over the kids." Tessa slipped her arm through the crook of Irish's elbow and leaned against him. "Thanks for bringing me here."

"I wish I could make everything better for you," he said.

"You do, just by being here," she sighed. "I guess we better get back. I've got to get ready for my date with my ex-husband."

"You don't have to go," Irish said.

Tessa nodded. "Yes, I do."

"Were you with him that entire night of the graduation party?" Irish asked.

"As far as I remember, I was," she said.

"What do you mean?" Irish looked at her.

"At some point in the night, I fell asleep on our blanket. I can't account for every minute of that night. Penny might not have left in that car. Randy could have been the one who strangled her and shoved her off the cliff. I don't know. I can't rule him out. He didn't show his violent side until things went south with his job. Verbal abuse, yes. Physical abuse didn't happen until then. But that doesn't mean he didn't have it in him. Either way, I hope we'll find out something tonight."

As they drove to the cottage, Tessa thought through all the information she'd gathered that day. From what Marcie said, Penny might have been accosted by someone. That someone could have been the person who'd ultimately murdered her. At that time of night, Randy was with Tessa, unless it was at one point that she was dancing and she'd thought Randy was hanging out with his football buddies. It was possible that he could have snuck off and made a pass at Penny.

Or it could have been one of the other guys. They still really didn't have a clue. When they reached the house, Irish went through it again and cleared it before he let her go inside.

Tessa carried the box with her sandwich in it and put it in the refrigerator. "You're welcome to eat this or anything you find in the fridge. I'm going to get ready."

She dreaded the thought of meeting her ex-husband again. He always made her feel so inferior, so small. But surely all of those therapy sessions had paid off. She squared her shoulders and went to her room with the idea that the better she looked, the better she'd feel and the more confidence she'd have when she faced Randy.

Knowing she didn't have to do it alone, made her feel even better. She liked having Irish around. He never judged her. He accepted her the way she was. It also didn't hurt knowing the sheriff's department would be in the vicinity if anything should happen.

Chapter Thirteen

While Tessa got ready for her dinner date with her ex-husband, Irish made a phone call to Trace Travis.

He answered on the first ring. "It's Travis. Whatcha got, Irish?"

"Just double-checking to make sure that you and Matt will be there tonight when we meet with Tessa's ex."

"Gearing up now," Travis said. "Matt just walked in the door. I thought I'd make it a date night with Lilly, so we'd have an excuse for coming to the diner. Matt will cover the exterior along with Deputy Jones and the sheriff."

"Good, I'll carry my handgun under my jacket," Irish said.

"We'll be ready if he tries anything with Tessa," Travis said.

"I'm glad. I don't have a good feeling about this."

"You think he'll try something?"

"Even if he's not the one who's doing this, I have a feeling that whoever is, might be watching and could make his move tonight. Or I'm just a Nervous Nelly."

Travis laughed. "You've had hunches before, and those hunches have paid off."

Irish sighed. "Well, let's hope my hunch is wrong this

time." He ended the call and sat at the kitchen table. Taking his 9 mm Glock out of his holster, he set it down in front of him. In less than fifteen seconds, he had it disassembled and laid out in pieces.

He dug his cleaning kit out of his duffel bag and spent a few minutes taking care of his weapon, cleaning the bolt and the barrel, and oiling them down. He checked the magazine and made sure that it was full. Then he loaded a second magazine to take as a spare. It might be overkill because it only took one bullet to kill a man, if you were a good shot. And as far as he knew, there was only one man who was after Tessa. And if it was her ex-husband, Irish might just enjoy putting a bullet in him.

When he was satisfied, he put the weapon back together, and tucked it into the shoulder holster strapped onto his back.

Irish glanced at his shirt. It was the one he'd been wearing when they'd gone around town this morning. If Tessa's attacker was not Randy and had been watching them, he would recognize Irish in the shirt. Heck, he'd probably recognize Irish anyway, but why give him any extra clues? He left the kitchen for the living room, dug into his duffel again and came up with a sky-blue polo shirt. Stripping off his shoulder holster, he pulled his T-shirt over his head.

He was standing shirtless in the living room when Tessa stepped out of her bedroom. and emitted a soft gasp.

She wore a sleeveless red dress that hung down to just above her knees, and she looked like a million dollars. No, she was even better than a million dollars. It wasn't just the cut of the dress that made it sexy, it was the woman wearing it. Her eyes were wide, her brows arched as her gaze swept over his bare chest.

"I'm sorry," he said. "I thought you'd be a little longer."

"No, that's okay," she said. Her face flushed a pretty pink.

He pulled the polo shirt over his head and down over his torso. Tessa's gaze followed his every move.

Quickly tucking the shirt into the waistband of his jeans, he let out a low and slow whistle. "Wow, that dress."

The pink in her cheeks deepened, and she glanced down at the dress. "Do you think it's too much?"

He chuckled. "It depends on what you are trying to accomplish."

She looked up. "What do you mean?"

"If you want your ex to regret that he'd ever lifted a hand to you in anger, that dress will do it. He'll be wishing that you were still his wife and getting down on his knees to beg to take you back."

"I don't want him back," she said. "And I don't want him down on his knees to beg me to take him back. But I guess I do want him to have a few regrets."

Irish grinned. "And he should. He let the prettiest girl in Whiskey Gulch get away."

She wrung her hands. "Maybe I should wear jeans and a T-shirt."

Irish shook his head. "No, you're wearing the right thing. Does it give you confidence?"

She nodded. "I went shopping the day after I signed the divorce papers. I guess you could say it was retail therapy. When I found this dress, it made me happy. And at that moment, I needed something to make me happy. To me, red is cheerful."

Irish smiled. "And bold."

Tessa nodded. "Bold and powerful," she said. "I wanted to feel a little bit of that power, and this dress does it for me."

"Then you're wearing the right dress," Irish said. "And you look amazing."

She glanced down at her outfit. "Yeah, but I'm wasting it on my ex."

"Maybe so, but you're not wasting it on you. Or on me." Irish gave her a wink. "Promise me that if we go out on a date, you'll wear that dress."

She smiled. "You're on."

Irish glanced down at his watch. "We have about twenty minutes to get to the diner. I got my computer out. I thought maybe we could look through the internet and see if we can find anything on the guys in your senior class. I don't know what, but I thought maybe we could poke around."

She followed him into the kitchen where he'd set up his computer. "What do you think we should be looking up? I know that Deputy Jones, Matt Hennessey, and Trace Travis have been searching for any police records on the guys that were in my class."

"Yes, they have, but I want to do some general inquiries on the internet to see if there's any information about any of those class members that might not be in arrest records. Let's look up Wayne. What was his last name?"

"Payton," Tessa said.

Irish keyed in Wayne Payton in the search bar. His name only came up in the obituary for his grandmother and for the announcement of his divorce to Marcie. Nothing particularly damning.

"Who's next?" Irish asked.

"Try Mike Bradley," Tessa said.

When he typed in Mike Bradley's name, hundreds of results displayed on the screen. "He might as well be named John Smith," Irish said. He added Whiskey Gulch to the search bar. Mike's name came up as the coach at the middle school in Whiskey Gulch, and there were several articles about him. Most were about what a great coach Mike Bradley was, and some of the charity work he had done.

Tessa smiled. "Told you he was a nice guy."

"Makes me want to meet him," Irish said.

"Stick around Whiskey Gulch long enough and you will," Tessa said.

"Next?" Irish prompted.

"How about Eddy Knowlton?"

Eddy Knowlton from Whiskey Gulch came up in several news articles about his football playing from ten years ago. One in particular detailed his injury, and how he'd had bleeding on the brain and been in the hospital for a week.

"Try Connor Daniels," Tessa said. Again, there were several news articles about his performance on the football field. And then there was also his social media page, where he displayed pictures of himself in uniform, graduating from firefighter training, and receiving a commendation from the city for rescuing a child from a burning building. He also had personal pictures with his hunting rifles and the buck he'd shot, his pickup truck with the knobby tires in the background. One image showed him holding a semiautomatic rifle.

"That's disturbing," Irish said.

Tessa laughed. "Half the guys in the county have

semiautomatic rifles. This is Texas. They believe it's their right."

"I can't complain," Irish said. "I own one, too."

"Yeah, but you were trained on how to use it and how not to use it."

"Makes me wish I'd brought my other gun. But it's hard to hide an AR-15 under my jacket."

Tessa glanced down at Irish's watch and sighed. "It's about that time. We need to get going."

He nodded, pushed to his feet and helped her out of her chair. "Are you sure you want to do this? You can back out right now if you want to."

She shook her head and smoothed her hands over the red dress. "No, I need to do this. If for nothing else, it helps me face my own demons. I haven't seen him since the divorce was finalized. I used to be afraid of him. I want to prove to myself that he doesn't hold any power over me anymore. I want to know that I'm finally free of him."

Irish nodded. "If at any point you feel threatened, all you have to do is say the word and I'll get you out of there."

She smiled and touched his arm. "Thank you. I appreciate that, but I want face him on my own. I want to be the one to walk away." She gave a crooked smile. "But it is nice to know that you'll be there if I need you."

They left the kitchen and passed through the living room.

"Do you want me to drive you there and drop you off?" Irish asked.

Tessa shook her head. "No. It's better if I go in my own car. I want Randy to think that I am on my own, and I don't have anybody with me."

Irish grabbed a baseball cap out of his duffel bag and slipped it over his head. "If I'm going undercover, I have to have a cover to go under." He winked.

She smiled. "You look good in a baseball cap. Makes you look like you don't have a care in the world."

"Good. Then my cover is working," he said. "And I want my looks to be deceiving." He touched her arm. "Because I have a lot of cares in the world, and they're all tied up in you."

Her cheeks flushed a pretty shade of pink. "Thank you."

She grabbed her keys and her purse and started for the door. He got there before her and held it open. Once out on the porch, he waited for her to turn the key in the lock, and he tested the knob to make sure the door was secure.

"You lead the way. I'll follow." He opened her car door for her and waited for her to get in, then closed the door.

He wanted to be with her every step of the way, but she had to do this in her own way.

Irish climbed into his truck and fell in behind Tessa as she drove out of the driveway and onto the street. He followed her the few blocks to the diner and waited for her to park before he pulled into the parking lot a few seconds later. As she got out in her red dress, he shook his head. Her ex did not deserve to see her in that red dress. He wished it was him that she was going to meet for a date. He'd show her how a man should treat a woman.

Tessa had arrived at the restaurant five minutes early for the scheduled meeting. As soon as she crossed over the threshold, Irish got out of his truck and went into the diner.

Fortunately, Tessa had chosen to sit at a booth next to another empty one. Her ex had yet to show. Irish walked past her and sat facing her from the booth behind hers. He winked and pulled his cap down low on his forehead, letting the overhead lights cast shadows, hiding his eyes and half of his face. He wished he could be in a position where he could see the expressions on both Tessa's and Randy's faces, so he could judge what was going on. But at the very least he could see Tessa's. If she showed any signs of distress, he'd be on it right away.

Irish glanced out the window just as Trace Travis's truck pulled up to the diner. Across the street in the parking lot of a real estate agency sat a sheriff's department SUV with, he would guess, Deputy Jones behind the wheel. In the far corner of the parking lot next to the diner, Matt Hennessey pulled his motorcycle into a parking space, got off, and pretended to check the mechanical functionality of the cycle's engine. The gang was all there. Now they just had to wait for Tessa's ex.

At that moment, a slick, black BMW sports car pulled into one of the parking spaces in front of the diner. A man wearing gray trousers and a white polo shirt climbed out, checked his reflection in the side mirror and then headed for the door. Based on the image in the yearbook, this had to be Randy Hudson, former quarterback and homecoming king. And Tessa's ex-husband. He had the swagger of a man who knew he looked good and took advantage of that knowledge. He smiled and waved at someone in the parking lot. And then he entered the diner.

Irish grit his teeth, his hands tightening into fists. He wanted so badly to wipe the smile off of Randy's face. The man was an animal for having beaten his wife. He didn't deserve to be in the same building as Tessa. He didn't deserve to be breathing the same air. Irish almost regretted promising Tessa that he wouldn't punch the guy.

The man stood in the doorway for a few seconds. He waved and smiled at Marge. "Hey, Marge."

Marge nodded and continued doing what she was doing.

When Randy spotted Tessa, he headed her way, smiling. Irish almost hoped that Randy would try something stupid, just so he would have the opportunity to plant his fist in the man's face.

"Tessa, sweetheart," he said and held out his hands.

Tessa kept hers in her lap and didn't stand to greet him.

"What? No hug for old times' sake?" He slid into the seat across from her, his back to Irish.

"I guess I had that coming," he said. "But I would have thought by now you would have forgiven and forgotten."

Tessa glared across the table at him.

Irish wanted so badly to go to Tessa, to pull her into his arms and just hold her.

But this was her battle. She wanted to fight it on her own.

Irish would have to sit patiently and watch as the scene played out.

TESSA CLENCHED HER hands in her lap, gritting her teeth so hard, she could feel her jaw twitch. Randy was every bit as handsome as he'd always been. In the distant past, his good looks had made her heart flutter. Now, she felt nothing but disdain for the man. And the sooner they got this meeting over with, the better.

She tipped her head, acknowledging his presence. "Randy."

"To tell the truth, I didn't think you'd come," Randy said. "What with the restraining order and all."

She didn't respond, waiting for her ex to get to the point of the meeting.

"You look really nice," he said. "Is that a new dress?"

She bit her tongue, wanting to tell him to shut up. He had no right to comment on her dress. She wasn't his wife anymore.

His brow puckered a little when she didn't respond. But that didn't stop him. "You must be doing all right if you can afford to buy fancy new clothes."

"I make my own money," she said, "and I spend it the way I like. Not on your fancy cars, or your expensive golf clubs."

His brow creased. "Hey, I bought those with my money."

"And I paid the mortgage on the house and bought the groceries."

Randy huffed out a breath. "I didn't come here to start an argument."

"Why did you come here?" Tessa asked.

"Is it wrong of me to want to see how my wife is doing without me?"

"Ex-wife," Tessa clarified.

Randy nodded, his smile tightening. "Is it wrong for a man to want to see how his high school sweetheart is doing?"

"Yes, if the divorce has been final for six months and she has a restraining order on him."

He raised his hands. "Hey, you didn't have to come."

She bobbed her head once. "You're right, I didn't."

"Then why did you?" Randy asked. "Could it be that you still have feelings for me?"

Tessa snorted. "Actually, Randy, I do have feelings for you."

He grinned. "Then aren't you glad you came?"

"I have feelings of regret," she said.

His grin broadened. "Think you made a mistake divorcing me?"

Tessa held back a laugh. "I regret that I wasted so many years of my life on you."

Randy's smile dropped and his eyebrows descended. "I would have though by now you'd be over being mad at me," he said. "So, I got carried away a little bit. I'd had a really bad day at work. I was laid off, if you recall."

"So, you came home and made sure that your wife had an even worse day, by beating her until she ended up in the hospital, with three broken ribs, a concussion, a black eye, and bruises over most of her body. *My* body. A girl doesn't get over something like that. It was the final game changer in our relationship," Tessa said.

"Fine," he said, "I got a little carried away."

"A little?" Tessa raised her eyebrows.

He shifted in his chair. "I was hoping you'd moved on by now. I came to tell you some news."

"I can't imagine you having anything to say that I would give a damn about," Tessa said.

"I got a new job," he said.

"Good for you." Tessa moved to get up.

Randy reached across the table and caught her arm. "I wasn't finished."

She jerked her arm away. "Well, I am," she said. Out of the corner of her eye, she saw Irish pushing to his feet. She gave a slight shake of her head, indicating that she didn't need him to step in yet.

He sank back into his seat, his lips pressed firmly together, his jaw tight, twitching.

Tessa raised her chin and met Randy's gaze directly. "Did I tell you I took self-defense classes."

"No, you didn't," he said. "Why?"

Her lips slid upward. "So that bastards like you can't use me as a punching bag ever again."

Randy sat back in his seat. "I can see this meeting with you was a mistake."

"You think?" Tessa said, still standing.

He rolled his eyes. "Geez, Tessa. I came to tell you that I'm getting married."

"Seriously?" Tessa blinked and sank into her seat. "Does she know how you treat your women?"

"No, and that's what I wanted to talk to you about. What happened between me and you—that was just a one-time thing. I saw a therapist and she helped me work through it."

"Why do you think I care if you get married?" Tessa's eyes widened. "You don't want me to tell her. You want me to keep it a secret that you beat me until I ended up in the hospital."

"There's no reason for you and her to ever meet. So, I'm not worried about it," he said, though he didn't sound convinced.

"Apparently you were worried enough to come talk to me and tell me not to say anything to her. She needs to know what you're capable of. She needs to take that self-defense class I took."

Randy looked right and left. "Could you keep it down please?"

"Why?" she said. "So your hometown doesn't real-ize that their former football star and homecoming king isn't as perfect as they thought he was? Are you afraid they'll learn that you're a wife beater? Because that's what you are."

Randy's frown deepened. "I told you that was a one-time event."

"Only one time that you put me in the hospital. The rest of the times, you just gave me black eyes or bruises. It happened more than once Randy. I'm not lying to anybody about that. And your fiancée has the right to know. I can't believe you want me to lie."

Randy leaned across the table. "I'm not asking you to lie. I'm just asking you not to say anything."

"Well, forget it, Randy. I'll do what's right. We're done here."

He reached across the table and grabbed her wrist. "We're done when I say we're done. If you hate me so much, why did you agree to meet with me tonight?"

"I'll tell you why I agreed," she said through her clenched teeth. "I want to know where you were the night that Penny died."

His brow wrinkled. "That was graduation night. I was with you."

"I fell asleep sometime during that night. Were you with me the entire night?"

"Of course, I was. I was asleep, too. I drank a six-pack of beer all by myself. I crashed." His frown deepened. "Why do you ask?"

"Did you ever have a beef with Kitty? Or Bethany?"

"The other cheerleaders?" He shook his head. "I had the prettiest cheerleader on the squad. Why would I have a problem with them?" His eyes narrowed. "Again, why do you ask?"

She inhaled a deep breath and let it out. "Randy Hudson, did you murder Penny?"

His eyes widened as he leaped out of his seat. "What the hell kind of question is that?"

"Did you murder Penny? And then did you murder Kitty and Bethany? And where were you the last couple of nights? Were you really in San Antonio or were you already here?"

He shook his head. "I was in San Antonio. My fiancée can vouch for me. I was with her and her parents, eating dinner. And the night before that, I was having dinner with my new boss and my fiancée. You aren't seriously accusing me of murder, are you?"

"I'm not accusing you of anything." Tessa blew out a stream of air. "I just figured if you could be angry enough to put me in the hospital, you might have enough anger to commit murder. Because you almost killed me."

He stepped back. "I never killed anyone. And if you start spreading any lies like that, I'll sue you for slander. If you think it hurt when I put you in the hospital, I'll make it hurt even worse when I make you go bankrupt."

She stood and faced him toe-to-toe. "Randy Hudson, you don't scare me anymore. Do me a favor and don't ever contact me again."

He grabbed her arm and squeezed it hard enough to bruise her skin.

"Let go of me," she said.

"I didn't kill anyone, and I'm not going to let you ruin my chances at my new job or with my fiancée."

"Excuse me?" a deep voice said behind Randy.

Tessa almost laughed at her relief when she saw Irish standing behind her ex-husband. The former Delta Force operative's broad shoulders eclipsed Randy's by a few inches, and he was a couple of inches taller.

Randy turned. "Butt out. This conversation is between me and my wife."

Irish took a step closer until he was practically nose to nose with Randy. "I believe the little lady said something about you being her *ex*-husband. That would mean she's not your wife anymore. Let go of her."

Randy released his hold on Tessa's arm. "There, you satisfied?"

"Are you all right, miss?" Irish asked Tessa.

She fought the smile that was creeping up the sides of her lips and nodded solemnly. "Yes, sir. Thank you."

"Can I escort you to your vehicle?" Irish asked, again as if he didn't already know her.

This time she did chuckle. "That would be really nice."

"So, are you gonna tell her?" Randy demanded.

Tessa stared him straight in the eye. "You need to tell her, and if you don't…"

"And if I don't—" he crossed his arms over his chest "—what are you going to do?"

"I'm going to file charges against you for assault and battery."

"That was in the distant past."

"Not so distant," she corrected.

His expression darkened. "It'll be my word against yours."

"The hospital took pictures. The neighbors heard my screams, and they saw you leave in your car. Are you willing to risk being hit up with charges and having a felony record?"

Randy's eyes slitted. "You're a mean woman, Tessa."

She snorted. "Pot meet Kettle."

"You won't do it," Randy said.

Tessa's lips curled up in a sneer. "Try me."

"We're done here," Randy said, and stalked out of the diner.

Tessa stood where she was until Randy's fancy BMW pulled out of the parking lot and raced down the main street and, hopefully, out of town. As soon as he was out of sight, the stiffness in her spine that had been holding her rigid seemed to collapse and she leaned into Irish's strong body. "That was hard."

He slipped his arm around her waist. "You were amazing. Like a Valkyrie on the warpath. I wanted to jump up and cheer 'Go Tessa!'"

She laughed. "Thank you for stepping in when you did."

"Do you think he's the murderer?" Irish asked.

She shook her head. "No, I don't."

Trace and Lilly entered the building.

"Was that Randy leaving?" Trace asked.

Irish nodded.

"You mean we missed the action?" Lilly asked.

"All five minutes of it," Irish said.

"Five minutes?" Tessa laughed. "It felt like a lifetime."

"And what's the verdict?" Trace asked. "Is he the one?"

Irish and Tessa shook their heads in the negative.

"He seemed genuinely surprised when I asked him about Kitty, Bethany and Penny. He only came to ask that I not tell his new fiancée that he's a wife beater."

Trace cursed.

Lilly crossed her arms over her chest. "You didn't agree to that, did you?"

"No way. No woman should ever be beaten, even if she *deserves it*, as Randy would say. Thank you for being here, and could you thank Matt and Deputy Jones?" she asked. "Now, if you'll excuse me, I'm exhausted and want to go home."

"You want to leave your car here and ride with me?" Irish asked as they stepped out into the parking lot.

"Sure," Tessa said, glad she wouldn't have to drive to the cottage. "I don't have to be at the hospital tomorrow morning. We can pick it up tomorrow."

Irish helped Tessa into the passenger seat and looked to meet her gaze. "Are you all right?"

She nodded. "I'll be better when I get home."

"You were amazing."

"I did what I had to do."

He climbed into the driver's seat and drove the few blocks to her house. Once he'd parked, he asked her to stay in the truck until he checked the interior of the house to make sure it was clear.

Tessa remained in her seat, shaking. It had taken every bit of her energy and her determination to face her ex-husband. Though she was proud of herself for keeping it together while she had been there, she couldn't help falling apart just a little bit now. The good news was, she was completely over Randy. And by meeting with him, she had shut the door to that chapter of her life.

Irish emerged from her house. "All clear," he said.

She loved that he was a gentleman and that he was a gentle man. The sooner they figured out who was trying to kill her, and who had killed Penny, Bethany and Kitty... Tessa might have a chance with getting on with her life. She might even let herself fall in love. Maybe even with a man like Irish.

Chapter Fourteen

Irish unlocked the truck door and swept Tessa up into his arms.

"I can walk," she said. "My foot is feeling better."

"Humor me," he said and carried her up the steps and through the open front door. "I'm still earning my armor."

"No, you're polishing it. You've earned it already." She wrapped an arm around his neck and leaned close to kiss his cheek.

He turned his head at the last second and captured her lips in a kiss that stole his breath away.

Without breaking contact, he lowered her legs, letting her slid down his body until her feet touched the floor.

Tessa opened to him and thrust her tongue through to meet his in a long, sensuous dance that only made Irish want so much more. "We have to stop," he murmured into her mouth.

"Why?" Tessa's hands circled the back of his neck.

"Because you're making me lose focus," he said, raising his head to stare down into her blue-gray eyes. "What if your attacker is outside this house, waiting for the opportunity to catch us unawares?"

"I'm willing to take that risk," she said and drew his head down for another earth-shaking kiss. When she paused for breath, she whispered, "I want you, Joseph Monahan." Then she kissed him again and pressed her breasts against his chest.

"You've had a rough day. You're not thinking clearly," he argued, trying to remove her arms from around his neck.

"I've never be more focused in my life. I know what I want. I'm not asking for forever. I'll take whatever I can get, even if it's only for a night." She leaned up on her toes and brushed his lips lightly. "Please."

His heart thundered against his ribs and his pulse raced through his veins. "Woman, you're making this harder than it has to be."

"Now you're talking," she said with a wicked little smile. "You don't have to sleep on the couch tonight. Stay with me."

Irish groaned. "If I stay with you, I might regret it in the morning."

"If you don't stay with me tonight, you'll regret it all night. I know you want to…" She rubbed her belly against his hardened staff.

Another groan rose up his throat. "I can't… Sweet heaven," he said through gritted teeth. "I. Can't. Walk. Away."

"Then don't," she said and slid her leg up the side of his, pressing her center against his thigh.

"Heaven help me." He bent, swept her up into his arms and carried her into her bedroom.

When he set her on her feet, it became a race to see who could strip the other the fastest.

Because Tessa was wearing a dress, Irish won. He had her naked in seconds, while she had only his shirt off and was struggling with the button on his jeans.

Irish brushed her hand to the side, flicked the button loose, kicked off his boots and stepped free of his jeans and boxers.

When they were both standing naked beside the bed, he cupped her cheek and brushed her lips with his. "You can change your mind at any time. Just say the word."

Tessa shook her head. "Make love to me, Irish." She reached into the nightstand behind her and produced a box of condoms with a grin. "I even have protection."

Irish laughed. "Were you planning to seduce someone?"

She lifted her chin. "I was planning on getting on with my life someday. I wanted to be prepared."

"Cheers for being prepared," he said, taking one of the little packets from the box and tossing the rest back into the drawer. "But first, I have to know your stance on foreplay."

She frowned. "Is this where I'm supposed to say foreplay is overrated?"

Irish rested a hand on her cheek and skimmed a thumb across her very kissable lips. "No." He touched the tip of her nose with his mouth. "It's where you tell me how you like it."

She chuckled. "No one ever asked me what I like. I really don't know."

He pulled her close in a hug that crushed their naked bodies together. "Sweetheart, tonight we're going to find out."

Once again, he swung her up into his arms. This time, he laid her gently on the bed and dropped down beside her, leaning up on his elbow.

"I'll start slowly," he said, trailing a finger along the side of her cheek, across to her lips and over the curve of her chin. He traced a path down the long line of her neck and across to one of her breasts.

"Your skin is so soft. I could touch you all day," he said. "How's it going so far?"

"Good," she said, her breath catching.

He laughed. "Just good?"

Her chest rose to his touch. "Everywhere your finger goes makes me burn there," she whispered.

He rolled her nipple between his thumb and forefinger until it hardened into a tight little bead. Moving to the other breast, he played with it until it, too, tightened and Tessa's back arched off the mattress.

"You're teasing me," she said, her voice ragged and little breathy.

"That's the idea," he said. His finger drew a path from her breast, over her ribs and down to her belly button. He dipped the tip of his finger in briefly before sliding still farther south to the apex of her thighs.

She sucked in a breath and held it.

"Are you ready?" he asked.

"Yes, please," she responded.

"Not yet," he said.

When she huffed, he laughed. "That's just the beginning. I want you to want me as much as I desire you."

"You desire me?" she asked, her voice hitching as his finger dipped between her legs.

"It's kind of obvious," he said. "But I'm not going to satisfy my urges until you've been thoroughly satisfied."

"What if I can't be...satisfied?" she asked.

Irish frowned. "Stop listening to your ex's voice in your head." He leaned over her and pressed a kiss to her lips. "You're a beautiful, desirable, and incredibly passionate woman."

She bit her bottom lip. "I've been told I'm cold in bed."

"Whoever told you that was wrong." Irish slipped his finger into her hot, wet entrance with a smile. "We have proof." Then he kissed her, stroking her center at the same time.

This beautiful, sexy woman was about to find that she was passionate and capable of coming apart with the right touch.

TESSA COULD BARELY BREATHE. Her pulse hammered through her veins, heating her body with every beat of her heart.

She'd never felt this way before. Sex with Randy had been okay at first, but he'd never taken the time to make sure she was as satiated as he was. He'd only sought his own gratification. She'd faked her release on so many occasions to make Randy feel better about his sexual prowess. He hadn't really cared about her needs or desires.

Irish touched her in so many places with his strong, gentle hands, taking the time to make sure she liked what he was doing.

When he slid his finger inside her, she was surprised at how wet she already was, and it made her even hotter at her very core.

When he withdrew his finger to the very tip, she raised her hips, wanting him back inside her.

Irish kissed her lips and slid that wet finger up between her folds, touching her there. That special little nubbin of nerve-packed flesh.

Sensations like she'd never experience before shot through her. Tessa arched her back off the bed, crying out.

Irish chuckled. "Like that?"

"Yes." Tessa moaned. "Oh, yes."

He stroked her there again, making her tingle.

"How... How...do you—" she moaned "—do... that?"

"It's not me. It's your body's reaction to being touched." He kissed her again and dipped his finger back inside her channel, swirling it around and around.

Tessa lay back against mattress, taking in deep, ragged breaths. She wanted more but she didn't know how to ask him for it.

She didn't need to. He knew what to do. His lips left her mouth and traveled across her chin and down the long line of her neck to where the pulse beat erratically at the base of her throat.

Tessa closed her eyes and moaned again.

"Don't," he said. "Don't close your eyes."

She opened them and smiled.

"I want you to see what turns you on." He slid down her body, capturing one of her breasts, sucking it into his mouth, flicking the nipple with the tip of his tongue.

His mouth felt so good on her breast that she wove her hands into his hair and pressed him closer.

He took more of her into his mouth and sucked hard.

Tessa's breath caught and held until he released her and moved to the other breast, treating it with the same finesse as he had the first.

When he abandoned both, he trailed his lips across her ribs, following the path his hands had taken earlier to the tuft of hair covering her sex.

Irish settled between her legs, parted her folds and touched his tongue to that special place she'd only just discovered could make her tingle all over.

He flicked it, sending sparks of electricity shooting through her body.

When he flicked it again, she gasped and her hips rose off the mattress.

The third time he touched her there with his tongue, she shot over the edge, her body pulsing to her release, every nerve quivering.

This was what it was all about, what she'd read about but never achieved.

"Oh, Irish," she called out.

He raised his head, his tongue leaving her. "Do you want me to stop?"

"No!" she cried.

He laughed and continued to apply himself to thoroughly satisfying her in every way.

When she finally came back to the mattress and the room around her, she sighed. Still, it wasn't enough.

"I want you," she moaned. "Inside me. Now."

He didn't have to be told twice.

Irish climbed up her body, grabbed the little packet of protection, tore it open and rolled it down over his thick shaft.

He bent to capture her lips with his. He tasted like her, making Tessa's core heat again.

Then he settled his big body between her legs and pressed his sheathed staff to her entrance.

"Are you okay?" he asked.

"Yes. Oh, yes."

He chuckled and slid into her slowly, letting her channel adjust to his girth.

Impatient to have all of him as soon as possible, she gripped his buttocks and pulled him all the way into her until he could go no further.

He filled her to full, his staff hot and hard. It felt so very good and right.

When he began to move, she moved with him, rising to meet each thrust. As he increased his speed, her body tightened with the same urgency inspired by his tongue earlier.

She peaked and shot over the edge for the second time that night, the tingling starting at her center and spreading throughout her body to the very tips of her fingers and toes. She rode the wave of sensations all the way to the end. Satiated, satisfied, and overwhelmed by the enormity of the passion burning within.

Irish thrust one last time, buried himself deep inside her and throbbed his release. For a long time, he held steady. When he bent to kiss her lips, he said, "Your ex was so very wrong."

She laughed. "How so?"

"You're a very hot, passionate woman."

A smile spread across her face. "It just takes the right partner."

IRISH SLID FREE of Tessa's warmth, rolled onto his side and pulled her back against his front, spooning her body.

"Wow," she said.

He chuckled. "That's all you have to say?"

"I have no words to describe what just happened," she said. "Please tell me you'll be around long enough for us to go through that box."

He laughed out loud and then kissed the back of her neck. "I can't think of anything I'd rather do."

She tucked her hand beneath her cheek and yawned. "I'm tired, but I don't want to go to sleep," she said. "I don't want to miss a thing."

"Don't worry," he said, brushing the hair back from her face. "There's always tomorrow."

"What if we catch the killer?" she said.

"I'm not going anywhere unless you want me to go away," he said.

"I don't want you to go anywhere," she said, and tucked his arm around her waist. "I never knew making love could feel so good."

"Like you said, it's only good when you have the right partner," he said.

"And am I the right partner for you?" she asked in a soft whisper.

Irish tightened his arm around her middle. "I'd give that a one-hundred-percent yes." He nuzzled the back of her ear. "Only, we should probably give ourselves more time getting to know each other. I mean I could be just your rebound from your ex-husband."

"There is no way that what I feel can be a rebound."

"But is it love or just lust?" he asked.

"Can't it be both?" she countered.

"We've only known each other for a few days," Irish said. He didn't want to tell her that, in his heart, he already knew. She needed time to believe in herself before she believed in them.

"Maybe you're right," she said, and yawned again.

"We need time to get to know each other. It's probably too soon to know whether or not it's love. And I don't want to be your rebound."

"You wouldn't be," she said. "And I don't want to saddle you with my hang-ups. I just got out of a really bad relationship. You deserve somebody who's not so mired in self-doubt. You left the Delta Force and fighting in foreign countries to start your life. That's hard enough without taking on someone else's problems."

"And you left your ex-husband to get on with your life."

"We both could be suffering PTSD," she said.

He kissed her temple and snuggled close. "Go to sleep, Tessa."

"You'll be here in the morning?" she asked.

He lifted her hand and pressed a kiss to the back of her knuckles. "I'm not going anywhere."

Soon Tessa's breathing became steadier and grew deeper, and she slept in his arms.

Irish lay there holding her, counting every breath and loving every minute he was with her. He had never been one to believe in love at first sight. And maybe that wasn't what this was, but certainly a person could fall in love within the first couple of days of knowing someone. He knew without a doubt, Tessa was the one for him. He just needed to give her time to come to the conclusion that he was the one for her.

He'd just closed his eyes when a cell phone rang in the other room.

Tessa stirred. "Is that my cell?"

"I don't know, but I'll go check." He slid out of the bed, padded barefoot into the other room, found her phone on the counter beside her purse. It stopped ringing about the time his cell beside hers started ringing. He pushed the answer button on his as he walked with hers to the bedroom. Tessa met him at the doorway as he answered, "It's Irish."

Trace's voice came over the line. "Irish, we need you and Tessa out by the interstate, ASAP."

Tessa's phone started ringing again.

"Allison? What's going on?" Tessa was talking on her phone at the same time. He could hear her saying, "I'll be there in a few minutes."

"There's a massive pile-up on the interstate," Trace

was saying. "Need all hands on deck to help. The fire department has every available man out there and it won't be enough. The hospital has called in all the nurses. They can use help out there on the scene ASAP."

"We'll be there," Irish said, and ended the call.

At the same time, Tessa ended hers. "Did you get the same call?"

He nodded. "Pile-up on the interstate?"

She nodded and ran for her bedroom. "Did they say what happened?"

"No, just to get out there as soon as possible."

Chapter Fifteen

While Irish pulled on his jeans and a T-shirt and shoved his feet into his boots, Tessa dressed in scrubs, pulling her hair back into a quick ponytail.

"Did they want you at the hospital?" Irish asked.

Tessa shook her head. "Allison said it's so bad out there, they want people on the interstate to help the emergency medical technicians who are overwhelmed. They're calling in as many first responders as they can get from surrounding counties. But I'm here, so I can get there quicker. Until the other units get to the site, I'm going to help. Then I'll head over to the hospital to receive the incoming wounded."

"We're riding together," Irish said.

She nodded as she looped her stethoscope around her neck. She rummaged through her closets, grabbing blankets. "Get the towels out of the bathroom," she called out. "I'm not sure what we'll need, but it's better to have stuff than not."

On the way to the bathroom, Irish grabbed his holster and slipped it over his shoulders, tucking his handgun into it. Then he shrugged into his jacket and collected all the clean towels he could find.

With the supplies in their hands, they rushed out to

Irish's truck and dumped the blankets and the towels in the back seat.

Tessa hopped into the passenger seat before Irish could get around to open the door for her.

He slipped behind the wheel and started the engine. As they pulled out onto the main road, Irish could hear the screams of sirens racing toward the interstate highway. He hit the accelerator, flooring it, speeding through town. He slowed as a truck pulled out in front of them with a rotating red emergency light clamped to the top.

Tessa nodded at the vehicle. "That's one of our volunteer firefighters," she said. "They're calling up everybody."

In front of that truck, an ambulance was just entering the on-ramp for the interstate, headed east toward San Antonio. Red, blue and yellow lights flashed further down the road, lighting up the sky.

They topped a rise and started down into the chaos. As they neared, they could see the destruction.

Tessa gasped. "Oh, dear Lord."

Trucks and cars were crunched between tractor-trailer rigs. Some had been thrown off the side of the road. Others had been lifted and piled like so many Matchbox cars. An eighteen-wheeler had smashed into the backs of other big trucks. Trailers had turned over, their contents spilled across the interstate.

Whiskey Gulch's fire department was already on the scene with their two big engines and their smaller emergency truck. Sheriffs' vehicles were stopping traffic to cordon off the area. Irish drove onto the side of the road and passed cars that were already stacking up trying to get through. When he reached the sheriff's vehicle parked horizontally across the road, he stopped.

Deputy Jones carrying a heavy flashlight, waved him down. "Sir, you can't go any farther."

Tessa got out of the truck. "I'm here to help and so is he."

When Deputy Jones recognized the two, she waved them past the barricade.

"What happened?" Irish asked as he stopped beside the deputy.

She shook her head. "From what I understand, a truck was holding up traffic, driving erratically. He sideswiped a car, which caused a chain reaction with the traffic backed up behind them. And what you see in front of you is the result."

Tessa was already hurrying forward, carrying her towels and her stethoscope. She stopped at the first EMT she came to. "I'm a nurse. Where am I needed most?" she asked.

He shook his head. "Nobody's made it up to the front of the line yet. You could start there and work your way backward. The main thing is to get them out of the vehicle if the vehicle is in jeopardy of catching fire. Then triage."

She nodded then moved forward, weaving in and out of the damaged vehicles, stepping into the median to get around some of the wreckage.

Irish followed, determined to stay with her.

Those who could, got out of their vehicles and helped those who couldn't help themselves. Some people staggered around, blood on their hands and faces.

Tessa had already made it to the fifth vehicle in line from the front.

Irish stayed right on her heels.

An eighteen-wheeler was smashed up against another,

and a car had run underneath the trailer, trapping the driver and the occupants in the wreckage.

"There are children in the back seat!" Tessa yelled. She stopped at the car and tried to open the back door. "It's locked." Inside, a child cried and a baby in a car seat was screaming at the top of her lungs. Their parents, still in the front seat, had blood on their foreheads, but they were conscious.

"Unlock the doors," Tessa called out.

"I can't," the father said. "It isn't working."

The mother, her face covered in blood, sobbed, "Get my children out of here. Please get my children out."

"I need something to break the window," Tessa said.

Irish pulled his gun from the holster beneath his jacket. He slipped the magazine from the handle and told the toddler in the back seat, "Close your eyes!"

The toddler ducked his head, closing his tear-filled eyes.

Irish slammed the handle of the weapon against the window. It cracked, but it didn't break. He hit it again, and this time the window broke. And he used the barrel of the gun to clear the glass. Then he reached inside and jimmied the door handle.

"The back doors won't open from the inside. The child safety locks are set," the father said.

Irish pulled a pocketknife out of his jeans' pocket, reached in and cut the seat belt holding the toddler in. Then he grabbed the toddler underneath his arms and pulled him through the broken window, and held him out to Tessa.

She took the child, shaking her head. "No, you need to hold him," she said. "I can fit through that window better than you to get to the baby."

He nodded and cleared the rest of the glass out of the way. Tessa handed the child to him and then shimmied through the window. When she reached the baby, she released the buckle on the child's car seat and extricated the baby. She had to sit on the seat beside it to turn around and hand the baby through the window. Several people had gathered around to receive the children.

Using the butt of his gun again, Irish yelled at the father, "Close your eyes, I'm going to break your window." The father covered his eyes and head. Irish smashed the window and cleared the glass, and then, taking the pocketknife from Tessa, he sliced through the seat belt holding the man in place. "Can you move your legs?"

"I don't know," the father said. "Let me have the pocketknife."

Irish handed the man the knife.

The driver leaned over and cut the seat belt holding his wife in the passenger seat.

"Oh, thank God. Thank God," she said.

Irish helped Tessa back through the window. The woman in the passenger seat reclined her chair all the way back and scrambled over the headrest into the back seat to climb out the window Tessa had just come through.

Once Tessa and the mother were on the ground, Irish tried to open the driver's-side door to help the man get out. It was jammed shut.

The driver tried to climb out the window but stopped, wincing. "I think something is broken," he said. "I can't move my leg."

A fire fighter appeared at Irish's side, carrying a crowbar. "Let us handle this. Move on to the next one."

Tessa made sure the mother, baby and toddler were

reunited and secure on the side of the road before she hurried around the overturned semi and trailer.

An ambulance had crossed the interstate's median and was parked in front of one of the first car's wreckage. The emergency medical technicians were working to extract the driver. The ambulance was from the next county over.

Tessa approached an emergency medical technician. "You guys got here quickly."

The man ran, carrying a crowbar. "We were at the truck stop on the interstate just two exits down when we got the call. Thankfully we were already fueled up. We were just pulling out. If we'd been back at the station, it would have taken us fifteen minutes longer."

She ran alongside him as he hurried toward a vehicle that had flipped over in the ditch. "How can I help?"

"I could use someone who's got a strong back to help me pry the door open on that vehicle. There's a man trapped inside. I think there's another car farther in the woods." He turned to Irish. "Sir, I could use your help. And, ma'am, if you could go get the stretcher out of the back of the ambulance and have it ready, that would be a big help. Have you ever done that before?"

She nodded. "Yes, I have."

"Good," the EMT said. "Go. The driver will help you."

While Irish ran down into the ditch with the EMT, Tessa hurried to the ambulance. A man came running toward her. "Tessa!"

She recognized him as Nathan Harris. "Nathan, what are you doing here?" she asked.

He shook his head. "I was in this wreck. I got out to see if I could help. There's something wrong with the driver in the ambulance, he needs your help right now."

Tessa ran alongside Nathan toward the ambulance. "What happened?" she asked.

"I don't know. He was in the back of the ambulance trying to get the stretcher out when he suddenly passed out. I got him into the ambulance but I don't know what's wrong with him. You need to check him out." When they got to the ambulance, Nathan swung the door open. As Tessa looked inside, she didn't see anyone in there.

"But it's empty." Tessa started to turn but was hit from behind, lifted and shoved into the back of the ambulance. Nathan climbed inside with her and slammed the door shut. Before she could get off the floor she felt something jabbed into her arm. Tessa fought, but he was too big, and suddenly her world became fuzzy and she couldn't control her body.

"What have you done?" she said, everything turning gray and hazy.

"What I have been trying to do for the last few days."

In the back of her fuzzy brain, her mind was screaming *No! No!* She opened her mouth. "Why?" She couldn't move. She couldn't fight. He lifted her from the floor of the ambulance and laid her on the stretcher, strapping her down.

"I got nothing but disrespect from you—from all the cheerleaders in our class. While I was out sweating on the field keeping your pretty boy from getting his face smashed in, he got all the glory. You girls only saw him. And I just got turned down by one cheerleader after the other, and slapped in the face. They never understood that ol' pretty boy Randy would never have made all the plays he made without me," Nathan sneered. "Well, he's not so pretty anymore."

"Wha…what have you…done?" Tessa said, her lips barely moving, words unable to emanate from her vocal cords.

"Your pretty boy is smashed up against a tree. His fancy car is worthless now."

Tessa fought to focus on the man's words. "It was you? You…killed… Penny."

"That bitch was the one who started all of this. I wasn't good enough for her. She slapped my face. She said none of you senior cheerleaders would ever go out with me. I was too ugly. I was never gonna go anywhere." He laughed as he tightened the second strap around her hips. "I showed them. I've been places. I've been all over this damn country."

"But you killed her."

"She fought me, but I was bigger. I was stronger. Stronger than your pretty boy. She tried to scream. I couldn't let her go crying to her friends. She slapped me. They'd take her side. So, I cut off her air so she couldn't scream. When she went limp, I couldn't leave her there for someone to find. She'd tell them. So I threw her over the cliff."

"Bastard," Tessa said.

"She slapped me. All I wanted was for her to dance with me like she danced with the other guys. A single damned dance." He turned toward the door.

"Why Bethany…and… Kitty?"

He spun back to her. "They were just like you and Penny. Too good for me. You-all didn't have the time of day for ugly Nathan Harrison."

"Didn't deserve to die…" Tessa said.

Nathan went on, caught up in his own tale. "I caught Kitty at home with her brats. She let me in like an old friend. She never treated me like anything but dirt back in school. It was too easy to take her. I threw her in the back of my trailer and drove her out of town. When I stopped, she was so cold. I told her I only wanted one dance. One lousy dance. I'd warm her up if she'd only dance with me."

His lip curled. "Just like Penny, she wanted to scream. And, like Penny, I cut off her air so she couldn't make a noise. I gave Bethany the same chance as Penny and Kitty. She refused to dance with me. She called me a freak and fought me like a wild cat." He lifted his chin and pounded his chest. "But I won in the end."

Tears spilled from the corners of Tessa's eyes. Kitty, Penny and Bethany died because Nathan felt rejected. The man was insane. And he wouldn't stop until he'd eliminated all the girls he felt had slighted him in high school.

Tessa tried to move but couldn't get her muscles to cooperate.

"It's time to go." The former football player stepped out of the ambulance.

As Nathan closed the door, Tessa tried to call out, tried to scream, but she couldn't. She was too woozy.

The sound of a door opening and closing at the front of the ambulance indicated Nathan had climbed into the driver's seat. The engine fired up and the ambulance rolled over the pavement, picking up speed, taking Tessa away from the wreck, away from Irish and anyone who could save her from the man who had attempted to kill her twice already.

This time, he would succeed.

Chapter Sixteen

Irish worked with the EMT, leaning all of his weight and strength into the crowbar, trying to force the door of the vehicle open. It had landed upside down in the ditch. A man and his small son were trapped inside. The man was unconscious, but the child was awake and sobbing quietly, suspended from his seat belt in his back seat booster chair.

"One more time," Irish said. "We almost have it."

They leaned into the crowbar once more. The metal door creaked and groaned, and finally fell open.

Irish and the EMT fell forward with the door and the crowbar.

Irish scrambled to his feet, got down on his hands and knees and reached inside the vehicle for the little boy. He carefully wedged his pocketknife between the boy's shoulder and the seat belt across his chest and sawed at the strap until it broke free and the boy dropped to the ceiling of the car.

Irish grabbed him beneath his arms, pulled him from the wrecked vehicle, and stood.

Two firefighters joined them from another unit that had just arrived. One of them took the boy from Irish's arms. "Thank you, sir. We'll take it from here." They went to work pulling the unconscious man from the wreckage.

Irish looked up, searching the darkness for Tessa. When he didn't see her, his pulse quickened. He turned to the EMT he'd been working with. "Did you see where the nurse went?"

"She was supposed to go get the stretcher from the ambulance." The EMT looked up. "Where's the ambulance?"

Irish's gut clenched.

At that moment, a motorcycle wove through the chaos and pulled to a stop beside Irish. He recognized the man riding it as Matt Hennessey.

"Do you need assistance here?" he asked.

"Yes," Irish said. "I can't find Tessa. I was helping out over there and she disappeared. From what I understand, so did the ambulance. Where was the ambulance?"

The EMT pointed toward the front of the crash site. There was a dark lump lying on the pavement at the spot where the ambulance had been minutes before.

Irish, Matt and the EMT ran toward it.

A man in an emergency medical technician uniform groaned and rolled over.

"Joe!" The EMT bent to the man. "This man is our ambulance driver." He looked at Joe. "What happened?"

Joe pressed a hand to his head. When he brought it away, there was blood on it. "I don't know. Somebody hit me. That's all I remember." He glanced around. "Where's the ambulance?"

"It left?"

"Who took it?" Joe asked.

"We assume whoever hit you," his buddy responded.

"Well, he couldn't have gone back through the wreckage," Matt said. "They must've headed east on the interstate."

Irish turned to Matt. "I need your motorcycle. I need it now."

"We don't know that Tessa's in that ambulance," Matt said.

"No, but that's why you need to stay here and keep looking for her while I go after that ambulance. I need to find her immediately. This entire disaster might all have been staged to get her away from me. If that's the case, he's succeeded."

Matt climbed off the motorcycle, removed his helmet and handed it to Irish. "I'll alert the others. We'll look here. As soon as we get a vehicle through, we'll follow."

Irish climbed on the motorcycle, hit the accelerator and sped down the interstate, his heart in his throat, his pulse pounding. His one job was to protect Tessa and he'd failed.

TESSA MUST'VE PASSED out for a few minutes. When she swam back up to consciousness, someone was fumbling with the straps holding her to the stretcher. She blinked her eyes open and looked up into Nathan Harris's face. As soon as the straps were loose, she tried to move her arms. They still wouldn't respond, even with the straps free. What had he given her? No amount of self-defense lessons would save her from this.

Without saying a word, he bent and threw her over his shoulder, stepped down from the ambulance and dumped her into the back of a tractor-trailer rig. He climbed into the trailer with her and scooted her away from the edge. Then he jumped back down and closed the door.

Darkness was complete and the floor was icy cold. The hum of the motor echoed off the walls of the empty trailer. Cold air blew through, chilling her skin. She didn't even have the muscles or energy to shiver. She realized she was in the back of a refrigerated trailer. No one knew where she was. Was this to be the end of her?

The trailer shifted, moving slowly. Tessa tried to open her mouth and scream, but nothing came out.

Why hadn't they come to this realization sooner? Nathan was the one behind the murders. They'd been thinking refrigerators as in a stationary building. Not a refrigerated trailer. As a truck driver, the man had the mobility to move around the country. It all made sense now. It was too bad that she was the only one who knew.

Tessa focused on her fingers and tried moving them. Her pinky finger twitched. It wasn't much, but it was better than nothing. She'd have to regain a lot more movement pretty quickly, or she'd freeze to death before she could free herself.

The trailer lurched as it was pulled forward, bumping across uneven pavement as it slowly picked up speed. It leaned to the right, as if turning, then back to the left.

Soon, the road smoothed and the leaning stopped. They were going straight. Tessa assumed it was the interstate. Good, if he'd chosen to take a back road, nobody would know where to look for them. She prayed that Irish would soon discover that she was missing and start looking for her. It would take a miracle for him to find her before she froze.

She moved the fingers on her other hand. And then she moved her hand. Her toes tingled, and she moved those. It just wasn't happening fast enough. The cold was seeping into her bones, lowering her body temperature, making her more lethargic than the drug. She couldn't even rub her body, her arms or legs, to generate any kind of warmth. Was this the way that she was going to die?

Surely, Nathan would stop the truck soon; he seemed to have taken pleasure in strangling his victims. Kitty hadn't died from hypothermia. He'd strangled her to death after she had already gotten frostbite on her fingers and toes. If Tessa could hold on long enough for him to open that trailer door again, and rustle up enough energy left to fight her way free, she might just see Irish again. And she wanted that so badly. He'd shown her what it was really like to make love, not just to have sex. He'd cared enough to please her, something Randy had never done. Was what she felt for Irish love? Or was she risking losing herself again when she'd only just begun to find the real Tessa?

Irish was worth it. He was gentle, caring, and amazing in bed. Tessa was willing to take the risk.

IRISH FLEW DOWN the interstate on the motorcycle, pushing the bike as fast as it would go. He saw nothing ahead of him. Nothing. The traffic usually traveling this interstate had all been blocked by the wreckage behind him. As fast as he was going, surely he would have caught up with the ambulance by now. It couldn't have gotten that big a head start on him.

He and the EMT hadn't taken that long to pry the door of that vehicle open. The ambulance couldn't have gotten too far.

Hope faded. On a long, straight stretch of the interstate, he saw no taillights ahead of him, but he did see an exit. Had the ambulance pulled off the interstate at this point? Maybe it had taken a different route? The interstate was too obvious. It would be too easy to spot an ambulance driving along it.

On a hunch, Irish slowed and took the exit. His hunches had paid off on many occasions when he'd been on active duty. It was all he had to go on, and Tessa's life depended on him. And then he saw it. At the side of a brightly lit truck stop, sat an ambulance, the back door hanging open.

As Irish pulled into the truck stop, a couple of eighteen-wheelers were pulling out. He drove straight to the ambulance and peered into the open door. As he suspected, it was empty. He looked around for anybody nearby who might have witnessed the people getting in or out of the ambulance.

A woman stood near the edge of the pavement, walking her two small dogs.

Irish drove the motorcycle over to her. "Excuse me, ma'am?"

She looked up. "Yes?"

"Were you here when that ambulance pulled into the truck stop?"

She glanced at the ambulance, her eyes narrowing. "Yeah, I saw it when it pulled off the road."

"Did you see where the people inside it went?"

She shook her head and bent to gather her two dogs into her arms. "No, there was a big truck parked right there. I couldn't see anybody getting in or out of the ambulance because the truck blocked my view. But after the ambulance parked, the truck drove away."

"Do you remember what the truck looked like? Could you describe it?"

She laughed. "Sure. It's that one right there." The woman pointed to an eighteen-wheeler crossing the road, headed away from the truck stop. It turned onto the on-ramp to the interstate.

"Are you sure?" Irish asked. "Are you absolutely positive that's the same truck?"

She nodded. "It's the only one I saw out here that had some kind of refrigeration unit on top of it. I remember being a little bit envious of the chill air it produces because the air conditioner in my car decided today was a good day to stop working. I thought, wouldn't it be nice if I had a refrigeration unit like that to keep my car cool for my little dogs?"

Irish didn't wait for her to finish her story. He hit the throttle, spun the back wheel of the motorcycle around, and raced after the eighteen-wheeler.

On a motorcycle, it wasn't like he could force the trucker over to the side of the road. And since the woman said that the ambulance had backed up to the rear of the truck, he assumed that whoever was driving the rig had transferred Tessa from the back of the ambulance into the trailer. That meant she was in the refrigerator unit. If he didn't stop that truck soon, it wouldn't matter. She'd die of hypothermia.

Wrecking the truck was not an option. He had to get to the driver. The only way to get to the driver would be to get inside the cab of that truck. He'd have to sneak up on it, or the driver could easily run him off the road.

As soon as Irish was out on the road and behind the rig, he switched off the headlights on the motorcycle. The truck built up speed on the on-ramp to the intestate.

Irish followed right behind the truck, sticking close to the rear of the trailer, so that the trucker wouldn't see him in his rearview mirrors. Already, the truck was moving faster as the driver merged onto the interstate.

Irish waited until the shoulder was wide enough for him to drive up alongside the truck. Then he made his move, swerving to the right of the truck pulling up alongside the trailer. When he was close enough to the passenger door of the cab, he noticed there was a handle next to the door. If he could just get his fingers around that handle, he could pull himself up.

Matching the truck's speed of fifty-five miles per hour, Irish took a deep breath and murmured, "Sorry, Matt, I owe you a motorcycle." He stretched out his arm as far as he could, grabbed the handle, and pulled himself up onto the side of the truck, on the running board. As he clung to the side of the truck, he watched as the motorcycle spun out of control and crashed into the ditch. At that moment, he knew he never wanted to be a stuntman on a movie set.

Once he got his balance, he tried the handle to see if he could open the door. It was unlocked. He yanked it open. The man behind the steering wheel turned to face him, muttering a curse. Then he jerked the steering wheel to the right.

The door flew out of Irish's hand. He clung to the handle on the side of the truck, trying to retain his balance. When the driver swung back to the left, the door started to slam shut. Irish jammed his shoulder between the door and the truck and took the force of the door slamming against his body. But the door remained open.

The trailer fishtailed behind them, and the driver righted the rig, straightening the wheels to keep it from skidding off the highway. While the truck was still going straight, Irish pushed the door open and dove into the front seat. The driver slammed on his brakes, throwing Irish against the floorboard. He hit his head but blinked and rolled to his side, pulling his handgun out of the holster. The driver swerved the truck to the right again and back to the left. Because Irish was already jammed against the floorboard, he didn't roll far. He aimed the weapon at the driver and shouted, "Pull over!"

Turning his head toward Irish, the man snarled. "Or what? You'll shoot me?"

"Yes." At that moment, Irish realized the man was Nathan Harris, the guy they'd seen in the hardware store. The one who'd had an issue with Randy *having it all*.

"What do you think will happen if you shoot me? The truck will crash and everybody in it will die, including you and your girlfriend."

Irish's gut clenched. It made sense that Nathan was the one. The refrigerated truck was a dead giveaway. And if it was cold back there, Tessa would die of hypothermia before they came to a peaceful stop. The way he saw it, Irish only had one choice.

He pulled the trigger, purposefully hitting the back of the seat near Nathan's head.

"You get the next one," Irish said.

Nathan jerked the steering wheel to the left, cursing.

"Pull over!" Irish shouted.

Nathan jammed his foot to the accelerator, sending the truck speeding down the interstate.

Irish leveled his gun and shot the man in the chest. As soon as he pulled the trigger, he pushed himself off the floorboard and grabbed for the steering wheel.

Nathan slumped forward. Though he was unconscious, or dead, his foot was still jammed against the accelerator and his heavy body leaning against the steering wheel made it hard for Irish to move it and keep the speeding rig on the road. As he fought to keep the truck between the ditches, it careened down the interstate, going faster and faster.

Irish leaned across and shoved open the driver's door. The truck swerved to the right. Irish fought to straighten it at the same time as he tried to straighten Nathan's body to shove it toward the open door. If he could just get him out of the seat, he could get to the brake and slow the truck down.

But the man was dead and, like a deadweight, he couldn't be budged. Irish ended up sitting in Nathan's lap, shoving the man's foot off the accelerator and then pressing his own foot on the brake. It seemed to take forever and a lot of gear-shifting before the truck came to a complete stop. When it finally did, Irish threw on the parking brake, squeezed out of the driver's seat, and leaped to the ground. He raced to the back of the trailer and disengaged the big metal latches holding the doors shut.

Lying on the floor of that refrigerator unit was Tessa in her scrubs, her skin deathly pale, her eyes closed. A lead weight settled in Irish's gut. Was he too late?

He shook his head. He hadn't come this far to give up yet. If she had even a hint of life in her, he'd make sure she lived to see another day. He scooped her out of the back of the trailer and carried her to the side of the road. Her body was so cold and he couldn't tell if she was breathing.

He hugged her close, trying to get his body warmth into her. It wasn't enough. He had to warm her quickly. Even as warm as it was on a Texas evening, it wasn't enough. He carried her to the cab of the truck and lifted her up into the passenger seat. The engine was still running. He switched on the heater and climbed in next to her, rubbing her arms, holding her close. He still couldn't tell if she was breathing. So he pressed his mouth to hers, pinched her nose and blew a breath into her lungs.

Her chest rose and fell.

"Tessa, sweetheart, breathe," he said.

She didn't respond.

He forced another breath of air into her lungs. "Come on, baby, you have to live. I need to tell you something important. You need to wake up so I can do that."

Still, her chest wasn't rising.

He breathed another breath into her lungs. "I need to tell you that I love you. I need to tell you that I believe in love at first sight. It's okay. Really. I'll give you all the time you need to come to the conclusion that you love me, too. I can be patient, especially if it means spending the rest of my life with you. You wanted to get on with your life. I want to start my life. I want to start it with you."

When she didn't seem to take her own breath, he pressed his mouth to hers again, ready to blow more air into her lungs.

Her lips twitched. He leaned back. Her eyes fluttered open. He let go of the breath that he had been about to blow into her lungs and smiled down at her. "Hey, beautiful, glad you could come to the party."

Her lips curved into a smile. "You found me."

"You bet I did. I couldn't let a good thing get away."

"How did you find me?" she whispered.

He grinned, his heart lighter than it had been in days. "I followed my heart."

Her body trembled and she started shivering. "I'm ss-ssoo cc-cold."

He adjusted the heater vent to blow right on her. Lights flashed in the side mirror, alerting Irish to an oncoming vehicle. A big black pickup pulled up beside the truck.

Trace Travis and Matt Hennessey jumped down and ran to the cab of the eighteen-wheeler. Trace climbed up on the driver's side and pulled the door open. His eyes widened when he saw Nathan's dead body against the steering wheel. He shot a glance across to the passenger side and smiled. "Oh, thank God. You found her."

Tessa glanced toward Trace. That's when she saw Nathan's body slumped against the steering wheel. "He's dead?" she asked.

Irish nodded. "He's dead."

"He admitted to killing Penny, Kitty and Bethany. He also caused that big wreck. He said he ran Randy off the road."

Matt Hennessey climbed up on the passenger side and opened the door. "They found Randy's body in his BMW, smashed up against a tree," Matt said, "We're just glad to see that you survived." Matt looked around, "How'd you do it? How did you get him to stop the truck?"

Irish gave him a crooked grin. "I had to climb on board like a movie stuntman. I owe you a motorcycle."

Matt shook his head. "I can replace the motorcycle. I'm glad you got to Ms. Bolton in time. That's all that matters. And now that the case is solved, she won't have to live in fear of being attacked again."

Tessa glanced at Irish, her smile fading. "You did your job, you kept me alive. Now you don't have to be my bodyguard anymore."

He tightened his hold around her. "Let's get you to

the hospital. We can talk about my next assignment after that."

With Matt's help, Irish transferred Tessa to Trace's pickup.

Matt stood outside the truck. "I'll stay here and wait for the sheriff. I'm sure they'll have questions and want to dispose of the body."

As soon as they had Tessa strapped into a seat belt, Trace drove his truck across the median and headed back toward Whiskey Gulch and the hospital there.

Once they arrived, Trace pulled up to the emergency room entrance, shifted into Park, jumped out and ran toward the door.

A nurse's aide ran out. "Need help?"

Trace nodded. "We could use a stretcher out here."

The aide ran back inside, returned with a stretcher and rolled it over to the side of the pickup.

Irish lifted Tessa out of her seat and laid her on the stretcher.

A nurse came out to help guide the stretcher into the hospital. "Tessa," she said. "You're supposed to be the one working, not being worked *on*." She smiled down at the woman lying on the stretcher.

"Thought you might not have enough to do," Tessa said.

"Sweetie, it's been utter chaos." She glanced up at Irish as they entered the hospital.

"We'll take her from here."

"I'm going with her," Irish insisted.

She smiled. "You must be Irish. I'm Allison. Tessa and I work together. She's told me so much about you. Tessa, do you want him to go back with you?"

Tessa held up her hand.

Irish took it and raised it to his lips.

"Yes," Tessa said. "I need him to breathe."

Allison chuckled. "Okay, then, come on in."

She wheeled Tessa to one of the examination rooms where a doctor checked her over, drew blood to be analyzed and, after receiving the test results, pronounced her all fit to go home to bed. "The drug he gave you will work its way out of your system in twenty-four hours. There should be no lingering effects. Get some rest."

"Could I stay and help the staff?" Tessa asked.

The doctor shook his head. "You need rest and plenty of fluids to flush your system. We'll handle things here without you."

Tessa nodded. "Yes, sir."

"Do you have someone who can stay with you for the night?" he asked.

"Yes, she does," Irish answered.

The doctor glanced from Irish to Tessa for confirmation.

"Yes, I do," she confirmed.

Trace met Tessa and Irish at the entrance to the ER with his truck. "Let's get you home," he said. "Once I drop you two off at Tessa's, I'll get back out to the crash site."

"I'd go with you—"

Trace shook his head. "You need to stay with Tessa. First responders from all the neighboring counties will be there to sort through the injured. As it is, I'm sure we'll just be in the way at this point. But we need to retrieve your truck, and I need to pick up Matt."

Trace drove them to Tessa's house and helped by opening the door for Irish as he carried Tessa through to the living room, laying her on the sofa.

Trace stood on the doorway for a moment. "Do you need anything before I leave?"

Tessa shook her head. "I have everything I need right here," she said, glancing up at Irish.

"She's right," Irish said, his heart filling with the look in Tessa's eyes. "We have everything we need right here."

Trace smiled. "When you're feeling better, I'll have Irish bring you out to the ranch for a barbeque. Lily and Aubrey would love to hear all about your experience." He grinned. "And so would I. We're all glad you're okay."

"Thank you," Tessa said. "I'd like to visit the ranch. I've always wanted to see it."

Trace left, closing the door behind him.

"Do you want me to carry you to your bathroom so you can shower and change into your pajamas?" Irish asked.

"Only if you'll shower with me," she said, lifting her chin.

His groin tightened, but he didn't want to read too much into her comment. "Do you need help standing? Are you still weak from the drug? Can I get you anything?"

Tessa pushed to her feet, swayed a little, straightened and then squared her shoulders. "I'm fine. I don't need help standing. I don't need you to wait on me hand and foot."

He frowned. "Sweetheart, you just went through a pretty traumatic event. I'm here. Let me help."

"I don't *want* your help," she insisted. "I no longer need a bodyguard or a babysitter."

"You don't?" His chest tightened. "Do you want me to leave you alone?"

"No," she said. "I don't want you to leave me alone. I want you to stay. But not because I need you."

"I don't understand," he said.

"I want you to stay because you *want* to stay. Not because you feel some obligation to help me."

"I *want* to stay," Irish said.

Her eyes narrowed. "Not because you think I'm too weak and too injured to be on my own?"

"Well...partly," he admitted. "But mostly because I like being with you."

"Not because I'm your assignment or your job? Not because you *have* to be with me?" she asked.

He shook his head and closed the distance between them. "I want to spend time with you." He gathered her in his arms. "I want to take that shower with you, to feel your body against mine." He pressed a kiss to her forehead. "I want to make love with you."

She melted into his arms. "When I was lying on the floor of the refrigerated trailer and couldn't move, all I could think about was getting out of there and back to you. I didn't want my life to end."

"Oh, baby. I was so scared," Irish said, crushing her to him, all the emotions he'd felt rushing back into his chest like a tidal wave. "When I couldn't find you, my world seemed to fall apart."

She wrapped her arms around his waist and pressed her cheek against his chest. "I felt cheated," she said.

"Cheated?"

Tessa nodded. "I'd finally found someone who understood me and didn't want to change me."

"You're perfect just the way you are," he said, smoothing a hand over her beautiful, silky, strawberry-blond hair.

"I'd barely had any time with you, and I wanted more."

Tears slid down her cheeks, wetting the front of his shirt. "I didn't want to be cheated out of getting to know you better and using up my supply in the nightstand drawer," she said, her voice dropping to a whisper.

He tipped her chin up so that he could stare down into her watery eyes. "Tessa, I wasn't going to stop until I found you. I shouldn't have lost you to begin with."

"We're here now," she said, her eyes wide and hopeful. "Do you think we have something growing between us?"

He grinned. "I'm sure we do. At least, I know I have feelings for you. I'd tell you I love you, but I'm afraid I'll scare you off."

Tessa's eyes widened and filled with more tears. "You love me?"

"Yes," he said with a grimace. "I'm one-hundred-per-cent sure."

Her brow puckered and tears slipped down her cheeks. "How can you be so sure?"

"Because I couldn't imagine life without you." He cupped her cheek in his palm and brushed away a tear. "Even though we only met a few days ago, I feel like I've known you for a lifetime. You're my heart and soul. You're the woman I want to have children with, to start living my life with."

More tears trickled from her eyes. "I'm afraid."

"Damn." He could have kicked himself for rushing his declaration. "I didn't want to frighten you with my confession. The last thing I want to do is pressure you into saying you love me when you're not sure. You can have all the time you need to figure out what's in your heart. I'll wait."

She leaned up and pressed a kiss to his lips. "Thank

you," she said. "Thank you for being you. It makes it so much easier to love you."

He heart skipped several beats then his pulse pounded hard through his veins. "Did you just say you love me?"

She nodded. "I was afraid to trust my feelings, after making such a huge mistake in judgment with Randy." She laughed. "And I've only just begun to like myself."

"Oh, baby, you're an amazing woman. You should be so very proud of who you are."

She nodded. "I know that now. And you helped me to realize it. I love you."

"I love you, too, but I promise not to rush you into anything else until you're absolutely ready." He hugged her close. "You love me. That's all I need to know for now."

"And you'll wait for me?"

He nodded. "As long as you need me to."

She wrapped her arms around his neck and pulled him down to kiss her. "And about that shower?" she whispered against his lips.

"I'm all in." He swept her up into his arms and carried her to her bedroom. "Until you're ready, no strings, no commitments, just pure love."

She laughed. "I can live with that."

He set her on her feet on the floor and kissed her like there would be no tomorrow. Thankfully, they would have many more tomorrows.

They would spend them loving each other. And that life he'd promised he'd start living when he left the military started with her.

* * * * *

COMING SOON!

We really hope you enjoyed reading this book. If you're looking for more romance, be sure to head to the shops when new books are available on

Thursday 3rd March

MILLS & BOON

THE HEART OF ROMANCE

A ROMANCE FOR EVERY READER

MODERN

Prepare to be swept off your feet by sophisticated, sexy and seductive heroes, in some of the world's most glamourous and romantic locations, where power and passion collide.

HISTORICAL

Escape with historical heroes from time gone by. Whether your passion is for wicked Regency Rakes, muscled Vikings or rugged Highlanders, awaken the romance of the past.

MEDICAL

Set your pulse racing with dedicated, delectable doctors in the high-pressure world of medicine, where emotions run high and passion, comfort and love are the best medicine.

True Love

Celebrate true love with tender stories of heartfelt romance, from the rush of falling in love to the joy a new baby can bring, and a focus on the emotional heart of a relationship.

Desire

Indulge in secrets and scandal, intense drama and plenty of sizzling hot action with powerful and passionate heroes who have it all: wealth, status, good looks…everything but the right woman.

HEROES

Experience all the excitement of a gripping thriller, with an intense romance at its heart. Resourceful, true-to-life women and strong, fearless men face danger and desire - a killer combination!

To see which titles are coming soon, please visit

millsandboon.co.uk/nextmonth

LET'S TALK

Romance

For exclusive extracts, competitions
and special offers, find us online:

 facebook.com/millsandboon

 @MillsandBoon

@MillsandBoonUK

Get in touch on 01413 063232

For all the latest titles coming soon, visit
millsandboon.co.uk/nextmonth

MILLS & BOON
A ROMANCE FOR EVERY READER

- **FREE** delivery direct to your door

- **EXCLUSIVE** offers every month

- **SAVE** up to 25% on pre-paid subscriptions

SUBSCRIBE AND SAVE

millsandboon.co.uk/Subscribe

MILLS & BOON
Desire

Indulge in secrets and scandal, intense drama and plenty of sizzling hot action with powerful and passionate heroes who have it all: wealth, status, good looks…everything but the right woman.

MILLS & BOON

MODERN

Power and Passion

Prepare to be swept off your feet by sophisticated, sexy and seductive heroes, in some of the world's most glamourous and romantic locations, where power and passion collide.

MILLS & BOON
MEDICAL
Pulse-Racing Passion

Set your pulse racing with dedicated, delectable doctors in the high-pressure world of medicine, where emotions run high and passion, comfort and love are the best medicine.

MILLS & BOON

True Love

Romance from the Heart

Celebrate true love with tender stories of heartfelt romance, from the rush of falling in love to the joy a new baby can bring, and a focus on the emotional heart of a relationship.